I am not such a villain as to send a lady of Miss Brabant's qualities onto the open sea," said the captain. "No, I think we shall keep her."

Windmera looked at the captain. "What, what do you mean to do with me?"

"Why, pretty moonflower, you are . . . a prize of war!"

Passion's Pride

Claudette Williams

FAWCETT CREST • NEW YORK

PASSION'S PRIDE

Published by Fawcett Crest Books, a unit of CBS Publications, the Consumer Publishing Division of CBS Inc.

Copyright © 1980 by Claudette Williams
ALL RIGHTS RESERVED

ISBN: 0-449-24278-1

Printed in the United States of America

First Fawcett Crest Printing: April 1980

10   9   8   7   6   5   4   3   2   1

To Phyllis, with love

1

Youth rambles on life's arid mount,
And strikes the rock and finds the vein,
And brings the water from the fount,
The fount which shall not flow again.
                                            —Matthew Arnold

One

1782

Godwin, Lord Ravensbury, stood, a lone figure on the craggy cliffs of Land's End in Cornwall. Before him lay the ocean, its whitecaps foaming around him, the jutting rocks harsh in their greatness, looking much like the weathered turrets of castles of long ago. He loved it, felt he belonged, and indeed he cut quite a figure against his background. His height enough to make a tall man raise his eyes, his shoulders such to make a quarrelsome chap a charmer, and his mien . . . that of a buck in his heyday!

He stood, his wild red hair frizzled in the force of the wind, his dark cloak dancing away roughly from his large frame, his black brows drawn over his dark eyes. He had come to Land's End to be alone with his thoughts, for a decision had to be made. He was twenty, he was lord and master of a his home, and his home was empty.

His parents he had lost when still very young. His elder brother he had lost to the sea some years ago; he had no others. He was lonely. He was Godwin, Lord Ravensbury, but he was alone.

He wanted a family. He needed a family, and though his years numbered but twenty, he'd been living as and taking on the part of a man for some years now. Children! 'Twas this he wanted. A brood of his blood carrying his name, tumbling, laughing, making mischief, breathing life into the staleness of his home. The thought of fathering such a pack made him delirious with pleasure, such was his nature.

A bride! A face came to mind, a gentle being whose full youthful body moved him to passion, whose name turned off such thoughts. Lisa? What was he doing thinking of Lisa?

A bride! She was Sara of Farenday, a lovely wench with hair the color of sun-ripened wheat and eyes the color of a clear sky. An innocent bride so different from the teasing Lisa. Yes, Sara. She would come to him, and he would teach her to pleasure at his touch, for he wanted her. Hotly she roused his blood . . . but did he love her? Here was the

9

quirk. How could he be sure? Bah! He was being foolish. Of course he loved her, how could he not? He would take the hand of lovely Sara Farenday. He would bring a bride to his castle to bear him children. He had made his decision.

Sara of Farenday sat among the sweetly blowing heather on her father's land. She was neatly clothed in a white muslin day gown. Her long loose bright hair framed her face. She was but seventeen, lithe and graceful. Her blue eyes took in her surroundings, gazed long at the modest but graceful Tudor home in the distance. She had always had all that she needed. At least, nearly all that she needed, for she wanted much more. She had a penchant for jewels that her father on his comfortable but not abundant income neglected to indulge. Indeed, even if he had been able to afford the trinkets she desired her mother would have put up a hand. Marriage? Of course. Marriage to a wealthy and noble peer of the realm! She would take nothing less.

She smiled to herself when she thought of Godwin of Ravensbury. He courted her now; indeed, she knew she was deeply imbedded in his mind. But it had not always been so. Once, he had looked to her friend Lisa of Cotham. Her smile deepened as she silently congratulated herself, for it had not been an easy trick to wean him from Lisa. Careful thought and planning had come into play, and both Godwin and Lisa had been duped.

She recalled the first time she had seen Godwin. She was with Lisa riding across the fields, as had been their wont, before the night of Lisa's ball. All had changed since, but then, then she was at Lisa's side, and before her came Godwin of Ravensbury! She recalled vividly the wave of envy that nearly conquered her better judgment as Godwin's dark eyes stroked Lisa's gentle face. He scarcely noticed the inviting look she threw him, such was his interest in Lisa. Sara marveled to herself, for Lisa was unfashionably small, unfashionably plump, and although she was quite pretty, her hazel eyes and curls of indistinct brown were nothing to the vision Sara saw in her own looking glass. Yet here he was, this large, quite handsome man with his title and his fortune and his interest all for Lisa. It was in that moment perhaps that Sara made a decision as well, and it was to have Godwin of Ravensbury!

They proceeded on their way, Sara and Lisa, the one filled with curiosity, the other wearing a quiet blush until Sara broke their stillness. "Lisa . . . I had no idea Lord Ravensbury was courting you."

Lisa's color heightened. She glanced at her friend and then hurriedly looked away. "Indeed, Sara . . . he is not."

"Oh, naughty girl, to lie so brazenly!" bantered Sara purposefully.

"Oh, stop! 'Tis no lie. He makes no formal court of me."

"But he does come to call?"

"Yes . . . he has paid my parents a few morning calls. . . ." Lisa hesitated. She knew her friend too well to confide in her easily. If she was not careful Sara would go about the countryside chattering that his lordship had proposed, when indeed Godwin had had but one lone interview with her.

"Do you want him?" Sara asked bluntly. "I should if I were you."

Lisa laughed, "You are outrageous . . . but, yes, I suppose I do want him. He is such a good man."

"Handsome is what he is . . . and affluent as well," returned Sara.

"Oh, Sara . . . you can be terribly calculating at times. I wonder at you."

Sara ignored this, for there were things she was impatient to learn. "What did you mean . . . he is such a good man? In what way?"

"In all ways. It is said he is the fairest landlord in all of Cornwall. And he has such love of children. Whenever he comes to call he allows all my brothers and sisters to clamor around him. He is a good man . . . one just knows it simply by watching him."

"Hmmm," said Sara, who was now busily in thought. Egad! His allowing Lisa's siblings, who she was quite certain numbered at last count no less than five, to pester him would certainly mean he was a man of patience if nothing else.

Thus it was that Sara plied her friend with questions, for she would know all there was to know about Lord Ravensbury! After that, her weekly visit to Lisa's home became a daily thing, and there by slow degrees she brought herself to Godwin's notice. She studied him well. He was not in love with Lisa, though he could be . . . but Sara was quick to realize that he was still vacillating. It needed only a nudge in another direction. Perhaps if he became disillusioned with Lisa? But how? Lisa was a nice person . . . and it would not be possible for her to whisper anything to the contrary in Godwin's ears for fear of appearing disloyal. No, it would have to be carefully planned and skillfully executed, if she was to win the heart of Lord Ravensbury!

Concentrated thought brought to Sara's notice her own cousin, Oscar Welby, a lad some two years her senior, home from Cambridge for the summer holidays. Long had Oscar wished for Sara's eyes to light upon him, and then suddenly, *voilà*, they did, like a miracle surely, or so the poor lad thought at first. However, though the pleasure of Sara's company sustained his dreams, doubts filled him. He accompanied Sara daily on her visits to Cotham and discovered there a warm and lively wench in the person of Lisa. So was he torn, for at every opportunity Sara made herself disagreeable to him, brightening the halo around Lisa's sweet head. Sara knew well her purpose, though no other did. As it chanced, or by clear design (one may only guess), whenever Godwin happened on the scene, he found Oscar very nearly alone in quiet conversation with Lisa. He had no way of knowing they talked earnestly not of each other but of Oscar's feelings for Sara.

The memory of Godwin's slow awakening tickled Sara as she mused, and she hugged her knees, relishing the scenes that had followed. Oh, but Godwin's frowns grew blacker with each visit, and he turned in his doubt to Sara, lovely, quiet in repose. And then came the night of Lisa's ball!

Lisa looked well in her white-on-white gown. Her hazel eyes were sparkling and her cheeks much flushed with her pleasure. Yet even so, Sara knew herself superior. Sara's curls of gold were cleverly adorned with dark-pink silk roses. Her gown of varying hues of pink hugged her tall graceful body, and she was well aware that many a man looked hopefully her way. But she wanted none of them. What were they next to Godwin of Ravensbury? But it was important that all who spoke her name did so admiringly and within Godwin's hearing. It would excite him to know how attractive other men found her. She could already see his interest in her had billowed. She bantered with him, laughed with him, teased, invited and used her eyes as no seventeen-year-old in the room knew how, and all the while did she work her plan.

Sara had more than wit with her this night. In her silk reticule she carried a potion. An herbal concoction the gypsy woman had assured her would do little more than make the victim slightly queasy. It was what Sara needed!

In her innocence Lisa came bubbling with her excitement

to her friend. She was well pleased with the round of dances she had already had, she was blissful over her growing friendship with Oscar and only slightly troubled that Godwin was holding himself aloof. She ascribed it to his recent odd humors and thought no more about it.

"Sara . . . oh, it is so wonderful. Mama and Papa are thrilled. They say nature has provided us with a beautiful night, the bakers with delights for the eye and palate, the muscians with the best of sounds . . . everyone cooperates!" She giggled at the happy ravings of her parents.

"Here, love . . . you need this lemonade more than I, for you are quite flushed," said Sara, holding out the glass. She watched as Lisa obediently took it from her and sipped slowly.

"Sara . . . your cousin . . . he says you will not dance with him. Is it true?" Lisa was frowning slightly, for she did not approve of her friend's cold-heartedness.

"Lud! Of course it is!" She pushed the glass back toward Lisa's mouth. "Drink up! The poor lad fancies himself infatuated with me. You don't think I should encourage him, do you?"

"No . . . no . . . I suppose you are right," said Lisa putting the empty glass down on a nearby table. "But he is so sweet. . . . I do so hate to see him suffer."

"Nonsense! He is more in love with *you* than with me," said Sara, purposefully putting the notion in Lisa's head.

"Me? Stuff! We are but friends," objected Lisa heatedly.

"So you are . . . but only because he has not yet awakened to the facts. Lisa . . . Lisa . . . what is wrong?" said Sara suddenly, immediately giving her friend a supportive arm.

"I . . . I don't know . . . feel so unsteady . . . and oh, Sara . . . I do feel something churning in my stomach. . . ."

Sara eyed her with some concern. "Come, darling . . . it must be all this excitement. What you need is to lie down for a while in your room."

"No!" objected Lisa fretfully. "I cannot—"

"Nonsense. You will only be gone for a short bit, just long enough to catch your breath!" chided Sara.

"Oh . . . people will talk . . . say I am a silly—"

"People will do no such thing! Why, what stuff. Can a girl not go off with friends if she so wishes." She looked toward Oscar, skillfully calling him to order with her eyes.

He came at once, his lanky form shifting as he hung about

13

hoping to be of unforgettable service. Sara brought him around just so, blocking Godwin's line of vision perfectly.

"Oscar, be a dear and accompany Lisa and me to her room. She is not feeling quite the thing, and your arm at this moment would be most helpful," whispered Sara.

Oscar admired Lisa and was sincerely concerned, for closer inspection made him certain that she was really feeling unwell. His arm went protectively round her small plump shoulders, and she leaned heavily, thankfully, into his hold.

Sara glanced over her shoulder and saw there Godwin watching them. Quietly she smiled to herself. "Come along before some biddy stops us to chat!"—with which she managed to get Lisa undetained out of the ballroom.

Godwin watched them leave the overfilled room. They made a cozy threesome. He was troubled. Deeply troubled. He was unsure of his feelings. He had been looking to Lisa with thoughts of a future, but recently every time he hoped be alone with her, there would be Oscar beside her, and the chit seemed well satisfied with the boy. There too was Sara. She was a beauty. In fact, many was the night he fantasized about her, saw himself possessing her. Sara of Farenday, he mused to himself now. Lord, but there wasn't a man in the ballroom tonight that didn't want her, and he could see, was nearly sure, that she wanted only him! It was a pleasant thought, especially because he felt slightly rejected by his first choice. Lisa, sweet, innocent, flighty and soft . . . Lisa, full-bodied, well able to mother a brood. But Lisa went off with Oscar's arm about her person! He cheered himself with the memory of Sara's tall graceful beauty and still felt a small sadness within.

He didn't realize how long he had stood in his corner frowning over his thoughts when suddenly he saw Sara enter the room. She moved sweepingly. But where was Oscar? And Lisa? He made his way purposefully towards Sara, for he would know the truth. In spite of all, his every leaning was to Lisa. He would have her if he could.

"Sara?" he called gently.

She turned, somewhat startled by his voice. His brows rose at her expression. "Godwin . . . oh . . . what is it?"—her tone as though frightened of what he might ask.

"What is it? What is wrong? Where are Lisa and Oscar? Tell me, Sara for I have a right to know!"

"Oh, Godwin . . . I feel you are sadly served in this. But it is not my place to say. . . ."

"Say? Say what?"

"Nothing. Please do not ask!"

"I see. Very well," he said. What was the use of pestering her when she was so obviously distressed? Besides, Mr. Cotham was approaching.

Sara looked up to see Lisa's father happily come upon her, and Godwin could feel Sara tremble.

"Well, well . . . enjoying yourselves?" called the man merrily.

"Yes, yes sir . . . very much." said Sara quickly, breathlessly.

"And where is that minx of mine?"

"Oh . . . I think she went for air in the garden, sir," said Sara hastily.

"Good. Good. She was looking flushed. Well then, go on . . . keep on having fun," he commanded, going off as happily as he had come.

"Excuse me," said Sara hurriedly before leaving Godwin's side.

He watched her in some concern. Lisa had not gone into the gardens. He had seen her leave the room and go toward the great hall. If she had wanted to go into the gardens she could have used the French doors off the ballroom! Really . . . what was afoot? He followed Sara out of the ballroom.

She sensed him at her back, God! Lisa's father coming at just that moment had been a stupendous piece of luck! Things were going perfectly. She slowed her pace, for she wanted him at her back when she opened the door to Lisa's room, where she had left Oscar in attendance.

Lisa had disgorged the evil irritating her insides only a moment after her friend left her in Oscar's care. It had been an embarrassing moment, but Oscar had been so good, so understanding. He had wiped her forehead with a cool cloth, and he had pressed words of understanding and comfort upon her. Oscar was so good, and as she lay resting against her pillow in the dim light she took his hand, because her nature was affectionate. "Thank you Oscar."

"For what? I did nothing," he said, blushing in the dark. In truth he felt he had done a great deal, but she was special, Lisa was, and he had been pleased enough to be there in her moment of need.

"But lord, girl . . . you are looking better." He patted her hand.

"Am I?" She breathed a sigh of relief. "I was so worried

that I would spoil the evening for Mama and Papa by coming down with something stupid!"

"Oh, Lisa . . . you are so thoughtful . . . so lovely . . ."

"Lovely? After that horrid display, I—"

"Nonsense!" he said at once.

"Oh, but Oscar . . . I was so embarrassed . . . and am so sorry you had to be a witness to—"

"Don't speak of it, Lisa. You are so good, so sweet . . . I was happy to be here, happy to help you in any way. . . . Oh, Lisa . . ." He leaned forward, for at that moment, with her eyes shining and her face still somewhat pale, she seemed a perfect beauty, and he wanted to cherish her. His kiss was gentle, soft and passionless as it touched her cheek. She took it in the spirit it was given, reaching her hand up to stroke his face.

Sara opened wide the door. Godwin hurried forward, and both stood frozen before Sara quickly shut it. Oscar and Lisa were so caught up in the sudden dawning of new feelings that they never noticed Sara's gentle handling of the bedroom door. They never noticed the two people in the hall or their expressions. Godwin was shocked, hurt, disappointed at his sudden realization, at his obvious loss. Sara's shock was genuine enough, for it had been more than she could have prayed that Godwin would find such a scene—it was for her beyond everything perfect!

Sara turned to find Godwin's drawn face. "Godwin . . . I . . ."

He offered her his arm at once. "Come, sweetheart—we dally here in vain, and I believe you had promised me this dance!"

"So I did, sir," returned Sara.

He smiled suddenly, dispelling the scene he had just witnessed. She was a beauty, was this Sara of Farenday, and he was pleased to have her interest in himself.

Sara's smile brightened her eyes. It had all been so easy. Lisa and Oscar had played their parts even better than she had planned! Oh, God . . . it was all really happening just as she had dreamed. Godwin would see Lisa no more, and Lisa would never even realize how she had missed out on such a catch!

Sara looked up suddenly, for the sound of a man's heavy footsteps on the hard earth path broke her trend of thought. Something caught in her breath as she watched the tall dark man smilingly descend upon her.

"Oh, Raoul, my love . . . I have so longed for today . . . and how I have missed you," she said feverishly as she went into his reaching arms.

He said nothing. He rarely spoke. His hand took up her face, and his mouth took hers crushingly. His body pressed against her, lowering her back onto the soft turf, and as he explored the delights of her body she felt herself released to her pleasure. Although he was her first, this meeting was one of many. She had met him several weeks before when procuring the potion that had so aided her schemes.

Yes, soon she would be Lady Ravensbury, but now she had her handsome gypsy and the pleasures he could so wondrously give her!

Two

So it was that in the fall of 1782, Godwin brought to Ravens-
bury a new and bright-eyed mistress. She entered the great
hall, and though she scarcely had eighteen years, her height,
her stature and her will commanded the respect of the servants. She had the confidence of knowing that she came from
good English stock and that she had married into better. And
still, on this her wedding night, she was restless, agitated and
unable to meet her husband's eye.

This Godwin very naturally took as virginal shyness, and
his tenderness knew no limit. His hand wielded her small pert
breasts, fondling, teasing, urging her reticence away.

"Come, Sara . . . I shall not hurt you," he said, raising the
skirt of her nightdress. "And I would see my bride," he said,
running his hand over her long smooth leg, finding the soft
tuft of dark-gold hair at the apex, cupping the triangle there,
feeling her response and bringing his hold firmer to bear.
"There, love . . . is it not good?" he cooed softly in her ear.
He had never dealt with a virgin before—this was something
he would treasure always, being Sara's first and only man.
She was his wife, his treasure, she would be the mother of his
children. Such were his thoughts even in his heat.

Her arms went around him. He was a big and wondrous
man, and his touch delighted and thrilled her, yet still she
could not dispel her tenseness. God! She had longed for this,
and even so dreaded the moment of his entry. Would he
know? Would he realize?

"I'll not hurt you, sweetheart," he said positioning his
manhood at her gateway. He was mildly, even pleasantly,
surprised to find she was already open to receive him. No
dryness halted his progress, and the sweet essence of her inflamed his desire.

The moment came for him to take her fully, to end the
foreplay with his plunge, and even still, because of what he
was, in spite of his bubbling veins, he was gentle and tender
lest he frighten her. She received him, and though her fear of
what he might now learn made her stiffen, he felt no breaking of her maidenhead. Deeper he penetrated, now caught up
in his passion, and the ardor of his movements brushed away

all thought. For the moment he did not question the fact that she seemed not a virgin, and later, he thought perhaps he had been wrong. He only knew she was his wife, he had chosen her, and the taking of her pleased him. And too, the taking of her, unlike the many women before her, meant the coming of children . . . children to bear his name!

She was lady of Ravensbury Castle. She had all she desired—her position, her clothing, jewels, the tender love of a man she admired. What more could she want? Peace of mind? Ah, peace of mind . . . what are all the rest without this?

She was with child, and how they all beamed and chatted! She was not due yet, for by her husband's reckoning if he had impregnated her their first night, their child would come in the spring, three months hence. She hadn't been eating well and she was thin, but her belly was swollen before her, and low . . . so very, very low! There were those who wondered if she would go full term, but Lady Ravensbury wanted but one more month. "Let my reckoning be wrong," she would pray. "Let me be off a few weeks . . . seven months . . . that would make the baby appear seven months . . . and perhaps with some effort all will be well!"

Her prayers, for reasons we can never know, were not answered. The coasts blew their harsh winds over Cornwall and sleet made travel impossible, but babies have no knowledge of such things, and 'twas time! Lady Ravensbury's labor had begun!

The midwife, a woman who had come to Ravensbury but a short time before, took command, for his lordship was too overwrought. His child . . . his child was coming, and what chance did it stand? No doctor . . . and the babe at six months would need a doctor. How could it survive? But she answered none of these questions. He was ordered out of the room; all others he sent in different directions. Her ladyship's water had broken but it would be a while yet before the child came. That would mean a hard birth. . . . She waited until she was alone with her ladyship before saying knowingly, " 'Tis no six-month bairn ye be giving him. 'Tis not even seven-month, m'lady . . . *but full-term!*"

"Yes, yes," said Lady Ravensbury quickly; she had planned what to say, "It is obvious, I suppose, that his lordship had me before he took me to the altar . . . but it doesn't matter."

"Aye," said the midwife wondering why then his lordship

would be worried about a six-month child. But she ventured nothing further on it. It wasn't her place.

Ten hours later, a healthy, albeit wrinkled, boy child was spanked roundly on the rump. He wailed his objection, a sound that made those within hearing ridiculously pleased. There was a great deal of commotion in Ravensbury Castle, for a male child had come to give them new blood!

Godwin demanded his son be brought for his inspection, and the midwife obeyed him. "But . . . he is so large . . . so pink! Just look . . . how lusty . . ." But his smile was fading. Godwin was no fool. How can one's fancies change in a moment? He had believed himself the only man in his wife's life. He had all these months been waiting for a child—*his* child—and here it was! *And it was a lie!* This was no six-month babe, but a full-term infant! *Not his, not his!*

He said nothing as this dawning took hold.

He went to his wife's room and closed the door, affording them privacy. She was flat on her back beneath clean sheets. All the blood had already been cleaned away. Her cheeks were pale, her eyes lusterless. He looked at her as though for the first time. She watched him and knew. Yet—he looked so gentle. Perhaps even now she could save herself. She looked upon his pain and thought of herself.

He was some distance from her, and his voice when he managed it was scarcely audible. "Whose babe did you birth today, Sara?"

"Godwin . . . he is gone . . . you are here. 'Tis yours. You felt its first kick . . . you cared . . . you care still."

Her words ripped him apart. He looked in her eyes and felt himself unloved. "Whose?"

"He was a gypsy. I fancied myself in love with him . . . and then he was gone."

"And I, I was there, wasn't I? Ready to play the fool." Still he did not raise his voice, but it cracked with his agony.

"Try to understand. . . . I needed a name for my child . . . could not bear to wear the scarlet cloak . . . shame myself. You drove all thoughts of him away, you were strong and wonderful . . . and I wanted to be your wife."

"You are beneath contempt," he said. "I deserved to be told. If you wanted my understanding, you should have told me. How could you let me go on thinking *it* was mine? Thinking *you* were mine. . . ."

"Godwin . . . no one need ever know," she said, thinking perhaps he worried for his pride.

He had not yet thought of outsiders or what *they* might think—his agony stemmed not from that—but her words served to exhibit how very far apart they were. "Did I ever know you, Sara? What did I see? How could I have been so blind? Did you laugh inside yourself . . . to hear the bovine Ravensbury say he loved you? Did you laugh when I handled you on our first night with such care? Did you?"

"No . . . I worried that you would discover my shame and leave me," she said on a sob.

"You worried for yourself. Of course. You never thought of me." He took a step toward her, for his anger was festered by his pain. She had said nothing to balm it, and every word drove the spikes in deeper. "And do you know . . . do you know that had you told me then, I would have loved you still! Then I would have understood . . . and taken the child as my own." But it proved to be too much for him to continue, and on an audible groan he turned and left her. He took the stairs to his library, where he locked himself in and thought of Land's End.

Sara believed all was at an end. All her planning had been for naught. Everyone would know if he went on in this fashion. She would be shamed in Cornwall. This was not London, where ladies of quality were notorious for producing spawns whose paternal parentage was questionable. She had to make him see that. This was Cornwall—cold, unforgiving, staid Cornwall. So it was that in an hour or so, in spite of her weakness, in spite of her pains, she raised herself off the bed and took the steps toward her door.

It happened quite suddenly. She felt nothing whatsoever, but at her feet was a pool of blood. It soaked through her gown, its warm stickiness streaming down her thighs. She saw it and screamed.

Godwin was in his cups. His brain was fuzzed with drink, but not so much that he did not hear. He sped like a man crazed and reached her room to find her in a faint upon the floor, her midwife screeching once again to the servants. He looked upon her, upon the blood, and cried, "Oh, my God! What have I done?"

It was not until the next day that the doctor could be obtained. Her ladyship's hemorrhaging had ceased, but there was infection. He kept her alive, but at the end of the week when he pronounced her no longer in danger, he took Godwin to one side. "I am sorry, my lord . . . but she'll bear you no more children."

Godwin stared hard at him. No children? Her sin he had nearly forgiven—if not really forgiven deep inside, he had taught himself to deal with it. She was, after all his wife, and these past few months with her had been good. But . . . no children?

The doctor tried to assuage the man's apparent grief. "Look here, my lord, you have a fine strapping youth in that nursery! Count yourself fortunate."

Godwin closed his eyes. A fine lusty bairn to carry his name . . . but it was a lie. There would be no more children. His bloodline would be ended within his veins, his chance at immortality shattered. He watched the doctor leave and then turned his back to the wall. Who could he go to? He was a man. He must keep his own council. They thought in different veins, he and Sara. Why had he never seen that before? And so, he went to the nursery. There he came for the first time that week to look upon another man's son. He looked down at the infant boy, and there was a pleasure in it. It surprised him, this sensation. The boy was not his—but it was a bairn, an innocent. He picked the babe up and cradled him in his large arms. The child looked at him, or so it appeared to Godwin, and his response was soft, protective. "Aye, son, you are a fine lad. . . ."

The days passed into months at Ravensbury. The servants would smile to see how warmly his lordship loved his son. Why, he had even the naming of him—Roderick, Roderick of Ravensbury. But they whispered about their mistress. She was a strange one, scarcely asking for the child, seemingly unmindful how he went on. The midwife, the one woman who could have told them a tale, had been sent up north to Sara's family, and Roderick was accepted as a true Ravensbury.

Three

1793

More than ten years had passed since Godwin had stood at Land's End and made his fateful decision. He was now one and thirty—the force of his youth had been swept away with his hopes, and there was that which marked time in his eyes. Youth's dreams, life's truths, had been exposed to the lad, leaving a man to carry on as best he could, and because he was Godwin, Lord Ravensbury, he brought a certain measure of contentment to his orderly life. He learned how to exist. He learned to adore his wife's love child, and Roderick was to him a Ravensbury.

Sara, Lady Ravensbury, learned to live as well. She filled her emptiness with social teas, routs, and gossip. Her nights with her husband were spent sometimes in passion, sometimes in the terrible loneliness of oneness, and never in friendship. Somehow that so important ingredient to marriage was denied them. To be sure, Godwin would have been the first to claim much of it his own fault. This because those first months were of his own making. He had never really forgiven her in the beginning, and it was exhibited in bitter remarks, resentful silences and cold disdain. Later, she reacted by avoiding his eye, displaying mannerisms not her own, and allowing guilt to lead her. So, they went on.

Godwin stood upon his rocky cliff gazing in earnest contemplation. They were so beautiful, the rocks, for they seemed to defy torture and time, boldly persevering. Proudly they jutted, sadly they whispered, but only to those who understood, for in the end they would yield to the sea. And he, Lord Ravensbury, felt a part of their might, a part of their destiny, as he stood towering among them.

It was then that he saw her! Raven hair glinting in the sunlight, its silken tresses swaying over her cloaked shoulder as she bent among the crags to gather her wild herbs. Her dark cloak blew about her graceful body, and he could just make out the profile of her face . . . and how it mesmerized him!

Then suddenly he saw her stumble, heard the instinctive

cry of one who knows a fall is inevitable, and she vanished from his view. He sprang to action immediately, hurrying his way down the razed slopes as fast as the steep terrain would allow, and there he found her rising to her feet, brushing the pebbles and sand from her clothes.

"Are you all right?" he asked hurriedly and in some concern.

She looked up, startled by his presence, and he was given the opportunity to note that her eyes seemed veritable violets, fresh and intense with their color.

"Oh, quite, thank you." She smiled ruefully as she looked herself over. "Discounting the injury to my gown. . . . Now if only I haven't dropped a morning's work into the sea . . ." With which she exclaimed gratefully, dived at a basket and nearly landed herself on the ground once again.

Godwin's great hand held her, preventing another such fall.

"Careful!" he admonished. "I've no mind to dive into the brine in April!"

She laughed, and the sound prodded a smile from him. "Nor do I, but I simply must get those herbs for my uncle, or he will say I am a lazy wench not worth my keep."

"Then stay put and I'll retrieve the basket for you," offered Godwin, settling her on a flat rock and scrambling after the wayward basket himself. This done, he set it at her feet. "There . . . and I don't mind telling you that you have an odd sort of uncle sending you off on such a dangerous mission!" He was smiling wide at her.

"In truth, these herbs can be had closer to home . . . 'tis just that I do so love Windmera and thought I might be able to enjoy it and get my errand off."

"*Windmera?*" he repeated, frowning.

She laughed lightly. " 'Tis what I call it. Look . . . they all meet here, don't they? I mean the sea, its marvelous winds . . . these rocks. It creates a peace. . . . Papa and I gave it that name. We used to come here together before he died."

"Yes, Windmera suits it. . . . But tell me, what is your name?" he asked, nearly blushing at his own boldness. He had never been a womanizer, he was not now, and he felt somehow guilty, sitting here asking this wench about herself. He knew well his motives.

She smiled. "Yes, it is only fair that you should know my name as I know yours, my lord."

"You know my name? How?" he asked, surprised.

"You are Godwin, Lord Ravensbury. Everyone in Cornwall knows that." She was smiling quietly, for she also knew there was a Sara, Lady Ravensbury.

"Very well then. As you said, it is only fair . . . ?"

"I am Heather Martin." She was no longer looking at him, but gazing out on the whitecaps.

"The vicar's niece?"

"The same." she answered, still not looking at him.

"But that is impossible!" he ejaculated.

"Is it? What an odd thing to conclude." She chuckled.

He flushed. "What I mean is—"

"What you mean is that you have heard the vicar's niece is a spinster of sorts . . . and I am far too attractive to fit that fiddle?" she interrupted him.

"Far too beautiful . . . and too young . . ." he floundered.

"I am one and twenty—near my dotage, you see. Up until last month I chose to teach in the school my father founded. However, the school closed—lack of funding, you see—so here I am at Uncle Martin's . . . driving them to distraction because I am not interested in the young men they present. . . . And gracious, what am I doing going on and on to you in this manner?"

"Please, don't stop. I want to know," he said, and his dark eyes had found hers.

Heather and Godwin were to meet often after that first encounter, and for reasons all too obvious to each of them. Heather told herself he was a beloved friend, someone who understood her, someone she felt whole with, no more. But honesty reared its hoary head and insisted she look! She lay on her soft mattress at night and questioned her motives. Yes, Godwin made her feel . . . all too much. Yes, she needed to be with him. Yes, he moved her heart. Yes, it was wrong! He was married! He belonged to Sara. But his marriage? It was a sterile thing, lifeless, giving him naught, and he, her Godwin, deserved so much, so much!

He, Godwin of Ravensbury? The vivacity of youth seemed to infect him. He only knew that his life took on new sparkle, that his heart felt light, that his nerves tingled and his blood bubbled. He only knew that Heather was the source!

There could be only one answer, and it came late one day in May of that very spring. They met at Land's End, between the crags she had dubbed Windmera. They met with but one shared thought—to make the other happy! Godwin watched her as she came to him and knew himself on fire. He reached for her, and she fell into his arms, for this their first kiss. It was enchantment. They cherished one another, and they drank of a fount that for them was innocent and pure. Forgotten was the world and its snares. Such was the joining of Godwin and Heather.

Afterward, she lay in his arms, his chin resting upon her head, and she listened hungrily to his words. "It cannot end with this," he whispered softly. "You must be mine in name as well as body!"

"Hush, Godwin . . . that cannot be." she answered gravely. This was not what she expected.

"I will not demean you . . . demean our love . . ." he returned harshly.

"What of Roderick? Would you shame him? Oh, my love . . . leave well enough alone. I am content." she argued gently.

"But my Heather . . . *I am not!*" was his answer. He turned her to him, holding her face, her eyes, with his glance. "I have lived a sham of a life with Sara. There is no love between us . . . only Roderick! I intend to see my solicitors. I intend to divorce Sara!"

"Godwin . . . no! You cannot do that to her . . . to Roderick!"

"Roderick will not be hurt by this. He is my son—my heir—and I shall provide for Sara's needs. No more, Heather . . . I will not suffer that marriage any longer."

She did not allow it to end there. She begged him long and tirelessly to give up such a notion. However, his mind was set. So it was that Godwin of Ravensbury made the second fateful decision there at Land's End.

Four

How could she sustain the shame? She would never be able to hold her head up! Oh, God . . . how the ladies of Cornwall would point and whisper! She would not let him divorce her, and so she said! She would not sign the deed of separation! Sara, Lady Ravensbury, tried everything to alter Godwin's decision, but he turned on her. As she paced now in her room, she could recall all too clearly the stone hardness of his eyes.

"Sign willingly, Sara . . . or you will live to regret what will follow!"

"No! What can you do? You have no just cause," she returned smugly. "You had better just forget your little jade."

He took a step toward her, his hand raised, but he controlled himself, though his body shook with the effort and her eyes opened wide before his wild emotion. "Never—do you hear, *never*—insult her again! Now listen well, Sara. I intend to have this divorce, even if it means dredging up the past."

"What do you mean?" she interrupted fearfully.

He answered her harshly, "I have no wish to hurt Roderick. I hope that I shall not have to."

He was bluffing. She would not believe him. "If you think that will answer, then do your best."

He stared long at her before answering. "You do not believe that I shall. I do assure you, it is not what I want. I love the boy, but I'll not sacrifice my future for either of you! You would both be ruined by such notoriety . . . but it will be by *your* hand, not mine!" he turned and left her then, but she still did not believe him.

She should have taken his warning more seriously. Godwin was not a hard man; indeed, his nature had always been pliable and gentle. However, he saw his life suddenly quite vividly before his eyes; He saw his past, he saw his future, and if it were to continue as it had he knew he would go to his dust without having made a mark upon the earth! He owed Sara nothing! He had given her his name and more, for in these past ten years of their marriage he had been fairly constant (for he counted not at all an occasional visit to a local bordello). She had made a place in society for herself, and she could still retain it if she would but give over grace-fully. How could she be so selfish? Such were his thoughts, and they did not deter him his purpose.

A month later, Lady Ravensbury sustained yet another shock. She had not seen Godwin overly much in this passing time, for he had taken to leaving the castle early and return-ing very late, and then never to her room. However, she had deluded herself into believing he had dropped the issue of di-vorce, that he was contented to play house with his doxy in that little cottage he thought no one knew about. Thus she was not prepared for Mr. Chale's visit.

An elderly man, Mr. Chale. He had served Godwin's fa-ther and was usually pleased to serve the son; However, he found this present task difficult in the extreme. He cleared his throat overly much and he fidgeted with the fobs at his plump belly, but in the end it had to be done. Godwin had confessed all to him with one sole purpose, to make Sara un-derstand how far he would go. And in the end, Mr. Chale made her understand. She sat before him, her gaze transfixed on nothing in particular and her voice scarcely audible,

"He is determined in this dreadful course?"

"I am afraid so, my lady. Though it grieves me to say it, his lordship will stop at nothing to obtain the freedom he desires," replied the elderly solicitor, the color making dark-red patches in his cheeks.

"Kindly advise Lord Ravensbury that I shall have to . . . study the situation before I give him my answer," she said, her mind racing.

"Very well . . . though he did wish me to make you aware that he will want your answer in the very near future."

"Mr. Chale!" she retorted austerely. "If he wishes to settle the matter of our . . . separation amicably, he must under-stand that I need time to adjust to . . . his proposals. It is, for me, an unbearable shame. I ask only a week. Surely a week is hardly unreasonable?"

"No, no, of course it is not," blustered Mr. Chale hur-riedly. His mind shot to Godwin's set words, his hard line, but really, Godwin would have to understand the woman needed time, he thought as he made ready to bow himself out of the room. "I will see to it that his lordship will be patient and give you the time you need."

Her chin was well into the air. She would not demean her pride before this horrid little man. She watched him as he departed. But now, now she had to think! Her first thought sent her back in time. It sent her to Lisa's ball. How she had won and now, now how Lisa and Oscar would gloat over her defeat! *No!* She had to find a way out of this. And because she was desperate, or perhaps because it was always in her nature, she found a suitable answer. Her blue eyes took on the luster of her youth before they narrowed, and as she formulated her plan, her lips took on a twist—such were her thoughts.

There were many things she would have to attend to, and some she would have to handle herself. But it was early yet, just enough time. Ha! What did Godwin think her—some soft and beaten creature? The years had made their mark on Sara. She had learned to find Godwin's reluctant forgiveness a bitter draft to swallow. Indeed, a part of her despised him for it. She had made him a fool! She had turned him from another woman with a false picture. He was a fool then, he was a fool still! Now, now he meant to challenge her, and she would make him long rue such a decision!

Then once more she thought of Lisa and Oscar. They had turned to one another in their disappointment. Their marriage, however, had been quite a success. She hadn't seen either of them since the ball, but they lived at no great distance. She wouldn't allow Godwin to so shame her in their eyes! Resolutely she crossed the oak flooring to a large well-worn gothic table of monumental proportions. There she took up her quill. What she needed first was Mrs. Abernathy. Indeed, that gross little skirter was just the one to carry out the second of Sara's errands. The first only she could handle—the first she could trust to no one but herself.

Heather strolled home to her uncle's modest but well-ordered household, musing pleasantly all the while. Her black hair trailed freely unhampered by the hood of her cloak. Over her arm a basket was slung full with wildflowers. In her throat a tune as lovely as her voice, and in her mind, thoughts of Godwin . . . and yet another.

She had not seen Godwin since their meeting at the cottage yesterday afternoon. She would not see him today, for he was away on business, and already she ached for him. She could still see his eyes . . . the way they looked when she told him she was with child. Oh, God, to give another such joy . . . why it just filled her with warmth.

Heather entered the kitchen to find the fire high in the

29

hearth, and she dropped off her cloak with a smile to Mabe, the cook. But there was no answering smile from the heavy woman. Heather remarked it at once, for she was used to the woman's coddling and this was out of reason odd.

"My goodness, you are looking dour. What is wrong? I am not late, for it scarcely wants ten minutes to five."

"Oh child, child," sighed the woman as she sank down upon a chair and made ready to tell her what had befallen them. She had known the moment she saw that miserable woman Mrs. Abernathy coming up the walk. She had known what would happen. " 'Tis best ye sit and talk with I before 'ee go to 'em."

Heather's brows met over her pert nose, and her violet eyes grew dark. There was a fear forming inside of her. "What is it, Mabe?"

"Mrs. Abernathy came to see yer uncle . . . and she made no secret of it, 'twas Lady Ravensbury who sent her. I know, coz m'boy listened at the door. I told him to."

"But . . . what does this mean?" cried Heather. She was alarmed. Her uncle barely tolerated her. He had taken her in only because it was the proper thing to do, and her aunt had little mind of her own.

"She made him know the worst of 'ee and himself. She come to end it." said Mabe, reaching to pat the girl's hand. It was wrong what Heather Martin was doing with himself, that she knew as a good Christian, but she was a woman too . . . and one that had been blessed with a heart for her man. Aye, she knew well what it was to love.

Heather jumped to her feet, "Oh Mabe . . . end it? I could no more end it than end my life!"

"Ye'll get nowhere speaking sech to the vicar!" said Mabe, shaking her head. "Lordy, girl, I've a fondness for 'ee, but still . . . himself be another's man. Think 'ee on it."

"But Mabe—" started Heather before cutting herself off. At the kitchen door stood a small but hearty lad of some thirteen years. He was round-faced and wide-eyed. He liked Heather and knew she was in for a severe scold. Many was the time he had received a frightening rendition from the master. He pitied her but gave over the vicar's instructions.

"Miss Heather . . . master saw 'ee coming down the walk . . . says to 'ave 'ee go to him in the study at once!"

She bolstered herself in the cook's warm hug. "There now, Miss Heather, buck up. It will be over soon enough."

Heather said nothing to this. Resolutely she picked herself

up, straightened her modest gown of blue muslin and left the kitchen at her back. Down the narrow hall, up the two steps to the main hall, down its length and across its width to the study doors. There she stood, staring and attempting to settle the beating of her heart. Oh God, she was frightened. The vicar would never understand. He and his wife were childless. He knew not the reliving of his youth through a child of his own. His only recollections were to justify his present. He would never understand. Indeed, how could he?

She took a long breath, sustained it, released it and opened the door. There he stood, a man of average height, balding, frail in his thinness, severe in his dark colors and his tight lips. He looked up, watched her come in with something close to pain in his faded blue eyes. She was so much like her mother, and now she had proved herself as loosely moraled, for he had never forgiven Heather's mother for marrying his brother.

"Close the door tightly at your back, girl!" His tone was harsh.

Heather obeyed meekly. She had often felt his treatment of her to be decidedly resentful, unreasonable, but she had never before been able to bring herself to face him with it. How could she now when he must feel she had sunk them into shame? She saw the sneer pull at the corners of his hard mouth, and because she was a gentle being, she nearly fainted with the thought of what was to come.

"Is it true?" was the question he threw at her. His voice was cold.

She wondered why he bothered to ask, for obviously he already believed that what he had been told was true. It piqued a feeling of disdain within her.

"Yes, it is," she answered softly, calmly—and was surprised by her calm.

"Faith preserve me, I have nurtured a creature of Satan!" was his reply. His hands were tightly clasped at his back, but they dropped to his side, and one formed a fist. It pounded the satinwood table at his hip. "You stand there, boldly admitting behavior most foul, without blushing, without shading your eyes from mine?"

"No, Uncle, I do not admit behavior most foul," she answered. From somewhere she was finding the strength to answer this cold man.

"Of your own free will you have just confessed—"

"You asked me if it were true? I assumed you meant is it

true that I, Heather Martin, love Godwin of Ravensbury. Yes, that is true, and I can not admit it to be foul!"

"You play with words? You stand here feeling no shame and . . ." He was overcome with sudden and, for him, strong emotion. "By God, girl, you deserve to be whipped!" He took a step toward her "You have participated in clandestine meetings with his lordship, and yet claim you have done nothing evil? Your actions are only surpassed in wickedness by your attitude."

"I am not playing with words or trying to win an argument, sir. You asked me how it was I did not blush, did not hide my eyes, did not feel shame, and I was but trying to explain. I find nothing wicked in loving Godwin. Nay, I am proud of it!"

"You engage in unlawful fornication with a man who is wedded to another. It is adultery!"

She did look away then for that was true. How could she make him understand, how could she explain?

"Ah! Finally I have succeeded in making you see!" he shouted with some pugnaciousness. It infuriated him to find that she was not cowered.

However, she met his glance once again. "No, that is not why I did not at once answer you. I merely thought the effort in vain!"

"By God, girl! Ravensbury is a married man. Does that mean nothing to you?"

"Yes, and had he been a happy man I would cut out my heart before attempting his! Do not speak to me of sins! God would not have put me in Godwin's way if He did not mean for us to meet, to love—"

"You are mad! Enough! I thought to bring you to your senses before sending you away! I see that it is impossible, which only strengthens my resolve that I am right in my decision."

This struck her a blow. Send her away? She had not expected this, not even from her uncle. She had expected him to try to extract a promise from her never to see Godwin again. She had not intended to submit to that, and all her words had been to that end. She never once thought he might send her away "You cannot mean it?" she breathed.

"Indeed, I have no choice. It is Lady Ravensbury's wish. Therefore you will find your bags in the hall, together with a pouch of bills to see you back to your Devon residence. I had sent for you believing I was doing my duty—believing you were a maid and therefore in need of protection. I looked to the proprieties. But, as you are not what I thought you, I can have no scruples regarding your future. I have no niece! You are to me, less than a stranger."

She sighed her relief. He saw it, and nearly went into an apoplexy. He had no way of knowing what her thoughts were. Heather had assumed that he was taking her in charge, sending her somewhere under guard. She had foreseen a time of trial ahead, but he was merely discharging her from the family. What was that? He and her aunt had never been her family! And there was the cottage. She would take her bags and go to the cottage. Godwin would not be pleased—he had not wanted widespread talk. But Heather cared very little for others' opinions.

She lifted her chin and looked at him boldly. "You are what you are. You will go on believing what you have done is the right thing. I wonder, Uncle, if you have ever known true happiness. I wonder, because I know that you will not in the future, and because of that I pity you."

He watched her go. Her words struck a nerve. For a moment he thought back to his youth. Had he ever known happiness? Yes, as a young man . . . the first time he had spent an afternoon with Heather's mother. But then she had given her hand elsewhere! Damn the girl! And even he knew not which girl he spoke of. Perhaps both!

Five

Not yet dusk, and Sara had accomplished much. She sat her horse well, her dark blue riding hat atop her yellow curls, her blue riding jacket hugging her body, her blue skirt flowing over her steed's back. One of the two men riding with her urged his horse forward and rode beside her. He glanced toward her and then lingeringly over her. She eyed him sideways and with a slight smirk allowed him his liberty.

It had been quite an afternoon! She had gone first to the widow Abernathy's small dower house. The woman was taken aback at first to find her ladyship condescendingly entering her home. She gushed over her with some effusion and then received Sara's tale with some relish. Sara smiled to herself. She had been so clever, allowing the widow to think it her idea to help. And then she rode into the town of Penzance.

The veil of her riding hat was drawn across her face as she made her way to the weathered tavern known as the Cat and Fiddle. She was tense lest anyone see her, recognize her, but she gathered up her determination and went through its doors.

Colin glanced up as the door squeaked on its hinges. His bushy brow went up thoughtfully. Hell, but she seemed a lady, this tall and elegant wench—what was she doing here? He watched her as she approached the tavern keeper, and something, he didn't know what, made him leave his men at their table and saunter within hearing distance.

Sara hesitated but a fraction of a moment. She wondered if but for a flitting passing of time, whether she was now passing the boundary, whether she was entering the world of true evil, but no sooner had such a fancy suggested itself to her than she blocked it off, swept it away. "I . . . should like to . . . hire some men." She took in breath and continued, "I have it that the Cat and Fiddle caters to the sort of fellows I am looking for."

"I don't take yer meaning, ma'am," said the tavern keeper cautiously.

"Eh, now . . . maybe *ye* don't, being dim-witted as ye are," put in Colin straightaway. "But me, now, I 'ave a mind to please the lady." He smiled widely at her. She looked as though her pockets were well lined, and Colin and his crew were in need of cash. Their last haul had gone to the brine, and they had never been able to retrieve it, for the riding officers and the revenue cutters had kept up too solid a patrol. It was why they had left Devon for Cornwall.

Lady Ravensbury turned around and looked him over. His hair was dark and unruly. His eyes were large and dark, though heavily lined. His build was husky, and in spite of the raggedness of his seamen's garb there was an animal attractiveness about him. Her eyes lingered on him, and he returned the compliment. It made her chuckle.

"Indeed . . . you look as though you may please me very well!"

His hand went around her shoulders, and her first reaction was to smack it off, but as she glanced at him sharply something within stirred. It had been a long time since Godwin had taken her to his bed. These past ten years she had been fairly contented to have only Godwin, discounting the times he was away and she had satisfied herself with a stablehand or a brawny tenant farmer.

She had come to Penzance with only business on her mind, but this burly stranger was reminding her that she was a woman, a desirable woman, and she liked the sensation it aroused.

"Aw now love, come over 'ere and ye'll be telling me how I might do that," he said, leading her to a private table in a corner alcove of the small dark galley.

He pulled out a chair for her before taking one himself and straddling it so that his knee idly bumped her own. He'd heard about quality ladies going after hard-living men such as himself, and he was enjoying his role. He was in spite of his hard heart and questionable life-style quite a ladies' man. Looking steadily into her blue eyes, he waited.

He was in her eyes a brute of a man, but still, for her he had a charm much reminding her of Roderick's natural father. The thought made her smile, for she had met her gypsy lover on an errand to win Godwin's heart. Here was yet another prospect, and the errand was much the same. "I shall be requiring your services—yours and your men. You are sailors?"

"Lordy love but what else would we be?"

"And you can obtain a vessel?"

"Aye. I am a man of means, sweetheart—got me own boat!" he said proudly.

"Very well. Then this is what I require of you," said her ladyship beginning slowly. When she had finished, Colin Stotes was sitting with his chin in his hands, his eyes narrowed and his face thoughtful. It worried her. "Have I come to the wrong man, sir?"

"No, ma'am . . . though it ain't our usual line of work. Smugglers we be, and proud of it. But this . . . coo, now, it will cost you!"

She smiled. "How much?"

"How much 'ave ye got to give?" he said coyly.

"One hundred pounds and no quibbling. It is all I have," she said firmly.

"I won't take a sou below two hundred," he returned, softly reaching for a lock of her hair.

She yanked angrily away from his grasp. "You will take one hundred. 'Tis all I have. Remember, I am buying the horses, and you'll be making a pretty guinea on the other side." She watched his thoughtful gaze find its way to the opening plunge of her bodice. She had deliberately undone her buttons while they were conversing. Her tone altered, and her eyes teased him suddenly. "It is all I have to give, sir."

"Is it now," returned Colin, catching the meaning at once. The hundred was in truth more than enough to keep him and his five-man crew for an entire month's lavish spending. Surely now the woman was a diamond, and he'd never bedded a real lady before. . . .

"Lord, but ye be a pretty mort. I'll have another fifty and the rest in merchandise, love. What say you?"

She didn't have enough to give him the fifty pounds and still be able to buy horses. Her eyes glittered as she moved close enough to give him a whiff of her perfume. "I was wont to think myself worth more, sir. You'll take one hundred pounds in cash . . . and one hundred in merchandise!"

" 'Tis a bargain sure!" said Colin, suddenly hot for her.

Thus it was that without at that point even knowing his name, or he hers, she was led up the tavern stairs to the narrow bedroom above where they concluded their arrangement.

It had been a long hard walk from the vicarage to the little cottage near Land's End. More than four miles. Her anger, her pride, her defiance, had carried her the first leg, but these emotions soon ebbed, for Heather was not a fighter by nature. Her belongings were not many, but the two portmanteaus seemed heavier as she reached her journey's end. Her situation loomed ugly in her mind, and her body was convulsed with a sudden weariness as she entered the dark two-roomed dwelling. The awesome questions reared themselves for inspection. Was she not selfish? Was she not wicked? She had come between a man and his home! Oh God!

She went to the hearth, and because she was shivering with the cold and with the prickling doubts of her conscience she started a fire. She had no way of knowing what was to come, what the smoke puffing from the cottage chimney of Windmera would mean to Sara. To Sara, yes, for Sara was outdoors. Sara was waiting.

Lady Ravensbury had planned well. Her timing was no less than perfect. The widow Abernathy had carried out her part and the vicar his, for Sara had given him, via the widow, an ultimatum. She had sent Mrs. Abernathy with the message, for she did not wish Godwin to know she had had a hand in this. It was simple enough; she wanted the vicar to send his niece away, *that very night!* She knew him well and never doubted his decision would favor her schemes. The girl would leave, but not for her Devon! Sara was sure of it. The girl would go to the cottage and thereby come into her hands. Oh, God . . . soon, soon it would be over.

She watched the smoke curl upward from the chimney and motioned her horse forward out of the dusky woods. Colin smiled and followed. The man at his back frowned, but he too urged his horse forward.

Farmer Burns closed his field gate. He stretched his well-worked limbs and sighed. It had been a long day. A long day. He hoped his spouse had made his favorite chicken pie this night, for he was tired of broth and bread. A sound ruffled his thoughts, and he looked up curiously to see horses cutting turf as they crossed the fields, jumped the fence and followed the road. Three riders they were, and as they neared he stood lingering, for one of the three caught his eye.

Well, well, he thought with some wonder. What would her ladyship be doing riding about with the likes of those two? Why, them blokes didn't look fit to feed pigs. He watched their progress, scratching his head beneath his straw hat over the problem. He settled it as he got a good look at Colin's manner of dress. Seamen! They were seamen sure! But lordy, he asked himself, why was her ladyship riding about with such as they?

Lady Ravensbury passed the farmer. He was some distance back from the open road, but near enough for her to realize that he saw her well. He was one of Godwin's better tenants, but she avoided his eye and quickened the pace of her horse's trot, stepping lively. A simple man, this Farmer Burns, she told herself soothingly. He would think nothing of her taking an evening's ride. At any rate, it could not be helped!

Heather stretched herself out on the hearthrug and gazed into the fire. She sighed gustily, for she could think only of Godwin and what he would say—do—when he heard how her uncle had treated her. Really . . . to send her out into the night believing she had yet to journey to Devon? *That* was wickedness, for it set out deliberately to hurt another being. She ran her hand down to her flat belly. There grew Godwin's child, and how she loved it already! She did not yet consider the future, for she was young, and youth rarely plans more than its immediate needs. She was nearly dozing, her head resting on her bent arm, when the door opened and Sara of Ravensbury stepped forth.

Her ladyship gazed at the lithe beauty stretched out near the fire. Heather was some ten years her junior, and Sara had never had the girl's particular shade of beauty. There was more than the perfection of features contained in Heather, and Sara saw this, and the hate within her welled and spilled over. She slammed the door shut at her back, finally getting Heather's attention.

"My, my . . . what a sweet picture you do present. One would hardly guess you have a slut's heart!" sneered her ladyship viciously.

Heather spun around, raising herself up to find Sara before her. She had seen the tall attractive woman many times before at a distance. The color drained from her face, not from shame but because of a sudden unexplainable fear that gripped her heart.

"My lady . . . ?" she managed as she stood, but floundered.

Sara, her head high, meandered through the cottage, saying nothing and expressing disdain only through several little snide movements of face and hands.

"What is it you want?" said Heather, stepping away as Sara came toward her.

"What I want is my husband!" snapped the woman before her.

"I . . . I have not the power to give him to you," returned Heather on a hush.

"No? You underestimate yourself . . . *and me!*" said Sara, opening the leather pouch she carried in her hand.

Heather watched, fascinated, to see Sara take out ink, quill and paper. What was she about? What was her purpose? What would Godwin think of this night's work?

Sara laid these articles down upon the round kitchen table and brought the candle holder near. With her hand she made a grand gesture. "There, Miss Martin, please be seated and I will tell you what you are to write."

"Write? To who?"

"Why, to my husband, of course," said Sara with much confidence.

The self-assurance of the older woman's voice sent a shiver through Heather. Something dreadful was about to happen— she sensed it, knew it. She saw before her a ruthless woman and knew herself doomed. But she maintained her composure.

"Write to Godwin? What would you have me say?"

"That you are leaving. That you cannot bring shame to his household, that you never want to see him again!" said Sara sweetly.

Heather considered the woman before her, choosing her words carefully. "It is a lie. Why would I give him a lie?"

"Quite simply, my dear. Come to the window." She waited, and as Heather did not budge, her voice became more insistent, "For Godwin's sake . . . come to the window."

Heather went as she was bid.

"See those two men?"

Heather nodded.

"Seamen, both. Actually . . . smugglers. They carry pistols, you know. They have agreed to murder Godwin for me, tonight, on his way home from St. Ives." She halted only to smile at Heather's expression of horror. "Indeed, 'tis a lonely road."

"You are mad!" cried Heather. "You would not dare such a thing!"

"No? I must admit to a certain reluctance. However, I would rather be a widow than a discarded wife!"

"Oh, my God!" said Heather on a faint cry. Her hand went almost instinctively to her belly, as though to shield her infant from such evil.

"You still don't perceive the situation, do you?" said Sara, on a weary sigh. "Very well—allow me to outline my thoughts. I will not divorce Godwin! Be that known. He means to shame me and my son in order to win his freedom. I could not bear that. I *will not* bear that. Therefore, I have but two roads left to me. One, getting rid of you. I cannot murder you without murdering Godwin, for he would surely run me to earth if I had you disposed of. Therefore, you must leave him. It is the only way. If you do not accept that, I shall take the other path, which is . . . disposing of both of you!"

"You could not succeed in such a nefarious plan!" objected Heather.

"No? Your uncle has disowned you—sent you off! People will assume you have gone home to Devon. My husband will have met his fate at the hands of highwaymen. Quite neat, don't you think?"

"You would do that to Godwin?" breathed Heather, trying to collect her thoughts.

"As I have said, I have no wish to be a widow—though to be sure, it may have its advantages. After all, sending you away may only make room for yet another slut, and I have no wish to enter into such dealings twice in my lifetime."

Heather gave the woman her back. What to do? What to do? She must humor Sara. She must pretend to accept. Save Godwin this night, and get him word later.

"It would appear, my lady, that you have left me no choice," she said at last.

Sara of Ravensbury knew well what Heather was thinking, but she stalled her tongue. Let the girl first do her bidding, then she would gloat. "That is quite correct. Now sit down and take down these words. You *can* write?"

For answer, Heather picked up the quill and took up a position at the table. Sara standing above and behind her began,

"Darling,
Too many are hurt by what we have done. I have shamed my family and must go. It is over. Indeed, it never was. Do not try to find me.
                                        Heather."

Sara saw Heather seal her name before picking up the letter, airing it, folding it and concealing it within her dark cloak. Then she turned and gazed with hate at Heather Martin. "Now, Miss Martin, you will go to your destiny!"

"I am far too weary to make any journey tonight, my lady. If you don't mind I shall not leave Cornwall until the morning."

"Fool! Do you think I leave you to your own devices? Did you really think I could be so gulled? You will never see your lover again, but you will see others . . . and in a French bordello!"

Heather jumped away from the table. "My God! What do you plan?"

"I have paid those men out there to take you to France, this very night, my dear. They are most willing, for in France they will sell you to a choice brothel, where you will get the opportunity to use your many . . . talents!" With these words Sara opened the door and shouted for one of the men.

Heather saw him looming above her, and her violet eyes looked up as she pleaded, "Please, sir . . . you cannot mean to do this. I am an Englishwoman, niece to the vicar—"

"Quit blabbing, mort—won't do ye no good! Paid to take ye and always do what I be paid for. Don't care who ye be—these ain't me parts—owe nobbut nuthin', so hush up or I'll have to clap a rag over yer mummer," said the large brute, holding her wrists.

"I believe it would be wise to silence her. She must be prevented from calling out to any chance passerby," put in Sara thoughtfully.

"Aye, then. *Bunky!* Hey there, Bunky!" called the man.

A tall thin lad of less than eighteen years came hurriedly to the open door. "Aye then, Colin, be ye wanting me?"

"Get the mort gagged, boy, and then afore ye on the saddle. We best be making paces to the sloop!"

Bunky looked across and found there Heather's eyes, and before her terror he blushed a deep shade of red. He ambled with some reluctance toward her, taking off the kerchief from his neck and coming around his older cohort. "Sorry, ma'am," he offered as he put the cloth into her mouth and pulled it into a knot at the back of her silken head. Fiend seize it, thought he, this is not the sort of thing I take to. Smuggling is one thing . . . but abducting women? Lordy, I jest can't take to it. But he knew Colin would have no more of him if he didn't obey, and he needed to make a living.

Heather did not struggle. She was sick with fright, but she knew struggling would do no good. She had only one hope.

Godwin would know she had not left him. She had only yesterday told him she was with child. They had shared a moment none could understand, and she knew he would not believe the note even though it was in her own hand. He would never believe it, and he would come . . . he would find her!

Sara watched her hired minions do the deed, and with a smile she took to horse and made for Ravensbury Castle. She would leave the note on his nightstand. He would find it tonight upon his return, but it would be too late, for Heather would already be on her way to France. Oh God, thought she fiercely, there is satisfaction in this!

Heather sat before the young lad Bunky on his horse, unable to speak, but she listened, for the youth seemed compelled to excuse himself to her. "Lookee, ma'am . . . I don't hold wit this, I don't. But, what I like . . . well, it don't make a ha'porth o' difference to the culls I sail wit. The woman . . . she come into Penzance . . . struck up a bargain with Colin some hours later . . . I jest be doing whot Colin tells me. . . ."

Heather turned her head around and answered him with her eyes. She said nothing, but he heard her clearly. We always have a choice! He was choosing the easier route. Lordy, what eyes this beauty had. He had never before seen their like. The color of wild purple crocus coming up dewy in the morn . . . sad they were, and why not? Torn from her home . . . why? It didn't matter why. They had no right to serve her so. Her fate he knew; Colin had laughed about it. She was to be sold to a French bordello. Lordy, but it went against the grain. However, long ago, coming out of the workhouse, he had learned well the manner of living with things he could not change. He would just have to live with one more.

They reached the cove; Colin had ordered his men to moor the sloop here and await his signal. The horses, provided by her ladyship's pocket, were set free. Colin lit the lantern and waved it in the air. Heather watched all this in silence. Her thoughts were less than dread, more than resignation.

The moon was only a smile in the darkness, but the unmistakable sound of oars scudding water were soon heard, for the sloop had sent out a small boat to fetch its winnings.

"There now, lass . . . up wit ye!" said Colin, apparently in an excellent mood, and why not? He had been paid to take this lady to France, where she would again earn him a pretty fee, and all this luck simply because he had chosen to take his Devon crew into Cornwall and evade the preventive officers for a time!

Heather saw the sails of the sloop shivering in the wind. She had her cloak tightly wrapped around her, but she was chilled all the same. Little hope was left to her now. She had but one—that no brothel would buy an unwilling English maid. More innocent she for such a hope!

There was some grumbling among the five-man crew, for though smugglers, they were for the most part law-abiding. An odd contradiction, to be sure, but nevertheless quite true. Abducting females, especially well-bred females, which the chit obviously was, and then selling her as a slave to a brothel . . . well, they had no liking for it! However, Colin was their captain, and they never went against their captain; he had seen them through too much to do that. And the money—there was no denying they had need of that, for each and every one had a family waiting in Devonshire.

Thus, Heather was taken on board and stowed at the bow of the boat. The only good that came from the guilt of these men was in the treatment they presented to Heather. None abused her; one, in fact, offered her a blanket, and all, observing Bunky's hovering care over the chit, silently decided among themselves to leave her to Bunky. Perhaps this came too from a desire to avoid the wench's eyes.

Bunky bent down and removed Heather's gag. "There . . . none can say naught now. I mean, who could ye call to?"

She glanced about the weather-worn vessel and then at the stretch of billowing sea and said ruefully, "That is a truth."

He sighed and went to the rigging, leaving her to her thoughts. She watched him for a time and then turned her gaze to Colin. He was a large man, and a moment's study told her he was also a hard one. No hope there.

Bunky returned to plop himself down beside Heather. A fine mist of sea spray had covered his lank brown hair, and he pulled out a wool cap and slipped it on. He cast her a sullen look, and looked away without speaking. And then his eyes found Colin. Damn, but it wasn't what he liked! He had in many ways looked up to his captain prior to this night, but he now saw a greedy aging man, unprincipled and hard to the core.

"Look, ma'am . . . I be that sorry . . ." he offered Heather.

She turned from her contemplation of the sea and cast him a doubtful look. "Are you? I suppose the hangman feels much the same. 'Tis, after all, but a job!"

He was stung and hastened to reassure her. "No, it won't be like that. Ye ain't going to any gallows." And then as he recalled just where she was going, the color drained from his youthful countenance.

"No, indeed not . . . at least not by a man's reckoning. However, I would rather be," she said quietly. Heather had never been a fighter. Her nature was grace and gentleness, and a certain bravery underlined these, but she would never pick up the cudgels in her own defense, and had they been put into her hands, she would have been hard put to use them. She sensed there was a chance with this lad. She felt she could persuade him to free her, help her; but she made no push to it, allowing the fates to run their course. And then she thought of Godwin. She would never see him more. A tear formed.

Bunky watched the path the glistening rivulet took down her lovely white cheek. It was unbearable. He had never seen this sort of sadness. He had seen and heard women shriek over many things. He had seen the keening over the dead, always frantic, always loudly calling for pity, calling attention. But this woman called for no pity. She bore her grief, her fears, in silence, and Bunky knew himself the lowest of miserable creatures.

The sloop of the Devonshire smugglers sailed into the sun, leaving the cover of night behind them. They would need it no more, for they were nearly in French waters. It was June, but no calm came to slow their steady progress, and by midmorning St. Pol-de-Léon was sighted. It was not with any great feelings of joy that they spotted French soil. Each time they made a trip to the French coast it was with a silent fear and additional doubt, for even if they were to win their way to and from Devon without an English revenuer taking chase, they had still to worry about the devilish French—for the Reign of Terror had begun two months past. And of late a dashing noble buck or two was crossing the Channel and making off with a head meant for Madame Guillotine. The French revolutionaries did not appreciate this. Anyone with a boat was suspected of trying to smuggle out French aristocracy. But Colin had been sailing his trade these twelve years and more and knew many people in the ports he could call friend.

By afternoon they were docked. Colin, taking two of his crew, departed in search of a cargo. He would be after brandy and silks. This left the boat with three men, one being Bunky. The other two took to playing cards to while away the hours. Bunky took to Heather. The lad was already worshiping at her feet.

"When do you think he will take me ashore and . . . give me over?" faltered Heather.

Bunky nearly choked on his answer. "By nightfall."

"Do you think, Bunky . . . I could have something to drink. My throat is parched."

He nearly stumbled in his rush to do this thing for her. He made his way to the water bucket, and as he drew a mug full he brought his eyes up to the bustling docks. There was the usual rush of peasants, the usual noise, a scuffle not far off between a market peddler and a dissatisfied customer. And there was something else. It was odd how it struck him, for he had seen such things before, even indulged now and then, yet at that particular moment, he was struck with horror. He saw a young harlot, no more than twenty. She was full-bodied and scarcely clothed. She made a selection, and the passing buck stopped to give her a grin and a pat on her rump. She slid closer to him and drew his hand into her bodice. Bunky watched and felt the color drain from him, feeling his life's blood turn cold as the woman exposed herself to her prospective client. He saw them go off toward an inn together, and he turned to find Heather graceful in quiet repose. God! Divine Power! He could not allow it. If he were to die at Colin's hand, he would not allow Heather Martin to be sent that road!

He sank down beside her on the deck. "I'll get ye away, ma'am, I promise ye and the Almighty. I'll get ye away!"

She sat up, excited, hopeful that the lad would see them out of this muddle. "But how?"

"We best wait until dark sets in proper like . . . then we'll inch nearer to the dock, I'll get ye up and over and ye run! It's bound to draw a crowd, all the hollering in English that will follow us. That'll be in our favor, coz Colin won't find it so easy to track us whot with Frenchies getting in his way."

"But where will we go?"

"I don't know that, ma'am. I only know I can't let ye go to . . . where they mean ye to go," said Bunky on a heavy sigh. Surely his future looked black.

Colin returned with the dusk. It seemed to Heather that

45

the cloak of night came with him. He spied her and Bunky sitting beside one another and leered, "Eh, lad . . . fancy her, do ye?"

Bunky flushed darkly, but he saw here a way, "Aye, that I do . . . but what can I do about it with all of ye gawking at us?"

Colin laughed gutturally. "Well, ye be a good lad. Why don't ye take her down to the inn for an hour or two. She be sold, but she don't go till morning. When we gets our shipment, we give her over . . . till then she be ours! I've already had me toss . . . so I put her in yer keeping!"

Colin had no suspicion. How could he? Bunky wouldn't dare let her go. How could he return to the ship and live if he did? And Colin took Bunky's constant presence at her side to mean but one thing, the only thing he could understand.

Bunky was beside himself. Colin was offering him a way! Not only could he aid Heather in her escape, but he could return to the sloop . . . say she knocked him on the head. At least he could return! "Mean ye I can 'ave her . . . now?" he asked cautiously, lest Colin was playing a May game with him, a thing his captain often indulged in.

"Aye. It's about time ye had a woman—never seen ye take to one afore—and jest to show ye how much I think of ye, Bunk, m'lad, I'll be taking ye to the inn meself!" said Colin, making the lanky youth a mock bow.

"Aw, now, Colin . . . I ain't a stripling to be led about," objected Bunky.

"Now who said ought about yer years? I jest want ye to be comfy with yer lass, and seeing as ye never stepped foot in France afore, thought it best to lend ye a hand," said Colin, leading the way.

Bunky thought it best to refrain from further objection lest Colin change his mind altogether. He gave Heather his hand and helped her to her feet. "Hush now, ma'am . . . say naught."

Heather followed him onto the dock, where she clung fearfully to his hand. He held her close, and Colin turned, saw and bellowed loudly, "That's m'buck! But jest wait now . . . 'tis only a few steps further."

They took the wharf to a two-story building of graying wood. It seemed to Heather that there was every good chance the building, which leaned heavily to the east, was about to collapse in that very direction. They entered. The odor of urine permeated the air, and she could see why, for not very far off an elderly Frenchman had freed his member and was watering the floor. Bawdy women, their breasts nearly bare, their hair twisted and snarled, sat atop tables and in corners, and Heather turned away from the sight.

Colin exchanged a few words with the Frenchman behind the counter, slipped him a coin and indicated to Bunky with a jerk of his head the stairs at the far end of the entrance.

Bunky whispered to Heather, "Hold tight now . . . don't look about ye, ma'am . . . for this is a terrible place," and he led her up the stairs. He glanced back to find Colin chuckling but making his way outdoors, and he sighed with relief.

"There. We'll jest give Colin a minute to make his way down the wharf . . ."

"And then?"

"Lordy . . . I dunno . . . first jest let me get ye out of sight."

Colin ambled toward the sloop, stopped and considered a notion. Aye, they had made a handsome sou this day! He was a generous man, wasn't he? Well then, he should be bringing a couple of bottles of whiskey to the crew! Aye . . . he'd just go back and get a few bottles for the men. Why not? They wouldn't be leaving till the morning!

Bunky led Heather outdoors. Oh, God, she thought, once outside, even the filthy scent about the docks was better than the insides of that inn! She allowed Bunky to lead her by the hand, still calm in spite of all she had been through. And then a shout stilled her heart.

"Eh?" shouted Colin, frowning at their backs. "Whot's this? Eh, Bunky!" Clearly it was a command to stop.

Bunky never looked back. His hold on Heather's hand tightened as he pulled her, and they were racing down the wharf. The shouts continued behind them, for Colin had obtained the aid of two French comrades, and the chase was definitely on!

They raced in a straight path, for there was nowhere to go, nowhere to stop and catch a breath, nowhere to hide. And then Heather spied the alley. It was her turn to lead. She tugged; he turned sharply, saw her purpose and seconded the motion. They sped down the alley, found yet another and took it. This led them to a fork. They took the wider avenue, not knowing where they were going, not knowing how far behind was Colin. It opened onto yet another wharf, another canal, but they could hear Colin and the Frenchmen not far behind.

Desperately Bunky glanced about and saw a well-built schooner. There didn't seem to be any crew about. There was nothing for it. They had to get out of sight before they were observed. He led Heather across its plank, onto its deck, down its waist and into the storage hatch. The hatch door clanged above their heads as Heather sank to her knees and gasped for breath. Bunky, panting, stood wobbling slightly, for his feet rested not on floor but on sacks of grain. He listened at the closed portal for a few minutes before dropping down beside Heather. "Aye . . . I think we've ditched them. Heard them shouting still, but the sound came from far off. Best we keep still . . . no saying that Colin wouldn't have all the port searching us out!"

"What? Stay here?" asked Heather, glancing about. She could see absolutely nothing in the total darkness. She felt the burlap sacks full with their grain and felt certain there must be rats somewhere about as well. Oh how she wished she were back at the cottage waiting for Godwin.

"Aye," he answered her. "Jest till morning. Then we'll lope off."

"How will we get back to England?"

"I dunno. I got some blunt. Mayhap we'll purchase a way. Don't fret it, Miss Heather. We'll be fine we will. . . ." he said uncertainly.

"Aye," she answered him, reaching out in the dark and finding his hand. She patted it gently, comfortingly. "Aye, Bunky, surely we will."

What of Godwin and his lady? Much had happened by the time Heather and Bunky found their way on board the schooner known as the *Liberté*.

Godwin returned to his castle near the hour of midnight. He was weary, for the day had been overlong and he ached for Heather. He thought of her as he shrugged off his blue superfine. Heather . . . carrying his child! Oh, God . . . was such happiness possible? Was it really true? He had his love and would soon have a babe, his very own babe? It was at this moment that he discovered a folded piece of paper propped on his nightstand. It bothered him. He didn't know why the sight of it sent a shiver up his spine, but it did. He reached for it, stopped himself and ran his hand through his thick red hair. He was being idiotic. He stretched out his hand and took up the paper and unfolded it.

Godwin saw the words. They swam before his dark eyes. He knew Heather's hand, it was her hand . . . but not her words! She would not go! Not of her own free will! He knew her. She would not take his child and leave him, not she! They loved! They loved! They loved!

"No!" The shout tore from his guts. "No!" and he turned to his door. "Sara!" This was Sara's doing, and he would wring a confession from her this very moment. He took the hall like a man crazed. No more could one see the gentle Godwin in his mien. "Sara!" he shouted as he shook her door. "Sara!"

His lady opened her door a crack, but his fist beat it from her hands, nearly taking her off her feet in the process. She faced him in her nightcap and white nightgown. "What is it, Godwin?"

For answer he shook the letter in her face. "How did this get to my room?"

"Why, how should I know?" she answered.

"Shall I call out each and every servant, Sara? Shall I?" he threatened taking up her arm.

She pulled herself out of his grasp, and as he reached for her again she stepped backward out of the room. He stalked her. "Answer me, madam! How did this note find its way to my room?"

"If you must know, Mrs. Abernathy delivered it to me. I put it in your room."

"Mrs. Abernathy?" he retorted. "What tale is this?"

"The vicar found out about your sordid little affair with his niece. He convinced her to go away. She gave the letter to him, and he gave it to Mrs. Abernathy, who then gave it to me!" snapped Sara.

Godwin heard her but knew there was a lie in it. A meanness took his spirit. He raised his hand into the air and sent it viciously across his wife's face. Sara fell and was startled into fear. He picked her up roughly by her arm, and she took a step away from him, out of his grip.

"So . . . you arranged it between you? You and Mrs. Abernathy . . . you made certain the vicar knew?" he accused. "And he, this marvelous man of God . . . what has he done with Heather?"

"I am certain I have no notion. Now let me be," she said, attempting to bypass him and escape to her room. He thwarted her efforts by grabbing hold of her shoulders. His shake was brutal, and her faded gold hair fell from her cap onto her shoulders. Godwin was himself no more. He had been trampled in his youth by this woman's lies; he would not be done in such a manner again by the same hand.

"Bitch!" he ranted. "I shall see you in Hell!" With which he pushed her aside from him, no longer able to stomach the sight of her.

He made for the stairs. She saw it, had to stop him. "Godwin—where do you go?"

"To the vicar!" he roared.

"Godwin . . . what of Roderick? Think of Roderick!" she pleaded, using the last weapon she had left to her.

It was not the moment. A man says many things in anger, and Godwin was in a rage. "Why in Hell should I? He is *your* son, your bastard . . . *not mine!*"

She took the steps, clasping his shirt sleeve in her hands, "Godwin, you can not do this . . . you will make a fool of me . . . of your name . . ."

He couldn't bear her touch. Brutally, he yanked himself away, hissing, "Get thee gone from my sight!"

"Godwin . . ." But again he wrenched himself free. She stumbled. Suddenly Sara was screaming; suddenly he was standing high above in mute shock, watching his wife bump and roll as she fell the length of the stairs to the marble hall below. He took the steps frantically, bending over her still form. "Sara!" he cried, demanded.

"Mama!" said a young boy's frightened voice from the top of the stairs.

Godwin stared with disbelief to find Roderick glancing accusingly down at him. Roderick? How much had the boy heard? He looked into his son's eyes and had his answer.

Roderick, heir of Ravensbury, had not understood all of what he had heard. The shouting had brought him out of his room, and most of its meaning had been lost on him, though later he would understand. But then he heard the one man he adored above all other beings, above his own mother . . . *he heard that man disclaim him!*

Ah, Godwin, a day to rue! Sara had robbed him of the lady of his heart and the child of his blood, and he had robbed himself of the boy he called son.

She groaned. Lady Ravensbury moved her head and groaned.

"Sara?" He waited not for a reply but shouted to Roderick,

"Fetch the servants . . . have them go into town for the doctor!" Then again to his wife, "Sara?"

She opened her eyes. "What . . . what happened?"

"You fell, Sara," he said, his brows drawn together in consternation.

"I . . . I want to get up," she said suddenly. "Help me up, Godwin!"

He attempted to lend her his support, but she was staring at him in horror. "Godwin! My legs . . . I can't move my legs!"

Six

The Liberté *chiseled its path through the choppy bay, and* its sails were full with the wind. Its captain, Maurice de Brabant, stood bent over the bulwarks staring at the receding shoreline, now barely visible in the night. The moon lit up his face, and his five-man crew were well able to discern his sadness. It was difficult, this final, this lasting break with France! But Robespierre had given him no choice. And thus it was that he, the comte de Brabant, would never return to his ancestral home.

No matter, he thought, now attempting to revive his spirits. Hadn't he made Barbados his home? Indeed, when his older brother had gifted him with this very schooner eight years before, hadn't he relished the notion of creating a life in that tropic isle? So he had gone to Barbados, and he had been granted a charter from King George III to begin a sugar-cane plantation, and he had made it thrive. And then the letters from home started slowing, and when they did come they were filled with fears. His brother, the comte, sensed danger . . . and then only four months ago his brother had gone to the guillotine.

Maurice had lost no time in returning to France, for he had still a sister, dear and beloved, and he would not have her go the same route. He had an old friendship with Robespierre; he would use it now! Louise Davenant had seen her husband guillotined for his speeches against the revolution, but her own faithful servants had spirited her out of death's way. Maurice had come, and he had fought with his old and now powerful friend, but in the end he had been granted his sister's life only provided he took her and left France and his ancestral home to the *citizens!* He had agreed; indeed, he had little choice.

Thus it was that the present comte and his widowed, childless sister made for the haven of an English isle.

"Bunky! Bunky!" whispered Heather, giving the boy beside her a shake of the shoulder. "Wake up!"

They had talked long into the night, telling each other the secrets of their youth and then falling asleep in separate corners. Something had roused Heather. She knew not what, but as she stretched she realized all at once what it was. The boat . . . it was moving!

"Bunky, please!" she pleaded, and sighed thankfully when he let out a yawnish growl.

It was still too dark to see much, but there was yet another fact Heather was certain of: it was day! Strips of gray light filtered in through the cracks of the hatch. Bunky stretched into wakefulness, and he too was struck by the sway of the boat.

"Whot the divil?" he ejaculated. "Oh, Lordy . . . we be moving!"

"Indeed . . . and must have been for some time, don't you think?"

"Aye . . . for day be coming through," he agreed. "Oh, saints preserve us! They'll throw us over, make no mistake. Captains don't take kindly to stowaways."

"But we are not!" declared Heather. "We are English! We shall present ourselves to the captain and beg that he return us to Cornwall."

"Nay, ye be daft, Miss Heather!" said Bunky. Then, remembering himself, he blushed for his rudeness. "Whot I mean is . . . if this be a Frenchman's yawl, they'll never set us in Cornwall. Whot's more . . . they might do much what Colin had in mind!" he added ominously.

"Gracious! There can't be so many villains in the world," she objected.

"Don't know naught about that, but I do know sailors! Crusty odd lot they be . . . out to earn their bread. It's a hard life, and they don't look too close how they come by their ready!"

"But, Bunky . . . they will find us. I mean, when they come into the hatch for supplies," said Heather in some consternation.

"Aye!" agreed Bunky dourly.

"Whatever shall we do?" cried Heather. What of Godwin? Was he lost to her for all time? Would she see him no more? There was no telling what Sara would do even if she did manage to return to Cornwall. Sara? A dangerous woman . . . ready to kill Godwin rather than free him.

"Whot I suspicion is this, Miss Heather. If this be a French yawl, she may be putting in for one of her isles. We might yet be able to slip away when she docks . . . if we can stay hid till then!"

"Oh, Bunky, I don't believe you are thinking. We can't stay holed up in here for days on end. And it would take weeks to get to one of the French colonies! We must present ourselves to the captain and pray he is a merciful man!"

"That be a queer start if ever I heard one, missy!" complained her companion. "Danged if I know what we are to do . . . but I ain't setting meself before no captain!"

She could see he was adamant on the subject and decided it best to let it go awhile. However, as she laid her head back she felt the first pangs of hunger. She hadn't eaten since luncheon yesterday, and that but a piece of cheese and a hunk of bread Bunky had procured for her. She decided to mention this fact to her friend.

"Bunky . . . I am hungry."

"Aye, bless ye . . . for ye ain't alone," said he.

"What shall we do? We must eat."

"Aye," he agreed.

She sighed, thinking his lively dread of the captain would see them starved and blinded if she didn't do something positive.

"Well then . . . shall we go above and request some food?"

He stared through the darkness at her, sure that there were maggots floating about in her upper works. "Eh? Do ye mean to get us fed to the sharks?"

She sighed and again gave it up. She would not go up against his will; she had not the right to so betray him. "Very well."

Soon, for lack of better activity, they drifted off again, and when next they awoke, no more light showed through the cracks of the hatch opening.

At Ravensbury Castle the doctor came and went, but in the end he gave it as his considered opinion that her ladyship would probably never walk again. This came as a blow to Godwin. He felt no compassion for the woman, but now a divorce was out of the question. However, this did not deter him in his search for Heather. To the vicar he went and there discovered not from Heather's uncle but from Mabe the cook that Heather had been sent out alone into the night.

The cottage? Could she be at the cottage? Almost joyfully he took to horse. He galloped across the downs to the small white stone building with its thatched roof. He jumped off his horse while the animal was still moving and opened wide the door. But Heather was not there. However, Sara had made one error—she had forgotten to dispose of Heather's baggage. It sat still where she had left it, unpacked, untouched. Godwin saw the trunks at once and strode quickly to them. He kneeled, he touched and he ran his hand through his frizzled locks. What had happened to Heather?

He took to horse, slowly making his paces this time, and was hailed by Farmer Burns. "Well, now, yer lordship. 'Tis that glad I am to see ye."

"Yes, and how is the family Burns?" said Godwin absently.

"Well, well . . . and her ladyship? I saw her the other night riding over the downs toward Land's End . . . but she didn't note me as she passed," he mused, scratching his beard.

Godwin turned his head sharply. "You say you saw her riding the other evening *here?*"

"Aye . . . going in the very direction ye jest come from. Had these two sailors with her," he added, watching Godwin's face. Something was afoot, he could just smell it!

"Thank you, Burns!" said Godwin, sharply as he made for home.

He was burning with anger, but this time he was in control. He made his way up the main staircase to his wife's room, and there he entered. Sara was sitting up in bed, reading. She put down the book at his entrance. "What do you want?" she asked harshly.

"Where did they take her, Sara? I know most of it now. You might as well tell me the rest!"

She laughed, and its tone lashed with bared claws at his heart, "Why not? It is too late for you to do anything about it. By now your precious Heather had been bedded by a dozen men!"

He wanted to kill her, to finish the job he had started the other night. His fists clenched at his side, and his voice was a low rasping blade. "Explain!"

"She was taken by Devonshire smugglers to France. There she was sold to . . . a bordello!"

Godwin closed his eyes. Shooting stars of fire swept past his blackened vision. A buzzing sound drummed at his ears, blotting out Sara's laugh. A sensation of nausea threatened, and his powerful legs nearly buckled beneath him. His Heather . . . his gentle love? He opened his eyes, and though he felt himself reeling, managed to steady the pulsating sway of his limbs. But there she was, there was Sara, sneering! It was more than mind and flesh could bear. He went toward her, sure now that he would strangle her, sure that in so doing it would end all earthly tortures for them both, and then a voice, a small boy's voice at his back, called him desperately to order.

"Sir? Sir?" cried Roderick. He had always called Godwin "Papa," but since that awful night, he had not been able to bring himself to it. *He was a bastard.* His mind pounded it into his heart, making sure he would remember for all time. His mother had brought him to this and for it, he hated her. Godwin? No, he could never hate Godwin, but there was almost a bitterness in him, a resentment of the man he had always thought his father. It was as though he blamed Godwin for allowing such a thing to be.

Godwin loved Roderick. The child's voice recalled him. He turned, moved resolutely away from Sara, looked down at the lad and touched the boy's thick curls. He was in agony, though, and he had to get away. If he stayed . . . surely he would kill her!

Godwin left the castle that night. He had but one person he could go to for they'd been friends since childhood. He and Captain John Pearson had romped through Cornish moors and sailed Mount's Bay and knew each other's hearts. It was to Captain John he went, pounding down his door near to breaking it, blasting his friend's name for both Heaven and Hell to hear and bear witness to his pain. "John! John! For the sake of mercy, John!" raged Godwin, waking his friend from a deep sleep and bringing him into, as it were, the thick of things.

And Roderick? He watched Godwin depart the castle with something akin to longing. And then he turned to his mother. He was overcome with emotion, an all-consuming beating made of love and hate, filling him with guilt, and with a need to cleanse himself, for the lad had come to think of himself as dirtied.

He understood something more now. He understood that Godwin loved another woman outside their home. He understood that his mother, Sara, had somehow managed to dispose of this other woman. Again, again his mother was the cause of something wicked in their household. Again he blamed not Godwin, but Sara. He gazed at her, perhaps a shade too accusingly, and then, caught up in his guilt, seeing her there helpless, a cripple, he went toward her, hoping to

56

give her comfort, hoping to derive some himself. He took on a man's work. " 'Tis all right, Mother . . . he will forgive us."

She stared at him blankly for a moment, incapable of understanding what he felt, what tortures he was himself experiencing, and her voice was cold with contempt when it came. He—this son of a gypsy—was the fault of it all! How dare he take part with Godwin? *"Get out!"* she ordered in her frenzy. *"Stupid bastard! Get out!"*

Roderick felt wounded to the heart. It was a scar never to heal. He would hear the word over and over a thousand times before age would harden his child's heart and turn his innocence. He ran, rejected, alone, confused, and a part of him formed for the future.

"That is it!" said Heather resolutely to herself *as well as* her companion. "We shall suffer no longer!"

"What mean ye, mistress?" asked Bunky with some concern.

"Bunky! Night has turned into day and day into night. We are weak with hunger. There is a stench surrounding us that is unbearable. And nothing, nothing, I tell you, is worse than what we now suffer," returned Heather.

"Aye. Let's not argle-bargle. Ye be in the right of it. So we've decided to give ourselves over to the divils and beg their mercy?" He too was beginning to think being thrown to the sharks a mild fate in comparison to his present aches. After all, one was a fancy, the other a reality.

He climbed up upon his pile of sacks and pushed hard at the hatch door. It opened wide, with a resounding squeak. He pulled himself up by his forearms and peered out. Good, no one about, thought he as he turned to Heather. "There now, mistress," he said, giving her his hand. "Use me knee."

She took hold of his strong hand and hoisted herself up by planting a foot on his thigh and allowing him to shove her upward. She took hold of the decking and pulled herself the remainder of the way.

A French crewman standing some space away observed a dark form move from a hold in the deck. It was a black night, and he was weary and unused to such mirages. True, the form seemed somehow alluring . . . but it had come from below, and to a superstitious man could mean but one thing. With a hand to his heart, he gave a yelp. *"Nom de Dieu!"*

This so startled Heather that she gasped and threw herself flat on the deck lest the Frenchman start shooting. Her swift movement sent Bunky off balance. He let go a howl, quite eerie to hear as it echoed from below, and this particular Frenchman was of the opinion that anything unusual that stemmed from below was surely not human. Reeling backward, Bunky landed heavily in a portion of the hold he had hitherto avoided and came face to face with an indignant rodent. This sent a shiver of revulsion through him, and as the red-eyed creature gave every indication that it was about to pounce and evict the intruder, he let out yet another screech of sheer terror and scrambled with newfound vitality up and out of the hole. Once out, he landed on his belly beside his mistress, who admonished him severely to be silent.

This series of unexpected and unprecedented phenomena so astonished and horrified this same crewman that he felt himself unable to move from his spot, and thus he stood, riveted, hand on heart, every inch of him wanting to run, and settling for second best he set up a screeching intended to bring down salvation. *"Ici! Bon Dieu! Ici! Capitaine! Ici . . . Louis! Ici . . . Bon Dieu . . . Satane!"*

This in its turn brought out the Louis he called for and yet another of the crew members. They came leisurely, laughing robustly at the sound of his terror, for this their compatriot had a reputation of being one given to flights of fancy.

"Eh . . . saucisse!" chuckled Louis. "What is the matter? You disturb the captain while he dines."

Heather listened to the French, a language she had learned in her schoolroom. At the same time she had to put a hand over Bunky's mouth, as he seemed on the verge of hysterics. Even so, he managed to get out, "They mean to throw us overboard! They be laughing over it, ain't they?"

She could see he was much distressed, but really this was no time for such talk. "Shhh," she commanded frowningly.

The new arrivals suddenly observed that something was moving not very far away from them. Two dark objects . . . crawling on the deck, or so it seemed. Shapeless atrocities were these things . . . moving . . . bent on doing them some evil in the night. Indeed, one was rising . . . rising . . . *"Mon Dieu!"* breathed Louis, joining his mate in fear. Then one of the dark objects boggled their understanding by actually taking on the shape of a woman, and this but after two days at sea!

"Quelle surprise . . ." mumbled Louis. *"Capitaine!"*

Heather thought it time to put an end to this shouting hysteria and moved toward them. Immediately, all three men stepped back. She sighed and gave forth in articulate but not altogether perfect French, "Sirs, I think it best that you call your captain calmly . . . or if you prefer, you may take us to him."

The three Frenchmen gazed long at her; their eyes were straining at the sockets. Then, feeling some further action was required of them, they turned and stared at one another.

Fortunately, their captain, having had his dinner disturbed by the howls outside his cabin, stepped forth to arrive on the scene. He was no less surprised by what met his eyes, but he was far better able to cope with the affair.

"What have we here?" asked the captain in his native tongue.

Heather braced herself, drew breath and said in French, "I beg your pardon, monsieur. My friend and I have, through a series of mishaps, come to be—quite unintentionally—captive upon your vessel."

"Aha!" interrupted the captain, eyeing the lovely before him with something akin to devastated wonderment. However, he had not reached his eight and thirty years without having had his share of pretty women. He had still his wits about him. "So you would have it, mademoiselle, that *we hold you captive* against your will? How very intriguing!" He had detected the English accent and had answered her in her own tongue.

Relieved to find he spoke English, she mentally brushed away the hint of sarcasm in his words. She measured the gentleness of his smile and responded warmly, "Indeed, how unhandsome it would be of me to suggest that. No, I meant no such thing, though indeed, we are at your mercy."

"What nonsense, to be sure." He chuckled. "But do let us proceed with first things first. I, mademoiselle, am the comte de Brabant, captain of this ship." He turned around as he heard the rustle of silk skirts, and his brow went up in some amusement at his sister's expression. Louise Davenant had appeared, her cashmere shawl tightly wrapped round her well-shaped shoulders, an expression of doubt tinging her attractive countenance, "Maurice?" she whispered at her brother. "Who is this woman . . . this boy?"

"As it happens, my dear," he answered her in English, increasing her curiosity, "I have not as yet discovered the answer to so pertinent a question. Come, let us all retire to my cabin and there learn the secrets of this affair."

Heather turned to Bunky and smiled reassuringly, for she could see her companion was still looking about himself in some trepidation. "You see, Bunky . . . they won't throw us to the sharks after all."

The captain heard her remark and with a roar of laughter assured Bunky that she was quite correct in this. He had no such intention!

So it was! While Heather Martin's future took shape on the high seas, Godwin near lost his mind on land. Godwin stayed with his friend Captain John Pearson in those first early days. Afraid of what he might do to Sara, he never went near Ravensbury Castle. Captain John put out with his yawl and made for St.-Pol-de-Léon, taking Godwin with him.

They went through the little French harbor town hoping for the best, dreading the worst, and finally found someone who had noticed Heather. He was an elderly sailor versed in the English tongue, for he had once in better times had his own galley and had done business on both sides of the Channel.

"*Tiens* . . . you would know of the pretty one. *Oui*, I saw the little flower with a ragged puppy at her side. They ran out of this very tavern. Then . . . *mon Dieu!* Everywhere sailors shouted after them . . . they run . . . they were hunted . . . and I believe not found. More than this I do not know." He pulled at his bristled gray beard and shook his head over the affair. He was tired and he was old, but as the gold coin was pressed thankfully into his hand he managed a smile that displayed the decayed teeth in his withered mouth.

Godwin held his friend's shoulder, overcome with deep emotion, "She escaped them, John!"

His friend was a big man and yet still looked up into Godwin's face. It had to be said: "Aye, man, so she did . . . but she hasn't returned to Cornwall. And Godwin, there is every chance that she won't."

Still, there was a comfort in knowing she had escaped the bordello. But where was she? There was nothing for it but to return to Cornwall and wait. Godwin had but one hope left, that somehow by some miracle she would find her way back to Land's End, to their Windmera and to him. His prayer nightly was, "Let her be safe, let the child she carries thrive . . . let me one day see them both alive and well."

Such was the man, such was his love. He stayed on with Captain John, who watched over him fretfully, for he knew the scars would leave their mark, he knew that time would wield no miracle here. So he empathized with Godwin, knowing the dream of Heather would linger and perhaps even twist him in the end, but it would not wither or be put aside. Had the Fates on their high and unassailable mount weaved a different net, had they put Heather Martin on a different ship . . . but that was speculation. Sad to say, they had set her apart from Godwin of Ravensbury, placing space and *fear* between them!

Summer's warmth enveloped the *Liberté* as it sliced water putting the rising white horses of the deep at its stern, sailing into cool aquamarine shades. Their destination, Barbados, the isle of sugar cane and rum. The isle of song, of long sweet nights and gentle charms. A haven for the comte de Brabant, and no less so for his sister, who had still to forget the pain of yesterday, but for Heather it held only sadness.

The decision was but misting before her eyes. The decision? She had to make one. The comte and his sister had heard her tale, and being what she was she had told them everything. Louise had taken Heather into her passionate embrace, for Heather's plight was that of love, and love had always a lure for a French nature.

The comte de Brabant had made her a very generous offer right at the outset. Upon their arrival in the West Indies he would immediately and at his own expense procure passage for Heather and her young manservant, Bunky, on the first vessel returning for England. It was all very simple, or so it seemed on the surface.

Life never is, though, that simple. How can it be, with all its multitudinous complexities? Heather had a fear, and it was for two beings, neither one herself. She feared for the babe she carried, and she feared for Godwin. Yes, she could return, and there would be Sara, waiting! A wicked woman, ruthless, heartless, Sara would stop at nothing to prevent Godwin from leaving her. Even if she were to somehow slink into Cornwall and meet with Godwin, how could she be sure Sara would not discover the tryst? How could Godwin guard himself from Sara's fancies? How could she guard their child? No, it would be impossible to do so every hour of the day. And there was no way to prove what Sara had done to her, for no one would take the word of a common seaman like Bunky . . . and Bunky could go to the gallows if he admitted his part. Oh, it was all so complicated.

If these doubts were not enough, there was still another. There was Roderick! What of the boy who believed himself Godwin's son? Heather had no way of knowing what Roderick would have to suffer if she came forth accusing Sara. She could not allow it!

She was a woman plucked from all nearer ties, wounded by the force of another woman's passions, confused by her own. She had never been a fighter, never would be a fighter; her nature was such that she would ever choose to yield to a gentler path, which in its turn was not always the easier one. She turned desperately to the captain of the *Liberté*, for he was there, ever ready to lend his ears, his shoulders and his heart, because in their first week Maurice de Brabant had fallen deeply in love with Heather Martin.

It was not surprising in spite of the fact that he had reached the age of thirty-eight and had managed to remain a bachelor. This oddity (and it was so for a man of his qualities and nature) came about because of circumstances beyond his control. He had squandered his youth in his studies, in his love for sailing and in his shyness (for he had been desperately shy as a young man). At thirty he had had his first real *affaire du coeur* when he was fluttering about the French court at the insistence of his brother, who felt he needed polish. A young beauty had caught his eye and proceeded to tease away his heart, wrenching it from him most brutally. He was a second son. His brother had held the title, the estates and the bulk of the family fortune. His brother had been married, and the family title and all its attractions would in all probability pass without getting into Maurice's hands. So thought the young lovely, so thought her family. They did not reckon with the Reign of Terror. Thus, the girl's hand went to another, and Maurice de Brabant sailed for Barbados. He had not blamed her, for he understood well the ways of the world, and after a time he was quite able to get over her, though never quite forgetting. And now, here he was again very much in love, and this time, the woman of his thoughts carried another man's child and had no heart to offer him! Unfair, but who is to say why such things are?

She leaned against the rail, the gown of red silk she had borrowed from Louise flapping carelessly round her graceful form, the sun full in her face, making her shade her eyes with her hand in order to observe Maurice's expression. He was looking sad, and she knew it was because of her.

"You have been thinking long. What have you decided?" he asked quietly, almost fearfully.

"I . . . I don't know. It is so very hard to know the answer. To return would hurt Sara and Roderick . . . perhaps it would put Godwin in danger . . ."

"Yes, but you could bear witness against Sara," he offered,

for he wanted her decision to be one arrived at without regrets.

"No. It would rake up scandal to Godwin's name."

"And what is his name, this Godwin of yours?" he asked curiously.

"That doesn't matter," she answered quietly.

"No, it does not. But the child you carry . . . it will want a name."

She turned from him. They had spoken about this before, but her problem was the same, and it upset her to think of her child being baseborn. He took up her chin. He had not spoken about his feelings for her, hoping that as they drew nearer to the isle she would perhaps undergo a change. He felt that she cared for him. The days had passed into many, the weeks into three, and he felt the time had come;

"Heather . . . do not go back. You know in your heart it is impossible . . . and I . . . I want to marry you!" he was begging.

She gazed at him, full into his gray eyes. Yes, she cared for him. He was good and kind. He was full of subtle witticisms that made her laugh. He was not unattractive. But she was not in love with him. "Maurice," she said softly, "I carry another man's child. I carry the dreams of another man's arms. . . ."

He winced, for truth is not always welcome. He knew what she said to be so, but he had no wish to hear it aired. "I know, my love, but I am . . . with the *malade d'amour*. My heart is full with you."

"No. You deserve better than I."

"*Mignonne* . . . have you no notion how *ravissant* . . . how wondrous you are to me? I would be husband to you . . . father to your child." He was begging her; gone was all thought of pride. He wanted this woman.

"How could I do such a thing to you? I do not love you in that way, Maurice."

"Give me time to make you, Heather. I will make you love me." Such is the cry of all lovers desperate to attain their goal.

"No. You are not thinking clearly. How could I take such advantage of you? How could I fault you in such a cruel way?"

"Cruel? My dear . . . to call you wife would be a joy! Fault me? 'Twould be my own fault if I did not succeed in winning your love."

"And what of Godwin?" she returned desperately, wanting him to see the futility of what he asked.

"He believes you lost to him by now . . . he will forget. Time has a way of dulling the senses, and he has his family to think of."

She knew in her heart that this was not so. Godwin would never forget her. She was Godwin's lifeline just as he was hers. She knew this, and because she knew it she shook her head sadly. "No."

His emotions were ravaged at this point, and he fought to change her mind. He took hold of her shoulders and shook her almost roughly. "Heather, what of the *enfant?* Have you the right to bring a fatherless child into the world when an alternative is offered? Answer me, Heather!"

His words formed an open hand and slapped away at her cheeks, causing her eyes to tear with the sting. She saw her dream's framework singed. The sparks grew until a flame engulfed it, relegating it to the past. Godwin was a beloved memory, put aside for the realities of life, and even as the horror of this thought forced her eyes open, she cried, "No." She turned from him, from his words. "No."

He was ashamed of himself. He had no right to torture her this way. He wanted to protect her. He wanted to shield her from the future as he saw it. He would take her to wife whether she loved him or no, or he would see her married to Godwin. He hugged her shaking body to him. "No, *ma belle, non, ma petite* . . . I will see you through this . . . your way."

She held on. She was in the grip of treacherous waters, and she held to the only life raft offered. "You understand, Maurice . . . you understand why I cannot marry you?"

"I understand, my love," was his answer.

Eight

Barbados! Heather stood on board the Liberté *as it was* safely docked in Bridgetown Harbor and thought perhaps all she had undergone the last few weeks had been worth the effort just to view this incredible isle.

Swan and Broad Streets dominated Bridgetown, as did their central marketplace, which was constructed in a spacious quadrangle where the hucksters sat. Their cries of "Fish hey, dolphin, 'nuseful limes" could be heard among the turning of wheels and mingling rush of bodies. An open center accommodated the more bulky foodstuffs, such as red and white yams, potatoes, coconuts and many other edibles. These were afforded shade by rows of bearded fig trees, from which the island received its name, for the Portuguese upon seeing the evergreen had christened it Los Barbados, meaning "The Bearded."

Heather took this in, and her eyes widened as the vision of swaying black women scantily clad in varying shades of cotton passed by, their baskets of wares neatly balanced atop their scarf-covered heads. Seamen exchanged ribald jests and hoots with the incoming vessels. Fishermen were putting away their nets, pocketing the cash they had earned from the day's catch. And human flesh, black human flesh, was being peddled in the center of all this!

Heather was stunned by it. She glanced at Maurice, surprised to find that none of it disturbed him, but of course he had lived here, thrived here, learned to accept and expect such things. She turned next to Louise, and the two women exchanged glances of mutual understanding. There was no time for more, however, for Maurice was ushering them quickly into a chocolate-brown curricle with the de Brabant crest emblazoned in gold across its doors.

Word had reached the comte's overseer, Jem Starkes, that the *Liberté* had been sighted, and he had quickly ordered the curricle to be readied. He stood now holding its door wide open, a pleased grin across his freckled countenance as he shuffled, inclined his head and welcomed his employer home. The driver, a black slave, awaited his turn to do the same, for

Maurice de Brabant, though a firm master, was also a kind one and well liked.

Heather's attention was arrested by the passing scenery. Unlike the picture produced by her imagination's artistic hand, the land was not rich in forests and riotous blooms. Much of the land was covered in fields of sugar cane, not yet fully grown because of the season. With something of surprise she turned to the comte.

"But, Maurice . . . it . . . all of it seems so much browner, flatter, than I thought it would be."

He chuckled. "Ah, yes. Our rainfall occurs from June to November, *ma petite* . . . and even then, we are not drowned as are our neighboring isles. The land is low, and much of it was deforested over one hundred years ago by your own countrymen." He smiled at Jem and included him in the conversation. "Isn't that so, Mr. Starkes?"

"Aye. What trees there were have long been felled to make way for fields of sugar cane."

"But . . . what a waste!" cried Heather in some dismay, visualizing the destruction of mighty timbers.

"Waste? Lordy, but that weren't the case, ma'am," said Jem, frowning, "We shipped tons of Barbados cedar, fustic and logwood to England." He stopped himself. " 'Scuse, me ma'am. M'lord . . . if ye'll look there . . ." He pointed to a lowland field sprouting sugar cane no more than two feet high.

"Good God, man! So you did it," said de Brabant, well pleased.

"Aye. It were as hard as I 'spected, but worth the sweat," said the Englishman, evidently proud of himself. Ordinarily he wouldn't have been happy to work for a Frenchman, but this one wasn't half bad, and there was no denying the fair wage the Frenchman paid him. "Though I got to admit, there was a time when I thought we'd never get rid of some of those old stumps."

Heather listened to them, but she was watching Maurice's profile. He was a good man, that was something she had realized immediately, but until now she had never recognized the fact that he was also a proud man. Proud of his heritage, of his capabilities, of his home. How it must have hurt him to have to beg her to be his wife and then be rejected! Yet he had taken it all so well. Why, any other woman in her predicament would have jumped at the chance! Something in her heart moved, and she began to admire him, respect him, and knew it was not enough.

Maurice felt a warmth engulf his heart, a trick perhaps of the mind, of the vision, for he knew suddenly that she was looking at him. And as always, whenever she glanced his way, hope filled his heart. He turned his head so that he was looking down into those magnificent violet eyes. Silently, gently, imploringly, he made love to her in that glance. He wanted her both physically and spiritually. He wanted her in a way he was certain no man had ever wanted a woman before. She saw it and quickly turned away lest he mistake her admiration for something more.

Louise, sitting beside Jem Starkes, watched them in silence. She observed in the quiet of her retreat, for the Reign of Terror was still a harsh reality to her. She wanted Heather to accept her brother. She wanted a sister such as Heather, for she knew Heather would be good for her brother. The child would be good for them all after what had passed in France. Yes, they needed new bubbling life. And then she caught a glimpse of the mansion that was to be her home, and she spoke for the first time on that ride. *"Mon frère, c'est bon!"*

Hastily Heather positioned herself to get a better view, for though she planned to leave as soon as a ship could convey Bunky (who had remained on the *Liberté*) and herself to England, she was curious to see the home Maurice had fashioned for himself on this island so different from England or France.

Brabant Plantation! Its house stood on high, on the crest of a rolling hill. Its position had been the first thing to catch Maurice's approval eight years ago when he had purchased the run-down and bankrupt estate. From its height the mansion commanded a view of much of its lands, and being an aristocrat, he had it deeply imbedded in his nature that a high location served to set his household apart from lesser beings.

Still, it was not only the mansion, a century-old manor house which had been remodeled and renovated in the tradition of the de Brabants' Bordeaux chateau. Its paned windows, its smoothly elegant lines, its mellow butter-colored sandstone and its foundation landscaping certainly caught the eye and demanded admiration, but it was the plantation whole that caught, fascinated and riveted securely the women's attention.

Two windmills, also on the peak of a hill in order to catch the wind, loomed in the distance, and Maurice explained with much enthusiasm how the wind created the power to grind grain in one, give them fresh water from the other.

They saw oxen pulling carts, and Maurice was quick to point out the large buildings where the carts were built from trees felled on their own grounds. "We have trained blacksmiths right on Brabant. . . . Look there, see that small lad."

They saw running beside the ox-drawn cart a shoeless black boy, shouting and wielding a whip. "Gee . . . cum, cum . . . hai!"

"He is a leader boy—he steers the oxen. On the last day of the crop he and the oxen will wear a necklace of flowers."

Heather was fascinated. Coconut palms stretching thirty feet into the air were neatly laid out, as were hibiscus plants, their lush colored flowers situated to catch the eye. But then there in the shadow of the house stood the rows of austere slave cabins. A thriving community was a plantation, self-sufficient, just as was any feudal parish four hundred years past!

A week, lovely, lazy and strangely stimulating, passed for Heather at Brabant. She was just entering her fourth month of pregnancy, and her belly had hardly begun to swell. Maurice took her riding over his lands and walking along the creamy sands, and they talked about everything. Everything but her going back, until the evening before he was to book her passage.

A night meant for lovers, it was sweetly slow, and when Maurice suggested the three of them walk along the beach before retiring only Louise declined. Heather chided herself now as she recalled. How stupid, how thoughtless she had been. They took the garden path leading to the painted wooden steps that led to their stretch of beach. Maurice took her hand as she reached the last step, but he didn't release it as she shrugged off her slippers and left them behind. His hand tightly clasped her own. She looked deep into the sky, staring at the enchantment of twinkling stars. Godwin. His name obsessed her thoughts, her dreams, as did her doubts. Maurice. His presence filled her days, and she had to admit to herself that she needed him, very much. There were times when she rode beside him in the curricle and his closeness, his warmth, his adoration forced her to look into herself and she knew that she wanted him too. If only she could love him.

The roar of the breakers against the long reef played out its willful song. The breeze played with her hair, pulling at the long tresses, and even in the dark of the night Maurice could see those violet eyes. He couldn't speak. For once he was at a loss, he was again a shy youth in the throes of an all-consuming love. He was again helpless.

Heather sensed some of this and meant only to set him again at ease. She meant only to assuage the pain as she moved her hand to his bronzed cheek. This wonderful, this good man was suffering because of her. In that moment it was her only thought.

He didn't know which was worse, the pain of her touch or the anguish he experienced without it. His lids closed over his bright eyes, and he set his jaw.

"Oh, Maurice . . . my Maurice," she whispered not knowing what else to say, what else to do.

Something deep inside him shattered. Perhaps it was his will, for he had been holding back, forcing himself to say no more to her, overpowering his need to touch her, kiss her, hold her. But under the strain of her nearness, her softness, the will dissolved, and his hands reached and found her shoulders. His mouth sought and won her own. Hungrily, ardently, feverishly, he kissed her.

She was taken aback. She was aroused by his need. She was reluctant to reject him any further. She was many things in that moment, so she allowed him his kiss, and another. She allowed him to press her close, closer still. In the flash of a moment she even thought she would let him take her. Perhaps then he would be able to forget her. Once he had had her, she would no longer be something he longed after. All this ran through her mind as he lowered her to the sand beneath their feet.

In passion he manipulated her bodice until her breasts were free; dexterously he teased her nipples until they were taut and ready for his mouth. Swiftly, urgently, he discarded her clothes, groaning over her beauty.

Heather felt a flood of a happiness surge through her. Finally, finally she was able to give him something of herself. His kisses, his touch, were pleasant enough to arouse the woman in her, and even as she thought of Godwin she felt no guilt. Her soul and her heart were with her only love. Thus, she moved willingly to Maurice's hand as his fingers sought the fluff between her thighs. She smiled warmly, encouragingly, as he hurried to shed his shirt, his breeches.

He positioned himself for his thrust, his lips nibbling at her ear. "Heather, my love . . . my love . . ." Deeply, ravenously, he plunged. . . .

With a start she jumped, putting the memory of last evening away, for Louise's hand rested upon her shoulder. "*Chérie* . . . you sit here alone? May I intrude?"

Heather had sought the shade and solitude of a palm tree, for she had to think, had to be alone . . . but she loved Louise. "Intrude? Of course you don't. Come sit beside me," she said, patting the cool grass.

"*Mon Dieu!* And ruin my beautiful white gown? *Non*, I shall sit on this, yes," she said pulling up a nearby wicker chair from its table set. She sighed as she sat but plunged right into the heart of the matter. "You sent Maurice to Bridgetown this morning. You sent him to book you and your Bunky passage to England, yes?"

"Yes," said Heather, remembering the stricken look that had crept into Maurice's eyes. Oh, she had hated herself. Last night had made things worse, not better.

He had stepped back as though she had struck him. He had gone red and spluttered, "Then . . . last night . . . last night . . . it was . . . ?"

"Goodbye, Maurice. It was goodbye," she had said quietly.

He had said not another word as he turned from her and left the room. Oh, God, she had made things so much worse! Louise's voice recalled her. "Heather. Heather, are you listening?"

"What? Oh . . . yes," she said, her voice scarcely audible.

Again Louise sighed, for she was not feeling well, had not been feeling well since yesterday afternoon. She had taken an early-morning ride with Maurice inland to inspect a piece of acreage he intended to purchase. They had lunched with the agent and returned. At first she had supposed it to be the heat, then she thought perhaps it was something she had eaten, but then later when she was soaking in her bath she noticed huge insect bites swelling over her arms and ankles. But no matter, it would pass, and now she had to do something to keep Heather from leaving them.

"I will speak plainly with you, *chérie*. Between us it is possible, yes?"

"Of course."

"Then you do not mind if I tell you this. In many things you are a good woman . . . yes . . . yes, do not shake your head. You are a good woman. That is why I am so puzzled.

You have told me everything. After my words, you may regret it. But I must speak. How, *chérie*, how can a good woman destroy the lives of so many people?"

Though the thought had flitted through her mind, Heather was shocked to hear it aired. "What . . . what do you mean?"

"Ah. You do not see . . . or will not see? This Sara . . . worthless, yes, but you go back, you destroy her. Her son, Roderick . . . is he also worthless? For if you return, he too will be destroyed. . . . And Godwin, this Godwin you love, will he also not be hurt by the scandal? Forgetting all these people, what of your child? Surely you realize that there is not enough time. You will not be in England before another five weeks have passed, and *chérie*, it will take months and months for a divorce. Your child will be born a bastard!"

Heather's face contorted. "Oh, God! But my child has a right to know its father. Godwin has a right to see his child. He must see his child!"

"You are stubborn or blind . . . perhaps a little of both. Godwin, you say. This Godwin will take to himself another woman. It is the way of men, and he will father another child. You must see, Heather."

Heather shook her head. Louise grew irritated with her and got to her feet. "You are being stupid! Maurice loves you. Last night on the beach, I let you go off together alone. I let you because I knew what would happen. It did . . . didn't it?"

"Yes . . . yes . . ."

"Then you are even a bigger fool than I thought you, stupid girl! Ah, *mon Dieu*. At first I thought . . . perhaps . . . perhaps she cannot with Maurice. Perhaps he is repugnant to her in that way. But *non*, I see you together and know . . . you are not unaffected by his charm. You care for him . . . you enjoy his company . . ."

"But I am not in love with him," wailed Heather.

"*Love!*" Louise spat contemptuously. "What is love? I was married to my husband in contract before ever I set eyes on him. But he was a good man, a good husband. One grows to love."

"No . . . it is not right."

Louise clapped her hands together in her agitation. She was feeling feverish and dizzy. She loved Heather. She wanted her for a sister. She loved Maurice, wanted him happy. It was spinning, buzzing in her head, her need to

72

make Heather see. "Heather, Heather . . ." And then suddenly bright white stars flashed in a black sky and she felt her knees go weak and collapse from under her.

Heather saw Louise crumple in upon herself and land on the green turf. She jumped to her feet, screaming, "Louise! My God, Louise!" She was beside her in an instant, touching her forehead, behind her ears, her wrist, and realized from her efforts that this was no simple faint. Louise's body was on fire. She was in the grip of a fever. She looked about her for assistance and saw four slaves working on the grounds. "One of you please go for the doctor," cried Heather. "The rest of you come here and help me get your mistress to her room. *Hurry!*"

Maurice guided his horse through the hubbub of Bridgetown, taking the main pike southeast for Brabant. Inside the inner pocket of his pale-blue riding jacket near his heart were two tickets for passage on the *Southampton* leaving for England in five days. He was wounded, deeply. He felt himself a fool.

He could remember vividly the touch of Heather in his arms. The sensation she aroused in him then was with him still. She had touched his cheeks, bringing to them all the heat her nearness infused in him. When she responded to his kisses, lay beneath him, spreading her legs, her heart, taking him to herself, he had imagined she had finally been won. Fool!

He chastized his ego unmercifully. Did you think yourself so perfect a lover? Did you? Naive bumpkin! Did you think that she would be yours after a night's lovemaking? Did you not see the goodbye in her eyes as you took her to her room? Of course it was farewell. It was Heather's way. Gratitude. That was all she felt for you last night. Only gratitude. He flinched beneath the cruelty of his thoughts and felt his heart contract within his chest. He felt old, worn and devastated. How does one part with one's life?—and Heather was that to him. But still he would let her go. For a defiant moment that morning he wanted to rail at her. He wanted to deny her the means to return to England. He wanted to force her into marriage with him. He wanted to force the safety of his protection on her. But in the end he gave over to his own gentle nature and took his horse to Bridgetown to purchase with his own hand, of his own free will, the way for her final thrust to his heart.

Across the Atlantic on a jutting rock at the height of Land's End stood Godwin. There was something different in his mien on the morning that Maurice purchased Heather's way home. There was something bright in his dark eyes. Captain John watched him from his horse with more concern than usual and would have called to him to come away, but he was stayed by the sound of a pony's hooves. He turned and found Roderick riding toward them. Captain John's brows drew together. Poor lad, he thought sadly, he has suffered no less than any in this. Roderick glanced at Captain John. "Please, sir . . . could I speak with my . . . with his lordship in private?"

"Aye, but don't be hipped, lad, if he won't talk with ye. He be not himself these days," said the captain gruffly.

Godwin turned at that moment and saw Roderick. He loved the boy. All that had taken place had not diminished that, and he realized in that moment that he had neglected, hurt, abused the youth. He smiled warmly. "Roderick . . . son . . ." His arms were open wide.

The boy was off his pony and running to those arms. His small world had been crumbling all around him. His ten years had not equipped him to handle the flight of one parent, the withdrawal of the other. He knew himself a dirtied being, and yet here was Godwin with arms outstretched. Here was his *god*. A man, yes, but to Roderick all-powerful. He saw him standing, red hair whipping around his beloved face, his smile warm, reassuring, and Roderick ran toward him, diving into those open arms. He forgot Captain John's presence at his back and fell into convulsive, shameless sobs. Godwin held him close, soothing him with whispered magic words.

At last Roderick spoke, his words faltered, tearful. "Please . . . sir . . . please forgive us . . . come home . . ."

Godwin stiffened. The thought of forgiving Sara was repugnant. The thought of living in the same house with her was revolting. But here was Roderick . . . and Roderick was his! The lad needed him. "Hush, lad. Your mother and I are beyond such things, but don't fret it. You have my love still, *you* always will . . . I promise you. I'll come with you to Ravensbury, because it is my home and you are my son, but don't speak to me of Sara!"

The lad nodded. He had won Godwin. Godwin would come home, and perhaps in time Godwin would love Sara

74

again and everything would be as it was. He was ten years old and thus hope was strong within him.

Godwin? He would go home to Ravensbury, but not to Sara. Heather would be home soon. He felt it, knew it. Heather would be here soon, and he would send Sara off, out of the county! He thought fleetingly of her crippled state, but here perhaps was the turning point in Godwin's nature, for he felt no guilt, no regret. Instead, he felt it was little enough punishment for all the pain she had caused Heather, Roderick and himself!

Nine

Louise tossed fitfully in her bed. Heather wiped her brow with a cool cloth dipped in rosewater, and she turned her eyes to the doctor bent over his satchel. Her brow was drawn, her eyes inquiring, but she said nothing as she waited for him to do something. Her eyes opened wider, her consternation plainly evident, as she observed him draw forth a glass bottle and carefully insert a pair of tweezers. Horrified, she saw him pluck a dark, slimy and very obese creature and bring it toward Louise. Heather jumped to her feet.

"Stop it! Stop it! You can't mean to use that on her?"

The doctor was old and tired. Little surprised him. It was not the first time a hysterical woman had tried to prevent him from bleeding a patient. "Now see here, miss, she must be bled," he said, still advancing on Louise.

Heather put herself between the doctor and his unsuspecting patient. "No! She does not believe in leeching. She has often said so. I won't allow you to put those dreadful creatures on her."

He had other patients to get to. He had little time to waste on this silly woman. "She must be bled," he repeated, then more kindly, "It will ease the fever . . . make her rest more comfortably."

"No, it will not. It will only drain her of her strength." It was what her father had believed and instilled in her as a young girl.

He sighed with some exasperation. "You have not the authority to interfere—"

"Oh, but she has!" said a firm strong voice from the doorway. "Miss Martin has as much authority here as I do."

Heather ran to him. He was here, finally, he was here and he would make all things better. "Oh, Maurice, Maurice . . . Louise . . . she has contracted some fever . . ."

"Doctor?" He had his brow up.

"Indeed, as Miss Martin says," he said somewhat testily, "your sister has contracted a fever not unlike malaria. However, at this stage I cannot be certain what it is. I am certain only of one thing, it is serious. We have had a few cases break out farther inland, and I have already lost two patients who have had similar symptoms."

"Inland, you say?" said Maurice, remembering the other day's excursion. They had stayed overly long at a stagnant pond, talking about the possibilities of cultivating the area. "What can we do for her?"

"As you won't allow me to bleed her, you must try to keep her quiet as best you can. The fever must break. I left Miss Martin some laudanum, but I wouldn't depend on it. I shall look in on her tomorrow."

"I see," said Maurice, standing aside to allow the man to pass. "Very well, doctor, I will see you out."

Louise was beginning to mumble again. Her eyes flashed open and she screamed. Heather soothed her with gentle words, shooing the nightmare away, cooling her head with the rosewater cloth.

Maurice reappeared, and Heather's eyes flew to his face. He was looking weary. Her heart went out to him. "Maurice . . . she will be all right. I am going to go down to the kitchens and make her sage tea. Papa often used it in the school whenever we had a child down with a fever."

"Thank you, Heather. I will sit with her," he said, taking up a chair. He was himself not feeling well. He had attributed it to his emotional defeat, but now he was beginning to wonder, for the room did seem as though it were unlevel, and the objects before his eyes did seem blurry. But he said nothing.

The kitchen was a huge rectangular room lined with pantry shelves and closets. One wall was totally dominated by the huge fireplace used as a stove. Within its crevices were niches holding copper kettles, and partly across its middle was an ingenious wrought-iron rotisserie whose turning spit operated on the principle of heat and air. The heat would rise up the chimney. This rush of hot air would cause a blade within the height of the chimney to rotate, which in turn would cause a chain to revolve on its course, and *voilà*, an excellent rotisserie.

The cook, a large round black woman whose floppy cap lay slightly askew on her short wiry curls, stood over an enormous pot of slowly simmering cherries which she was preparing for jam. She stopped her ministrations, leaving the large wood ladle in the pot, and turned anxious eyes on Heather. Whatever was a white woman doing in her kitchen?

Heather smiled reassuringly. "You must be Belle. How his

lordship raves over your meals . . . as do we all." Until this moment she had never seen the cook, as Louise had been managing the household and the daily menu.

"Thankee, miss," said Belle rather uncertainly.

"I need your help, Belle. Your mistress is ill with some unknown fever. I can only assume it is the dreaded swamp fever I have often read about. I should like to prepare her some sage tea, as I believe it might help. Have you sage in your cupboards?"

"Yessum."

"Good. And honey . . . oh, and some lemon juice too." She watched the black woman scurry off and called after her that she would set a pot of water to boil.

"Yessum," said Belle, rushing about, but to her mind if Mistress Davenant was suffering from swamp fever, it was tamarind pulp that was needed! But she wanted no part in suggesting it; more than likely if something went wrong, she'd get the blame of it!

Abovestairs, Louise tossed violently. Now and then she would whimper, call her dead husband's name, curse Robespierre, and then moan enough to wrench and twist her brother's heart.

"Non, ma petite soeur . . . it is over . . . non, non . . ."
He felt flushed, and as he tried to settle back in his chair, he felt unbalanced. He wanted air. That was all. Telling himself this again, he attempted to rise.

Heather came in, carrying the tisane on a tray. She opened the door and found Maurice unconscious on the carpet. "Oh, my God . . . oh, no, not you too, Maurice," she cried, laying the tray on a nearby stand. She lost no time in pulling the bellrope, and as she knelt over him and felt his pulse, his fevered head, she prayed.

Two days had dragged by, and neither Maurice nor Louise showed any sign of improvement. Heather was near total exhaustion as she worked between them, and her heart was wearing down. She couldn't bear to hear Maurice pitifully calling her name, begging her not to leave, crying in his delirium. It was too much. The sage tea she continued to prepare, was preparing now in the kitchen.

Belle stood nearby frowning over her problem. She was a white woman, this Heather Martin, but instinct told the cook she was different from the others. It was certain that sage tisane was doing naught to help the master and his sister. Was best now to put in a word.

"Mistress?" she said hesitatingly. "Mistress . . . there be a tree, they say it do be good for swamp fever and such. . . ."

"Oh? What is it, Belle?"

"They call it tamarind. We grows it right here on our own land. I keep the pulp handy, if you want to try. . . ?"

"Of course I do. How do we prepare it?"

Belle smiled broadly. "Jest a minute, mistress . . . I'll be back." A moment or two passed before Belle returned with the dark pulp. She dropped it in the pot of already boiling water. "We is got to boil it and strain it after it cools, and then we can make 'em swallow it every two or three hours. That will break the fever, see if it don't!"

Heather smiled warmly. "Oh, Belle, would that it may! Pray God that it may!"

At first Heather thought this too would fail, for neither of her patients seemed to improve, and then after two hours Louise was forced to sip some more of the bitter brew. Heather left her only a few moments while she got one of the servants to hold Maurice as she sent the lukewarm liquid down his throat. Again he was laid upon his back, and she crossed the hall to look in on Louise. She approached the bed, reached down and stroked the woman's cheek. "Oh, darling, please, please, Louise . . . do get well."

Louise's eyes opened and a faint smile flickered. She attempted to speak, but settled instead for a weak nod. Heather nearly cried with joy. "Oh, Louise, Louise . . . the fever . . . oh, Louise, you must drink some more, darling. Here, try," she said, holding her around the shoulders, tipping the cup toward the woman's mouth. She saw her comfortably settled, called her black maid to sit with her and went again to Maurice's room. There she took up a chair and hoped for still another miracle.

But it did not come. Maurice seemed to get worse with every passing hour. She couldn't bear it, she thought, if he died. Not Maurice, not this kind, wonderful man. He meant too much to her. She knelt by his bed and held his sweating hand. "Maurice . . . it is my fault . . . you don't want to get better! It is all my fault. Maurice, please, please, my darling, *hear me!* If you get well, if you try and you get well, I will stay. I will marry you. I promise, Maurice. Get well and make me your wife! Please, oh please, Maurice, hear me."

Still he did not stir and still the fever did not break, but Heather was to repeat her promise over and over through the night. She would take his shoulders and spoon the tamarind brew between his clenched teeth and she would beg him to hear her.

Maurice dreamed many things. The French court fluttered by, and in its center was Heather. She was naked but for the jewels around her throat and the jeweled slippers on her feet. He wanted to shield her from prying dirty eyes, but she would dance just in the center where all could see. He would scream her name and she would look his way and put out her hand, but it would be just out of his reach, and he cried. Over and over it repeated, this dream, and then suddenly, finally, he reached her hand, clasped it to his breast and pulled her away. He was covering her beautiful naked body with his coat. She was smiling at him and he heard her say, "I will marry you, Maurice. Hear me, I will marry you."

He choked on the words as his lids fluttered open. His mouth felt dry as he attempted to speak. "Will . . . you?"

Heather sobbed onto his chest. "Oh, thank God. Thank God. Yes, yes, I will marry you, sweet Maurice. Get well for me. Get well, please."

He fell again into a sleep, but this time, it was quiet, it was blissful, and Heather was safely wrapped in his arms.

She sobbed with thankfulness. He would recover now. The fever had been broken. She would marry Maurice de Brabant and give him all she had to give. She wanted him, she needed him. And love . . . perhaps in time. Perhaps in time forgetfulness of Godwin would come and she would love Maurice in that special way. It didn't matter. She knew she couldn't go back. Cornwall held too much pain. And here . . . Maurice needed her, and she needed him. He would be father to her unborn child. She would make him happy. She would. Louise was right. This was the only way. And in going to Maurice, a portion of Heather Martin was put to rest, perhaps never to be recalled.

Such was the joining of Heather Martin and the comte de Brabant!

2

Swift as a shadow, short as any dream,
Brief as the lightning in the collied night,
That, in a spleen, unfolds both heaven and earth,
And ere a man hath power to say, "Behold!"
The jaws of darkness do devour it up:
So quick bright things come to confusion.

—Shakespeare, *A Midsummer Night's Dream*

One

February 1812

Variegated shades of green oscillated at her side, rising heavenward in a sky that one felt was all around. Narrowly stretched the creamy sand beneath her bare feet. Huge boulders of aged gray coral rock traced a path to the translucent sea of jades and aquas, looking much as though some great god had planted them there as markers of another time. She walked amongst the isle's offerings, her roan doggedly following her steps in the sand.

The maid's hair was a thick black gift of silk reaching her slim waist, swaying at her well-shaped back. Her brows were well defined in their jet flight above eyes whose violet hue was lush and full-bodied. Thick black lashes curled around those violets, and a pert nose sniffed the fresh salt fragrance above lips full with their youth's blush. Any would have taken her for Heather Martin! *But she was not.*

A white peasant blouse scarcely concealed the fullness of her youthful breasts. A gathered muslin skirt was hiked up at her waist to allow freedom of movement. She had little care for the proprieties, for her parents were no more . . . she had no one to account to. She really didn't think her flightly Tante Louise would notice. She was *Windmera, mistress of Brabant!*

She had been born to Heather and Maurice some nineteen years before. Her life had started on a wild December night, wild because the island had been struck with the tail of a hurricane. The gale blew fiercely, making it impossible to ride for the doctor, but the babe would come! She had arrived fighting for breath, determined to take her rightful place . . . and she had.

Windmera had come to the seat of Brabant, heir to all Maurice had built and shaped for himself, his bride and the daughter he had quickly learned to love. However, birthing Windmera had taken a great deal out of Heather. She was never again to enjoy the robustness of good health, and shortly after Windmera's fourteenth birthday, Heather de Brabant had died.

Heather had brought to Maurice and to the plantation much joy in those years, and she had learned a quiet contentment, but she breathed her last secretly thinking of Godwin.

Maurice de Brabant mourned her passing and found that time healed him not at all. Wine replaced his wife and stilled the ache. Even Windmera, whom he adored, was unable to bring him around. Indeed, the older she became the more she grew in her mother's image and the harder it was for Maurice to cope. He wanted to die, to join his wife, but until three months before he had lingered. A stroke, devastating in its force, took him from Windmera, leaving her heir to the plantation, leaving her to Louise Davenant.

Windmera was her mother's image, a duplicate in all but her nature. That was as different as the moon is from the sun—and Windy was the sun. Her parents and everyone on the plantation had spoiled her lavishly, and she grew a maid full with her willfulness. She was headstrong in everything, and yet modifying such faults were her capacity for compassion, her ability to love the smallest and meekest of God's creations, her scampish charm and her naughty wit. She was a fighter, a rebel, and even the passing of her adored, her beloved parents had not left her broken.

She had turned to Bunky in her crisis. Bunky, who had come with Heather to Barbados. Bunky, a cherished being, more an uncle than a servant, and he was always present to lend her his worldly wisdom. There too was Tante Louise, who could always make Windy laugh. Such was the way of it when Captain John Pearson happened to see her walking that sandy path by the sea.

It near took his breath, such was his amazement. She was her mother all over. He had come to Barbados for a shipment of sugar and rum. Trade wasn't his calling in those days, but the time had come when he needed ready cash, and that was a way to it. And then there she was, just as he remembered her nineteen years ago, when she had been taken in by her uncle, the vicar, and had enthralled Godwin. Heather Martin? A second glance told him that the maid he was staring at could be no more than nineteen, twenty . . . and how, how could Heather have remained so young?

"Heather! Heather Martin!" he called.

Windmera looked up. Someone was calling her mother by her maiden name. How odd. She stopped and looked at the tall man in a merchant captain's garb. His hat was tilted back over a swarm of thick gray hair. His beard was short and full over his neck and up his cheeks. His eyes were pale-blue and bright.

"What did you say?" she asked, just to be certain she hadn't been daydreaming. "What did you call me?"

"Er . . . my mistake, lass. You put me much in mind of a woman I knew many years ago in Cornwall," said Captain John, still staring.

She brightened. "Then you did call me Heather Martin." She came forward smiling, hand extended. "Heather Martin was my mother."

He took her hand somewhat lamely, and to put him at his ease she smiled sweetly. "I am told I am much like her."

"Yes, yes, you are . . . the very spit and image of her! But . . . I'm being rude, lass. What be yer given name?" he asked, scarcely able to suppress his glee at finding her.

She was amazed at the man's excitement, and she gave him the fullness of her smile because of it. He must have been a good friend of her mother, she thought, but it was odd her mother had never mentioned him. "My name is Windmera de Brabant, sir."

His smile vanished ludicrously. "De Brabant?"

She chuckled. "Why, yes. My father was the comte de Brabant. But please . . . who are you?"

He gave her his name quickly, almost impatiently. "But . . . your mother . . . where is she? Where can I find her?" All he could think of was Godwin. Godwin still waiting in Cornwall, and Heather married to another man here in Barbados. Godwin's child carrying another man's name.

Windmera's lush violet eyes darkened with sadness. "Oh . . . I see you did not understand me. My mother has been dead these five years."

It hit him hard, and it showed. Windy went to him at once, touching his arm sympathetically, and he was struck again with her eyes. So much her mother's . . . yet there lay in them a spirit Heather never had had. A different girl, this.

"Oh, sir . . . I am so sorry. I should not have been so blunt. I should have realized that as her friend you might take it as a shock," said Windy.

"Aye . . . a shock . . ." he answered stupidly, for again he was thinking of Godwin.

"Come along," said Windmera, taking command of the situation. Again he was struck by her nature, so different from her gentle mother. Here she was, a slip of a girl, taking command of an uncomfortable situation.

They walked together for more than an hour, and they talked about her mother. He was careful never to say too much, but it came to him that she knew something, something her mother had hinted at but had never explained. However, he kept silent. He had no intention of bursting her pretty bubble.

So it was that Captain John Pearson sailed home for Land's End and Godwin, bearing news he was in a dither to relate to his old friend. His thoughts were many. Perhaps all in all, he mused as he looked out to the northeast and home, perhaps Heather's passing was for the best. Perhaps Godwin would now be able to get on with his life. He had no way of knowing the news would drive Godwin to further madness. How could he have known?

In Mystic, Connecticut, thrived a seaport of growing dimensions, and with it flourished the Landons, a small but hearty brew and of English noble stock.

It was just about the moment when Captain John Pearson docked his vessel at Land's End bursting with his news of Windmera that the wheel of the future brought Lance Landon into its gyrations.

Lance Landon stood on the docks of his father's shipping domain, the very broth of a man. His deep-blue eyes were twinkling with that devilish glint that so shook the maids' hearts in Mystic. At twenty-eight he was what any father could wish his son to be . . . and more, perhaps a shade more than Jules Landon wanted, for Lance had his mother's Irish temper, zeal and will. They stood there, two tall oaks unmoving, but only Lance's eyes were lit with amusement, for his father found himself balked. He regarded his son, noting not for the first time that Lance had inherited his mother's obstinacy.

"There is not one reason in the world that you must personally fetch Isabelle's sugar!" snapped Jules Landon.

"But you mistake, Father." Lance chuckled, his glance not wavering. "There is every reason. *I desire* to do my sister's bidding."

"Do not play on words, Lance. I won't have it!" objected his father strongly, glaring at his son. "We have any number of excellent captains who can make the trip."

"Father, Izzy will not rest until she gets the sugar for that settlement she and Jim are so proud of up there. True, any number of captains could do the trip . . . but you know we were lucky to negotiate this consignment with the comte de Brabant, and besides, I need the exercise. I've been stagnating here and shall be better at sea!"

Jules Landon regarded his son's full head of black hair. It was the color of Irene's silken tresses, and Jules's eyes troubled over. What would *she* do? He wished, not for the first time, that Irene were still alive to guide him. It was true, Lance was too restless these days. Oh, he liked the business his father had built into an empire, and he showed every promise of capably carrying on . . . yet, he was forever taking to the sea in that schooner of his.

Jules hesitated before saying slowly, "Lance . . . we received no reply to our letter advising the comte that our ship would be departing for Barbados this month. And that was some three months ago."

"Don't fret it, Father, one cannot be dependent on the mail packets these days, what with all the trouble we have been having with British vessels—" As soon as it slipped out he regretted it.

Again the heavy look came into Jules's eyes. "Precisely why I don't want *you* making the trip to Barbados. 'Tis British waters!"

"I must, sir."

It was a quiet reply, but Jules Landon heard and understood the tone. There would be no discussing the topic any longer. Lance Landon would not be dissuaded. *"Drat the sugar!"* he said testily, a hand going through his steel-gray hair.

Lance laughed out loud. "That is not what you said six months ago when we received Izzy's request for the stuff." An affectionate arm went round his father's wide shoulders. "If I remember correctly, your words were: 'Sugar? My child wants for sugar? She will have enough to supply an entire town!' "

Jules Landon regarded his son with some annoyance. "It is all the fault of that . . . that impertinant puppy she has married!"

"Again, as I remember it, *you* gave your blessings." He sidestepped and threw an order to one of his crewmen on board his schooner, the *Sea Hawk*.

"That was before the devil of a lad took it into his head to go up north to Canada to do his doctoring! The very idea! Impudent, I say!"

"Indeed . . . but they are not really in Canada, sir. It is Buffalo, New York."

"Outlandish. Might as well be Canada . . . and with my grandson on the way!" He turned on his only son. *"And you!* Tossing first one wench and then another . . . but marrying none. *I want grandchildren.* Do you hear me, Lance? Grandchildren!"

"And on that note I take my leave of you, Father . . . for the sun grows bright already and we must set sail." Strong hands clasped one another, and it was a moment of feelings.

So it was that a sleek schooner, swifter than most and but lightly armed with four cannons, took to the sea with Lance as its captain. The *Sea Hawk* put Mystic behind it and set its sails for the West Indies, its destination Bridgetown, Barbados. The Landons had no way of knowing that Maurice de Brabant had died, that he had lost his overseer and that his estate was now run by incompetent solicitors. Perhaps knowing would not have mattered, after all; the goods they had contracted for had already been paid for by bank draft. But Maurice's death would make a difference . . . and that, that whispered trouble!

Roderick had grown to be a fine-looking young man, with curls the color of russet and eyes of cool marsh brown. He looked upon Godwin still with a worship few sons give their natural fathers. He was in the village, as it happened, on the afternoon Captain John Pearson went rushing to Ravensbury Castle. Roderick was wooing the girl he thought to marry, for at that time he didn't think anything would come to stop him.

Godwin heard his friend's name announced and jumped to his feet with genuine pleasure. He had so few of them. He went forward, and Captain John noted that time had done little to alter his looks. At least not to an outsider, not to someone who hadn't known him as a youth, for he had still his red curls, though they were faded by the years. He had still those bright dark eyes, though the pain was readable in their recesses. His height, his build, still spoke of his virility, yet the aging was there.

"Captain John! You old sea dog! Come back, have you? And with what news?"

Captain John could hardly contain himself. He knew Godwin's question was but an idle one; he never expected word of Heather.

"Godwin . . ." said the captain, making certain the library door was closed. "Godwin . . . we must talk."

Godwin's smile faded into doubt, as though he sensed what his friend was about to impart to him. "Sit down, John . . . I will pour us some brandy," he said, going to the decanter.

Captain John watched him pour, looking for the right words, but he was a simple man and his words came out blunt all the same.

"Heather . . . Godwin . . . she died . . . five years ago!"

Godwin dropped his glass of brandy, and John watched the contents spill over the oriental rug. He stared at the seaman, and his face was contorted into pain. And then he gave his friend his back and walked toward the fireplace.

Captain John couldn't see his face, but he knew what Godwin was feeling. He was the bearer of sad news . . . but good news too, for there was Windmera! "Godwin . . . Godwin . . . listen to me, man. You've been blessed with a daughter!"

Godwin turned at the words, but John couldn't be certain he had heard, for he was staring past him to another time, another scene.

"Godwin! Didn't ye hear me, man? Ye've got a daughter. A fine lass . . . every inch of her the image of her mother!"

That took hold of him. "A daughter?" he whispered. He went to his friend. "A daughter . . . mine? Our child . . . lived? Where? Where is she?"

They sat together then, and Captain John told him all that he knew, and when he had done, Godwin made him repeat everything. It troubled Godwin when he learned that Heather had married a Frenchman. He was torn between knowing she had been cared for and the jealousy common to a man who loves strongly, passionately. But he set aside his jealousy, aware that she must have had her reasons not to return to Cornwall, not to brave it out with him.

Over and over he made John repeat his daughter's words—how she had looked, how she had sounded. He couldn't get enough of what she was like. He'd whisper her name and that faraway look would come over him. Satisfied he was that Heather had named her Windmera. It meant much to him. It was a message of her love.

At that moment Captain John was content. He felt he had done the right thing, and he relaxed on the sofa. At last, at last, Godwin would rest, settle down. Then suddenly Godwin was up and pacing. The more he moved, the more frenzy would creep into his eyes. John watched, puzzled, for the last time he had seen Godwin like that was the time of Heather's disappearance. It worried him.

"Godwin . . . what—" he started.

"Hush, John!" interrupted Godwin sharply. "I've got to think. My God! A daughter!" He stopped and raised his eyes as though in silent prayer, quiet thanks. "A daughter . . . our Windmera. Heather's and mine! I shall have her, John! *I shall have my daughter here . . . at Ravensbury!"*

Two

Roderick watched her glide down the garden path toward him, and he waited, his heart beating with desire. Small white hands found his own slender fingers, and he took her to him, bending to kiss her lips.

She giggled and pulled away coquettishly, and he found himself enraptured by china-blue eyes. Soft winding curls bobbed about her heart-shaped countenance as she shook her head and wagged a finger. "Naughty boy!"

"Not so! I protest, Clara, but you do ill use me," he bantered, playing the game with her as his arm went around her and his other hand clasped the small waist. He could feel the youthful suppleness beneath her blue silk gown. Lord, but he wanted her! Love? He looked down past the graceful white neck to the swells of her small breasts. Ah yes, he could love her very well. Marriage? Perhaps . . . if it was the only way he could have her, and why not? True, she was not as highly connected as the heir of Ravensbury had a right to expect, but then Roderick had never really attempted that road. He had his fears. He had his skeleton hidden away and avoided with some care the lures of loftier maidens. Why? He wanted no one to look too deeply into his past. He wanted no one to ask questions, for he was a bastard, and he had no way of knowing how many people from the past were aware of it. No, a noble family having been presented with his suit might look and find his dreaded skeleton. Thus it was that Roderick always chose to look beneath his station when he courted.

His mouth closed on hers. He could feel her body yield to him, bend to his sway, and it excited him further. Audaciously he plunged his hand down the front of her gown and found the soft satin flesh of her budding youth, and his finger teased the nipple to its perfection. She groaned and attempted to pull away. "No . . . Rod . . . what if Father should see?"

"Ha! The old devil wants this to happen!" he said roughly, once more covering her mouth with his own, this time sending his tongue deep into her, taunting her into submission with his expertise. Clara was but seventeen and he twelve years her senior, yet he knew well her father looked for a match here. They would not be disturbed. Already he was lowering her onto her back. She objected softly, but he ignored it, sending his cape with a swift snap of his wrist before her. He had chosen the spot well, for they were hidden by the shrubbery.

"I want you," he whispered hoarsely.

"Do you? Oh . . . Rod . . . do you love me?"

He never hesitated; he had no such conscience. "I adore you."

She allowed him to raise her gown, to find the soft tuft of dark-blond hair at the apex of her thighs. She allowed him to please her with his ministrations, but she was not as foolish as her appearance would make one think. At the crucial moment she stopped him. "No, Roderick . . . not that! I am afraid."

"Afraid of what, my darling? I shan't hurt you," he attempted to convince her.

" 'Tis for marriage only . . . if you love me . . . ?"

He stopped and looked down at her lovely face. He could see the chit meant business. *She meant to have his name.* And why not? He was tired of the life he had been living. It might be nice to take a wife . . . start a brood. It would please Godwin!

"Will you marry me, Clara?" he asked suddenly, his eyes bright.

"Yes, oh yes, my darling," she cried, hugging him to her. At last, she thought, at last.

"Do I now have permission to proceed?" He was teasing, for even as he said the words he was lowering her skirts. All desire had fled with the gravity of the future he had just taken on.

"No, sir, you may not! But on our wedding night . . . you may do what you will with me."

The seduction in her voice thrilled him, as did the movement of her lips, the light in her eyes. He remembered the look of her as he took the ride back to Ravensbury Castle, and he felt elated. Yes, Godwin would be pleased with him. Godwin wanted him to choose a bride, start a family. His mother? She lay still a cripple in her bed, but she had a strange will. She would not like it. She had grandiose ideas and notions. Sara would want him to seek higher for a bride. But he didn't really care what Sara wanted! Godwin would be pleased!

Such thoughts carried him pleasantly to the library, to his father, for he wanted to break the news immediately and see the happiness come into Godwin's eyes. However, he stopped short when he saw Captain John seated with Godwin. They had never been close, the captain and Roderick. Perhaps it was because Captain John had witnessed his shame that long-ago day on Land's End. Perhaps he was jealous of the deep friendship Godwin shared with the captain. At any rate, some of his elation ebbed at the sight of his father's guest.

"Oh . . . captain. Good to see you," he said politely, coming forward to shake the old seaman's hand.

"Aye, lad, how fare ye?" asked Captain John, smiling warmly, thinking the boy had something bursting in him to tell.

"I am fine, sir, just fine," Roderick said, dismissing the captain and turning on Godwin. "I have news I would share with you at once, sir."

"Have you?" said Godwin, eyeing his son strangely.

Roderick was too excited to notice the oddness of Godwin's tone or the glint in his eyes, and he proceeded, his smile wide. "I have decided to get married . . . to Clara Boswell." He waited expectantly, sure of Godwin's approval.

Godwin glared for a long strained moment at Roderick before finally releasing what it was he had on his mind. Captain John fidgeted in his seat, sure this had something to do with the girl, Windmera, sure it boded ill, wondering if he had been right to tell Godwin he had a daughter.

"So . . . you have a wish to be married, Roderick? Excellent, lad, for I have been wishing you so these many years," said Godwin, but he wasn't smiling. He was deep in thought.

Roderick sensed something was wrong in spite of his father's words. He glanced doubtfully at Captain John, looking for an answer. What was wrong with him? Whatever had happened? He looked at his father, seeing the disturbing change in Godwin. "Yes, sir. Then you don't object?" He wanted his father's felicitations, he wanted joyous celebrations, not this strange quiet. "I had a notion you wanted me to settle down . . . start a family."

"Start a family?" repeated Godwin, an uneven light coming into his eyes. "Yes, that is what I want of you . . . but not with Clara Boswell!"

Roderick was surprised. He fiddled with the fobs at his waist. "Not with Clara? But sir, I thought you rather liked Clara."

"Clara Boswell is a lovely girl, and had I not another in

mind, yes, I would have countenanced such a match . . . though your mother would not."

"Another . . . another in mind?" said Roderick stupidly, for in fact he was stunned by this announcement.

It was then that Captain John understood. He saw it all clearly before him. He jumped to his feet with his objection, but couldn't at first speak. He could only stare at his friend. Had Godwin lost his sense of reason? But Godwin ignored him.

"Yes. Her name is Windmera." He had said it quietly, but its impact was that of crashing thunder, leaving everyone speechless.

Roderick stared idiotically at Godwin for a long time before repeating the unknown name. "Windmera? But . . . I know of no such woman."

"Ah, but you will, Roderick. You will leave Cornwall for the isle of Barbados. You will seek out Windmera . . . de Brabant, and you will make her your wife. You will return with her to Ravensbury Castle, and here the two of you will reside and give me grandchildren. Grandchildren! Oh, God . . . of my own blood, and they will carry on the line!"

Roderick was hit hard by the last of his father's words. Suddenly he believed he understood. It was the reference to the bloodline that took his mind into the past. He remembered the missing Heather, who had carried Godwin's natural child. So, Windmera was his daughter. But his thought was first that he was not Godwin's son, and all the wishing had ended with his youth. He was not of Godwin's blood. But Windmera, *she was*. He knew this, yet he pressed on. "Why, sir? Why have you chosen a girl thousands of miles away, a girl you have never seen? Why?" It was something of a challenge. Something inside him dared Godwin to air it at last.

Godwin frowned, for he loved Roderick well, yet still he would not be balked in this obsession. "Enough! It is my will, and as my son you owe me the filial duty to obey!"

Roderick's voice trembled, and Captain John winced as he watched in silence. *"Obey?* I have always obeyed you . . . in everything! But I will marry where I choose . . . when I choose!" He had taken a stand, not because he wished to defy Godwin but because he was in the throes of jealousy, a jealousy he did not recognize, could not understand. Jealous of a girl who carried not Godwin's name, but his blood!

Captain John found his voice, for he could see the fire in Godwin's eyes and wanted to spare them both. "Godwin? Ye can't do this. It won't work . . . what you are planning. It is not right—"

"Won't work! You are very much mistaken, John!" Godwin said in a calm cool voice.

"Ye can't be thinking . . . the girl . . . Windmera . . . she is the image of her mother. People . . . they would remember Heather—"

Roderick slammed his fist on the table. "So, that is it! You mean to bring her here! You have found that woman and she has a daughter and you plan to bring them here! So be it. But you can't foist the girl onto me!"

His father crossed the room and brought his open hand across Roderick's lean cheek. It made a sound to silence all others, and there they stood, Godwin in a fury and Roderick stunned by the first blow he had ever sustained at his mentor's hands.

"*Don't you ever* speak to me in that way again!" roared Godwin, out of his usual control. "You will marry Windmera. Do you hear me?"

"Yes, I hear you . . . but I shall not comply with your wishes," said Roderick bitterly, his lips twisting on his words.

"You will comply or you will lose Ravensbury! I swear it. If you do not go to Barbados and marry . . . *my daughter* . . . and bring her here to Ravensbury to enjoy her heritage, I shall make certain *you* do not!" There, it was out in the open.

Captain John moved away from them, closing his eyes, blaming himself for having brought this onto Godwin, onto the lad. This was Godwin no more, but a creature made by torment, piling his disillusionments onto Roderick's head. It wasn't right, but he knew there wasn't anything he could do.

Roderick stared, for he couldn't speak. He knew what he was. He knew that Godwin knew this, but never before had Godwin showed a sign that it was so! Not since that night . . . He stood there, the pain driving through his chest. Needles whose ends were lit with fire singed his heart. His eyes burned, and he longed to answer, longed to say he didn't care to have Ravensbury under such humiliating conditions, but he couldn't. He loved Ravensbury, needed to continue under its disguise of legitimacy, and there was still too much of him that worshiped Godwin.

"Yes, Roderick, now that I have said it, make no mistake, I mean it. Your mother sent the one dearest being out of my reach, caused my child to be raised by another, with another's name. You are not of my blood, we both know it, so there is no incest in the marriage I plan for you, and only we three know that Windmera is mine."

Again Captain John attempted a word. "But Godwin . . . she will remind people of Heather."

"What does that signify? Does she look like me?" he growled.

"No . . . but . . ."

"People will then assume that Heather married and had a child. It is all very simple. Windmera will attain her rightful name through her marriage to Roderick. I will achieve my end. I will have my own flesh and blood . . . here beneath my roof! She will bear me grandchildren . . . carry on the Ravensbury line . . ."

Roderick stood during this madness. He was nine and twenty but he had the look of a beaten boy. He cringed within himself. Over and over again a pitiless voice yelped at him, telling him he was a bastard, and in that moment a sore that had been paining him for too long split open. It did not bleed as do most open wounds. No, not this. It gave itself over to infection. So started the thing to fester, for though he adored the man before him, he knew suddenly that he hated him as well, and this new unthinkable acknowledgment blew his soul to smithereens.

Three

The sails of the Sea Hawk *were full of wind. The hand-*some schooner sliced the deep blue, whispering lovingly among its folds. They were a pair, formed for one another and much in harmony. Captain Lance Landon stood at the wheel in his shirt sleeves and leather jerkin, the sun full on his bronzed face. The salty breeze played with his black billowing hair, and his blue eyes were bright with his pleasure. They were making excellent time, and three weeks at sea saw them nearly at their destination. He loved the open water. She was a naughty mistress, plump and full with life, ready to tease, to caress . . . to devour, if one allowed her. But, and he smiled at the thought, *he'd* not allow her. It was not that he knew her too well. It was not that he trusted her, for he had learned early never to trust such a mistress. It was his confidence in himself, his self-assurance in his judgment and his belief that his very distrust of her capricious will would keep him ever cautious, ever wary, and therefore one step ahead.

Suddenly the pleasantness of the morning was broken by the call from the watch overhead, *"A brig to leeward!"*

Lance Landon gave up the wheel to his first mate, a young lad, no more than twenty, but one he had taken beneath his wing many years ago. "Keep her on course, Jackie, steady now," he said quietly as he took up a spyglass. Leveling it, he saw the huge, heavily armed vessel. He saw too the flag; *it was British!*

At the very same moment, the brig, bearing the name *Hornet*, observed the schooner's sails. Its captain issued swift orders to tack, for he had every intention of boarding the *Sea Hawk*.

Lance Landon's mobile black brow went up, and its match dived in a frown, for his thoughts were not in accord with those of the *Hornet's* captain. England and the United States were not yet at war, but there was certainly a great deal of talk regarding its possibility in the near future. Relations between the cousinly nations were at best very strained in this year of 1812. The causes for their disputes were many, and the men of the times would certainly argue over which reasons were paramount, but all would agree that the problems they were facing on the high seas certainly were among the chief concerns.

"Free ships make free goods." It was the principle upon which Americans expounded their rights. The British did not countenance this doctrine. Indeed, it was very much otherwise. England was at war with Napoleon. The English felt they were on the side of right. They felt that in fighting Napoleon and France they were fighting for freedom for all and therefore were entitled to do everything necessary to win that war.

The Americans called themselves neutrals. However, they conceded to a compromise, agreeing that certain ports, certain goods, would be blockaded. The problem lay in defining what was contraband and what was not. Americans felt that only the goods that directly aided the French war effort were contraband articles. The British did not feel this way. Furthermore, the British felt they had the legal right under their hazy agreement with the American Congress to board, search and seize, if necessary, whatever items they considered contraband. Needless to say, American merchants did not see eye to eye on this point with the British Admiralty. In fact, they felt that any search by a British navy should be limited to their papers. A problem indeed!

Perhaps this in itself may have been resolved. But in addition to boarding and turning American merchant ships topsy-turvy in their search for contraband, the British naval authorities began employing the ugly tactic of impressment while on board American vessels. This on the excuse that they were searching out deserters from their own legions. The British felt that once an Englishman, always an Englishman, and therefore whenever they came across an Englishman who appeared to be a deserter, they impressed him on the spot. This sole decision could be made by any officer of the Royal Navy.

It is quite easy to understand that this did not find favor with Americans, who to begin with considered impressment inhumane. They believed that the practice of seizing these men while they were under the protection of the American flag was an insult to that Flag. No nation that allowed its citizens and those applying for citizenship to be seized and put into virtual slavery could consider itself a nation free!

Thus it was that feelings were hostile between the two nations, especially on the sea. Lance Landon was a proud man, protective of his schooner and his crew. He had not himself encountered any trouble from the British before, but he had heard the accounts of those who had, and he would allow no mishandling of his ship or his men.

Within fifteen minutes the brig sent out their longboat with its captain at its bow, and the *Sea Hawk* was boarded. Captain Landon stood, his hands folded at his back, his legs apart, as he looked down on the smaller captain.

The British captain presented him first with an official document.

"I am Captain Cabe. You have there a warrant to board, search and seize French contraband," said the British captain. He did not smile.

Lance Landon did smile, widely, and his deep aqua-blue eyes glittered quite dangerously. A more perceptive man than the British captain before him might have wondered just what the look portended.

"Board you have, sir, but search you most certainly will not!" said Lance Landon. He produced from his leather jerkin his own set of papers and rather roughly took up the captain's limp hand and smacked them into it. "You have there *my* papers. To save time, I shall tell you that we disembarked from our home port, Mystic, Connecticut, with naught but provisions and a legal tender to receive a shipment of sugar from the comte de Brabant of the Brabant Plantation in Barbados. We carry no French contraband."

"Nevertheless, I shall have to see that for myself," said Captain Cabe, unwisely.

"Sir! You misread. You are speaking to the captain and owner of this vessel," warned Lance Landon.

Captain Cabe hesitated. "It is . . . our policy—"

"The devil take your policy!" snapped Lance. "Are you calling me a liar?"

"Captain, I assure you . . . we have no quarrel with the Americans—"

"You will have, though, I promise you, sir," interrupted Lance. "Now, if you don't mind, I would appreciate it if you would return to your brig and allow us to proceed on our way."

"I am afraid that is not possible. In addition to the fact that we must search for contraband, we are also looking for British deserters. Your men must offer themselves up for our inspection."

Lance did not at once answer him. His men were set, with

purpose, throughout the boat, innocently it would appear. However, he now sent a glance to Jackie, who in turn put up a brow, and so it was carried. Muskets and pistols suddenly were aimed, and their targets were the British crew standing behind Captain Cabe. The Englishmen nervously noted this and awaited the end result.

"This . . . this is madness!" spluttered Captain Cabe, looking down the barrel of a deadly musket.

"Is it now? How so? I have ordered you off my boat. I am a merchant vessel on its way to an approved *English* port. I am being detained illegally. I have ordered you off my ship, and you have not complied." He turned once again to his young blond first mate. "Hoist up, lad. These gentlemen . . . will be leaving us!"

"Captain Landon!" exploded the harried British officer. He wanted no trouble. He was not in a position to take forceful action with a merchant vessel not at war with England, but at the same time he felt hardly used. "Your behavior is . . . highly irregular!"

"So is your boarding my ship!" snapped Lance Landon angrily. He held the British captain in contempt. He saw him the weak-natured man he was, and he knew intuitively that Captain Cabe would not take violent action. If a war was to start between the Americans and the British, Captain Cabe would want no responsibility for firing the first shot.

So it was that the good captain of the *Hornet* took his men and his leave, the American seamen shouting ribald jests at their back. They watched the longboat as it was rowed back to its waiting brig until they heard their captain shout at their heads, "Well, my fine lads! Unfurl those sails . . . get a move on . . . come on, you blasted lubbers! Keep a sharp eye and a firm hand, and its rum you'll be swigging before long!"

They loved their captain. They had sailed beneath him for many a year now and they were loyal to his call. But none knew then how very soon their loyalty would be called upon, or how very much their captain would be needing it!

A moon lit up two figures in a large open bed whose mahogany backboard overshadowed their movements. An island breeze ruffled the flimsy drapery which hid the open glass doors to the stone terrace outside, and a woman's soft groan hung in the air.

The movements, the sounds, were not new ones to this particular room. The chamber had seen these same two lovers in each other's arms many times in ecstasy, in sadness, in laughter, in regret, but always, always in passion. Even now, after nearly sixteen years, still in passion! Louise Davenant moved away and lay back a moment on her pillow. Layers of light crossed her features. The blush of youth was no longer there. Yet the years had been kind to Windmera's aunt. The ravages of wrinkles had not yet marred her beauty. She was still at fifty quite lovely of face and her brown curls scarcely yet gray. Her figure, though as plump as it had always been, was womanly, desirable, and she thought ahead to the future, for Louise Davenant after all these years was about to take on another husband! And he was not the man lying beside her. He was not the man she had grown to love more than life . . . but a stranger.

He was asleep, her love. She propped herself up on her elbow and watched the movement of his eyes beneath his closed dark-brown lids. He was dreaming. His black short frizzled hair was tinged with silver. His face had the look in sleep of deep peace, deep contentment . . . but he did not know, she had not yet told him, she was going to be married. Her lover was beside her, flat, his legs sprawled out, and she moved her hand adoringly over his black glistening muscles. Her lover. How odd to think it, whisper it. Her lover . . . a black slave.

She could remember still the first time she had seen him. It had been years since she had seen her husband killed at the guillotine. Her husband. He had been the only man she had ever known. It was not a love match—few marriages of her day in her class were—but she had loved him in her own way, for he had been a considerate man, good to her. With his passing so passed her whole way of life. She was caught up in a new life in a new land, and then her body began to make its demands. Odd . . . she could have gone to bed with any number of white Englishmen. Enough invited it, enough were available. But somehow none attracted her, none intrigued her. And then she had seen Jokai.

All these years, and she could still recall that first time. Maurice and Heather had taken her for an outing to a neighboring plantation. They had lunched, and Lord Brayward and his wife were giving them a tour of the plantation. She had been hot and bored as she wandered over the grounds, duly noting the modern workings of the sugar plantation. Everywhere men and children, all black, all half-naked, bustled at their work. The odor of the processing of sugar filled the air, and suddenly she felt she would be suffocated by it all if she didn't get away. She held back her steps, and then in a burst, as though she were once again a schoolgirl, she escaped down a path. It took her through sugar cane rising some six feet in the air. All around the stalks grew, their withered leaves, called trash, hanging loosely, for they were ready for the reaping that would soon start.

And then he appeared. He stepped out, the large black boot-shaped cutter called a bill hanging limply in his hand. He saw her and stopped, frightened. He was a slave, owned by a lord who was not unkind by nature yet was well able to dole out punishment when he saw fit, and Jokai was never sure when his owner would see fit. Furthermore, he was not where he was supposed to be. He had been aiding another slave and had taken time out from his field work, and if this was not enough, here before him was a white woman. A beautiful white woman alone, and there was no telling but that she might start up shouting, for white women were known to do such things!

He hurried to forestall her scream, for indeed the suddenness of his appearance produced a startled gasp from Louise's lips.

"Mistress . . . ah mean yuh no hurt an' will be out yuh way torectly." So saying, he bowed his head and eyes and pressed himself along the outside edge of the narrow path.

Louise Davenant cocked her head, for it suddenly came to her mind that the man before her was a particularly handsome creature. He was tall and wide-shouldered. His brows were finely etched. His nose was almost patrician and his lips sensuous. All at once she had an uncontrollable urge to speak with him. She had never really conversed with a slave before other than to give orders.

"You are frightened. Why? And why do you avert your eyes? Am I so hard to look upon?" She couldn't believe it of herself; she was actually dallying with him.

He glanced up quickly, sharply, and his eyes met with her own. "Mistress . . . I am always frightened of my betters." He had learned well the knack of survival. Inside his gut raged with indignation at his words, but it was necessary.

His large black eyes struck her with their intelligence . . . and more, something much more. Was he laughing at her? She put up her chin. "I would not have you . . . or any man . . . afraid of me! It is not the sort of . . . sensation *I* like to inspire in men!" she answered tartly, somewhat peeved that she had not set him aquiver with feelings other than fear.

"Yes, mistress," he answered, and this time she was certain she saw a flame of amusement in the depths of his eyes. She was about to dress him down when her brother's voice called to her admonishingly.

"Louise? Ah, so here is where you have got to. Come, Lord Brayward wishes us to return to the house for lemonade before we return to Brabant." He was looking at her and then at the tall glistening slave, aware of something in the air and yet telling himsef he was imagining it. He had spoken in French to his sister, but oddly enough she answered in English. She answered in English, though it was not her native tongue, for it seemed somehow rude to speak over the black man's head, and for the first time that afternoon she saw him, really saw him, and thought of him not as a slave but as a man.

She turned to take up her brother's extended arm and caught the black man's eyes following her. She caught too the expression, and saw that he glanced at her as a man looking at an attractive woman. It thrilled her, and she stopped Maurice, turning her head to the slave. "Your name?" she asked softly.

"Jokai, mistress." And again his eyes were on the ground.

"Good day to you, Jokai," said Louise, startling her brother into thoughtfulness.

It wasn't long afterward that Louise talked her brother into purchasing Jokai from Brayward. Maurice worried about it, but she was dear to him, and as it pleased her . . . what harm, then? So it was that Jokai came to Brabant. He came wearing naught but his trousers frayed at the knees. The thin material fit his muscular thighs tightly, and his torso glistened in the sun as he rounded the corner in search of his orders for the day.

Louise, on her way out of the house through a side entrance it was her wont to use, came forth and collided heavily with him, landing very neatly in his arms.

"Oh . . ." she breathed, startled and a little frightened lest someone observe, yet excited all the while.

"Yuh scotched, mistress?" asked Jokai, anxiously looking around lest some white male come upon them and think he was taking a liberty.

"Scotched?" she asked, looking up into his face, backing away slowly.

"You hurt? I just about knocked you down. Didn't see you," he answered.

She frowned. "But no . . . and it was all my fault. It was I that came stampeding out." She cast a doubtful look at him, "For gracious sake . . . you are again looking at the earth! Am I the dreadful Medusa? Shall you turn into stone, monsieur, if you look at me?"

He looked at her full then, and in a way that near took her breath directly from her lungs. Aye, she pleasured his eyes. He was nearly three and thirty and had sired many a black child on this isle. A good breeder, was Jokai—so had said his master when he was sold to Brayward. Thus it was that Jokai rarely wanted for an evening's pleasuring, but more than that Jokai had never had, never felt. It wasn't good to feel. There was never any security in it. What would he do if he loved and then some white master chose his love for his bed? What could he do? No, he would never allow himself to shed his armor. But then he looked into Louise Davenant's light-brown eyes, and something inside them both churned.

Still he answered, "Now, mistress, I don't look on you cause I know 'tis not my place."

"Jokai!" hailed Maurice. "There you are. Come, let me take you to the smithy, where you will be trained for your work here at Brabant. I think you will find our plantation runs somewhat differently than Brayward's . . . and I think too you will be far more suited to your new chores."

Louise watched them go off. She stood frozen, taking in every line of Jokai's back, admiring every sinew, and she knew a deep stirring in her womb. She felt it again that night and the next morning when she awoke; and it was that stirring that sent her out that day with but one intention.

She timed it well, for she had Jokai sent into Bridgetown on an errand, and she had him sent not in the wagon but on horseback. A single horse would be far easier to conceal in the fields. Then all she had to do was waylay him on his way back. It was easy enough. He reined in the old nag they had given him to use, and his brow went up with some interest, for she had such a look about her.

"Mistress . . . are you well?"

"No. I was out walking, Jokai . . . and twisted my leg." She raised her muslin skirt and wrapped her hand around her ankle, wincing all the while.

He dropped off the unsaddled cob and came to her at once, his face troubled. He bent, and his large black hand hesitated as he sought her ankle. She raised her skirt higher and encouraged him further. "Yes . . . right there . . ."

He inspected the ankle but could find no swelling, no injury, and he glanced at her doubtfully. Quickly she answered his doubt.

"If you could just carry me to a shady spot . . . and bring your horse . . ."

"Best if I put you on the horse and take you back."

She snapped, "I shall decide what is best . . . and what I need is to be away from the house . . . from the lovebirds . . . my brother and his wife. It is very difficult for me, you see . . . being a widow." She gave him a long look. "There now, Jokai . . . please?"

He lifted her in his large arms and allowed her to direct him. The cob followed, nibbling at the tender grass, and then he was lowering her onto the turf, but her arms did not release him. He allowed it. He told himself that it would mean his undoing, but he allowed it. His heart began beating so hard he thought for sure it would burst from its walls. He wanted to speak, to tell her how he felt, but no words would come. She was a white woman! Again, again he was being used! Had he no pride? But her eyes drew out his heart, and he wanted her! Something inside of him yearned, and already the dark staff of his manhood was pulsating to the churnings of his desire. Silently she found his hand and put it to her breast. Her other hand worked his staff until they could stand no more. Such was the joining of slave to mistress.

Such was the joining then, and now sixteen years later he was still her slave, but she was his as well. He worked at Brabant as a slave by day, but by night he was free, free to climb through her window and to her bed. Maurice and Heather had always known, but they had never said a word. She had her own wing in the house, and it had been her own affair. Affair? Odd word, that. She had been so much to Jokai . . . lover, teacher. Oh yes, she had done the forbidden, she had taught him to read and to write. She had taught him to love . . . and now, now what was she about to teach him? Betrayal! But she had no choice. Dear God . . . she would have to make him understand. The plantation was Windmera's, and at any rate, it was no longer prospering. She had naught to keep her in her passing years . . . and Lord Brayward, now a widower, wanted her. He had always wanted her, and it now appeared that he would get her!

Brayward! How Jokai despised the man. Always Jokai had had to watch Brayward watching Louise. Always Jokai had had to hold himself in check whenever Brayward took a liberty, forced his attentions on Louise. In the past, Brayward's wife had kept his lordship off . . . but she was gone now two years, and with the passing of Maurice, Brayward was a constant visitor to Brabant. Jokai would not take the news well, and soon Louise would have to talk to him, tell him what she was planning.

It wasn't fair! It wasn't fair of Maurice to leave things in such a mess at Brabant. Poor Maurice. Heather's death had left him useless. Each year had seen him more and more dependent on wine and less capable of running Brabant. His will left everything to Windmera. His funds were depleted and his bank account was almost empty, so she would have to look out for herself. She would have to accept Brayward's offer. Oh, God! If only she could still go on with Jokai. Perhaps . . . perhaps she could, somehow? Perhaps if she were to arrange to meet him here at Brabant from time to time? How could she give up Jokai? Life, she thought, had dealt her a blow, devastating in its totality. Life had made her white, had made him a black slave, and had made her without the means to ignore it all!

Windmera's quarters were situated on the opposite wing of the large French-styled country home. The hour was late, and Windy lay asleep in her high-canopied bed. A sea breeze fluttered her light organza hangings and played with her hair. She could hear the toss of the waves against the rocky reefs through her sleep, and it stirred her movements. Pale shades of flimsy floated about her lithe body, for in her restlessness her covers went to the floor. Black thick tresses of hair were twisted in her fingers, and she weaved the long strands unconsciously as her dreams worked havoc. She dreamed and she frenzied with troubles, but they had naught to do with her aunt. How could they when she knew nothing of her aunt's problems?

Of course, Windmera knew all about Tante Louise and Jokai. She had noticed the unconcealable alliance long ago and had gone to her mother with it. Heather had explained in her own way, and Windy had understood. Louise had a black slave for a lover. . . he was head groom at Brabant, and it was not the thing! However, she didn't think her aunt was wicked, only that society was oddly put together. Even so, she never broached the subject to her aunt and Louise never spoke on the matter. It was something everyone at Brabant was aware of, and something none spoke about. Such had been the policy during Heather's reign, such was the policy still. However, Windy had no notion that things were beginning to change for her aunt. She had no way of knowing that Louise was suffering spasms of concern over her future or that her aunt was thinking of marrying Brayward. In fact, Windy had no notion that Brabant was in financial difficulty. What then caused her restless sleep?

Windmera de Brabant was nineteen, a woman full-grown, full-blossomed. She had a woman's needs and more, for Windy's heart was given to passions. Mind now, the maid was a virgin with every intention of giving her maidenhead to none but her future husband (whoever that might be). But still, she was a well ripened lass. The bucks came strutting, and more than one virile fellow caught her eye. She had a mind to speculate, and did it by allowing a kiss here and there. There were some that pointed at big Joseph McKane and said if any were to win Windmera de Brabant's heart it would be him, but Windy . . . she thought differently!

Big Joseph was a rogue of a fellow, young, strapping and with a winning way about him. He came courting, and being fine-looking he caught Windy's interest. Got her fired up enough to walk out alone with him and used just the right words to wheedle a kiss from her. His lips had tickled her desire, burning her ripe body, so that boldly he sent his hand to explore. A deft movement and he found his way down her bodice, where he groaned at the touch of her full breasts. Luscious fruit they were, and he rushed to tease her response. What he got was a gasp from the lady. Strong-minded was Windmera, a wench determined to keep her body from ruling her future. She was not in love with Joseph McKane. Slap went the hand and off went the lady!

So it was that her dreams were restless, for she couldn't deny to herself that it was a difficult thing indeed to be virtuous. The Fates watched all this, never halting their needles, for Roderick of Ravensbury was nearing . . . Roderick, who'd been ordered by her natural father to bring her back as bride of Ravensbury.

Lanky Bunky McGuire was skipper of the Liberté. *Not yet* forty, he'd weathered into something of a man. A shock of faded fair hair always in disarray and framing a face browned by the tropic sun. Eyes squinted and darted and a smile lit the corners of his mouth. Bunky was well liked in Barbados. Well known and well liked, for he had built himself a reputation for being a fair-dealing man.

There he was most times just as the sun began its steps downward. And so it was this hot late afternoon. He sat there, bare feet raised, corncob pipe stuck between his teeth, contemplating the black women, baskets of fruit atop their heads as they swayed past. Dark water lapped at his ship, and its music blended well with the sounds of the end of the day. It was paradise, this isle, and more than once did he give silent thanks to the night he had made off with Heather Martin.

"Eh, Bunk . . . coming to welcome the two new vessels?" called a passing comrade from the dock.

Bunky smiled at him and shook his head. He was comfortable, tired from sailing tourists round the isle. Maurice de Brabant had made him a gift of the *Liberté* long ago, and Heather had come up with the notion of sailing sightseers around the Island. He'd done well for himself, too. He was a happy man. Losing Heather was a blow . . . but then he had Windy to pick him up, and she did. He had a strong love for the lass. A father's love . . . perhaps a little more.

"Give over, Bunk, and come with me," cajoled the sailor. "The *Sea Hawk* has docked, from America, and there is another from Cornwall, they say. Ain't Cornwall yer home?"

Bunky made a disgusted sound. "Whot? Cornwall? Never say so! I be a Devon man! Naw . . . go no wit ye. I 'ave a mind to sleep well into the night."

"Ye be getting old, Bunk me man, ye be getting old." The sailor laughed and sidled off.

So, almost simultaneously had Roderick of Ravensbury and Captain Lance Landon landed in Bridgetown. They had come, and what they promised to the future . . . it didn't bear guessing on then.

Dusk was settling, but the sky over Barbados was shaded in wisps of layered blues. Soft it was, and welcoming. Scents of wildflowers and those planted by design filled the air as the afternoon surrendered itself to the evening. Roderick loosened his collar and undid his fasionable neckcloth. The humidity and heat were a new experience for him. The women, they too were something to contemplate. Black half-naked bodies, or so it seemed with their scanty chemises clinging to their sweating flesh, moved across the market square, most of them carrying baskets full with their wares upon their heads. He had a curiosity about them, a sudden urging to get the prettiest among them into his bed. But he turned such thoughts off. Now he had a mission. Ha! A mission indeed! He had been commanded and had no choice. However, it was too late in the day to find his way to Brabant. He had a plan well laid, for he could take no chances, and therefore he would have to play carefully, very carefully. God! Until he had set foot on this tropic soil he had not really believed this was truly happening to him. But it was, and now there was no turning back. Still, with any luck he might be able to end with the winning hand.

Such were Roderick of Ravensbury's thoughts as he made himself comfortable in the Georgian Inn, overlooking wharfside and Broad Street. His door was opened then, and he found himself confronting a small, well-proportioned black maid. She held in her hand fresh towels and asked in sing-song fashion if he wished his bath to be readied. He smiled wide, for indeed he did.

Captain Lance Landon saw his crew well established and his vessel neatly secured, then sought out an inn for himself. The Georgian was well situated, and its style he liked. Flowers hung from window boxes of dark wood. The pink walls and arched opening suited its island setting. He went in and after a short span of time was shown to the second floor above the lobby. His quarters consisted of two huge rooms painted in cream. The furniture was of dark wood. The bed was a most admirable size and surprised him by being some three feet above the floor and provided with a set of steps. He grinned and moved across to the long glass doors. There were two sets, one facing wharfside with a small rectangular balcony encased in black wrought iron, the other facing southeast and overlooking shacks and other town buildings.

He sighed and threw off his leather jerkin. What to do

first? There was Frank Holmes, a friend of his father's, whom he had promised to call upon, and there was de Brabant. Oh well, it was too late in the day to be searching either out. Good, then he could attend this night to his needs. His needs? Obvious. A bath, a good dinner and a wench! He hadn't had a woman in more than four weeks, and he had every intention of rectifying that want! However, he had no intention of taking a black woman. It was not that he did not find them attractive, for indeed their exotic beauty was most compelling. It was that Captain Lance Landon did not approve of slavery. He wanted no woman who gave because she feared to do otherwise. He wanted a woman who gave freely, without fear. He wanted to seduce a woman who wanted to be seduced! There it was plain and simple, and so he would seek out a particular sort.

Windmera? 'Tis time we spoke of her day as well. It had been dull, leaving her edgy and resty. Having no wish that the coming of dusk would find her in the same mood, she made her way to the stables. There she found Jokai. Now, she and Jokai had never been close. Knowing about him and her aunt made her shy of the large black man, and she was never able to be herself before him, but she liked him well enough. Jokai, on the other hand, liked her strongly. She was a good lass, and he wished only the best for her. There too, maybe because she was his Louise's niece he took a special interest in the girl. So it was he spoke up when he saw she meant to take her roan out.

"It be coming on dark, miss," he said, his neat brows drawn in a frown.

"So it is, Jokai . . . but I must ride," she answered quietly, marveling at this new side to him. She couldn't remember his ever voicing any objections before, but before her father had been alive.

"Ah would be that honored if you would tell ole Jokai where you be bound," he said carefully.

She smiled. "You needn't worry, Jokai . . . I shall be back before my aunt notices." She saw he was still not satisfied and added kindly, "I am only going to Bridgetown to visit with my friend Bunky."

He returned her smile. "Bridgetown be a good seven miles off, missy . . . and you won't be back before dark."

She reached for the blanket herself and slapped it onto her roan's back, neatly squaring it. "I've been out in the dark before, Jokai," she started. She was frowning slightly, wondering at all this concern over a little jaunt into town.

He hung his head slightly. "So you have miss, but they do say two ships come into harbor today . . . and they'll be those sailors looking for *basa-basa . . .*"

She laughed openly. "Well, they won't find it with me. Never fear, Bunky will guard me well enough."

"Will he see you home, miss?" pursued Jokai daringly.

She smiled warmly. He was a good man, this man her aunt loved. "If it pleases you I shall ask him to do just that."

He knew he had never been mistaken in the girl. He smiled from his heart. There was a solid feeling there. She was white and by law she was his owner, but somehow, because of his Louise, Windy had become his family as well. It was an odd feeling.

Off went Windmera, heading her roan northwest toward town. She was scantily dressed as was her habit in a white peasant blouse and loose-fitting long skirt, now hiked up and tucked in at the waist to allow her freedom of movement on the horse she rode. Light leather sandals protected the bottom of her dainty feet, and a straw hat of weathered brown made from the inner branch of a coconut palm covered her head and gave her eyes shade. Tanned she was, contrary to the fashion, but a sight, lordy what a sight! She had little care for the proprieties, which forbade such a riding habit for a lady, daughter of a plantation owner. She loved her freedom too well and had been spoiled for too long.

Sugar cane is reaped from February to May, its harvest time was nearly at an end, and she passed fields upon fields empty now but for the trash of leaves left behind. New stalks were shooting up everywhere, but they barely reached eight inches in height. Brabant's crop had been completed, and the plantation was now in full swing with new plantings. The road passed by a sugar-processing bin, and the entire area smelled of candied yams, or so it seemed to Windy.

A long furry creature, a mongoose, scurried across her path, and she smiled at its haste. Now and then the road rose and dipped and gave her a view of the ocean. Brabant Plantation was housed on the windward Atlantic side of the island, unlike Bridgetown, which saw the beginnings of the Caribbean, known as the leeward portion. The sea was breathtaking. Balls of deep peacock blue seemed nearly surrounded by lighter shades of aqua which melted into lime which further melted into minty blue. Exquisite to look upon.

She loved it. She would always love it, but every now and then she thought what it would be like to travel . . . to see other lands, other people.

Bridgetown was approached and entered. White people, fashionably dressed, passed in their covered curricles, many of them nodding or waving to her. Some of the dowagers shook their heads gravely to see her so dressed and would have stopped to lecture her had she given them the opportunity. She did not, but hurried her horse along to the wharf. There she heard the cry of young black boys in the water calling to the sailors to throw a coin, promising to dive and retrieve it for their amusement.

She spied the *Liberté* housed in its spot and sighed thankfully. Bunky would pick up her spirits with his tales and his happy outlook. He always had the power to tease her out of the dismals.

There on his balcony stood Lance Landon. A bath awaited him, but something kept him from it. Aye, something indeed. He had spotted Windmera as she tooled her horse through the town traffic. He had seen her hailed by lady, by gentleman, by sailor, slaves and servants. She was herself dressed as a servant, or so it seemed to him. He had no way of knowing that the blouse and skirt she wore were made from the finest silks the island had to offer, such that no serving maid could afford. No matter—he wasn't thinking on her clothes. Her jet-black hair streamed in thick waves down her back. She had lowered her skirt as she entered the town, so there was no more of her leg to be seen, but her woven straw hat had fallen a bit back, giving him a view of her features, and they quite caught his breath . . . and interest. Thus he allowed his bath to wait and followed with his eyes the pretty's progress.

"Windy!" he heard called, and turned to see a tall smartly dressed youth winding his way through the crowd in his attempt to catch the girl's attention. "Windy!" cried Joseph McKane, waving his arm frantically.

Windmera saw him, put her chin in the air and deliberately urged her horse out of his path. Lance Landon's brow went up with interest and his deep-blue eyes followed her still. He could almost reach out and touch her, she was that close it seemed, for the *Liberté* was docked directly across from his room's vista.

"Windmera?" cried Joseph again.

She turned then, furious with him for shouting her name abroad.

"Ill-mannered wretch! Go away and speak my name no more! Brute!" was the answer he received for his efforts.

He grinned widely, taking it in stride. He was somewhat out of breath as he reached her. "Eh now, girl . . . don't go on so . . . it wasn't less than you deserved . . . looking the way you do." It was definitely the wrong tactic to use with Windmera de Brabant.

Up went her leg, and her foot planted itself neatly on his chest. With every ounce of strength she could summon she hurled into that thrust and sent the boy reeling into the crowd. A burst of laughter issued forth as she jumped off her roan, handed the reins into a white linkboy's hand and asked him to water the animal.

Bunky was leaning over starboard, grinning wide at her play. Aye, that was his Windy, plucky wench, full of spit and fire. Her mother in body . . . but certainly not in spirit. No, Heather was all softness and ease . . . but not her daughter!

"What brings ye, lass?"

"Boredom," she answered at once, plumping herself down on the poopdeck bench and smiling up into his light eyes. "Boredom, Bunky. Nothing ever changes here on Barbados. 'Tis always the same. The same people, the same places . . ."

"Aye, ye've got the itch, m'gal. 'Tis plain as a pikestaff. Sooner or later ye'll be needing it satisfied," he mused out loud.

"But how?"

As Bunky proceeded to attempt an answer, Lance Landon hurried down the hotel steps to the wharf. He had to meet this wench. She seemed a serving girl . . . with the mien of a duchess. Who was she? He had to find out!

Out came Lance Landon, the sinking sun's rays shimmering across his black hair, which billowed about his lean hardlined face as the breeze took it. His shirt, also taken by the wind, pressed against the hardness of his body and it couldn't help catching Windy's eye as she conversed with Bunky. Caught it and held it as she followed his progress.

Lance sauntered casually toward the *Liberté* and moved his head to see her, and their eyes met. Windy couldn't move. She felt caught in a net, felt as though she had been struggling for hours and had no strength, no will to fight it any more. She couldn't move. His eyes, deep in their blue, held her prisoner. He, he felt much the same. Egad! Violet eyes! He'd never seen their like before. So they were in a moment joined in the magic of silent meeting.

Windmera had never seen a man such as Lance Landon. Tall and erect as an oak. His stance bold, self-assured, sophisticated in spite of his careless garments and arrogance.

Captain Lance Landon saw a free-spirited woman-child whose violet eyes bewitched, whose smile sent a quiver of anticipation, whose form reminded him of the stirring need in his loins. And it was he that first broke the spell of their silence. He sought that moment to charm her further with his deft address. He stepped forward, and though he wore no hat, he tipped his hand to her and made her an impressive bow.

She was amused. He was without a doubt a rogue. Handsome, to be sure, but a rogue nonetheless. She was certainly intrigued, but she was a de Brabant, a lady, and knew well what was her due. He was a stranger, taking a liberty! She turned her head, ignoring him completely, and though Bunky put up a brow at these proceedings he followed her cue and began conversing with her again as though nothing had occurred.

Snubbed! 'Twas Lance's first thought. The wench had actually snubbed him. A new experience for such as he. Snubbed indeed, but undaunted, he acknowledged the setdown with a lift of his mobile brow and the curving of his sensuous lip. He moved off, indicating to the wench should she be interested that he would intrude no further. A fair and somewhat lively shrimper whose skirts were hiked up enough to display a well-formed leg passed nearby, and though the odor of fish repelled, her smile invited. He threw her a compliment, and she threw him a hip. All this Windy caught from the corner of her eye, and though she kept her face averted something inside her moved. But then the audacious fellow was gone from her sight, and Windy sighed. Good riddance, she told herself. He was no doubt a rake . . . and she had probably seen the last of him.

Five

Roderick of Ravensbury lay on his back in his high four-poster bed. Sleep would not come! There was an ache in his loins still, for he had not been satisfied earlier. Hell and fire, what an unpleasantness had come out of the matter of the little black wench!

She had come to him with towels and an offer to have his bath prepared. He had liked the look of her, the form of her butt beneath the gray linen she wore. "A bath, of course . . . have a bath prepared." He had watched her scurry off to do his bidding. It was an easy thing to plan. He would simply ring after he was in his bath. He would ring for more towels.

Two black boys prepared the hot water for his tub. He waited for them to leave him alone before disrobing and sinking into the soothing warmth. He soaped himself down, poured rinse water over himself from the china pitcher, stood up and went to the bellrope. She appeared a few moments later.

"Come in, child," he said quietly.

She looked frightened, probably because she was frightened. She was no more than thirteen, small, neatly packaged, with full budding breasts, enough to make a man like Roderick forget her age. The hotel owner treated her kindly, she was not hardly used as some black female slaves were, and so she was still a virgin.

"Yes, m'lord," she said anxiously. What had she done? Hadn't she done everything the master told her? What had she forgotten? And this white man . . . he was naked . . . naked! She had never seen a white man in the raw before.

She stood still by the door. He frowned. What was the matter with her? Why did she hesitate? She should be thankful for his attention. Hadn't he selected her? He, Roderick of Ravensbury, white, noble . . . hadn't he selected her? He was a little angry now. "I said, come in here . . . and close that door!"

She came in at once. She was too well trained not to obey a direct order from a white person. She could not speak, though. Something, instinct, told her she was about to be used in the way of her sisters. She wanted to cry. There was a boy . . . a black youth who worked at the hotel . . . if she was to be used, she wanted it to be him, no other, please no other, and not this white man with his hard cruel eyes!

Roderick was completely out of patience now. He took long strong strides across the room. He wanted to see those black tits bared, and he would have his way now! One rough hand took hold of the gray material and ripped it away from the small body. He took the time out to stare. He had never seen a black woman bared before. She was beautiful and tantalizing . . . he would see more!

She backed away, horrified. It was her only good dress. The master had bought it for her when he had elevated her to parlor maid. Her only good gown, ruined. A large tear formed and rolled down her smooth cheek. White people . . . they were so cruel! His hand reached out again and took hold of her round firm breast. His touch was violent, and the child cried out. How could she endure this? No more . . . please, no more! She screamed!

Meanwhile, snubbed by the mysterious beauty, somehow deflated when she took herself out of sight by going below with the skipper of the *Liberté*, Lance Landon decided to return to his bath. He made for his quarters at the end of the long wide hall and stopped, for he thought he had heard the sound of a girl, a young girl's distress. Then the scream! He was a man of action, was Lance Landon. Another might have called to the hotel manager, another might have called out a question, another might have at least knocked, but not Lance. He decided in a moment where the cry came from and charged the door with a strong thrust of his leg. It opened wide and banged itself against a receiving wall. There the sight of a child being raped by a man somewhere near his own age disgusted him. Quick were his strides that brought him face to face with Roderick of Ravensbury, quicker came his fist landing the fellow a blow.

Without a word he took the covers from the bed and put them around the young girl's shoulders and led her from the room. What she needed was to be seen to immediately.

Caught off guard and naked, Roderick had taken the blow and the intrusion with astonishment. It grew into indignation which further found its way into rage. She was a slave! Here to do his bidding! How dare that swaggering devil interfere? But it was done, and he had received the worst end of it. No sense making a further cake of himself. In the end he had decided to allow the incident to pass.

However, this allowed him no satisfaction. He was frustrated on too many counts. There was the ghost of a yellow-haired lovely back in Cornwall haunting him. There too, images of the black girl's full rounded breasts teased him. He had to have a woman. Thus thinking, he tossed off his covers irritably. He'd go to the tavern down the road and see what was available.

As it happened, Lance took the girl to Master Evan, owner of the Georgian Inn, an elderly man with a heart not sympathetic to slavery. He assured the captain that the girl would be taken care of, and not put in Ravensbury's way again. This done, the captain finally returned to his now lukewarm bath. Dinner was downed some time later, and thoughts of going to the local tavern were discarded in favor of sleep. What a night this was turning out to be, for try as he might, sleep would not come!

He had not taken on the buxom shrimper, though her full body pleased. He had not even tried after that to find another. Why? He didn't know. He certainly should have been in the mood. What he needed was to get the picture of that poor black child's fearful eyes out of his head, for if he wasn't remembering violet-shaded orbs snubbing him, he was thinking of the distasteful incident with the Englishman.

Thus it was that both Captain Lance and Roderick of Ravensbury came to the White Hart at the end of Broad Street. They nearly bumped into one another as they entered from the dark into the dimly lit tavern. They stood a moment, each with words on his mind, neither wishing to take it further. The captain thought there was no sense . . . the man before him wouldn't learn by it, he was already formed. And the captain had administered an unrequited blow. Best to leave sleeping dogs alone.

Roderick first thought he'd hammer into the American and return what he had received, for he was no coward in this respect. But then it might come out that he'd been rejected by a black wench! He wouldn't like that. No . . . best leave things as they were.

So it was that nearly shoulder to shoulder they proceeded into the tavern and caught a barmaid's eye. "Coo," said the maid, casting a glance over the two. Hard to choose between them it was. One a well-polished handsome blade, the other rugged and good-looking with eyes to steal the heart away. "Coo," she uttered again, this time out loud.

Roderick saw her. Bright fair hair was touseled about her heart-shaped face. No more than twenty she was, but well experienced, any man could see that! He cast his eyes down to the overflowing breasts. Enough to feed four men. Well hipped she was too. Lance noticed the same, and they both had visions of riding the lass that night. However, 'twas Roderick that reached out first and found her waist. She made no objection as he pulled her close, though the fellow sitting beneath the bumper of ale that spilled over shouted angrily.

"Pretty girl . . . have you a ready bumper for a thirsty man?" whispered Roderick, nibbling at her dainty ears, ignoring the scent of rum that hung about her.

The captain leaned up against an oak pillar and grinned wide to watch the play. Clearly he was out, and from what he could see of the remaining lasses, none was to his taste.

The girl chortled, and her hand went to Roderick's cheek. "Lordy, guv . . . I got whatever ye be wanting."

Roderick glanced over her head at the American. It pleased him to have the winning hand. He smirked when Lance made him a mock bow, and more to spite the captain he sent his hand to the girl's butt as he led her away.

Lance sighed and shook his head to be bettered by such as that, and turned to find himself hailed by most of his crew. He grinned and made his way to them.

Windy had no better luck at sleeping than did those two men. Thoughts of a stranger with deep-blue eyes troubled her mind. Bunky had seen her home, a thing she noted pleased Jokai to no end. The thought now brought out her smile. She had never really thought about Jokai before, what he was really like. It felt odd now to do so. With an exclamation finally of exasperation she threw the covers off.

"I can't sleep," she said out loud. Under such circumstances there was but one thing left to her. She'd go for a swim. It was something she had been wont to do with her mother. They had had their own private little cove. There would be the devil to pay in the morning when she would have to wash the salt and pebbly sand out of her hair, but it was worth it!

Quickly, quietly, she threw on a loose shift, banding it at the waist with a long satin ribbon. With a swish she tied a shawl about her shoulders and made for her long glass doors.

Better to use this exit out of the house, she thought with a mischievous smile. Down the trellis she went, catching her sandal as she reached the bottom. It fell before her to the ground, making a clunking sound on the flagstone in its path. Hurriedly she retrieved it, and hopping on one foot while she donned the thing she made her way to the stables. It was late; everyone would be asleep. She was right, and she tacked her roan without hindrance, threw a blanket over his back, hoisted herself up and was off. She took him over the lawn slowly, so that she'd make no sound. It was better this way. If she woke the servants they would tell her aunt, who might make a fuss. Tante Louise was so ill-tempered these days. . . .

The fingernail-size frogs were hiding well, but their song was everywhere. Whistling frogs they were called, but their bleeps sounded more a chorus of song to Windy. She guided her horse past the plantation's slave housing, past the carts full with the remains of the harvest, past the rows of coconut trees to a private road. It was a shortcut to a stretch of beach she considered all her own. Brabant land was extensive and hugged a slice of the ocean, most of which was too rough for swimming. However, in the horseshoe-shaped cove she sought, coral reefs divided the ocean from the beach and thus created a natural pool for her. She made her way to it. The scent of salt filled her senses, and it was good. She could hardly wait to shed her clothes and dive into that blue-green haven.

An hour had passed for the captain in the White Hart with his crew. He joined in their jests and mirth, but he was restless, itching for more. He looked about him suddenly with a frown and sighed, "Gad, but I'd like to get on a horse and ride the beach!"

"Why don't ye then, cap?" said an older man who had joined their company a while ago. Not one of the crew, but an American eager for American company.

"Too late to lease a horse," said Lance.

"I got mine jest across the street. Ye be free to make use of her. I won't be needing her tonight, and ye can give her over in the morning."

"That is very kind of you. Thank you, I think I'll take you up on that offer," said Lance, extending his hand.

The older man shook his hand amiably. "Her name be Mary. Use her kindly, she's a love."

"I'll do that," said Lance, getting up.

A few moments later saw him riding out of town. A crude map had been constructed for him by the tavernkeeper, and he smiled to himself ruefully. Odd time of night to go exploring, and he laughed as he remembered the tavernkeeper's expression over it. But exploring was just what he needed to tire himself out enough to sleep, and besides, he had a notion to have a look at Brabant Plantation, so it was in that direction he headed.

The air he breathed deeply pleased with its mild intoxication. He liked the odor of processed sugar and stared through the dark at the processing plant he passed. The fields seemed barren now that harvesting was nearly done, but he smiled to see the fullness of the breadfruit trees bearing their ripened fruit, and he thought of the *Bounty* and Captain Bligh. Mangoes hung heavily upon their branches ready now for picking, as did bananas. He reached out and picked a banana. It was small, and though its color was a pale green it was ripe and sweet to the taste. Smiling, he continued along his way and after some moments saw the sign that indicated Brabant Plantation. He turned his horse onto the drive and took it nearly a mile before sighting the dark shape of the French-styled house. So, this was Brabant. Good, he would find his way easily tomorrow. As he sat his mare, he heard the distinct sound of the ocean beating its music against the rocky cliffs, for the house was situated on an elevated crest just over the ocean.

It struck him to take a path off to the side and search out the beach. It would be good to have a nice long run on the sands. So he tooled the mare down the same narrow path Windy had taken only moments before. Right at her back he was!

The sound of the ocean smashing its rolls against the coral reefs resounded in Windy's ears as she drew her horse up. Stars glittered in a velvety sky, and the moon lit upon the entrance to her special place. To another perhaps it might have appeared eerie and foreboding. To another the bent trunks of the tall trees reaching out and meeting with the giant coral boulder, forming an arch, may have seemed like the opening to a strange new world, cold and repelling, but not to Windmera. To her it represented another time, an age ago, but one filled with happy memories of her mother. She left her horse tethered to the giant exposed roots of one of the tall trees and stepped through the arch, for on the other side was her cove.

Off went the sandals, off the light shift as she ran toward the large enclosed ocean pool. She had naught to fear, for it was her own private dwelling where none would dare to intrude . . . or none ever had intruded before.

Captain Lance followed the path in its gradual descent, and then the glimmer of the moon's rays lit upon a track in the sand. A horse's track. It might have been an old one, but something told him it had been made recently, very recently, and out of curiosity he followed it, allowing it to make the choice for him when the path finally forked. A dark shadow met his eyes first, and then the body of a roan. The steed turned its head, looked the captain over and snorted good-naturedly. Whether it approved of the captain or the captain's mare is anyone's guess; at any rate, it did not fuss at the intrusion.

Lance Landon observed his surroundings. He was not put off by the starkness of exposed tree roots bending and twisting in their path from the rock and dirt cliffs above to the sand below. He was not put off by the archway created by boulder and tree trunk or by the hint of mystery on the other side. He slid out of his saddle, tethered his horse beside the roan and boldly stepped through.

He was met immediately by the sight of a cove enclosed by coral reefs in the sea and cliffs well into the sky at his flanks, as though this cove had been created especially for privacy. He smiled at God's handiwork, and then his perception found a gleaming fluff of white silk lying carelessly on the creamy sand. Puzzled, he moved forward, bent and retrieved the flimsy article. Shaking it out, he determined that it definitely belonged to a female. Further inquiry elicited a pair of sandals, a shawl and a satin ribbon. Slowly the curve of his lips deepened into the naughtiest of grins. Thus armed, he turned seaward and gazed in pleasant anticipation. He had not long to wait.

Windy had stepped into the cold ocean. The pool gathered depth quickly, and but a few long steps found her waist-deep in water. She dove and swam quickly. Reaching the encrusted cover of reef that protected her from the open ocean, she turned and swam back toward the shallows. Shaking the water and salt from her hair, she stepped forth from the foam.

121

He watched fascinated as the waters seemed to part and gave her up to him in all her youthful glory. Black hair glistened brightly in the moonlight as though she had taken the stars from the heaven and affixed them about her well-shaped head. Rivulets of salty water cascaded over her full white breasts so much in contrast with the tan of her neck, shoulders and arms. He could see the sweet nipples pert with the cold. She wiped the water away from her face, not noticing she was not alone. She moved quickly, rushing up the sand, for a force of wind made her shiver, and Lance Landon's amusement was lost in the stunned silence of growing desire.

"Now where did I . . ." she started to say to herself in some exasperation when she did not at first perceive her shift. She cut herself off, however, when her vision brought into focus a tall being of striking mien. She froze from both astonishment and shock. She gasped. She was naked before this stranger . . . but he was no stranger. He was the man with the deep-blue eyes whom she had seen earlier that evening in Bridgetown! What to do? What to do? A useless movement brought her hands across her chest and then across her belly. *He had her clothes!*

"I suppose you want these?" he said, holding them out to her.

She was furious, embarrassed, indignant, but yes, she wanted them! She made a sound, unintelligible but something to that effect, and took a hasty step toward his outstretched offering. In so doing she never noticed the rather large crab that was at that moment crossing her path. The creature was quite intent on his journey and when a foot presented itself to deter him he knew himself balked. What could he do? Retaliate . . . so he did! Scrunch went those two frontal claws, catching Windy's large toe. She jumped, yelped and brought down another foot in exchange for the damaged one. Again, the crab, feeling threatened in the extreme by what gave every appearance of being a full-scale war, took the defensive line and snapped with vigorous effort, causing his unwitting opponent no little damage before the dreadful little creature hurried along its way.

This last attack left Windmera crying out and holding the bleeding extremity with both hands. Lance, who had witnessed the whole, was unable to suppress a round of indecent mirth, but he did at this moment come forward. His strong arm went around her waist with every good intention of lending her support during the tricky operation of inspecting her bleeding toes. She objected loudly to his generous offer, which in turn threw her off balance, as she was unwise enough to strike at his offending arm. She certainly would have fallen at this juncture had he not been keen-witted enough to reach out and prevent it. Up she went into his arms like a babe, and off he went with her, making for the natural archway at their backs. Here he set the wiggling lass down, but not without sustaining a swift kick to his shin.

"How . . . how dare you!" cried the lady, leveling her attack. "Cur!" Upon which she spied the shift he still held in his hand, grabbed it, felt some surprise to find that he gave it up without objection, then turned her back upon him.

He sighed and, ignoring the pain in his shin, leaned against the gray coral boulder, folded his arms across his chest and proceeded without the least trace of shame to observe the lovely before him. Odd, he thought, watching her, how women usually give a man their backs in such circumstances. One can only surmise that they feel there is less there to observe. The thought widened his grin.

Windmera looked back over her shoulder and caught the scampish grin curving his lips. She was strangely thrilled by it and annoyed with herself as well, so she seethed.

"You could at least have the decency to turn yourself about!"

"That wouldn't be decent, my love, 'twould be stupid," he answered, smiling at her rage.

"Oh! You are insufferable!" And then, as though an afterthought came to her, "I called you a cur . . . but you are a hundred times worse than that!" With this closing statement she became entangled in the neck opening of her shift.

Lance's bright-blue eyes watched her sensual movements. He noted well the ripe youthful breasts glowing in the moonlight. He felt an urgency suddenly take command of his humor. This wild young wench was the finest he had ever clapped eyes on. Lord . . . she was worth some effort. He decided to exert it. He was beside her in that moment, helping her with the folds of her shift as they stuck to her damp body. His voice came quietly, thickly, tantalizing her with his whisper, with the sudden change of his mood. "Aye, love, but you are too fine to be covering up. It's a sorry state I must be in to be helping you at it." Upon which his sturdy hands took hold of her small tight waist. He brought her to him in one swift movement.

It happened so suddenly, quite before Windmera knew

123

what he was about. She felt his grip, and it sent a shiver of shameful delight through her, and just as she was overcoming this, looking for words with which to scold his daring, his lips locked on hers, parting them open, and his tongue found its path. Heat, fiery bullets of heat, burst through her veins and exploded before her eyes. She saw flashes of flame, bright shades they were, as sensation taught her to yield. Windy's legs went suddenly weak, and to keep herself from falling she held the man of iron whose embrace seared her soul. She held him and felt his hard burning body singe her flesh. She felt the hardness of his growing desire press against her thigh and realized in her volcanic haze that he had lifted up her shift.

It was like nothing she had ever experienced before. She had no way to measure this new sensation. She only felt this stranger's kiss and knew in that moment her body was alive for him. She wanted him to take her, and the thought so shocked her that she felt as though cold water had been thrown into her face. She was Windmera . . . a de Brabant . . . a lady. She had her virtue, she had her dreams! What was she doing allowing this stranger such a liberty? She pulled away and slapped his face a striking blow.

Lance was surprised by it, for he could swear the chit pleasured at his touch. He held her, kissed her, passioned for her and knew too she had responded . . . yet her hit had been flush, and there had been a look of fury in her violet eyes! Could he have been mistaken? He watched her rush off, leaving her sandals behind. He watched her as she struggled to mount her roan, laughing out loud at her frenzied effort, and he made no further attempt to conquer.

It wasn't that Lance Landon no longer hungered for the lovely. Indeed, he felt himself a starving man. Having tasted her honey, having touched her bewitching flesh and looked deep into those violet eyes, he knew he would have to have her. She had fired his blood, this well-formed maid, and as he watched her ride off he wondered if she was a virgin. She had held him like a woman, yet there was that of the innocent in her eyes. He had no wish to seduce a virgin. He wasn't the sort to hurt innocents. Still, the thought of taking this one did strange things to his fancies and wobbled the earth beneath his principles.

He stepped forward to the shawl and discarded sandals and bent to pick them up. The shawl had the feel of fine gossamer silk. . . . Odd, that . . . had she borrowed her mistress's shawl? He wrapped the sandals in the shawl. She would need these. Perhaps she would seek him out in search of them . . . and then? Aye, Lance Landon . . . and then? The question plagued him on his ride home. Best to forget the wench. . . . He had his business at Brabant tomorrow . . . but damn, before he left this paradise he would find the black-haired beauty and continue the game!

Six

The glass doors were open wide, allowing the island's ever sweet winds to cool the library, yet in spite of the gentle breeze Louise felt overcome with heat. It was not from the heat of the summer's day. It was Brayward. Brayward standing too near. Brayward's hand on her bare shoulder. Brayward's eyes, round, protruding, demanding!

She glanced at him and then quickly away. How she loathed his stance, his paunch, his red blubbery cheeks and his nearly bald head. But he was wealthy, and she . . . she was getting old and had no means. . . . Here was the man she had chosen to marry, a man whose every touch made her recoil within herself. Oh, Lord, chosen? 'Twas not by choice. Windmera had a ridiculous saying, some nonsense about always having a choice. But it was not true . . . not in the real world. Perhaps for Windy in her fairy-tale world . . . but even for Windy . . . soon she would learn. Yes, soon her poor dear niece would be selling herself as well. Life was so hard! And Jokai? What of Jokai? How could she marry a black slave? It was unthinkable! Even if she were financially independent she could never marry Jokai . . . but it wouldn't matter if only they could be together. . . .

"Louise! Louise . . . have you been listening?" said Brayward somewhat testily. She seemed miles away.

"What? Oh, yes . . . but I do not understand," she said absently.

He sighed. "I was explaining to you that you cannot at this time honor your late brother's recent sale to the Americans!"

"Brayward, dear, such things elude me. You will of course guide us in all such matters, *oui?*"

He puffed up in consequence. Her ignorance of such matters added to his self-esteem. "Of course, my love. However, as it is your niece's estate, I thought it best that you make her understand regarding this matter. The sale Maurice made to this Landon fellow in America was long before . . . before we were certain war was about to break out between England and the rebel colonies. You will send the Landons a letter advising them that their money will be returned to them as soon as we have placed the shipment elsewhere." He sighed heavily. "Besides, Maurice made a very poor bargain. He sold the sugar for far under its present market value."

"Oh, please, Brayward . . . this wearies me greatly." Louise sighed, for she was earnestly wishing the fellow well away. She had never had any head for business, and less so now. "It may do so, my dearest, but I fear that Brabant Plantation is in need of some well-executed moves to ensure profits in the coming season. I cannot promise you a future for this plantation if it does not recoup its present losses." He eyed her and found to his satisfaction that his words had done exactly what he had wished. Yes, she would come to him. "Therefore, I have taken the liberty of offering this particular crop to an English firm. Quite respectable, I assure you. They have often dealt with me, and I am certain they will meet the price I have put to them. My solicitors have arranged with yours to enter in my name a finder's fee . . . but never mind that, it is quite nominal, and I am certain Windmera would make no objection."

"*Oui*, Brayward," she answered, swishing it all away with her hand, wishing fervently she could do the same with the man.

He looked at her calculatingly for a long moment. He knew all about Louise and her black slave. He knew, and it repulsed him not one bit. In fact, it made her all the more desirable. What passions the woman must contain in that well-rounded body! What passions . . . and after eighteen years with a cold wife . . . egad, but he meant to have her, had always meant to have her and now had the power to obtain her!

Brayward had married for financial gain. His bed had never given him the satisfaction he required. He sought out tavernmaids and their like, but there too there was always something lacking. Perhaps it was love? He didn't bother with this thought. It didn't matter. What he felt for Louise Davenant was something that worked up his blood. He went to her and led her to the sofa. She was reluctant, he could sense it, but it didn't matter. Even in her reluctance he could feel a passion that his wife had never been able to arouse in him. He pulled her down beside him silently, and his pudgy hand went to her chin, turning it toward him. His hand strayed from her face to her bosom, where he lay it flat on the swells above her bodice. "How lovely you are, Louise."

"*Mais non*, Brayward . . . not here . . . not now," she objected feebly.

"Here and now, Louise," he said defiantly, pushing his hand down the front of her gown to capture the large soft breast. It tantalized him to frenzy, and his mouth sought hers.

His lips were wet, and she was repelled by him, but she allowed his kiss. She had to allow it, she told herself, but she wanted to cry. His hands continued to fondle until their insistence became almost violent and she feared he would go too far. She pulled away roughly. "Please, Brayward . . . you take unfair advantage! My niece could at any moment enter."

"Hang it, Louise, I want you . . . all of you!" he insisted.

"And you shall have me . . . in our marriage bed," she said quietly. She was resigned to it. She felt flattened, without will.

"So I shall. And in the meantime . . ." he said hoarsely, fingering the large nipple his hand had found beneath her bodice. His other hand went to her neck, then down her shoulder, over her arm. Oh God, her heart cried and her mind ordered, endure! You must endure! But how? How? She must, she told herself. Was she not about to turn fifty? Was the plantation not failing? Was she not without means in her waning years? *She must endure!*

At last he released her, but it was with reluctance, and it was only because at last Windmera did come.

"Oh!" exclaimed Windy at once. She loathed Brayward. She knew not why her aunt allowed him private interviews, and now, now she had seen her aunt in his arms. Clearly she could not be mistaken, and Tante Louise looked relieved to have her interrupt, but then why . . .? "My lord." She nodded formally. This was her house, and if this man was bothering her aunt she would have him out immediately.

Brayward got to his feet and made a perfunctory bow to Windmera. "Miss de Brabant," he said with a smile—after all, soon she would be his niece. He had never been able to seed his wife, but that must have been her fault. Such were his flashing thoughts.

He received no answering smile. Windmera had never been very good at hiding her feelings. She did not like the man. She would not, could not pretend otherwise. She was not even sure he was due the normal civility, but she gave it coldly by nodding to his greeting, then turned to her aunt. "Tante . . . cook is in such a fluster over the luncheon menu. Perhaps you could see her and straighten things out?" It was a bald-faced lie, but she could see that her aunt was looking pale from her encounter with this horrid man.

"Oh, *mais oui* . . . but first, there is something Lord Brayward wishes you to know about the plantation."

"Really?" said Windy, putting up her brow. "And may I ask what Lord Brayward has to do with it? Surely if there is something we should know our solicitors would have brought it to our attention."

"It seems, Miss de Brabant, that they were not aware until recently of the problem. I offered to help, and they accepted," said Brayward.

She did not like the patronizing tone of his words. Her dander was on the rise. "I am certain that is very kind of you, my lord, and I will take the matter up with Mr. Willes when next I am in Bridgetown." Clearly it was a dismissal.

Brayward was not slow to realize that for some reason he had antagonized the girl. Well, no matter, sooner or later she would come around. He nodded and allowed her to show him out. When next Windmera returned to the library it was with a question on her mind. Her aunt was sitting in a shroud of gloom, and this deterred Windy's attack, softened it. She came to her and took up her aunt's hands. "Tante Louise . . . won't you tell me what it is that is so troubling you?"

Louise's eyes darted to her niece's face. Her niece perhaps not in blood, a secret well guarded, but her niece in every other way. She loved the child. "Oh, my darling . . . how can I explain?"

"Why don't you start at the beginning?" urged Windy, taking up a place beside her on the yellow damask sofa.

"The beginning . . . ah, bah! How do I tell you . . . Windy . . . the plantation, it does not go well. When your father lost Heather . . . he gave up, you see, but even so we managed. Now with him gone as well . . . I have no head . . ."

"And Brayward advises you? asked Windy, frowning.

"He does more than that. He wishes to marry me," said Louise, averting her eyes.

Windy jumped to her feet. "That is disgusting!"

"What mean you, disgusting?" inquired her aunt, startled by her niece's vehemence. "The man makes me an offer. At fifty, my dear, one does not get too many offers!"

"That is nonsense. It doesn't matter how old you are . . . only what you are. Look at you, Tante Louise . . . you are beautiful. You cannot mean to give yourself to that . . . that pig!"

"But I do." She said it in a strange tone, one that Windy had never heard her use before. Then suddenly she was smiling and looking her niece over from head to toe. "Why, *chérie* . . . you are wearing that new gown I purchased for you only last week. It pleases me . . . and surprises me."

Windy blushed, for she dared not think on why she had put up her long black hair into a semblance of fashionable curls. She dared not think on the reasons for donning the low-cut yellow muslin with its short puff sleeves and *haut ton* high waistline. She had no intention of mentioning the events of the previous evening to her aunt or the fact that she meant to go into Bridgetown and search out the man who she felt certain was keeping her shawl and sandals. The notion of seeing him again both set her cheeks aflame and excited her all at once.

She answered her aunt faintly, "Oh . . . do you like it on me?" She had been quite pleased with the effect as she gazed upon herself in the long looking glass in her room.

"Ah, but of course. You look a flower . . . elegant, yet hinting of much naughtiness. Most enchanting, love."

Windy hugged her aunt and was patted gently for her efforts. "There now. Tonight you will further please me by donning that new red ballgown I had made for you. We go to the Holmes ball . . . and no, do not look like that . . . we *will* go!"

"But Tante Louise . . . it is too soon."

"You will mourn no more! It is folly, and Maurice would not wish it. *Ma petite* . . . you are youth, and youth . . . ah, but it passes far too quickly to waste time in mourning. What good does it do? It brings them not back to us. In this I will be obeyed. Tonight we go to the very nice American family and dance at their ball. Yes?"

Windy's violet eyes glistened warmly, and she squeezed her aunt's hand. "If it is your wish and if you feel it is right."

"I do, for it is," said her aunt simply, then sighed. *"Eh bien."*

"It is not finished," said Windy, bringing the subject around once more to her aunt. "You have not really put me off with talk of gowns and balls."

"Enough. You do not understand." She saw the hurt come into her niece's eyes and she took up her Windy's hands. *"Chérie* . . . leave me to myself in this. Go enjoy . . . and worry not over such things."

Windy would not have dropped the matter there. She would have nagged until finally her aunt talked about it, but at that moment the library door was opened and a black butler stepped rigidly into the room and announced: "Captain Lance Landon of the *Sea Hawk* from America."

After such an impressive introduction, both ladies were stunned into quiet observation. However, it is to be noted that the two experienced quite different sensations.

Louise Davenant recognized the name at once. How could she not when Brayward had repeated it half a dozen times that very morning? She also realized in that same moment that she was about to be involved in a difficult situation. It was all very well to put someone off in a letter but quite another thing to do it face to face, especially when the face was as warm and attractive as this gentleman's! How could she advise this handsome blade that she would not deliver his shipment? She composed herself and, with her eyes opened wide and her hand to her wildly fluttering heart she went to him. After all, she told herself, she needn't deal with the problem. She would send him to Brayward!

In he stepped, filling the doorway with his height. His long black hair swept in waves framing his bronzed face. His blue eyes, alive in the morning sun, startled the viewer with their depth and hue. He was more fashionably attired than the night before and looked the gentleman in his white superfine and pantaloons. Still, Windy had no trouble recognizing him as the heathen brute who had accosted her on the beach.

My God! What is he doing here? The silent question hit Windmera as she stared in stupified awe. What can this mean? How dare he track me to earth? Whatever shall I say . . . do? Whatever will Tante Louise think?

The object of all these cogitations stood frozen, himself quite taken aback. Jesus! The girl . . . the girl standing here in this room? Good God! She was certainly no longer dressed like a serving wench, and the hair that had been damp and pressed against her naked body was now shining in long ringlets from the top of her head . . . but she was the same!

Thus did all three confront one another. However, it was Captain Landon who found his voice first and with some effort pulled his gaze away from Windmera to her aunt. He stepped toward her and took up her now extended hand, making her an excellent bow and saying on his way up, "Enchanted, madame, but may I first offer you my sincerest condolences on your loss." For he had learned of Maurice's death only moments ago in the stables.

"Er . . . thank you, monsieur," said Louise. She observed

131

his glance toward her niece. Ah, excellent, thought she, we can divert him from business. "My niece, monsieur, Mademoiselle Windmera de Brabant, my late brother's daughter."

He stepped toward the lady in yellow, and there was a bold smile playing with his eyes and curving his sensuous lips. The lady could not help but notice and felt the color stain her cheeks as she met his eyes.

"I fancy . . . I have seen mademoiselle somewhere . . . but I can't seem to recall," he said, bowing over her hand.

She withdrew her ungloved fingers almost violently and snapped, "Monsieur's memory is very poor. We certainly did meet . . . and *I remember it quite well.*"

"Ah yes . . . it comes to me now," he said mockingly. "But I fancy you looked . . . different at the time."

She gasped and backed away as though fearing another such episode with the arrogant blade. Her aunt broke in on the exchange, saying lightly, "Monsieur, may I offer you coffee? This," she said, indicating the coffee tray, "is no longer hot, but I shall have a fresh pot brought in."

"Thank you, no," he said turning around, his gaze most reluctantly leaving Windmera's outraged countenance, and his thoughts taking a vein that would have sent hot rivered blood through Windy's being. "I would, however, like to discuss the delivery of my shipment of sugar."

"Delivery . . . yes, of course. I regret, monsieur, that we are unable to supply you with your purchase of sugar," she said, feeling faint at the look that came into his eyes. He was a demon, this one, and she was not the one to have to be telling him such things. Drat Brayward! She would send him to Brayward!

This was it, of course, thought Lance as he gazed beneath drawn brows at Louise de Brabant, who was wringing her hands. She moved away restlessly. This was the feeling that had been nagging him these past weeks, that something was going to go wrong. He knew it, sensed it. "Perhaps, madame, you will be kind enough to explain?" he said, mustering up a calm he did not feel.

"I? Explain? No, no, how can I, for I do not really understand it myself. You must go to Lord Brayward . . . our groom will point out his direction. Yes, yes, go to Brayward . . . he will explain."

"Indeed, but I should like to know who this Lord Brayward is and what he has to do with Brabant and its dealings.

I have purchased a harvest of sugar cane from the late comte, as evidenced by the papers I carry with me. This shipment was paid for in full some months ago. Now what I should like to know is why you cannot supply it."

"Sir! I have already told you I cannot and will not explain what *I* do not understand," snapped Aunt Louise, going on the attack because she felt on the defensive.

Windy was frowning. If what this man said was true, why then were they not giving him his sugar? Something was wrong. She had no liking for this but would not say anything at the moment, for it was a private matter to be discussed with her aunt in this man's absence.

Captain Lance Landon made her a formal bow. "As you wish, madame, but believe me, the matter is not ended here." He turned sharply and nodded at Windmera before taking his abrupt leave of them.

Windy waited only for the closing of the door before rounding on her harried aunt. "Now, Tante Louise, you *will* answer *me*. What has Lord Brayward to do with Brabant? Why in Heaven's name should anyone who has made an arrangement with my father now have to go to Brayward?"

"*Chérie, chérie* . . . all this heat? What matter is it whether your solicitor Mr. Willes or Lord Brayward lends us aid . . . as long as we attain the help we need?"

"Oh . . . I cannot believe this!" said Windy, moving her hands irritably. She rarely had patience with subtleties. She wanted always direct answers. "I have asked you why Brayward is involved with the dealings of my plantation, and all you do is go around in circles."

"But what does it signify, my pet? You would understand it no more than I," said her aunt, mildly surprised at her niece's interest in a matter she considered to be at the very best tedious in the extreme.

"Not understand? My sweet but definitely naive aunt, I understand what Brabant needs far better than either Lord Brayward or Mr. Willes! You are forgetting that my father often discussed business matters with me—"

"When he was not wallowing in his drink!" snapped her aunt. "You will leave it to me . . . and to Brayward!"

"Until I become of age I have no choice but to leave it to you, but not to Brayward . . . and still I would know why this American must go to him for an answer!"

"Oh dear . . . you are upset. Very well . . . sit and I shall explain what Brayward has told me only this morning," said Louise.

And so Windmera was told how things really stood at Brabant and how they must go on. She did not like it, not in the least!

Seven

Roderick of Ravensbury was led to a large, richly styled
study. Shelves upon shelves housing hundreds of books, few
of which had ever been opened by their present owner, lined
the stainwood walls. Silk hangings of satiny cream were
drawn wide to display the neat lawns and exotic blooms outdoors. The fragrance wafted into the room. A well-appointed
desk, between two walls of (one might assume) family por-
traits, held stacks of documents. Lord Brayward had been
thumbing through these, but his mind was elsewhere; he was
thinking of Louise. It was all he did these days. He had come
to Barbados, titled but penniless, and he had met the woman
who later became his wife. A marriage of convenience. But
not this new marriage he planned, no, not this. Such thoughts
were interrupted by the resonant announcement of
Ravensbury.

Ravensbury? The name meant something to him, but the
young man standing at his study door was unknown to him.
He smiled a welcome, but there was puzzlement in his eyes.

"My lord . . . we have never met, but I believe you knew
my father well. You were at Cambridge, were you not, with
Godwin, present Lord Ravensbury and"—he hesitated—"my
father."

"Godwin?" a light hit in his memory. Egad, but they had
sported well together as youths! Of course he remembered the
wild red-haired devil. Godwin. He lived in Cornwall . . .
they had lost track of one another. No matter. "Of course,
lad. Your father and I were cronies indeed. Many is the tale I
could tell you of our escapades together. You are not much
in his like . . . favor your mother, I suppose?" he said, getting up and extending his hand.

Roderick took his hand and smiled warmly. Here was his
introduction to Brabant, to the girl Godwin would have him
wed. "No, the devil of it is that I don't seem to favor either
one!" He curved his lip in a half smile.

"Eh?" Brayward chuckled, enjoying this. He poked Roderick conspiratorily with his elbow. "No matter. Got the
name, that's all that counts!" He was jesting, but it hit home,
though he knew it not.

Roderick looked away and made some mundane comment about the island's beauty, and then added, "But whatever does one do here for social entertainment?"

"Entertainment, is it? Well, I tell you what, lad. There is a ball being given tonight. By the Holmes family . . . not very high in the instep if you know what I mean . . . been here some ten years or so. Holmes has his origin in America . . . but he is a good sort. At any rate, anyone worth anything on this island will be there. You come with me!"

"I should like that very much." Roderick smiled.

Again the butler appeared, again a name was announced, but this time Brayward had no trouble whatsoever in recognizing it. Egad, he thought. The devil here already?

In stepped Captain Lance, his face drawn in set lines. His blue eyes found Roderick, and his dark mobile brow expressed his surprise and displeasure. This was turning out to be a morning indeed. "My lord," started Captain Lance, ignoring Roderick, who moved to watch the interview from a corner of the room. "I was asked by Madame Davenant to come here and put my questions regarding my consignment of sugar to you."

Lord Brayward grimaced. Wasn't it just like Louise to put the burden on his shoulders! Very well then, he would handle it. He had no liking for the bold attitude of this young man. "Indeed. Just what would you like to know?"

"More than six months ago my family purchased a harvest of sugar from the comte de Brabant. A contract was entered into and paid for in full. I arrived yesterday with my vessel to take delivery of that shipment, yet Madame Davenant advises me that she will not or cannot deliver. She is at a loss to tell me why and has suggested that the person to explain this is yourself."

Brayward sighed heavily. He was caught in a bind. Dangerous fellows, these Americans. No manners, always ready to raise their fists and their arms for the slightest provocation. However, there was no turning back now. "You will, of course, have your money refunded to you as soon as we have been paid for the shipment from the new buyers."

"Am I to understand that you think you can sell this shipment elsewhere? May I remind you, sir, that I have documents—"

"Your documents will no longer be honored. The comte is dead and the estate is now in the hands of the solicitors. We cannot deliver to you at the price you managed to wheedle

136

poor Maurice de Brabant into accepting! Furthermore, as our two countries are about to engage in war, I doubt that you have any recourse but to accept my kind offer and sail home and await the refund of your money!"

Captain Lance was infuriated. He took a menacing step forward, and his eyes flared in anger. "You expect that I shall take this quietly, I suppose? You are mistaken, sir . . . very mistaken!" With this promise, he turned on his heel and left the room.

Brayward turned to Roderick. "I don't like the tone of his words," he said slowly. He was again thinking of all the brutish things he had heard about Americans, no matter their background. It worried him.

"My lord, the heathen sounded as though he was threatening you," suggested Roderick slyly. "Perhaps you had best report him to the local magistrate." There was no suppressing the gleam in his eye.

"No . . . no . . ." responded Brayward thoughtfully. "He has not as yet done anything to warrant that, but no doubt the man bears watching."

"Absolutely no doubt at all, and I shall be happy to lend you whatever assistance you deem necessary," offered Roderick at once. Aye, the lad was well pleased to see the bold American in difficulties, well pleased!

The captain was in no pleasant mood over this. He'd been dealt a backhanded blow. It was both unethical and illegal, this withholding of his sugar, but he was a man with his head squarely situated on his shoulders, he knew what ground he was walking. He was an American on English soil! Brayward was right—he'd heard the talk going about, and it did look as though America and England would soon be at war. All the more reason to get his hands on that sugar! Lord, but there was no denying that his position was precarious. He could obtain the services of a solicitor, but legal action would take months. What to do?

There was Uncle Frank, of course! Francis Holmes had left Mystic some ten years before with his wife and brood of young children to take up his inheritance on Barbados. During his life in Mystic he had become fast friends with the Landons, and Lance had grown up calling him uncle, though no blood made him so. It was time he called on Uncle Frank; it was just too bad that he would have to hit him with a problem straightaway. It made him feel a child! Damn, but that annoyed him all the more. It flitted across his mind that the English dandy in the corner of Brayward's study had looked well pleased over the thing, and he wondered if the man had taken his spite to this extreme. Had he anything to do with it? No matter, it was done and what he must now do is handle it. Therefore, first to the Holmes plantation!

Brayward played with the sapphire pendant he had just placed around Louise's neck. "It looks lovely on you, my dear," he said softly, attempting to place a kiss upon her rosy lips. She gave him instead her cheek. He settled for it because of young Ravensbury's presence.

"You are too generous, my lord," Louise said coyly. She was always able to flirt; it came to her naturally even with men like Brayward. If only she could leave it at that and not have to go so much further! "I don't know what is keeping Windmera," she said lightly, glancing at Ravensbury speculatively. He certainly was an attractive young man . . . all the way from England. Wealthy, too. She wondered if he would catch her niece's eye. There was never any telling with Windy! "Ah," she said, catching sight of her niece at the parlor doors. "There you are, love."

All eyes turned very naturally to the newcomer, and Roderick had his first look at the woman he was being forced to pursue. There was no denying her beauty, and it was his first thought. Windmera stood enswathed in red silk. Its off-shoulder effect suited her figure to perfection. The low cut of her bodice revealed alluringly the full swells, and the small waistline accentuated this. Her long black hair was swirled into cascading curls all about her well-shaped head. Around her large violet eyes fluttered lashes both thick and curling. Her black-winged brows moved with some surprise as her eyes found Roderick of Ravensbury. Her first thought; Hmmm, interesting . . . unexpected and most interesting. Such was her age.

"Come, darling, and meet Lord Brayward's guest. Roderick of Ravensbury. He comes all the way from Cornwall on a holiday."

Windmera came forward and found her hand taken up by Roderick. As he put the gloved dainty to his lips and murmured a greeting, she smiled. "From Cornwall? My mother was from Cornwall . . . near Land's End."

"Really? Our lands run along there, stretching as far east as Penzance."

She sighed. "Mother spoke rarely about her home . . . but I have often had a yearning to visit Cornwall and explore."

"Come, come . . . my coach awaits outside, and we are already quite late. I pride myself on being punctual," said Brayward cutting in on their conversation and ushering them toward the door with an extended hand.

Roderick of Ravensbury smiled and offered his arm. Windy was pleased to take it. A most charming young gentleman, was Roderick. A few moments later saw them well situated in the coach heading toward St. Daniels farther inland and the Holmes ball.

Jokai watched the coach lumber off into the night. He fidgeted with his distress. He had no liking for what was happening right before his eyes. It wasn't the first time Louise had attended a ball during their sixteen years . . . but this time it was different. Before she had always gone on her brother's arm . . . and it was because he knew a woman needed to dance, to be flattered, to socialize, especially a woman like Louise. He'd never be able to give her those things, but he would never begrudge them to her. How could he? She had given him so much.

Tonight, however, he did not feel this way. It was, of course, because of Brayward's presence. It was because Brayward had come for her!

She had never allowed a single man to escort her before. What could it mean? She loathed Brayward . . . or so he thought. Damn the man! His lordship was constantly turning up at Brabant! And too, this morning . . . that young captain . . . he had come to Brabant with a smile and left in a rage. He had asked for directions to Brayward's plantation. Why? Tonight when she returned he would confront her. Yes, that was what he would do. He had a right to know. She was his woman, and he had that much right . . . she would not deny it to him . . . not Louise! His fists clenched, because for the first time in his life, living, enduring, no longer mattered. There was something more important, something he had to have, and it was more important than staying alive. If he didn't have this, life was meaningless. He had to have Louise's respect, he had to have her love, he had to be a man!

Windmera had always liked Frank and Martha Holmes. Their American background had not helped their emergence into the English dominant society of Barbados, but they had emerged all the same. It had something to do with the success of their plantation and their wealth.

The Holmes children numbered eight, from age twenty-five, the eldest, a young man just home from his studies at Oxford, to a sprite of a daughter, age seven. Windy liked them all and was looking forward to this outing. The fact that her escort was a polished gentleman hindered her pleasure not in the least.

The doors, forming a semicircle, were open wide to allow the breeze to cool the ballroom. Torches were lit on the veranda and scattered on high stakes throughout the garden. An orchestra worked their violins from a raised platform in a corner of the well-lit room, and everywhere fashionable *ton* mingled, danced and enjoyed themselves.

Louise Davenant's entrance with Lord Brayward was marked, and a few of the dowagers' brows went up. "She means to have him," whispered one.

"Poor dear man, he doesn't know what she is," said another.

"Whatever do you mean?"

"Never say you have not heard the rumors!"

"No . . . what rumors?" The gleam was in the eye.

"About Louise and her . . . *black slave.*"

"My God!" But the head was turned and the smile was on the lips. "Louise . . . darling . . ." She went forward to encompass the Frenchwoman in her flabby arms.

Windmera watched her aunt taken away, an amused light in her eyes. She saw Brayward engaged by some of his cronies and breathed a sigh of relief. She looked up and saw coming toward her young Peter Holmes. His fair hair was neatly combed, and he was well dressed for the occasion. However, it was not his appearance that surprised Windy, it was his companion.

"Windy! Devilish glad you decided to come. Mother wasn't sure you would," said Peter, smiling broadly. They had been friends a long time and were on easy terms. "Want you to meet our houseguest. Friend from the States and quite a favorite, so you must be kind to him! Captain—"

"We have already met," said the captain quietly. "How are you this evening, Miss de Brabant? But I can see that I needn't ask. You look . . . as usual . . . quite superb!"

"Lord, but he do turn a neat compliment, don't he?" said

Peter, and then turned his eye upon the tall dandy at Windy's side.

Windy acknowledged the captain's compliment frostily but politely. She was actually in a quandary as to how to behave. She felt he was being done an injustice by Brabant Plantation, yet she could not put out of her mind the fact that he had manhandled her the previous evening. She felt a flush rise and tried to subdue it. Turning partially toward the man at her side, she made quick introductions, ending with, ". . . and Captain Lance Landon . . . of America."

"I am afraid Ravensbury and I have already been unfortunate enough to have had an . . . introduction, of sorts," said the captain, a sneer distorting his lips.

"Unfortunate is too gentle a word, sir." Roderick smiled evenly. He then turned his back on both his young host and his enemy and spoke quietly to Windy. "A country dance, Miss de Brabant?"

She had not liked the way Roderick behaved, but was not in any position to remark upon it. Then too she wanted to dance, and he certainly was a most attractive partner. Whatever problem he had with the captain must be justified—hadn't she her own reasons for disliking the bold American? Graciously she put her hand on his bent arm and allowed him to lead her out onto the dance floor.

"Peter. m'lad . . . what do you know about Ravensbury of Cornwall?" asked the captain thoughtfully as he watched Roderick manipulate the steps of the dance with great expertise.

Peter Holmes had been only fifteen when his parents had uprooted the family and come to Barbados. Shortly thereafter, he was sent to England, first to Harrow and then to Oxford for his education. During his stay in England he had learned to enjoy the meanderings of *haut ton* life. He had learned its subtleties and the names to look out for, but still, Cornwall had been a long way from London. He frowned. "Ravensbury . . . seem to recall his name being used in connection with the ladies . . . but nothing really grand. Why?"

"It is curious, don't you think? That dandy out there looks as though he would never be out of a London drawing room if he had the choice . . . yet of all places, here he is in Barbados! Why?"

"Got a point there. But don't worry your head over the fellow. Come along, let me introduce you to some of our

141

flowers." Peter was joyful to be taking the lead. He had as a boy looked up to Lance Landon as a god.

"Sorry, lad. There is but one flower I have a mind to."

"Oh?" said Peter, following the line of Lance's blue eyes.

"Aye . . . a moonflower," said Captain Landon.

"A *what?*"

The captain laughed out loud and moved in on his object. The country dance was at an end. Roderick he had observed going off in the direction of the punch bowl. No doubt playing the gentleman but the fool as well, as it left the girl unattended, mused Lance as he made his way deftly to her side.

"So, Miss de Brabant, not a shade of guilt do I see in your wondrous eyes?"

Startled, Windy turned to find the captain towering above her. She felt her body quiver in spite of her resolve not to be so affected by this man. Why did she feel this way whenever he was near? What was it about him that set her blood bubbling? She must not allow his good looks to intimidate her this way. "I? Guilty? I don't understand your meaning, sir."

"Really? You mean you haven't refused me my shipment of sugar simply out of spite?" He knew this was not so, but he baited her, and he was well satisfied to see that she took up the offering.

Oh, my God! It was her first reaction, and it showed in her eyes. He thought she was behind it all? How dreadful! "Of course not, sir!" It was nearly a shout. Then, lowering her voice, "Your action last night deserved a glove across the cheek. Unfortunately my father is not alive to administer punishment . . . and still I would not do anything so backhanded!"

He was surprised, and pleased as well. Perhaps here was the solution. It was what Frank had suggested. Talk the de Brabant woman into reconsidering. He had said it was the only way . . . and the method intrigued the Captain, very much!

The waltz was fairly new and not totally accepted in all drawing rooms. However, it was in the Holmes house quite a vogue. Peter had brought it back with him from London, and often in the last few weeks they had set up practice in anticipation of this night. The young Holmes lad made his way across to the five-man orchestra with a pretty upon his arm and made a request for one now. As it filtered through to the captain's ears, he smiled. A new dance this, but one he had been quick to learn. What man would not when it allowed him with perfect propriety to put his arms around a fair maid's form?

Before Windmera could object, he had her in hand and was twirling her around the floor. His eyes smiled down into hers. Lord help him but she was too lovely! He said as much. and found the lass's blush enchanting. It was the right time to broach the subject, but he wished he could forget about it, forget about it and concentrate instead on Windy's charms. "Then tell me, Miss de Brabant. If you do not approve of the treatment I have received at your aunt's hands . . . why do you allow it? It is, after all, your plantation."

"Yes, it is mine . . . but I am not yet twenty-one. It is therefore in the hands of my trustees . . . namely my aunt and the solicitors."

He frowned. "Then you are helpless to aid me in my cause?"

It was her time to frown darkly. "I don't know about that. This was not my aunt's notion but Lord Brayward's! What he has to do with Brabant . . . well, he should not have anything to do with it. I intend, sir, though I am certain I don't know why, to go to my solicitor, Mr. Willes, and advise him of my feelings in the matter and see whether or not he can persuade my aunt to reverse her decision."

"That is very kind of you," he said slowly, hesitating but a moment, for he could not resist adding, "You said you don't know why you should be helping me. May *I* hazard a guess?"

There was a teasing quality to his voice. He was flirting, nothing more. She could see it in his eyes . . . such eyes, their blue twinkle hypnotized her nearly into responding in kind. However, she caught herself before allowing such a thing. She looked away and said sharply, a bit too sharply, "No! No, you may not attempt a guess, sir. It is not necessary. I really . . . do know why I wish to help you. You have been served a trick. It is not what my father would have liked. *That* is the only reason I am taking your side."

He felt a warm rush flood his veins in spite of her cold words. There was something about the way her body shivered so close to his own. There was something about her that told him she was not as unresponsive to him as she would have him believe. She was attracted to him, he could just feel it. He wanted to tease her into admitting it, if not to him, then at least to herself. His lips were too close to her ears, and his voice sent her away to another place, perhaps to her ocean

143

cove, perhaps to the moment he had first taken her in his strong arms.

"My beautiful moonflower . . . is that what you really believe?"

He had gone too far. He saw it at once. She would not be backed against a wall, not she! She pulled away on a gasp, and there was a seething to her low words. "You are insufferable! Conceited and . . . and . . . and a boor!"

She was off in the moment, leaving him on the edge of the dance floor no longer partnered. As it chanced, Roderick stood directly in her path. He'd been standing rum punch in hand, and he offered it with a familiar, almost possessive smile. She took it, because in her rage she did not know what to do first. She took it and smiled almost adoringly at Roderick, whereupon she took his offered arm and allowed him to lead her off. Her fury was fathomless at that moment. She couldn't think. How dare he? How dare he hint that she might be attracted to him? He was so puffed up in his own self-esteem that he thought every female was ready to fall at his feet! Oh! Hang the conceited cur . . . the gall of him! Well, Captain Lance Landon, thought the lady sternly, I shall show you how very wrong you are. Very wrong indeed! Drat you!

Eight

Jokai paced the polished dork wood flooring ceaselessly.
The whites of his eyes were bright with his frenzy. He
stopped and glared at the woman he called his own. She had
not answered his many questions satisfactorily. She had left
him feeling empty and frustrated. She sought to evade. He
knew it, and it hurt. Deep in his throat he felt a welling con-
striction, and it was hard to speak now, but he had to pursue.
She must satisfy him.

"Louise . . ." He had stopped his pacing, he had extended
a hand to her, and he waited.

She saw his pain, and it cut through her sharply. In that
moment she made up her mind. Oh, she had no intention of
giving up Brayward's money. She would marry the man no
matter what. 'Twas not that under her consideration. It was
only, how would she tell Jokai? Her decision was simple. She
would not tell him at all! Marry Brayward in secret, leave the
telling for someone else, be not present during his first en-
lightenment. Be not present during his first wave of shock
. . . and perhaps fury.

She saw his extended hand and went to him at once. She
fell upon the hard muscular chest and sighed. "Jokai, Jokai
. . . he is nothing. Remember that always. Brayward is nothing to me. He is necessary right now to Brabant . . . he is a
means of survival. In truth I detest him, I always will."

He kissed her silken locks. Her words were soothing. They
brushed away his anxieties, they cooled his temper. He believed her. Why should she lie? Indeed, she did not. His lips
sought her own, and his hands began working the buttons of
her gown. He needed more than assurances, though . . . he
needed her pledge, and this he would have in their bed.

In the opposite wing, Windmera lay on her back, one arm
behind her head. She stared up at the creamy ceiling, but she
saw many images, and they took form. Roderick. He had
made quite an impression. He was handsome, polished, full
of anecdotes of a life she had longed to know. His charm
concealed his mind, and she sensed this. It made her leery of

145

him . . . and still she was attracted to the man. How could she not be?

Captain Lance Landon. He conjured up mystery, excitement, adventure. It loomed all around his person. He was a man of action, a taker. But was he a giver? She had no way of knowing and decided perhaps wrongly that he was not. He was also in her opinion a detestable brute who forged his way despite all obstacles. He was arrogant, conceited, self-assured and thoroughly raffish. Still, she found him alluring. She found herself remembering his kiss, his arms . . . oh, she hated her weakness! She must put him out of her mind. But first . . . she must get him his shipment! Tomorrow she would visit with her attorney and arrange the thing. It would give her great satisfaction to manage the affair and be rid of Captain Lance Landon! With this last thought she fell off into a troubled sleep.

Roderick, now situated in a guest room at Lord Brayward's estate, leaned against his wrought-iron terrace and drew long on his cigar. He puffed out the smoke and watched it form patterns in the air. He pulled a face at the taste and flicked it over the rail. He had never liked "blowing a cloud," as his cronies called it. So, it would appear that Windmera Brabant would be no easy conquest! There was no one else the chit was interested in, of that he was nearly certain, though he had no liking for the way she had of gazing at Captain Lance Landon. He didn't even think she was aware of it, but she did look at the man overly much. Well, no matter, the American would soon be out of the way.

She had a mind all her own, did this lovely wench, but in the end he would have her. By God! He even found himself wanting her. He thought about her beauty, and his desire grew. But it was not that. He knew deep in his heart that it was not because of her haunting beauty. She was a natural Ravensbury. Conceived out of wedlock, but of Godwin's blood! She was the image of a woman Godwin had loved with all his heart, and unconsciously Roderick had ever aped his adored Godwin. Yes, he wanted her, for she was the blood of Ravensbury. Having her would make him all the closer to Godwin. Dangerous are such thoughts, for out of them come obsessions!

Captain Lance Landon took the rear door and made his way up the stairs in the dark. He needed a walk after his host's ball. He was now staying at the Holmes plantation. His walk had cleared the air for him, helped him to think better. He was getting too fired up over Windmera de Brabant. He must get her out of his mind. She was not for the taking! He was confident that given enough time he might be able to lay her bare before him, and Lord only knew he was itching to do just that, but he was fairly certain the lass was an innocent. She behaved like a schoolgirl when he flirted with her. Unused to the art of dalliance, she had responded with anger. It amused him and warned him to steer clear. But still . . .

Enough of that! He put these thoughts away. At least Windmera de Brabant had promised to do what she could to help. With any luck he would soon have his cargo of sugar and be heading homeward. In the meantime, perhaps he would take young Peter Holmes's suggestion. He laughed to himself to think of the boy who had followed him around now all grown and fully knowledgeable in such matters. When he had mentioned his need of a woman to Peter in passing, the lad had patted his shoulder and said he would take him into Bridgetown the very next night to a particular bordello he was fond of frequenting himself! Peter, who had hero-worshiped him, now leading him! It was almost laughable! Well, perhaps a visit to the local cathouse was just what he needed. Then for no good reason the image of Windy's wild violet eyes came into view, as did her long black hair floating about her bare shoulders, her pert white breasts glowing in the moonlight. Damn, he thought almost viciously, damn but he wanted her!

There was no stemming her irritation as she tooled her perfectly matched bays homeward. Windy had donned her finest pale-green linen habit. She had tilted her green matching top hat quite sophisticatedly upon her high curls, and she had gone to town in the open curricle usually reserved for her aunt. All this to impress her solicitors with her maturity. It had not moved them one iota! All they would say was that her aunt was her guardian until she was twenty-one and that Lord Brayward's proposal was sound and therefore they would not interfere! Infuriating!

It was enough to try the soul of a maid of patience, and she had never deemed herself lucky enough to have this enviable attribute. If that was not enough to harass her for a morning, here was Peter Holmes with his detestable houseguest coming her way! Lord, but she wished she could avoid them . . . however, might as well get the humiliating thing over with.

"Ho there, Windy m'girl!" cried Peter jovially. "We were just on our way to Brabant!"

"Were you? Well then, if you accompany me, we can dine together." She smiled at Peter, nodded coldly at his companion, noting reluctantly that the captain's eyes did him credit. Odd how one so arrogant could have such speaking eyes, such sensitive expressions. She had invited them to lunch because of her long friendship with Peter, but she hoped heartily they would decline. They did not.

"Splendid notion, Windy. It seems Lance here has some problem with Brabant. I suppose we can iron it out with your aunt over the table . . . what do you think?"

"Oh, I don't know, Peter . . . I've just come from the solicitors, and they won't go over my aunt's head, so if we are to iron it out, I suppose it must be with her. The ridiculous part of all this is that they have informed me that the sugar has been refined and is sitting in the Jackson Warehouse just waiting for shipment! Oh, it is provoking."

"You say the sugar has already been processed?" asked the captain, speaking for the first time.

"Yes," she said, looking up at him without thinking. By God, he was a handsome man. Because of this thought she scowled and looked away. "The refined sugar sits idly in a warehouse right in Bridgetown. Really, the entire situation is totally unbelievable."

"Indeed it is," agreed Peter, who had learned the way of things from his father. Frank Holmes felt responsible for this predicament because Jules Landon had written first to him for a consignment of sugar. His entire harvest had already been booked by a firm in England. Frank Holmes was a friend to Maurice and knew that the Frenchman was in need of a sale . . . it was only natural that he should advise his friend Jules to write his friend Maurice. He now felt it lay on his shoulders to do something about the nasty turn of events. While Peter and Lance were off to speak with Louise, he was off to see Brayward. Peter had taken on his father's conscience. He could see too that there was some antagonism between Lance and Windy, a thing he found most surprising, for he would have thought the two would get on famously. He thought them much alike. "What surprises me, Windy, is your aunt. I can't imagine why she should be giving Lance here such a difficult time."

" 'Tis not she . . . at least not directly. She is acting on the advice of Brayward. But shhh, Peter, I am thinking . . ."

They had by then reached the Brabant stables. A few moments later saw them entering the Brabant sitting room, where they were met by Louise Davenant.

"Ah, Peter . . . how good to see you," said the Frenchwoman, fluttering gracefully his way and giving him her cheek.

He kissed it perfunctorily and then wagged his finger, "Tante Louise!" He had called her so ever since he could remember; it had been at her instructions and he had liked doing so. "I am here to tell you how surprised I am at you."

"Peter . . . how can you speak so to me?" cried Louise, genuinely taken aback.

"You have served my friend Captain Landon here an inhospitable turn," he said, reducing the lecture he had planned, coating the edges, for when confronted by the woman he found it impossible to take a harsh tone.

"Oh, but you are unfair. I have done nothing. The solicitors have done it all. It is they. I know nothing of the running of a plantation."

"Tante!" objected Windy. "I have just come from Mr. Willes, and he tells me they are acting on the sole advice of Lord Brayward."

"So they may well be! He knows best." she said, and there was an obstinate look to her eyes. She did not like everyone hounding her, and she was most put out with her niece for going off to the attorney this morning. The very idea!

"Now, Tante Louise—" began Peter.

Louise stomped her foot, "Enough! Oh, you have all spoiled my day! I cannot do anything about this dreadful business. Now leave me in peace!" With which she turned and fled the room as though she were no more than ten years old.

It left Peter feeling embarrassed. It brought her niece's mouth wide open, but she knew her aunt, and had half expected this reaction. It brought a puzzled expression to the captain's profile. He had been detached from the proceedings, looking on with only mild interest . . . because he had seen from the very outset that they would get nothing from Tante Louise. She was a woman whose compassion was turned off simply by separating herself from the ugliness. She needn't feel if she didn't see. He hoped that his Uncle Frank would

149

have more success with Brayward, for it appeared to him that Brayward's word would be final in this affair.

"Drat Brayward! How could we have foreseen his involvement in this matter?" said Peter, slamming down the glass of port he had poured out for himself. "Louise would never behave in such a manner if he had not set her to it!"

"Hmmm . . . that is another thing," said Windmera. "I can't imagine why she is allowing him to influence her so strongly." Then after a moment's thoughtful hesitation she went to the door her aunt had left ajar and closed it quietly. Having done this, she set the latch and turned to find both gentlemen keenly interested in her movements. She smiled and began portentously, "It would appear that we shall have to enact plan *two!*"

The captain had taken up the glass of port Peter had served him earlier. He toasted this at Windmera and said, his eyes twinkling, "Plan two? I was not aware there existed a plan two."

"Oh yes. I formulated it on the way down the drive. It was when you asked me if the sugar you had purchased from Brabant was already processed. Remember?"

"Vaguely . . . but—"

She interrupted, "Well, Captain Lance Landon, you will have your sugar, but I am afraid you will have to . . . *steal it!*"

"Steal it?" spluttered Peter, choking on his libation. Then, turning to the captain, "The girl is quite mad. Has always been so, you see, but I always thought there was no harm in her."

"Shh, Peter. Don't you understand? Oh, you are a ninny!" She sighed. "I was only speaking figuratively. In truth, it is the captain's consignment of sugar. He has his correspondence with Father to prove it, and he must have receipts showing that he paid Father in advance."

The captain thought it time to put in a few words. His tone was low, thoughtful, because he could not help but think that the girl had a notion worth investigating. "I have paid receipts, yes, but I am afraid I do *not* have a bill of lading! Without that in my possession I very well could be charged with stealing."

"Nonsense! 'Tis your cargo. You have paid for it. Besides, you will have it loaded onto your ship and be off with none the wiser until it is too late." She added lest he doubt, "Peter and I shall help you."

150

"We shall?" squeaked Peter. He gave it quick consideration. "By Jove, we shall. What a rare kick-up this is turning out to be! Famous good sport, Lance."

"Indeed," agreed Windy, her violet eyes alive with anticipation. "We shall have to discover when the guards go off duty . . . the best route to your ship . . . oh, all sorts of marvelous things!"

The captain's lips quivered. Children, these two were children, nothing more. "Let us first hope that Uncle Frank has had more success today with Brayward than you have had with Tante Louise, shall we?"

"Oh pooh!" remarked Windy, surprised at his lack of spirit.

Nine

Roderick of Ravensbury's name was announced at the Brabant library doors. Windmera was sitting alone in her breezy library devouring the pages of *Childe Harold*, written by the new young poet Lord Byron. She heard Roderick's name and looked up quickly. The sight of him, well dressed, russet curls fringing his forehead, winding around his ears, twirling at his neck, brought a welcoming smile to her lips. He was good-looking, very good-looking. His eyes, though . . . they bothered her. They were a cool brown flecked in their recesses with specks of gold, but they told nothing, nothing at all.

She put down her book and extended her ungloved hand. It was not exactly the height of propriety to be receiving him alone, but her aunt would not come downstairs. Louise was still at odds with her conscience. At any rate, she would allow him but a few moments.

He took up her dainty fingers and noted their color from the sun. The girl was a free spirit, not given to fashion. Most intriguing. Another would have worn gloves to protect hands meant to be white. She almost saw his thoughts and smiled to herself, but when his lips brushed the tips of her fingers she felt a flurried sensation filter to her brain.

"Fair charmer, have you a moment to give me?" He was already sliding down beside her on the yellow damask sofa.

"I fear, sir, if I did not give it, you would most certainly wrest it from me." She flirted with her eyes, with the shift of her body, as she allowed him to sit beside her. He was in her mind an approved suitor. She was a maid looking for love. She knew not what that well-talked-of emotion felt like and had every intention of exploring!

His eyes moved over her dreamily. His hand had not yet released her own and again he put it to his lips, this time kissing the palm, allowing his voice to display his ardor.

"You need not fear me, Windmera. I want only to please you . . . always."

Such a word is 'always'! He had learned early in his philandering to use it, for it seemed most women needed to hear it.

However, that was not the case with Windmera. It was all

moving too quickly, this flirtation. *"Always"* came as an alarming thing she was not ready to accept. The proximity of his body, the intent of his move, made her aware of what he intended next. Oh no, thought she, not so fast, my handsome buck!

She retreated by getting to her feet." Well, Mr. Ravensbury . . ." She needed to change the subject; her movements brought her near the discarded spencer of her traveling habit. "Have you had the opportunity yet to see any of our lovely island?"

His gaze rested on the green linen spencer lying negligently over a chair back. She had been out riding? Where had she been? With whom? He was already possessive of her. He was already thinking her his very own. "No," he said as he too got to his feet. "I have not as yet been fortunate enough to find anyone willing to give me the tour, and traveling alone is at its very best a lonely occupation." He was studying her. Not just appraising her charms, but tracing her mind, attempting a penetration. She could almost feel it as she turned to meet his fevered eyes. She moved away farther still.

"What you need is a guide," she said lightly, without calculation.

He took it up immediately. "But would *she* be willing to take me in hand?"

"She? Whom do you mean?" she asked, half in curiosity, perhaps half in jealousy. Females are by nature a jealous lot. This extends to all males within their scheme of things, and she had not yet ruled Roderick of Ravensbury out of her schemes.

He smiled, pleased at her reaction. It took him less than a moment to reach her, to take her chin between his forefinger and thumb and tilt her face up to meet his eyes. She was stirred by him, and she allowed it.

"No other *she* holds my interest, Miss de Brabant. Wouldn't you consider taking me in hand?"

"I doubt that any woman could do that," she said, attempting levity, enjoying too the game they played.

She tantalized him, this beauty. He forgot for a moment that she was Godwin's daughter. He thought only that she was lovely and that he wanted to possess her. His hand went to her waist, drawing her nearer still. "You are wrong, Miss de Brabant, for I know one and one only quite capable of doing just that!"

Again the library doors opened. Again the butler's voice.

153

"Captain Lance Landon!" said he, and as Windy jumped away from her suitor's embrace she thought she saw a trace of amusement in her old retainer's eye.

Captain Lance Landon stopped short. He was quick to note Windy's hasty retreat, quick to understand its meaning. He glanced over at Roderick with something of distaste and wondered at Windy . . . but then there was never any accounting for a woman's fancies. A strange churning filled his gut. Lord, but he wanted to plant the smug dandy a facer, but he was ever a smart blade not wont to give over to his emotions. In he stepped as though nothing untoward had passed . . . but a friend would have noted the storm in the captain's blue eyes.

Windmera saw his eyes and quietly sucked in air. What a man was this Lance Landon! What force was contained in his virile body! She felt strangely at odds with herself, and when his voice called her to him she nearly jumped.

"Miss de Brabant, I am sorry to intrude, but I thought it necessary to continue our discussion of this afternoon. I hope you don't mind."

"I am afraid I do mind." She realized how rude she was being and yet could not help herself. "I thought we had settled everything between us when you were here with Peter." It was a statement, not a question. She was humiliated that he had seen her in Roderick's embrace.

He took her words to mean she wished Roderick to know she had not been alone with him. It pinched him into irritation. "It was Peter who suggested I return and go over the matter with you more thoroughly. However, I can see that I have come at a bad time." He started to turn to walk away.

She couldn't bear it. She wouldn't let him leave like this. It was terrible. How could she have treated him so uncivilly in front of another man?

But before she could speak, Roderick snidely returned, "Indeed you have come at a prodigiously bad time, Landon!"

She nearly stamped her foot at Roderick, so heightened was her agitation. How dare he step in, take over? How dare he? Roderick and Landon were at odds. She knew not why, and at the moment didn't give a fig. She only knew she wouldn't allow Roderick to rule her manners. She put in quickly, far more kindly than her tone had been a moment ago, "Perhaps, captain . . . if you could return later this evening, and with Peter . . . ?"

He smiled. "Yes, of course, as you wish," said the captain

inclining his head, taking his dismissal in good grace. As he turned to go, Miss de Brabant called out, "Wait, captain! Mr. Ravensbury was just leaving as well. You two may . . . walk out to the stables together . . . unless you would like me to ring. I can have you wait here until your horses are brought?" She put up a questioning brow, and there was the hint of a twinkle in her violet eyes. Only Lance saw it and responded in kind. So, she would not allow the English dandy to behave as though he had full ownership of her. Interesting, thought the captain as he made her his bow.

Roderick was surprised at Windmera's trenchant design. However, he took his loss well, bent low over her hand and marched somewhat erectly out of the room. Captain Landon he chose to ignore. Again he thought of Windmera's spencer. He thought of the captain's words: ". . . continue *our* discussion." Evidently the lady was not above dangling two suitors simultaneously. He had no liking for the crude American's emergence on *this* scene. Windmera was his, or would be, no matter what he had to do to make it a reality!

Windmera smiled at Landon's expression as the captain watched Roderick proceed before him. Amiably the captain followed, stopped at the door, turned to smile at Miss de Brabant, winked at her as well and was gone. She sighed and felt burdened by a sudden sense of loss. How dull the afternoon would now seem with no one about. She picked up her book again and began where she had left off. So engrossed did she become with the dashing *Childe Harold* that she never heard anyone enter through the open garden door. She never heard anyone step purposely across the room. She only knew that as she read out loud, "Had sigh'd to many though he loved but one," a pair of dusty Hessian boots came into view. She followed their line upward, her heart beating violently as she stifled a scream, for there stood Captain Lance Landon, a grin lighting up his ruggedly handsome features.

"And that loved one, alas! could ne'er be his." He made her a mock bow. "They say Byron has taken London quite by storm. I must admit having a fondness for his verse myself."

"Oh!" she managed to breathe at last. "You gave me a start, you horrid beast! What are you doing here? How did you get in?"

He dropped unceremoniously down beside her, loosening his neckcloth with some abandon, not in the least chastized or ashamed. He pointed at the open garden door. "Through that portal, my love." He stopped, moved his body so that he sat facing her, one boot bent over his knee. "Now, we have much to discuss, you and I, and with the English popinjay gone—"

"Oh! How dare you call him that? Mr. Ravensbury is no popinjay, sir. He is far more a gentleman than you!"

"Is he? No doubt that is why after knowing him but a day you allowed him to take you in his arms?" His words he had meant to be bland, but something in his tone cut through her.

"You are insufferable! Do you know that?" She seethed, leaning away from him, her eyes burning with her indignation, her cheeks flushed with her emotions.

He sighed. "So you have been telling me. But before we proceed, Windmera, what is Ravensbury to you?"

"I did not give you leave to use my given name!" she snapped, because she had no answer for him.

He was already in position; he had but to move his arms around her. He accomplished the next with a dexterity that surely would have brought applause from Don Juan himself. She was tightly wound in his embrace, his face just a breath's distance from her own, and his words came low, huskily. "Have you not noticed, my love? I am a taker." With which he began to prove to her the truth of his statement.

His mouth found hers in tenderness. Gently did he part her lips, sweetly did he take her breath, give her in return his tongue. As he tasted her, his hand moved to her hair, released it from its pins, enveloped its silk in his hold.

She gave herself to his magic. There was a drumming in her head, and her knees were so weak that she gave thanks she was not standing. Flames shot up before her closed lids, and a hot yearning lit in her loins. She wanted this to go on. She displayed this by shoving roughly at his chest. His chest, it felt like a mold of hard steel, only unlike the metal it was warm, and there beat a heart beneath its layers. She could feel his heart palpitating wildly, and the sensation further singed her flesh. No, no, no, said her mind to her body. She reacted by hitting his chest with her small fist.

He released her, or rather, he set her from himself. He was frowning, but as he saw her expression his frown softened into a smile. She was unprepared for his next attack, for then in the midst of her confused state he dropped a kiss upon her nose. "There now, my moonflower, shall we to business?"

"Oh!" ejaculated the lady, finally discovering her voice. "Oh!" She picked up her volume of Byron with every intention, even at their close proximity, of throwing it at him. He caught her wrist, removed the book and shook his head.

"Tsk, tsk, 'tis no way to treat a work of art." He laughed out loud. "Don't be angry with me, lass. I am but a mortal man, and you are too beautiful to resist. But see, am I not holding myself in check?" He hesitated a moment and then threatened, "And if you wish me to continue to hold myself in check . . . perhaps we had better address ourselves to my sugar!"

Under her breath she leveled a curse or two at his merry head, but thinking it wise to take his advice, she listened to what next he had to say.

"I have outlined a number of things you and Peter will have to find out for me. I have already gone over Peter's part with him. Now, this is what I need from you. . . ."

Neither one heard the rustle at the garden doors, or noticed the shadow move across the lawn.

Ten

Windmera sat up in bed and gazed at her nightstand clock.
The hour was nearly twelve! A nervousness came over her,
and another feeling as well, one she could not name. Three
nights had gone by. Tonight was the appointed night. Tonight
Captain Landon would have his cargo safely onboard his *Sea
Hawk* and he would sail for his home . . . and she would
never see him again! Odd, for the notion left her strangely
out of temper.

It had been an exciting three days. She felt sorely being
left out at the last minute, as did Peter, but the captain would
have none of them this night. He had allowed Peter to visit
the warehouse clerk during the day and pilfer an empty letterhead, for he planned to use it to get the guard's attention.
He allowed her to nose about the warehouse, flirt with the
same clerk and learn the hours, the shifts of the men. It was
all so simple, and now she was totally deflated, for it would
soon be over! And he would soon be gone.

It doesn't matter, she told herself. He is an arrogant brute!
She remembered how he had kissed her that very afternoon.
He was always taking her by surprise, taking her in his arms,
and then reluctantly, as though it took great strength, great
will, setting her aside. There were moments when she wished
he wouldn't do that, when she wished his kisses wouldn't
stop. It was all so confusing, for there was Roderick as well!

Roderick. She wasn't sure what she felt for him, but he too
aroused her . . . in a different way. He aroused visions of a
new life, a social extravaganza which she had dreamed about.
He was a skillful lover, his touch titillated her, stirred her.
She had allowed him a kiss last evening when they walked
out after dinner at Lord Brayward's. It had been natural to
allow it, and there was no denying that it had aroused her
womanhood into wanting. Oh, God! It was all so confusing,
and she had no one to turn to with these conflicting emotions.
And soon, soon Captain Landon would be gone. It was the
one recurring thought that taunted!

Jackson Warehouse was no more than a hundred yards
away from the wharf, not more than two hundred yards from

the *Sea Hawk*. Lance had discussed the scheme with his young first mate, Jackie, and then with his remaining six-man crew. They had all agreed heartily that there was nothing else for it. If they were ever to leave this island and return home heads up, they would have to take what was rightfully their own. It was how they saw things.

They came armed with an empty wagon, a gun a man, and Peter's acquisition of a Jackson letterhead now duly filled out. However, all that appeared at the rear entrance was a wagon, one driver, one loader and the captain. The night watch sat on an overturned crate eating his pewter bowl of okra and rice. At his back was the high-ceilinged wood shack of a building. Weathered it was, for the salt air had taken its ravages in spite of the fact that it was but some eight years old. He heard the sound of wheels and looked up from his late meal. Whot's this? He sighed, put the bowl down and took up the torch stuck into the wall holder. It would be naught, there was never any excitement at the Jackson Warehouse, and that was just the way he liked it. But then his torchlight loomed forth and there was the wagon and the three men.

"Who be ye, gents? Whot be ye wanting?" called the guard.

A cultured male voice, deep, authoritative but not at all English, answered him, "Would this be the Jackson Warehouse, friend?"

"Eh? What would ye be wanting at this time of night, 'ere?" asked the guard suspiciously. He waved the torch before the captain's eyes to get himself a better look.

"Move that torch out of my way, my man, or you will find yourself in straits!" warned the captain amiably.

"Uh . . . oh . . . all right, then. Give over and be after telling me your business 'ere."

The captain jumped down from the wagon. He brought the letter from out of his pocket and devoutly hoped he had been right when he assumed that a night guard would not be able to read. He waved it before the heavy-set man's eyes before flicking it open with an impressive wrist movement.

"This authorizes us to take charge of our shipment of sugar," said the captain, motioning for his men to alight.

"Hold there . . . no one told me—"

"No one need tell you. This paper is enough," said the captain portentously.

"Maybe so. But they would 'ave told me . . . always do . . . never gave over a cargo at night."

"There is always a first time," said the captain, hoping the fellow would not make it necessary for them to put him out of the way.

"Eh? Like I said, guv, maybe so . . . but I'll jest have to be calling after the beadle. He'll go over to Clerk Rawl—"

The poor man was never allowed to finish. He was never allowed to take another step. From behind, as previously planned, came the remaining five men, one of whom was Jackie, the first mate. And it was Jackie who brought down the back of his pistol unto the man's thick skull. "Sorry, mate," offered Jackie to the unconscious man, "but it seems you take your work too seriously."

The captain ruffled his first mate's head, "Devil! Have pity on a poor working man down! Our fight was not with him."

" 'Twas his own fault, capt'n—he was about to balk," objected Jackie, grinning widely.

The captain shook his head but called out softly, "All right, then, m'lads! Step lively!"

On this command they set up a line, using a relay system to get the bags of refined sugar out to the wagon. The captain took up a station outside on the wagon and felt very much like singing as he caught each bag thrown to him and laid it down.

He'd been at it for not very long when a shot split the air and all work stopped.

The captain peered through the darkness down the long drive that led to the street, and there he made out a small regiment of soldiers. At their lead were two men. One was Lord Brayward, who ordered angrily for them to put up their hands. The other was Roderick of Ravensbury!

The captain cursed softly to himself and told his men firmly, "Give 'em no resistance, lads. I want all of us alive in the morning!"

"But capt'n—" objected Jackie, closest to him.

"Hush there, Jack. We'll come out of it. Just believe in me awhile longer!"

"Aye, capt'n."

Through this all, Captain Lance Landon's mind worked. How did Brayward know? Why was Roderick looking so self-satisfied? It was more than catching him at his deed . . . it was more, he could just feel it. And how . . . how did they know the day, the time? It was uncanny.

Roderick was looking strangely exultant. He had wanted to rid himself of this captain from Windmera's thoughts! It wasn't enough to have the man return to the States . . . he had to ruin him! He had to make Landon hate Windmera and never want to see her again! He had to do this, and at last he had found a way. They had given it to him.

He meandered leisurely toward the captain as the guards relieved the sailors of their weapons and took them under arrest. The captain had already jumped down from the wagon, and as he had his hands tied behind his back by a dragoon, Roderick smiled.

"You are, of course, wondering how we managed to . . . arrange this little welcoming party for you?"

"Am I, Ravensbury?" said the captain sweetly. "No doubt you will tell me when it suits you."

"Tell you? Of course, I have no objection to telling you. You see, Windmera and I are . . . very close. When she told me what she had agreed to do for you, we discussed it at length and thought it best to allow her little joke to proceed. She allowed you to think that she went along with your scheme when in reality she was planning this as your end!"

The captain felt something sharp jab at him. No! There was Peter. If this were true, wouldn't Peter have known? But then, perhaps it was her way of getting back at him for that night on the beach? No! She wasn't like that! But . . . how then did Brayward and Roderick know about tonight? How? How . . . if not from her?

The morning came brightly. No sign of rain, but Windy awoke feeling that it should be pouring. Had he not gone? However, she had not long to dwell upon these thoughts, for no sooner had she washed and begun calling for her clothes than she heard a rider on the drive outdoors. She looked out her window and one winged brow rose. Peter? It was Peter?

She hurried with her dressing, but still a maid with a message from Mr. Holmes arrived at her door before she had completed her toilet.

A note written on his card said only, "Come down at once!"

Concern suddenly filled her heart. Something had gone wrong! Without finishing the dressing of her hair she picked up a ribbon and tied the long silky curls at the nape of her neck and proceeded to the study, where Peter Holmes awaited her. However, Tante Louise was there as well.

"Peter . . . ?" said Windy, going forward to take his extended hand.

"It's gone wrong, Wind. Everything has gone wrong. They were betrayed. Captain Landon and his crew are at this very minute imprisoned in that hole . . . Savannah!"

Savannah was a stark building used as a prison for whites only. It was little more than a breeding ground for death. "But, but that is unthinkable! Why there?"

"Lord only knows. They've impounded their ship as well . . . taken it up the coast to Holetown!"

"Are you certain? Who told you all this?"

Peter Holmes was the only son in a family that numbered seven after him. Six of those girls were now in finishing schools in England. The last was a minx of a child so well liked that she was often found in nearly anyone's home. It was she who had come home after an overnight visit with a close friend whose father just happened to be a corporal in the regiment that had conducted the arrest. However, even so, Peter had gone into town to verify her story. He had come straight from Bridgetown to Windmera. It was left now to Louise to clear the captain. He turned to her now.

"It is true, Tante Louise. You must do something now. Brayward has overstepped. That shipment is rightfully Captain Landon's."

"I . . . I have no notion what you two are talking about," said Louise, sincerely confused.

"Of course . . . how could she, Peter?" said Windy. "Tante . . . listen to me. The captain, acting on my advice, tried to take his shipment last night. He has been arrested for stealing . . . he and his crew! They have taken him to prison!"

"Oh dear. That is dreadful. But it was wrong of him . . . to try and take the shipment after I told him he must not."

"Tante . . . you cannot mean you will not speak for him?" cried Windy.

"I? Speak for him? He tried to steal the shipment, Windmera," said Louise, much surprised. "What can I do now?"

"You can speak to Brayward," said Peter hopefully. "Ask him to have the captain released . . . at least to my father's custody."

"I . . . I don't know . . ."

"Auntie, please!" cried Windy.

"Look, it shouldn't be so difficult. My father is with the authorities right now attempting to arrange it, but it will be much easier if you or Brayward put in word."

"Very well . . . But I think you should leave now, Peter . . . I would speak alone with Windmera about this terrible thing."

"Oh . . . of course." He bowed and left them abruptly, surprised at Tante Louise. Really, he had never thought she could be so hard-hearted, so unconcerned with another's troubles . . . especially when he considered that a great deal of the fault lay with her!

Louise turned to Windmera and sighed. "Windmera . . . what I tell you now is a confidence."

"Yes, Tante."

"I am going to marry Brayward. No, do not look like that. It will be a secret wedding . . . for I do not want . . . anyone to know of it until after the fact!"

"But . . . but Tante . . ."

She put up her hand. "I will not discuss it with you! I am telling this to you because I want you to understand why . . . why I must bow to Brayward's decisions in these matters, why I want you to stay out of it."

"Stay out of it? It is my plantation, my crop of sugar, my responsibility . . . how can I stay out of it?"

"Nevertheless you will stay out of it. I am only thankful that women are not allowed near Savannah! God only knows—you might feel it necessary to visit the American there."

"Of course I shall—"

"You will not, Windmera! Promise me! All else, perhaps . . . but you will not go in person to such a dreadful place. If not for your reputation, think of mine. People will say I have no influence on your actions . . . people will say—"

"Hang them all!"

"Yes, sometimes I wish I could . . . but Windy, I can bear no more problems now . . . please . . ."

"Yes, Tante . . . I promise not to go near Savannah," said Windy, feeling as though she were giving away a part of her being.

The captain's place of imprisonment, Savannah, was some two miles southeast out of town. His guards, a regiment of English dragoons whose barracks lay perpendicular to his prison quarters. They were separated only by a stone rectangular courtyard some thirty feet in width. His cell, a narrow room no more than eight by ten feet. His light came from an opening six inches square on the back wall high above his head. His bed, a lump of foul-smelling straw. His sanitary facility was a gourd. And still, he was in his aloneness somewhat better off than his crew next door.

They too had a narrow cell, but all of them shared it! For beds, they had the stone floor. Their means of natural relief were also gourds, and these were left continuously in the cell, festering the air with an unbearable odor. But still they looked to their captain! Landon would pound at the mutual wall they shared and regale them with amusing anecdotes, calling Jackie to aid him in this. He bucked up their spirits well enough and he gave them hope.

Hope? He dwelt on it now, for he had just been allowed a visit from his Uncle Frank. Egad, that had been an ordeal to sustain. He, attempting to look undaunted by all this . . . Frank, attempting to do the very undoing he was doing for his men . . . give hope! Francis Holmes had done his very best. He had already visited with the governor this day. He had argued that this was no place for the son of an English nobleman to be housed, no matter the accusation. The governor had not seen things quite that way, for he had already heard from Brayward.

The governor had responded, "Is not the man an American? Did he not attempt to steal a cargo that had been specifically denied him? Did not his father fight on the side of the colonies? He will stay where he is pending a trial!" He would not be moved. Thusly did Francis Holmes report to Landon, again saying that their only hope now was to appeal to Louise Davenant. Well, Captain Landon knew better than to look to help from that quarter. And Windmera? She had betrayed him. He believed this to be true. It hurt him to the very core. He was unused to such treatment from women.

Lance Landon was a man who had grown to think of women as treasured beings worthy of attention, worthy of respect and admiration. His own Irish mother had been such a creature, and his sister, dear to him, had always been a treasured kitten, a pet, a fond being upon whom he had doted. Women . . . yes, he had always enjoyed them. This Windmera was a new breed! She had betrayed him, that was now fairly obvious. Why? He could only assume she must have some devious, spiteful reasons of her own . . . but her eyes . . . how they had fooled him!

Lance Landon was hurt. It was a deep cutting wound, and

oddly enough, the very first he had received at the hands of a woman. It angered him to think how she could have lied. How she must have laughed. He was not by nature a vengeful person, but he knew an itching to teach her a lesson, and every night he spent in his prison hole, this itch grew in its intensity.

Eleven

April was nearly gone! The thirtieth day had come, and Lance Landon and the seven-man crew of the *Sea Hawk* had spent five nights in their cells with little prospect of escaping. However, they still were not without hope.

Peter Holmes had wheedled his way into Landon's cell. A dragoon guard stood outside the door, but the man was busily engaged in conversation with another soldier. Still, Peter and Lance spoke in whispers.

"It is useless. Tante Louise says that Brayward will not budge in his decision, and Windy says—"

"Never mind what Windmera says. She is not to be trusted!" snapped Landon. There was a full growth of tough blackness beneath his cheeks, around his mouth and beneath his chin; coupled with his sudden ferocity he gave off a demonic quality that quite startled his youthful friend.

"But . . . but Lance," objected Peter, his eyes opened wide, "Windy can help."

"As she did before? How the deuce do you think we got into this hellhole?"

"Brayward must have found out from Tante Louise," suggested Peter, who had been wondering on and off about this very question.

"Nonsense! And if such balderdash were true . . . how did *she* find out?"

"She might have overheard." Actually he was certain it had *not* been Louise who had told Brayward, because he could still recall sharply how surprised she was to learn of Landon's predicament. So his tone was more than half doubtful.

"You no more believe that than I!" returned the captain hotly.

"No, perhaps I don't! But I do know what I believe, and that is that you are completely out with regard to Windmera! Look, Lance . . . she could no more have turned you in than . . . I!"

The captain's rage against the lady had increased substantially since his first night's incarceration. If he had logically thought then that she might have slipped and mentioned something to Roderick, he now was certain that she had told Ravensbury the whole, and not by accident. He sneered at the image this conjured up in his mind. "Not to Brayward! No, she betrayed us to Roderick! She gave us over to a popinjay!"

Peter frowned at this. It bothered him, for he had seen Roderick at Brabant more often than not, and Roderick was a houseguest of Brayward's. The captain was quick to note the consternation that flickered over Peter's brow.

"Ah ha! So! I have finally made you see!"

"No! Not at all," countered the lad. "I mean . . . well . . . what I mean is . . . Windy had naught to do with this filthy business. Yes, I do agree that Roderick found out somehow and took the information to Brayward. But I insist on one thing throughout . . . no matter how bad it looks for her, Windy had naught to do with all this! Indeed, the girl is most disturbed about your being here!"

"Is she?" The captain sneered. "Is she indeed? No doubt so disturbed that she daren't face me?" It had bothered him that Windy had sent him no word, had made no attempt to see him. Somehow it increased his belief that she had betrayed him; otherwise, surely she would have come to him. It was what he expected of her, though he didn't know why.

"Now really, Lance, that is too bad of you!" returned Peter, rushing to her defense. He and Windmera had never really been playmates, but they had known each other a long time, and during that time had learned to be open with one another, leading to a closeness few males and females had in their era. "How can she come here?"

"How indeed? I would have thought the lady equal to anything." The Captain smirked. He meant it as no compliment, but Peter took it as such.

"Yes, and so she is, but her aunt would hear none of it." He patted the Captain's shoulder. "Buck up, Lance . . . we still have a hope. I posted a letter on yesterday's packet to London. It goes to Brummel . . . a friend of mine whose relationship with the prince regent may help. I have asked him to see what he can do with Prinny . . . perhaps the regent will send a letter to the governor demanding your release."

"Ye gods! That will take months!"

"I know . . . but in the meantime, I have managed to get permission to have proper meals sent in to you at our expense . . . and we have a friend among the soldiers here who has promised to see to it that you get what we send."

"Awright . . . awright . . . ye be gabbing like a couple of morts . . . time was ye be leaving, Holmes," said the fat-bellied guard, sidling up to the peephole at the door's center. "Out wit ye . . . and capt'n . . . ye best be standing back in a corner whilst I let him out."

This done, the captain remained standing a long moment as the sound of Peter's steps receded in the distance. He thought again of Windmera. Guilty! Aye, the lass was guilty . . . though her eyes . . . but hang it, she was guilty! He would get out, and when he did, Lord but he would teach her! He had handled her so gently, he had put her aside when every inch of him had wanted to lie with her. He could have had her, he was sure of it . . . but no, not he! He played the fool in her hands, but not the next time. Oh no, Windmera de Brabant . . . not the next time!

He walked over to the wall that separated him from his men.

"Eh, lads! Wake up and get to work! Bend those knees . . . stretch those arms. We'll be getting fresh meat and fruit tonight! Do you hear me, lads?"

"Aye, we hear ye, capt'n!" cried Jackie, picking himself off the stone floor and stretching for the ceiling, "Look alive, men!"

So he had them exercise a good part of that day, but they were already losing their spirit. They were sore of body, sore of morale. It would have to be soon, thought the captain of the *Sea Hawk* . . . they would have to get their freedom soon.

May 1, 1812, started out much like any other day on the isle of Barbados. The sun came up strong and bright. The air was a living thing filled with the softness of turtledoves cooing to one another; blackbirds cackled incessantly as sparrows dove in search of their breakfast. The windward breezes of the Atlantic spread their vibrant strokes, bending the tall lean coconut palms, shaking the trees' fronds, sending to earth an overripe browned shell.

A day much like any other, though the harvesting at most of the plantations was done. The sugar cane had been picked, most of it had been sold and delivered. Only a rare plantation had still another month's crop left to them.

Fishing vessels had gone out early that morning and were

now returning with their day's catch. They hauled kingfish, redfish, albacore and a local fish called dolphin onto the docks. Bunky watched them as they opened up their nets and began the busy, cunning production of bargaining. Broad Street was filled with wagons of fruit led by single donkeys or oxen. Everywhere people bustled about the open market, for the day was already in full swing.

He smiled to himself as he saw a flying fish take to the air with its silver blue-green body. He had only to turn to find a diminutive black hummingbird sucking at the flowers of a nearby hibiscus shrub. Aye, this was the life! He had taken the day off. He and his three-man crew were doing naught but lying about the *Liberté* soaking in the sights and the sun. Perhaps later they'd take her out for a sail and a swim . . . but not now. He had even turned down old man Brewster, who had wanted to hire him and his vessel for a day's trip up to North Point. He had told him no. This because the preceding weeks had made him enough cash to live leisurely for a while, and that was just what he intended to do. He was his own man, and as he had never been overly ambitious, just making his living was enough.

"Wake up, you old slug!" said a pretty maid's voice. "My word! Such deplorable laziness. There should be a law against it. Bunky . . . come on, you old charmer . . . get up, I say!"

He opened only one eye at this and found there enough to open the other. "Windy, m'darling." He sat up and pulled up a stool for her and motioned for her to sit. "Where 'ave ye been these five days and more? Getting tired of yer old friend, are ye? New and better taking me place?"

She sighed and took up the stool, plopping down upon it heavily. "You know better! Oh, Bunk. These last five days have been miserable! Tante Louise has forced me to go everywhere with her! To this one's for tea . . . to that one's for a Venetian breakfast! To Lord Brayward's for dinner! And when we have not gone out, she has insisted I remain at home and help her entertain her friends! I have been in a prison!"

"Never say so!" ejaculated Bunky, much surprised. "That don't sound much like your aunt."

"And it is not! But she is so dreadfully afraid that I will make some attempt to go to Savannah Prison and see Captain Landon."

"But 'ere now! Why would ye be doing that?" asked Bunky, puzzled.

"Oh, Bunky . . . it is all my fault . . . his being there!"

"Heard about that muddle over at Jackson Warehouse. Didn't half believe it. But there . . . he was caught red-handed, wasn't he?" He looked her over penetratingly, "Yer fault, ye say? How's that?"

"It was I who suggested he take his shipment and be off!" wailed Windy. "If I hadn't put the notion in his head . . . and then encouraged him afterwards . . ."

He rubbed his chin. "So . . . that's the way of it?"

She stopped and sent him a sharp look. "What do you mean?"

"Me? Naught . . . but be after telling me why a man should be locked up for taking that what he paid for."

"That is just it! He shouldn't be! He has not even received a refund for the shipment my aunt and Brayward have refused him! Oh, Bunky, I don't know what to do."

"Aye. But the man ought to go free. Hear tell the Holmes family been beating a path every day to the Governor's House. There's those that say sooner or later the guv he'll 'ave to give over! Well-connected are the Holmeses, even if they be Americans."

"Yes, but in the meantime . . . Captain Landon and his men are in that filthy place! If only Peter could think of something."

"Is he trying, then?" asked Bunky quizzically.

"Oh, you must know Peter is determined to break him out!" said Windy earnestly. Then, seeing the look in Bunky's eyes, she half smiled. "Well, he is! One mustn't underestimate Peter. He is forever surprising me with his knowledge. Why . . . just the other day he told me that he is on intimate terms with Beau Brummell."

Bunky grimaced. "Now, how is his friendship with a dandy going to help your captain?"

"He is not *my* captain! And Brummell is not just a dandy! He is very important and a good, good friend of the prince regent's! That should mean something to the governor!"

"Aye, and by the time it does, those poor souls in Savannah may be dead!"

She went white. "Don't say that! Don't even think it! Besides, Peter is working on it . . . he just has to find a way . . . for I swear, Bunky, if he does not . . . *I will!*"

Peter did have a plan. However, he had not wanted to mention it earlier either to Windmera or Landon. He wanted to give no false hopes to Landon, and he feared that Windy would no doubt dive without looking, and this was something that needed clear thinking and precise action.

He showed his pass to the sentry at the Savannah gates and walked through undeterred to the rear courtyard, where he again flashed his visitor's pass. It was the only thing the governor had granted the Holmes family . . . a visitor's pass! His steps were sluggish as he made his way toward the prison building, toward Lance Landon's cell, for his mind was heavy with its meanderings. He had to work it out so that he and his father would not be implicated! Tricky . . . very tricky.

And then suddenly, without warning, nature lent her unpredictable hand. Capricious is her character, and no one in Barbados expected this. Indeed, nothing before had ever been like it! Even gales and storms gave warnings, gave signs to those who knew how to recognize them . . . but this, this phenomenon promised dilapidation to the fairy isle!

Those in the fields threw up their hands and fell to their knees, crying to God to save them. Others wailed that Satan had at last won his battle . . . that the end of the world had come. Whether it was God's work or Satan's, all agreed, the end had come. So the cry was picked up from the fields, taken to the great houses, still onward to the towns and villages. Mighty was the fear, and they had good reason, for mighty were the forces at work! It had started with the sun, for it had become quickly obscured and then all at once nearly totally darkened. The heavens seemed to open up, and out poured their rage of vengeance, or so it appeared to the Bajans! Grayish-white it came . . . in clots it came, thick and heavy . . . and havoc was reaped with all its accompanying panic and fears!

And then the screams began! They echoed from field to field and were carried by the winds by those looking for safety, from village to village and from village to . . . prison! What would later be known to all as the May Dust had come to cover all in Barbados. To the isle's inhabitants, those hours were terror-filled, but to Lance Landon they were joy!

Peter had approached the one guard outside Lance's door just as the sun's rays became shaded. He waved his pass, and the guard inserted his large brass key. Suddenly the sun was blackened, and in some surprise the guard turned halfway to gaze up at the sky. "Whot's this . . . a storm, ye think?" he exclaimed, for the day had given no sign of it.

171

Peter too turned his head skyward and frowned. The sun was no more! No storm this! "I . . . I don't know."

The guard clucked his tongue, pulled up the latch and opened the door inward for Peter to enter. Just as Peter started forward, it came! The ash was upon them! Thickly it fell, and startled by the heaviness of the clots the guard stood in the open doorway.

The captain had seen the darkening of the sun. He had witnessed the falling of a mass of gray-white substance and was quite sure it was not snow. He reached up to his small barred window and touched an accumulation of it. He put it to his nose and took a strong whiff, and then dawning came. He was well traveled, well educated, and he knew exactly what this grayish matter portended. He then observed the guard standing in the open doorway staring idiotically at the sky. He saw the man's hands stretch upward as though to take to himself the heavens' offerings, he saw the man's total absorption . . . and more, he saw that outdoors some commotion was afoot.

Ever an opportunist, the captain knew well what he must do. Out went his arm, catching the guard beneath the chin, tightening his hold on the throat and dragging the man into the recesses of his dark cell. Peter's attention came into focus. He opened his eyes wide but immediately moved into action, for he saw the guard's hand move to his waist, saw there an overly large and quite deadly pistol stuck into the man's wide belt. He would have to stoop to immediate dissimulation if he was to aid his friend and yet protect himself and his family.

"I say there. Landon!" he called, admirably shocked. "I say . . . Landon! Do let the fellow go. What do you think you are doing?" He had already managed to get the gun from the man's waistband, and he waved it at Landon.

"Drop that gun, Peter! Drop it now . . . or I swear I will break this poor man's neck!" returned Landon, understanding immediately.

The guard's eyes followed Peter as he moved around him to Landon's side and one could see the man's consternation for Peter was still waving the gun, "Drop it? Oh, very well . . . I suppose I have no choice?" he said.

The guard heard and saw no more as Peter rendered him unconscious.

He had offered the gun, handle first, toward Landon, and just as the guard looked away, the butt of the gun came down with just enough force to ensure them an hour's time.

"Well done, lad!" whispered the captain, grinning wide. "Now . . ."

He dragged the fellow into a corner and laid him to rest for the time. The ring of keys he found still dangling from the keyhole in the studded door. These they took up, and sticking his head outdoors he threw back, "Now . . . if only they will not notice . . ." In this he was to have his wish.

Outdoors confusion at its height reigned supreme. There was perhaps a man or two, well traveled, well read, who like the captain had guessed the meaning of this phenomenon, but they were splinters in a forest. Such was the force of the growing panic that none could hear anything but his own terror. Everyone was certain the time had come to face death. It was the end of the world! What to do in such a crisis? It is interesting to note that so many had the same single notion in mind . . . *to run!* For that is what they did. Everyone began running and most in separate directions, each perhaps looking for a portion of the isle that was not under Godly attack.

The Bajans then had no way of knowing that St. Vincent, a neighboring island, was suffering the eruption of its live volcano. They had no volcano on Barbados, and no understanding of such things. Tons of volcanic ash poured from the sky, and they believed themselves doomed. They were, of course, in no real danger, but at the time how could they know this? Thus they panicked, and they formed screaming trampling mobs, and the soldiers were caught between their own fears and the fears of their people. They never gave the captain and his crew (safely imprisoned, as they believed) a thought.

The captain moved swift and sly. Out came his men, all seven of them, slinking in the dark. There were soldiers running across, to and fro over the courtyard. Some had torches, but they never looked their way. Dark it was, blacker than night for there were no stars, no moon. The captain bade his men to hold low and close to the wall. So they moved as one unit to the prison walls. Up and over the five-foot brick wall in less than two minutes. And there staring them down was a team of oxen harnessed to an empty wagon!

The captain stared through the darkness and grinned wide.

"Godsend, eh, Peter?" He laughed, slapping the lad on the shoulder. "Come then, we mustn't turn such an offering down!"

Peter looked around for the owner, but the man was nowhere to be found. "What then? An oxen team is valuable."

"So he must have thought his life was as well! Ran for cover, more than likely . . . just as any sane man might. But no more, we must be off."

"Aye then, capt'n . . . but what is this?" cried Jackie, shaking a handful of the falling ash in his palms.

"Volcanic ash, and it won't interfere with our escape, lads. We shall turn it to account, see if we don't!"

"Lance . . . where do you mean to go? How can you get to your vessel in all this?"

"You said the *Sea Hawk* was in dock at Holetown?" He was smiling, pleased with the plan he had in mind.

"Yes . . . but . . ."

"Well, then, I mean to get my cargo of sugar, I mean to take it to Windmera de Brabant's vessel . . . the *Liberté* . . . yes, she has often mentioned the *Liberté* . . . and I mean to sail her to Holetown and there transfer my goods onto my schooner and sail for home!" He looked at his men. "How does that sound to you, lads?"

"Aye, captain! Let's be after doing it!" shouted Jackie. His cry was picked up by the men.

Peter was frowning. " 'Tis not a de Brabant vessel, Lance! It was given to Bunky, her skipper, some years ago."

"It makes no difference . . . we only mean to have the loan of her, Peter, nothing more, and 'tis the least a friend of a de Brabant could do for us after what they have put us through. Don't you think?"

"Yes, but . . ."

"Go home, Peter. Your family will be worried about you," said the captain firmly.

"Yes . . . but . . ."

"Off with you!" said the captain, extending his hand.

Peter took it up and shook it vigorously. "Godspeed, Lance . . . good luck!"

"We'll be needing it!" With that he sent the oxen forward, and the men of the *Sea Hawk* made their slow but steady progress through the darkness, through the falling ash to the Jackson Warehouse.

Twelve

Windmera held two glasses of freshly squeezed lemonade as she made her way from the kitchen galley below deck to the companionway and up the narrow companion steps to the top deck, where Bunky awaited her. The stairway door was open wide; however, she came nearly to a halt, thinking perhaps someone had accidentally shut it, for certainly it was far too dark. She stood midway on the worn steps peering through the darkness until finally with a sense of awe she realized that the door was open and the blackness was nature's work.

"What . . . ?" she breathed out loud, completing her ascent and coming up on deck. She gazed heavenward, and her voice was sharp with her sense of dread. "Bunky . . . the sky . . . whatever is going on?"

He was standing, staring upward, as were his men at the bow of the vessel. He looked her way a moment and came to take up his drink, but then the ash began to fall.

He brought the glass to his lip and opened his eyes wide with his objection as he got a mouthful of ash. "Stap me, girl . . . what the deuce did ye put in this?" he spluttered.

She didn't have to answer, for the grayish-white substance was now coming down in abundance. She reached out and brushed a mass of it off his shoulders. "Bunky . . . Bunky . . ." she said, her voice low. "What is this . . . what is happening?"

"Lord, love ye, child . . . I've never before seen the like of it!" he said, staring at the pile of ash collecting at his feet.

It was just about that time the screams began. Windy stared at the crowds, unsure exactly how it had started, for all at once people were throbbing with fear. Two definite sentences rang out from the mobs passing before her: " 'Tis the end of the world!" and "Satan has finally come into his own!" It was repeated with a frenzy she had never before witnessed as people ran to and fro seeking shelter.

"Bunky . . . Bunky . . . what are they doing? Has every living soul in Bridgetown gone mad? It is but some quirk of nature . . . only that, is it not, Bunky?" She wanted reassurance that her logic was sound.

He put his arm about her shoulders, "I can't say fer sure,

175

darlin', but what I can say is this. There ain't no Satan coming fer us and it ain't the end of the world! But still . . . we'd best be locking ourselves below a spell. I'd say we be in more danger from them mad fools roaming out there than from any storm!"

It was true, of course, and she agreed readily. "Yes . . . the mobs are in a panic. But my horse, Bunky . . . Brabant . . . Tante Louise . . ."

"Don't be giving me any foolishness. Yer horse be well stabled. 'Tis a fact that Brabant be land and as such is subject to nature's fancies. Yer aunt will be as safe as we . . . so I want no fretting!"

She sighed. "Very well . . . but what of the captain . . . in Savannah?" She told herself again she was responsible for his imprisonment. If she had not talked him into stealing his shipment, he would not now be there. If anything happened to him during the storm she would never forgive herself.

Bunky scratched his chin. "Lordy, girl . . . I don't know what ye want from me. But yer captain will be safe enough. At least as safe as ye'll be. Come along now, Windy, ye'll be having to make us another batch of that fresh lemonade . . . that first was spoilt." He could see the trouble in her eyes and wished he had the magic to soothe it all away. Keep her busy, that was the answer. Keep her busy in the galley below. He called to his men standing abeam. They were mumbling about the strangeness of the storm, but they were as levelheaded as himself, he reasoned. He'd have them all calm in a matter of minutes. "Come on, ye old blokes . . . we're going below."

The men of the *Sea Hawk* found the Jackson Warehouse easy prey. Its handful of laborers had fled in the first wrath of the sky's outpouring. They left the building but one man to service the public, its owner, Mr. Jackson. He sat now at his desk in the middle of a crate-filled floor. A branch of tallow candles illuminated his position, for he was working on his accounts. His glasses hung low over his thin nose, and the flickering flames gave off a glow to his balding head. He was clucking his tongue out loud, still put out with his employees for having left him. He looked up from his work, for he thought he heard a sound.

"Eh? Someone there?" he called. He waited. Nothing. He sighed and returned his glance to his ledger sheet.

Again! The distinct sound of a man's heel on the creaky

wood floor. "Someone is there!" he accused. "Speak up! Come back, have you? Saw it was naught but the workings of a storm, eh? Well, well, have a good mind not to give you the job back!"

From out of the shadows stepped a tall, lean figure. Black hair fell around a distinctive rugged countenance. The broad shoulders wore no coat, and the shirt, made of white fine linen, was now ragged and dirtied. But even this in no way diminished the aura of the man.

"Good day to you, sir!" said the captain of the *Sea Hawk*, inclining his head.

"Good God! Who the devil are you!" demanded Mr. Jackson.

"I am Captain Landon." Lance grinned.

"Captain? But . . . you . . . you should be in prison!"

"I beg to differ with you on that point." He sighed. "However, I have no time for amenities, sir. I have come for my shipment, and when I have it, I shall trouble you no more."

"Your shipment!" snapped Mr. Jackson. Slyly he had already slipped his hand into his right drawer. "I'll see you hanged first!" With which he attempted a deft movement, aborted however when a foot came up from behind and slammed the drawer hard on his hand. He howled with pain until he was finally allowed to remove his damaged but empty hand. Jackie grinned broadly, well satisfied with himself for this feat, and waved the pistol Mr. Jackson sought in the air. "Lookee 'ere, capt'n! Sneaky little devil, ain't he?"

Six additional men had emerged from the shadows, and Mr. Jackson closed his eyes with defeat. Smiling rogues these were . . . he could only pray they would leave him his life!

In answer to Jackie's comment, the captain gave a brisk command. "Stuff his handkerchief in his mouth and then tie him up with some rope. I want no more out of him!" He watched Jackie and another of his men take his order into firm action before gathering the remaining five men. "Well, lads, we'd best hurry and get our wagon loaded. I want every Brabant sack in this place!"

"But . . . but . . . you cannot!" objected Mr. Jackson before he saw the white linen handkerchief leave his pocket. "Only forty sacks were originally marked for America!" he managed to spout before the linen found its resting place.

"That may be, sir, but things have changed! The additional sacks we take today will go toward making up for the trouble the de Brabants have put me to!" answered the captain, and this time no smile lit either his eyes or his lips.

All was quiet. No more did the air vibrate with thunderous hooves and stampeding humans. No more did the docks feel the cry of frantic havoc. In the galley below the *Liberté's* topdeck, Windy sat and listened to the sudden stillness. She moved in her hard wood chair and stared through the dimness of the scantily lit room at Bunky. He was quiet too, listening as she was, but unlike herself, she could sense that he was frightened.

How could he not be? Here he was, Bunky McGuire, come up from nothing, from the workhouses to a smuggler's sloop, to Heather, to the *Liberté,* to Barbados, and finally, finally to peace! He'd never seen the like of what was happening outside, and he was afraid, afraid that all the happiness he had finally acquired would be torn asunder.

His two mates, grizzled with the humidity and the rum they'd swallowed, had fallen into a slumber. They didn't care. If all was terror and insanity out there . . . well, here they were, safely within.

Windy? She was excited by it all. Something stupendous was happening outside. Yes, it was frightening, yes, it was awesome and terrible . . . but it was real, and she was cowering here like some fearful animal, missing it all! Well, she would not!

"I can't bear it any more, Bunky! I want to go topside!" she breathed at last.

Bunky frowned, scratched his gray-stubbled cheek and sighed. "Do ye?" A musing reminiscing look came to his eyes. "Ye put me in mind of yer mother. Topside, is it? Well then . . . up wit ye!" he grunted as he got to his feet and stretched his limbs.

"I'd like for ye to stay below jest a wee bit, darlin', jest to let me 'ave a look about," he suggested as an afterthought.

"Ho! I am not so poor-spirited, Bunky. Think I'd let you have all the fun? Oh no!" She laughed, excited by the prospect of leaving their closed quarters.

He sighed, displaying resignation, and turned to his men. They were slumbering heavily, one nearly whistling, so profound was the man's intake and output of air. Bunky grinned at the sight and turned to follow his lady up the stairway.

She knew it would be dark at the top. Their open porthole had already informed them that the sun was still hidden by the strangeness of the darkened sky, yet still the blackness felt disconcerting. She stepped into it, gazing upward, never once looking ahead of her, and in so doing she walked directly into the arms of Captain Lance Landon!

Windmera Brabant felt a wave of alarming heat rush through her veins as she realized just who it was that held her arms in a vise grip. She couldn't speak, so great was the rushing of air that took place in her lungs. She was shaken by the encounter, shaken by the nearness of him, by his magnetic vitality and by the unbearable excitement he engendered in her being.

"Captain . . . Captain Landon? How . . .?"

Here she was! Her slender bare arms in his hands. Her full lips pursed in surprise. Her eyes, her damnable eyes . . .! Hell and fire! Here she was, this two-faced, this lying, traitorous wench with her bewitching body and her deceiving eyes! He wanted his measure of justice. He had in these last five days learned to despise Windmera Brabant for her treachery, yet here she was at his mercy and all he could do was want her! Then he saw Bunky at her back, and he hardened against her still further. What a sly young slut was this wench! Was she not here playing with sailors old enough nearly to be her father? Was she not? God, but something inside him wanted to slap her innocent face. How dare she have such a childlike countenance and yet be what she was?

"How indeed, Miss de Brabant!" Then, still gripping one of her bare arms, he pulled her to his side and turned to his crew. "Escort the skipper below and make sure he and his men are comfortable!"

"What the devil?" thundered Bunky, yanking his arm out of Jackie's hold. "What do ye mean by this?"

"I mean to load your vessel with my cargo and sail her to Holetown, where I will leave you and your ship unharmed!"

"Come on then, skipper," urged Jackie, taking Bunky's arm and sticking the horse pistol he had acquired at the warehouse into Bunky's ribs. "We ain't got the time to be jawing.

"And the girl?" demanded Bunky, standing firmly.

Captain Landon's mouth took a hard line. "Never mind Miss de Brabant. She will be with me!"

Windy watched Bunky leave reluctantly and then turned unhappy eyes to the captain. There was something disagreeable about him this evening, and his hold on her arm was beginning to wear. "Captain? Would you mind releasing my arm?" she asked politely, thinking only to bring him to a sense of what he was doing. She never doubted that he would immediately obey her. She looked haughtily at his darkly bearded face, waiting.

"Mind? Indeed . . . I would mind very much!" he answered curtly, then ignored her to throw out a command to his crew.

"Oh! Really? Well, that is just too bad!" she snapped, attempting to pull away her arm. Finding his iron grip had not budged, she shouted at him in something of a temper. "Release me at once, sir!"

"No!" He was glaring down at her now, his blue eyes dark with his welled anger. "Traitorous bitch! Think I don't know 'twas you who got us into Savannah? Think I mean to allow it to pass?"

She felt the color drain from her cheeks, and then a heat deep within started her blood rushing so that she went white and then red in quick succession. So, he did blame her! Just as she blamed herself. It was her first thought. It made her look guilty, for indeed she felt guilty.

"I . . . I had no . . . idea . . . how . . ."

"Spare me!" he snapped, disgusted with her feeble attempt. Her reaction, her expression of guilt, sent his hot temper flying. He had hoped, really hoped, she would instantly deny his allegation. He had hoped that she could prove her innocence, and her answer only served to convince him how futile such a hope had been.

Then suddenly he was yanking her by that same arm, pulling her toward the topdeck captain's cabin. He opened the door, shoved her roughly inside and spit at her in some fury, "We'll settle our differences later, my girl, but don't worry . . . you don't have long to wait!"

He slammed the door shut, locking her within. He had to get the vessel launched. The dark sea was covered with floating volcanic ash. It fell still; however, he could see the quantity would soon diminish. Soon . . . soon the darkness would be swept away. They would have to hurry! He moved into tight action, hurrying the deposit of his shipment on deck for easy transfer to the *Sea Hawk*. He was in a vile temper, and his men exchanged glances of understanding. Just let a woman enter the picture and there was no more reasoning at all!

At last, he saw the sails unfurled. At last, he saw the *Liberté* make for the open Caribbean, and his course was set

for Holetown. He left Jackie in charge, and with some anticipation, some burning he could not explain, he crossed the
deck from aft to waist to bow. He stood at the cabin door a
moment before opening it wide.

She was standing, her long gleaming black hair floating
over her back. She wore her simplest clothing, the white linen
peasant blouse and frilled skirt. Her eyes were bright with
unshed tears, and they glistened in the dark.

He closed the door at his back, and his strides were hard,
long and determined. He had but one purpose, to make her
his. She saw him, and thought him a wondrous man, and
then she saw the expression in his eyes. Hungry they were,
hungry with lust, and she knew a certain sudden fear!

There was no tenderness, no jesting, no twinkling in his
blue orbs. None of what she had seen in the previous weeks
was apparent now. She stepped backward, and this seemed to
harden him further. He reached out for her wrist and yanked
her forward until she was against him. She felt his muscular
sweating body press her against the wall. She heard his mean
accusing whisper. "You fooled me once with those eyes.
Don't think you can do it twice!" His mouth took hers in
wild ferocity, parting her lips to take still further. His hand
found the neckline of her blouse, and in one rough movement he tore the thing from off her body. She gasped and attempted to move out of his hold, but it was useless. His hand
held her arm bent backward, his other hand held and fondled
her breast as he forced her down onto the narrow bed.

Her trepidation quickly took on horror. She had to make
him stop! She couldn't allow this violation of her will. She
would not be taken in this manner . . . no, never against her
will. She kicked wildly, no longer thinking of her nakedness
before him. She had but one aim, to free herself. She cried
and she begged, but he yanked up her skirt and not bothering to tear it away proceeded to her small clothes, pulling
them off in one swift movement. She couldn't believe this was
happening. She couldn't believe he would so harm her. Why?
Why now? He hadn't forced her that first night on the beach
. . . he could have raped her then with no one the wiser, but
he had not! So, why . . . why now? She was crying still as
she saw him undo his breeches with his one free hand. She
managed to get up to a sitting position and with all her
strength tried to pull out of his hold. Roughly, without

181

concern for her well-being, he pushed her backward again, winding her with the might of his thrust.

He wasn't enjoying this part of it, though in truth he was excited by it. He didn't want to compel her with such brutality, but she would fight. And why? Why did she fight him when it was obvious that she was easy with others? He was on fire. Every inch of his body yearned for their joining. He wanted her in a way he had never known possible; all mind, all nerves were in tune to take her. But something was wrong, terribly wrong. The wench seemed truly frightened. How was that possible? No virgin here! He knew of at least one who had had her—the English dandy, Roderick; and perhaps another, the one he held captive below. This particular thought further enjoined his wrath to action. God, she was beautiful. Her skin glowed with its creamy satin texture, and the tuft of black curling hair at the apex of her glorious thighs seemed to demand his exploration. Her breasts taunted him as she wiggled beneath his hold . . . yet, she was crying and her fear was genuine.

He was glowering at her, holding her wrists well above her head, keeping her knees parted with his firm legs, and his mouth was very near her own. "Don't cry, Windmera . . . no, there is no need for tears. I shan't harm you. I want only payment for your treachery. Justice for the five days you made me spend in that filthy hole. I want you, Windmera." His voice was low, and the quality sent her to another time, a time when he had kissed her in tenderness and she had liked it . . . very much. But no, that time was past, and she was here now, disgraced, ill-used!

"You . . . you shame me! You say you mean me no harm . . . yet you have torn the clothes from off my body. You have . . . prepared me for a violation I have never before known. Sir . . . I am maid still." She was humiliated beneath his gaze. Her cheeks blazed with her shame.

He stiffened and gazed hard at her tear-filled eyes. Violet pools of infinite beauty. Innocent in their dread of what was to come. But he had been fooled by her before. "Virgin! You would have me believe you a virgin? What do you take me for . . . some moonling? What is your game? For what purpose do you put me off? Am I so repulsive that you would stoop to any lie to keep me off? It won't work."

She felt the pressure of his hard pulsating manhood at her door; she knew there would be no stopping him now and closed her eyes.

"Then get it over with and have done, but know yourself a rapist, know yourself the vilest of men, for I have told you that I am a maid . . . an *unwilling maid*."

Whether she lied or no, she had ruined the sport. Her words tugged at his heart, brought him to a sense of himself. Yes, she had been a treacherous bitch. Yes, she probably lied now about her maidenhead, and yes, he was probably a fool for not taking his pound of flesh, his moment of revenge, his price for the five days taken out of his life. But he was a Landon! He had always believed himself an honorable man, and if she was a maid still . . . 'twas something he wanted no part of!

"Virgin, you say! I doubt it!" he said contemptuously, but so saying he had already risen from the bed. "However, I find I no longer want you!" He pulled up his breeches, buttoned them, laughed to find that in his haste to have her he had forgotten to remove his boots. He crossed over to the wardrobe closet and removed a faded blue shirt from Bunky's meager collection and tossed it to her. "Put it on . . . we shall be arriving at our destination shortly!"

And so saying he left her, to her quiet astonishment. She sat watching the closed door with something of disbelief. What manner of man was he? He had not believed her, but he had put her aside nevertheless. And what the deuce did he mean, he didn't want her? He was infuriating, was this Lance Landon!

Thirteen

Holetown! Nestled quietly in the west coast, it lay but seven miles north of Bridgetown Harbor. Its major claim to notoriety was the landing in 1605 of the *Olive Blossom,* an English vessel whose men proudly inscribed upon a tree their arrival, constituting the island as a possession of the English crown. The tree no longer stood; in its place a cross had been erected in memory of the men and their moment. But Holetown Harbor held still something more. It held the *Sea Hawk* captive.

The vessel had been guarded well until this afternoon, when the captain of the guards had taken with him two of his men to Bridgetown in order to obtain instructions with regard to the unnatural behavior of the sky. This left the schooner with but two sentries on its deck, both armed. It was a prize, this vessel, and one the men in authority in Barbados meant to claim as their own. After all, they reasoned, were they not about to enter into declared war with the United States?

Captain Landon was well aware that the admiralty of Barbados might be thinking along such lines. He wanted no outcry, no firing of guns, for while he was certain he and his crew would manage to set sail, he wanted no warships at his back. His vessel was made for swiftness and while armed with cannons was still not created for battle. He put up his spyglass and saw, outlined by the torches lit on the *Sea Hawk*'s deck, a man both aft and fore, each carrying a flintlock. He had still the cloak of darkness to aid him in his plan, and he had Windmera! Ah yes, he meant to use her well.

Into the skipper's cabin he strode, and his steps were hard with something of his tension. Windmera's violet eyes found him, and they held defiance as he reached for her. It angered and stirred him all at once, and the touch of her flesh in his hands sent hot rivulets skimming through his veins. He ignored it and pulled her roughly to her feet.

"Listen well, woman, for I'll be warning you just this once!" he said harshly, adding credibility to his words. "You have a man below. I don't know what he means to you, but

184

if you wish to see him alive in the morning, you'll do what you are told!" He glared at the defiance in her eyes and shook her slightly. "Understood?"

"Understood," she said, her voice low, controlled, in spite of her own raging temper. There was Bunky to think of . . . Bunky below, trusting; would this hell-and-brimstone captain really harm him? She couldn't be sure, and she wouldn't take any chances.

"What do you want of me?" she asked quietly, feeling a calm take command of her senses. She wouldn't show this brute how unstable she felt. She wouldn't demean herself!

"Much . . . but we'll let go of that and concentrate now on managing but one thing—to part, my fine lady, and never see one another again!" he hissed.

"That is fine with me!" she snapped, yet felt something inside of her churn. She believed it was but her anger.

"Then you will follow my lead, nothing more, nothing less. Come along!" With which he pulled her out of the cabin and across the waist of the vessel to the small boat.

He turned suddenly and scooped Windmera cradlelike into his arms, holding her close against him. She struggled, and he chuckled spontaneously as he released her. She came down hard onto the wooden bench of the small boat, and she glared at him. There was a light in his eyes that moved her, and she looked away rather than acknowledge its power. She heard him order his men to work the great wood pulleys and felt her boat wobble as it was lowered to the sea. Half surprised that he was not with her, she looked up curiously, only to see him climb over the *Liberté*'s side. She watched, half in sullenness, half in reluctant admiration as he managed the athletic feat and came nimbly into the belly of the boat. Silently he picked up an oar and with a signal to his men began sculling toward the *Sea Hawk*.

He was looking past her, and for no particular reason she studied his face. It was set with determination and something else, something that intrigued further inquiry. He was staring at his schooner! The torches on its deck gave off a warm glow, and they were reflected in his blue eyes. She noted it and suddenly realized the depth of his feeling for his vessel. The realization moved her.

Captain Landon saw his schooner within his grasp and felt charged with excitement. Here she was . . . his vessel . . . his pride. He appraised the *Sea Hawk*'s lines lovingly. It was a schooner of his own design, his own being, for he had poured into her all that he felt was the epitome of his sea. The *Sea Hawk* was for him a living, vital, breathing thing, always enchanting, always disturbing, never satiating! Such was his feeling for his vessel. Different for him than for his father. For his father, for Jules Landon, it had always been a business. Shipbuilding was nothing more than a successful industry, an enterprise undertaken and made profitable. Not so for his son. For Lance, ships and sailing were the essence of his existence, they were the very air he breathed, and watching him now Windmera noted some of this and became even more troubled by the man. The man? She questioned his composition silently. What manner of man was he? Had he not earlier commanded total power over her? Had he not for some obscure reason thrown her aside? He had humiliated her. He had in every way from the moment of their meeting treated her with disrespect! But then a shadow crossed her mind. That was not totally true. There were those days, just before his arrest, when he had shown her tenderness, gentleness and something more. . . .

That was gone. In its place was the present, and the present offered an entirely different man. He was unforgivable. He was a black-hearted scoundrel! Not a man . . . but a devil! She put up her chin and looked away.

Lance was looking at her again. The *Sea Hawk* would soon be his once more. In a few hours Barbados would be at his back and home would be just ahead. And even as he thought of home, still did his mind touch on the woman seated before him! He wanted her still. There was no denying this to himself. No gainsaying the fact that with her so close, within his grasp, so very much at his mercy, he was in a fever pitch to keep his hands off her. She was a woman. Women were made to please men . . . and he knew she was not as indifferent to his touch as she would have him believe. He was far too experienced a lover of women to believe her dispassionate. He had incited her body even if her mind had recoiled, that he knew. Windmera de Brabant! Hell! He would be well pleased never to hear the name spoken to him again!

"Ahoy!" called out Captain Lance Landon some minutes later to the men aboard his schooner. "Ahoy there!"

The taller of the two approached the starboard side and looked down into the brine. They were some distance from the docks, anchored seaward, approachable only by boat, and there was a security in that. He thought of this but fleetingly as he made out two forms in the small boat below. He could see one was a large well-built man and the other was a well-formed lady. It piqued his interest, but he held his flintlock steady all the same. "Ay! Who goes there?"

"Easy now, mate! I've brought ye a lady I have . . . Miss de Brabant by name. She comes with news from Bridgetown! There now . . . give us a hoist up!" rejoined the captain, falling into an easy dialect, disguising his own American accent.

"Miss de Brabant, ye say?" called the sentry. "Hold, then." He turned toward his comrade standing guard at the stern. "Whot then . . . do I lower the ladder?"

"Miss de Brabant eh? She be the owner of that Brabant Plantation . . . ye know, 'twas her sugar that American devil tried to prig! Ay, best be throwing her the rope ladder . . . though I can't fathom whot it is *she* be wanting with us . . . especially with the skies gone crazy!"

The smaller sentry grunted, indicating that he agreed fully with his mate's line of thought, but he searched out and found the rope ladder all the same. He hauled it over the side and called out its readiness.

The captain secured the small boat and called Miss de Brabant to her feet. His tone was not pleasant as he urged her at the ladder. "Up with you . . . mind now, my men have orders to end it for your aging sailor at the first sign of trouble . . . so no tricks!"

She pulled a face at him and then steadied her foot on the first rung of the ladder. She felt his hand at her butt and turned around to grimace at him, but he had a strange grin lighting his features and there was the devil in his eye. It was then it happened! She felt the tug at her skirt. Her violet orbs opened wide with the sudden realization that she was going to fall and why! He had tripped her up purposely. He was causing her to take a plunge . . . the beast! It was her single thought as she met the cold sea below.

She made the required splash. As she struggled in the depths of the sea fighting to swim to the surface, weighed down by the skirt suddenly heavily laden with brine, the captain initiated a commotion above her head. Both sentries were now hanging over the bulwarks trying desperately to understand what was afoot, and the captain called to them in a simulated frenzy, "Lads . . . hurry . . . I can't swim well enough to fetch her meself!"

"Damn!" said the smaller of the guards, but his jacket and

boots were off and were laid aside with his flintlock. Perhaps there would be some reward in this after all. Over he went while his mate looked on. They were too busy to hear or make note of the fact that a small boat was being rowed some distance from their port side.

Lord, but he was quick! No sooner had the young sentry hit the water than the captain was upon him. The splashing went well, and it took but two blows to put the man out. Into the small boat he went just as Windy was able to bring herself to rights in the water. She kept herself afloat as she tried to inhale air, and she heard the captain call out to the sentry waving a torch above, "Your man seems to have hit his head on our boat! Best be giving me a minute to bring him around!"

"I don't like this!" shouted the sentry from the bulwarks. It was just about that moment that he heard something, the dripping of water perhaps on the well-polished deck. He caught a movement abeam and turned swiftly, but not swiftly enough.

Four wet sailors were upon him before he had moment or thought to take action. Yes, they had planned well, Captain Landon and his crew. They had swum the short distance from where they had anchored their small boat and were up and over in a trice. The *Sea Hawk* was, without firing a shot, in the hands of its rightful crew once again.

Windmera was holding now onto the side of the small boat; she saw Jackie wave a torch at the captain not far from her. "All's well, capt'n."

"Unfurl those sails, you lubbers!" the captain laughed. "I'll just see off my cargo and then it's home!" He was in the small boat almost immediately with nary an effort, and he reached over and hauled in his wet human instrument. She glared at him, but had now her breath. "Of all the despicable things . . . you could have warned me . . . I might have drowned!"

"No. You wouldn't have drowned . . . I've seen you swim," he said quietly, his eyes alight with mischief.

She was at a loss for words and sat shivering in her wet clinging garments. The residue of wet ash had soiled her clothes, and she made a feeble attempt to brush at her shoulders and arms. He gazed at her while he rowed, the unconscious guard between them. Her black hair glistened around her well-shaped head, but she was slightly pale from the suddenness of her experience and he could see that she was cold. The knowledge brought a deep frown to his eyes.

The *Liberté* was reached; his remaining three crewmen were on deck awaiting him and set up a cheer as he came into view. He grinned boyishly at them and called out instructions to have the guard, now raising his head, taken on board. A rope was tied around the dizzy man and he was hauled up before the captain saw Windmera before him on the rope ladder, and this time she was allowed to complete her ascent untroubled.

He came up sharply behind her and without warning took her up over his shoulder like so much baggage. She gasped with her rage. Oh! The man was a heathen brute. His men laughed ribaldly to see their captain handle the woman well, and rather than give them further show, she went limp over the captain's shoulder. Very well! She knew enough not to struggle and give them a further spectacle.

He took her to the skipper's cabin once again, put her down, closed the cabin door with the swing of his heel and strode toward the bed. She eyed it and him, wondering if he had had a change of heart, wondering if he meant to have her after all, and she felt a sudden rushing of blood at the fancy. He did not, however, make any attempt to draw her there. Instead he swooshed up the blanket and came toward her.

In spite of the fact that she was trembling with the cold water still running down her flesh, she struggled to ward him off. It angered him, and he forced the blanket around her shoulders, drawing her near.

There was a challenge in her violet eyes, and noting it he laughed suddenly, dispelling the heaviness of his mood. "So frugal with your favors, my love? No, I think not . . . and since we now part . . . shall we not part friends?" Still closer he came, he seemed driven by a white blazing heat. "Ah, moonflower . . . no more shall we meet . . . come, do let us kiss our farewell."

His mouth took hers gently, slowly building up its tempo, slowly igniting her timbers, commanding the essence of her own passionate desires to respond. His kiss wooed, his tongue teased, his hands engendered a sensation she wanted desperately to deny. He was going away. He was going away. This was the last kiss, the last insult, the last touch . . . and for some inexplicable reason the thought caused her some measure of troubled emotion. His strong arm crushed her to him, his wide wonderful hands found the fullness of her breast and cupped it, touched in power, teased with intent.

189

Suddenly she knew her body needed this, and she pressed herself to him for one wanton moment in hedonistic agony. She gave her kiss with an ardor that matched his own.

He felt exultant in that space of time. He wanted to dive full force and take what it appeared she was offering . . . but the time was past. His schooner and his crew awaited. The time was past. It was too late. He felt a sharp and terrible ache, but he set her aside. There was something of bitterness, something of longing in his words. "Moonflower, pretty moonflower . . . it just wasn't meant to be . . . the time has flown . . . and I must be off." He turned his back and went to the door, meaning not to look back, yet he did and their eyes met, but his words belied any feeling. "You will be locked in . . . but you are a resourceful wench . . . no doubt you will manage to escape this cabin, free the guard tied to your mainmast and be reunited with your sailor."

He was gone! She stared at the locked door in the darkness and felt deserted and empty. She heard him in raillery with his men as they took to the small boat. Soon after, she heard the oars scrape with water and wood. He was gone!

Something deep inside of her cried, and her heart ached. Her mind? Her mind called good riddance, but the tears came all the same.

Fourteen

Dimly did the candlelight dance on Jokai's damp shoulders.
Louise scrubbed his back and giggled as she dropped a kiss
upon his neck.

"Ah, Jokai . . . with me at your back, who then is slave?"

He turned around and eyed her ruefully. "Ah, mistress, ask
that question of me by light of day!"

She hugged him, pressing herself against his wet back.
"Jokai, Jokai, I love you, and well do you know how much I
want you free to love me at all times."

He moved in the tub and twisted to face her. "Mayhap I'll
be free one day."

She sat back on her thighs. "What mean you?" It worried
her, the look in his eyes. There was talk of the slaves organiz-
ing under the leadership of Bussa, an African slave. "Never
say you have met with Bussa? Oh, do not say it, Jokai . . . it
is so dangerous!"

"If it displeases you I won't say it," said he quietly.

"Jokai, Jokai . . . you have met with him!" she accused.

"And why not, Louise?" He made a frustrated sound.
"Your assified government, what does it say? Three years
ago, they say, 'No more slave trade!' Eh . . . say they not
that? No, they want no more slaves brought in . . . but do
they free us? No, we be animals to them! Bussa, he says
they're wrong. Bussa, he says—"

"Stop it!" She put her hands over her ears. "I won't listen
to you!"

He frowned. "Why? Why do you not want to hear me?"

"Because you will break your heart and in the end mine as
well! We, all of us at Brabant, want an end to slavery, but
Bussa preaches insurrection, rebellion! I have seen what
rebellion does and want no more, no more! Do not go to
him, Jokai . . . he will end in getting his people murdered!"

He grunted angrily. "Whot . . . am I an auntie-man to be
led by my woman?"

"No, you are no *mamapoule, mon cher* . . . but still would
you so have me worry?" she coaxed.

He got up from the sudsy water and stood before her dripping as he reached over for a cloth and began drying himself.

"No more talk of Bussa. We talk now of Windmera." He stepped out of the bath and walked across to his favorite easy chair and stretched himself out. He smiled wide, pleased with the sensation he was experiencing. He was a man in this room and this plump lovely woman was his. He motioned to her, and she came willingly to sit by his feet and nuzzle his knee. He sighed. "I's worrit about Missy."

"Are you?" she was puzzled and looked up at his face. "But why?"

"She is not herself these days. Ever since the ash storm she is . . . eh now, jest not the same . . . is she, Louise?"

"Oh, I don't know . . . she is more quiet . . . but well pleased. That young Englishman, Roderick . . . he means to wed her."

"Don't like him," said Jokai uncompromisingly.

"But why?" He was forever surprising her with his knowledge of the world. She had her own doubts with regard to Roderick, but nothing she could pinpoint.

"Don't know." He grinned then and touched her chin. "I got ye a poesy, woman . . . want I should say it?"

She smiled to herself. It was sweet, so very sweet, this moment. She recalled how they had strained over his letters so many years ago, how determined he had been to read and write well. Spelling his name was not good enough for Jokai . . . he would read Shakespeare himself, he had said . . . and now, here he was about to give her his verse. How she adored him. "But of course, *mon cher.*" She folded her hands in her lap and waited.

He puffed up in self-consequence and then grinned wide as he began,

> "O ain't I the cheese, ain't I the cheese,
>   Out by the Serpentine under the trees
>   As I stroll in the park with my pretty Louise?"

No Shakespeare he, but his meaning had not been lost on her.

"Oh, Jokai, my beloved, would that I could promise you that one day we would stroll together in the park . . . under the trees . . ."

The sun's rays enveloped Windmera. She felt the heat of the warm blanket beneath her and a soft breeze touch her cheeks. She was comfortable, rested and secure in her island paradise. Their picnic had been enjoyable, his company desirable. His shadow fluttered her lashes open, and her violet eyes were dark as she took in Roderick's features. He stood above her, looking down on her stretched-out form, and there was such a look in his bright eyes. She knew what was coming, anticipated it with some excitement if not longing. She waited.

He came down beside her onto his hip, his arm slightly touching her midriff as he propped himself up by one hand and gazed hard at her. But he said nothing. There was too much churning within him. It was now more than eight weeks since the day the American had stolen his shipment of sugar and sailed away. He had made good time of the American's absence, for suddenly Windmera had turned to him, but still she held back.

Windmera noted the troubled crease on his forehead and sat up. She touched his arm with concern. "Rod . . . what is it? What is wrong?"

"Don't you know?" he asked, and his tone indicated that he believed she did.

"No . . . no . . . I don't."

He came closer and his hand took her chin. "My God! Can it be that you still do not understand? Windmera . . . I want you. With all my being I want you."

She blushed hotly. His advances had increased each day; his demands on her were few, but this one she had been unable to supply. He wanted to marry her and she could not answer him either way! He wanted her for bride and she was unsure what she wanted! There was a part of her that wanted him, wanted the life he offered her. He was charming, amusing, sophisticated. She enjoyed his flirtation, welcomed his courting and was certainly not repelled by his touch. In fact, many times she felt herself aroused by him in many ways. But . . . marriage?

"I . . . I . . . don't know how to answer you yet," she stammered, worried lest she hurt him, worried lest he give up on her.

Exasperated, he put his hand through his curly auburn locks and looked away momentarily. There was no one about here on the Bathsheba Coast. They were alone with the cliffs, the sea pounded the reefs below, and they had the music of hummingbirds to accompany his romancing. He had tried everything except physical seduction. This because at first she had warded him off and he had been careful not to offend,

193

but now, now he felt the time had come. He turned back his glance to her face, allowed it purposefully, slowly, to follow the line of her throat to the full swells of her breast above the pretty embroidered white-on-white muslin gown she wore. Further went his gaze to the small waist, and then because he knew she was blushing furiously, back to her eyes again.

"Windmera . . ." he said softly, coming forward, taking her into his embrace, folding her tightly to him as his mouth discovered her sweet lips. His kiss was gentle, urging, inviting her to respond, and she did. Her arms went around him, and as she felt his hand stray from her back to her waist, she returned his kiss furiously. Again his hand began to stray, finding the full jutting breast and fondling it in spite of the cloth keeping her flesh from him. He couldn't bear it; he pulled away at the low bodice just enough to allow him to plunge in his hand and take up her luscious breast, find the nipple and taunt her passion. Windy's eyes were shut tight. She was incited by his touch and yet she thought of another man's hands, another man's kiss, another man's twinkling blue eyes. Oh God! What was she doing? How could she let Roderick touch her and yet think of Lance Landon? In disgust with herself she pulled away roughly.

"What is it, Windmera?" Roderick was puzzled, frowning.

To reassure him, to dispel the sudden gravity that hung over them, she touched his hand. "Naught, Rod . . . it is just that you . . . take too much . . . too soon."

His brow went up. "You think me not in earnest? Windy . . . what exactly are you afraid of?"

"I? Afraid? No, I am not. It is just that I have certain notions . . ."

"Of propriety?" he ejaculated, his tone scoffing the word. "Then why did you come up here with me alone? 'Tis more than two hours' drive from Brabant." He took up her shoulders. "You came to be with me! You want me to make love to you! Why won't you admit it and have done?"

She held him at bay, and her chin was up. He had not hit the right chord. "I came to picnic with you because the Bathsheba Coast is majestic . . . because I enjoy your company . . . because I trust you, Roderick! As to the rest . . . I don't know."

She could hear her mother's voice, see her mother's face as she turned and looked at the whitecaps so far below. "Windy!" It was not Roderick's voice but her mother's. "Windy, darling . . . I have not long and there is something I would have you promise." She had promised to do whatever it was her mother wanted, for Heather had been dying.

"Windy . . . you must never give yourself to a man unless he loves you! First you must love him . . . and he you . . . and then marriage. One does not necessarily go with the other, but I wish for you they would. I want no loveless marriage, no marriageless love . . . not for you."

"Rest, Mama . . ." Windy had cried to see her mother distressed. She was only fourteen, she couldn't understand fully, she never had known what her mother had suffered, and it was strange to hear such words.

Roderick recalled her to the present. "Windmera . . . please, look at me . . . forgive me?"

"What? Oh . . . of course, Rod." She was smiling, touching his lips with gentle fingers.

He took up her hand and fervently placed his kisses upon them. "Windy . . . have I not been patient? Have I not tried to wait out your indecision? But I see you no closer to deciding today than you were yesterday . . . and I must have an answer!"

"Not today, Rod."

He sighed, but stilled her words with his fingers. "My lovely girl . . . there are such things I would teach you in our marriage bed . . . such things I would teach you now."

She got to her feet and picked up the picnic basket. "Come . . . if we are to obey my aunt's wishes and arrive at Brayward's for tea, we must hurry!"

He looked up at her. "Ah, I have trespassed beyond what you like. So be it, but there is tomorrow . . . and be it known, my Windmera, I shall teach you to want me!"

She smiled benevolently. "I have no doubt that you will *try*." With which she threw him a challenging glance and ran off toward their open curricle. She wondered if he would pick up the tease, take up the chase.

He did not. He bent and picked up, instead, the blanket, smiling to himself, for he was Roderick of Ravensbury, self-assured and determined to one end. He would have her. Thus he followed leisurely.

Again did Windy's mind wander off. Her fancy lit by a pair of twinkling blue eyes. How would he have reacted? Would he have taken up the challenge . . . understood the banter? Yes, Lance Landon would have had her now securely in his arms, hang the blanket and all else. Lance Landon would have. But the American was out of her life . . . and good riddance! But still there was a nagging, and once more she thought of the war.

The war! They had received word in Barbados in the last week of June that war between the United States and Great Britain had been officially declared. It was now the middle of July. Was Lance Landon fighting on the high seas? Was he safe? Devil fly away with his memory! Why should it matter if he was alive or dead? Maimed or whole? The day of the volcanic dust, the May Dust, was in the past. Those moments were gone, never to return.

"Windmera . . ." It was Roderick as he picked up the reins of their team. "Windmera . . . whatever are you thinking of?"

"Naught," she said resolutely, putting away the image of moments spent, returning to her present. "Ah, but the day drenches us in far too much heat! Lud, but I am hot . . . are you not?"

He looked at her meaningfully. "Yes, my love, very hot indeed."

Fifteen

"*They should be here, Brayward! Whatever is keeping them?*" fluttered Louise as she moved restlessly about the Braywards' richly furnished parlor.

Lord Brayward put down his glass of sherry. He sighed. For his part he gladly would have dispensed with what was about to follow, but Louise had insisted. He moved toward her and caught up her hands. "Now, now, my dear . . . there is no need for you to get into a pucker. They will be here in good time." He kissed her fingers and looked directly into her warm eyes. Such eyes. It seemed no matter how much he looked he couldn't be satiated. There was such promise of passion. "Louise . . . Louise . . . how I wish we had more time to be alone before their arrival." There was meaning in his tone.

She looked away, but not from shyness. "We shall have so many hours together . . . and this, this is so important, especially, Brayward, because of the manner in which—"

"Hallo! Are we very late?" Roderick smiled easily as he stepped aside to allow Windmera to precede him. It was already some minutes past four, and he knew well enough that his host had pointedly requested him to return with Windmera precisely at four. He had thought it odd at the time, since it was also his host who'd suggested he take Windmera all the way to the Bathsheba Coast.

"It doesn't matter," said Louise, going forward to envelop her niece affectionately.

Windmera smiled, but she was startled by the force of her aunt's bearhug. She tilted her head to have a better look at Louise's face and found there enough to bring a crease to her brow.

"Come, *ma petite* . . . come . . . sit," said Louise, directing Windmera to an elegantly upholstered lady's chair. She remained standing while Windy obeyed.

"Ah . . . good . . . now I . . . oh, *mais non*, Brayward," said Louise, suddenly reaching for Brayward's hand, "I cannot! You must!"

He chuckled and kissed Louise's trembling fingers before attempting to enlighten his audience. "Indeed we have very exciting news. Windmera . . . Roderick . . ." He smiled proudly at the woman at his side. "Lady Brayward!"

Windy closed her eyes. No! It couldn't be . . . Louise married to this pompous . . . oh, God! Now it all made sense. Louise's insistence that she go on a picnic with Roderick in spite of the fact that Louise had no great love for Roderick. It all fit. In secret, in haste, Louise had committed the remainder of her life. And what of Jokai? How had he taken it?

Roderick had already gone forward to shake Brayward's hand vigorously and offer his felicitations, but Windy could not move, could not speak. It seemed as though she felt all around was but a haze.

Louise was looking anxious. She bent to her knees and took up her niece's hands. "*Ma petite . . . ma belle . . .* Windmera . . . look at me!"

Windy brought her violet eyes to her aunt's countenance. They were dark with her sense of foreboding, her pity. "Oh, Tante Louise . . . dearest aunt . . . what have you done?" It was whispered, barely audible, but with power enough to bring the tears to Louise's eyes.

"*Non, non . . .* only wish me well."

"I do," said Windy. "I could not wish you anything else . . . but I am feeling fatigued from the heat of the day." She turned to Roderick and managed a smile. "What say you, Rod? Shall we leave the newlyweds?"

"An excellent notion!" agreed Rod.

Windmera made some brief attempt to soften the abruptness of her parting, but it was difficult indeed, for all her instincts pounded against this marriage. At the door of the parlor, Windy hesitated, turning to find Lord Brayward putting his arm around his wife. It was wrong! All wrong! It screamed at her from within, but she was helpless to do anything. Roderick took up her arm, and she allowed him to guide her steps, for indeed, her vision was blurred. Her eyes saw not a happy couple, a lovely union, for instead she saw images of Jokai. What, oh what, was Jokai suffering now?

The answer was more than mere words can describe, and even as Roderick drove Windmera to Brabant, Jokai had arrived at Brayward. Yes, he came. He came to see with his own eyes betrayal most foul. He came to accuse. He came with some slight hope, for over and over again he saw her face and knew she was not capable of such treachery.

Was it only an hour ago that he had worked with a smile on his face? Was it only an hour ago that the earth did not tremble beneath his leathery feet? What must he be doing when he first heard the word? Smiling! Smiling like a bovine clown! Working with naught to trouble him! He felt the anguish in his throat exploding, and he screamed as he ran. Rage and hurt mingled as one and rent the air with their piteous sound.

A wedding! It was the whispered word that black maids carried to young stable boys. Brayward had called a minister to his home to marry him and a woman . . . but not just any woman! No, Brayward had taken to him Mistress Louise Davenant!

His smile had faded as the words took hold. His head seemed to twitch as the words filtered through his body to his heart. He made a wild grab for the young cackling maid and he shook her.

"Speak, woman! What are you saying? Not mistress . . . not she to Brayward?"

"Leave go, big'un. Mistress, she done took her a husband. Best forget her and look another way." She was inviting him with her eyes, with the sway of her body.

Jokai saw not her wiles. Something inside of him was splitting open. He clutched at his belly as though to prohibit further rifting, but still did it gorge out a path shattering the muscles of his diaphragm from throat to groin. He felt warm blood come gushing out, filling his gut, choking, clogging the canal of his throat. He doubled over in his agony, and to escape the pain he began to run. And he ran and ran, needing to escape the merciless anguish, but it followed. And then Brayward House stood before him.

Here was the answer! Here would be Louise! Hadn't she always soothed the miseries of the day away for him? She would do so now! She would give him an answer that would banish his hurt! He must find Louise! Oh, thought he as he looked through one window and then another, slinking through the bushes, hiding lest he be found before he find her . . . oh, the white man's God was cruel!

With Windmera's sudden departure, Louise felt depleted. She felt a cold barrenness ooze its way into her mind. She could hardly speak to Brayward and was thankful when his man of business called him into the study to attend to some minor estate matter. Hastily Louise escaped the suffocating parlor and made her way to the garden room. Among its exotic blooms her fantasy softly took hold. Jokai. She could see his face everywhere she went. His adoring eyes, his innocence of soul. The fragrance of passionflowers recalled her to easier times, and she closed her eyes, hoping to capture the moment of a memory. But then reality pushed its way.

Unthinkable! Cruel woman! Voices shouted their tauntings. You have left Jokai to strangers! You have left him to hear of your marriage from strangers! He will have no one to comfort him. Rationalizations came to her rescue. He was a man. Men did not love as strongly, as deeply, as women. He would get over this. He would take to himself a pretty black woman and forget her.

A breeze cooled her tear-stained cheek and she opened her eyes to the open glass door, already knowing what her sight would bring her. Jokai stood, his black mountainous body glistening with his sweat, his beautiful face distorted with his pain, and his eyes, they shed no tears and yet still they cried enough to wound her ears.

"Jokai . . ." It was a hushed sound, and she moved toward him. She could see he was hurting. She could see it, and the knowledge drove a wedge into her heart.

"They say . . . Louise . . . they say . . ." attempted Jokai, going forward, looking askance, his eyes begging for hope and instead finding in hers the truth, "Oh no . . . say to me . . . no, Jokai . . . I not do it! Say to me . . ." He had her shoulders in his firm grasp, his fingers were cutting through her sheer muslin gown, but she did not feel the pressure. There was an anguish in her heart overriding all physical realities.

"Jokai . . . try . . . try to understand . . ."

"*Understand?*" He shook her fiercely. "Understand what? you came to me in my bondage! You came . . . you gave me love . . . taught me love. You brought to Jokai learning . . . taught Jokai to know things a black man should not know in a white man's world. Now, you say, Jokai . . . no more! You set me free, Louise . . . and now I am slave again. You are my woman!" A large tear rolled down his cheek as he grabbed hold of her hair and touched her forehead, "In thought . . . mine!" He touched her full breasts voraciously. "Yes, Jokai's woman . . . in body! Jokai's woman in soul! Say it so, Louise."

"Yes, beloved . . . I am your woman. I shall always be

your woman. You are right. All thought is for you. But Jokai
. . . the world deems us apart . . ."

"No! It is not the world that parts us . . . but *you,* Louise!
I have carried weights, Louise . . . all your people would
have me carry . . . so I have done . . . to survive! Then . . .
then . . . when survival seemed no more to me worth the
trouble . . . you came and made it sweet. You gave me my
manhood . . . now you would tear it away? No! I will bear
no more! Jokai will take no more!"

He moved away from her. He was striding hard toward the
door. Louise became frightened, not for herself but for him.
She was frightened for Jokai, for if Brayward were to find
him here thusly, he could have him whipped . . . or worse!
She reached out to hold him back, but he was in a rage and
flung her roughly away. She fell backward, crashing into a
round marble-topped table. It tilted, throwing her to the floor,
and before she knew what had happened she felt the weight
of the marble upon her hips. She cried out in pain, and it
brought him to her at once.

He lifted the marble off and jerked her into his arms.
"Louise, my Louise . . ." His hands were all over her, his
kisses wild. She attempted to reason with him. She only knew
she had to get him out of the house before Brayward came
down upon them.

"Jokai . . . go home. I will come to you in the morning."

He set her from him. "No, Louise. No dog to go with my
tail between my legs. I will go . . . when you go with me!"
With which he lifted her in his arms and began crossing the
room to the garden doors.

"Hold there, boy!" It was Brayward. Not only had he
heard the crash of the falling table, but he had had a visit
from one of the servants who had seen Jokai go into the
garden room. Brayward had taken time out only to arm himself with his pistol. He held it now well aimed.

Jokai turned to face his lordship. He saw the gun, and because he would not hide behind his woman's skirts, he allowed her to slide to her feet, whereupon he set her behind
him.

She saw Brayward's gun and screamed. "Brayward . . .
there is no need for your pistol. Put it away!"

"As soon as this Brabant slave leaves us! Tell him, Louise
. . . *tell him we want none of him here!*"

Louise pulled on Jokai's arm. "Go now . . . please,
Jokai . . ."

He looked down at her. "Deny him . . . come with me . . . tell him there is no marriage . . . that you belong not to him!"

Tears glistened in her eyes, spilled over and left their mark upon her cheeks. "I cannot! I am Lady Brayward, and you, Jokai, have no business here!"

He looked at her with disbelief. Hurt welled in the depths of his being and petrified there. Upon its mounds rose anger, and it charged from his constricted gullet, tearing through the air. Such was the agony of his scream as his hands clamped around his Louise's throat.

Yes, in that moment, swiftly came a chapter's end. Brayward needed no further prodding to loose his temper. He saw a black slave daring to lay filthy hands on his wife. He saw a black slave even in rage far more intimate with Louise than he had ever been, ever would be. Deafening was the report of his gun, deadly its purpose. Jokai received the bullet in his back, though it lodged itself well near his heart. He gasped and stared at Louise with the horror of this final parting, and he crumpled to his knees. Louise grabbed for him, went down with him, and her cries were soul-shattering as she realized her Jokai was dying.

He heard her grief through his pain. He said nothing, but in his last moment Jokai raised his hand to her lips. And then did a black slave die. Louise gave over to her guilt, to her sorrow, and there was not a one in the house that did not hear her cry. She wailed as though demented. French words of passion and grief intermingled and called for her own destruction.

Brayward was flushed red, stunned by her behavior, ashamed, angered, and he sought to end her foolishness by wrenching her away from the black man's body. *"Louise!"*

She turned on him, her teeth clenched, her eyes bright as any attacking tigress protecting her brood. "Don't touch me! Do you hear? Murderer! You shall not touch either of us!" It was her stand. It eased her heart not at all, for it came too late. Too late for Jokai, and indeed, too late for herself.

Sixteen

Buffalo, New York

The windows of Jim Foster's colonial home were thrown open to let some of the evening breeze conquer the heat of the summer night. Wax candles burned in pewter branches and in sconces attractively hung on the papered walls. The parlor was a favorite room to Isabelle and Jim Foster, but it was presently occupied by three males. They sat about near the fireplace, though it held only unlit logs at this time of year. Isabelle had not joined them, for she was abovestairs in the canopied high four-poster bed she shared with her husband. She was holding her newborn babe in her arms.

"Oh, you are a martinet, you terrible creature," She pouted at her maid. "Leave him with me . . . just awhile longer . . ."

Her maid pursed her lips. She had been taking care of Isabelle since long before her marriage and she knew well how to handle her.

"No, my love. You need your rest, as does this little fellow." She pried the fair-haired infant from his mother and saw him comfortable in the cradle that had been his father's before turning to tuck in her mistress. "Sleep now, Mrs. Foster, you'll feel better for it."

Izzy Foster sighed contentedly and turned on her side, whereupon she fell blissfully, totally, into slumber. Belowstairs, her men were very much awake.

The talk in the parlor was jovial as well as cockish, each man in his turn taking whatever credit he could think up as his alone for the beauty of the husky male child peacefully sleeping upstairs.

"But you cannot deny, you young scalawag, that the lad has my ears!" put in Jules Landon, poking his son-in-law with his pipe.

"I shouldn't dream of denying any such thing." Jim chuckled. He stretched back with a sigh and ran his hand through his fair thick curls. Izzy had had a long hard labor, and he had suffered right along with her. Birthing a child had always been a wondrous joyous thing, one of the best parts

203

about being a doctor, but bringing into the world his own son! It had been an all too euphoric, a kingly experience. And then to make it all perfect for Izzy, in pops her father and brother! Their timing couldn't have been more perfect, for they had entered his comfortable home just as he had been slapping his new son's rump.

They all sipped their brandy in companionable silence. Jules Landon broke the pleasant stillness. "Look here, Jim . . . with the baby here now . . . well, it is time to think of bringing Izzy to Mystic!"

Jim frowned and chose his words carefully. He was a good man, and he knew that Jules was lonely for his daughter, but he had his father's practice to continue there in Buffalo. He couldn't just pull up stakes because Jules was lonely. "I understand how you feel, sir . . . but it is impossible at this time."

"Damnation, son!" said Jules, getting to his feet. "Don't think it's because of me! Look here, Jim. I want my daughter, my grandson, I want them near, but that is not why I am bringing up the issue at this time!"

Jim's frown deepened. "Then . . . why?"

Jules made a sound that clearly indicated his impatience. "Where have you been . . . in the clouds? There is a war on!"

Jim flushed. "Of course there is . . . but what has that to do with moving to Mystic?"

Jules glanced at his son for help. He was not surprised to see a look of detachment about Lance. Something had happened to him in Barbados, something more horrible than his imprisonment, but what it was he could not guess. He only knew that Lance was troubled, moody and ill-tempered these days . . . that is, when he could be brought into a conversation. Still, he enlisted Lance's help.

"Speak to him, Lance! You went to school together. You must know how to get to him!"

Lance smiled. "Ah . . . but he went on to medicine at Harvard, Father, so there is never any knowing what he will say or do!"

"Lance!" insisted his father.

Captain Landon sighed. In truth he did hope that Jim would bring Izzy to Mystic. It would mean his sister would be relatively safe and his father would have something to occupy his thoughts, for he meant to be taking to the seas again, and soon. He hadn't yet told his father, but his recent trip to New York had been to see Commodore Rodgers. He had been commissioned to sail the Atlantic on a special mission.

"I believe what father is trying to make you aware of is your proximity to the British forces. It is not desirable, Jim."

"British forces!" he said derisively. "Why, everyone knows that Wellington keeps the best officers in the Peninsular to fight the French. What the Canadian market gets is the rubbish of every department. Lord, Lance . . . you must admit they are wretchedly commanded."

"Yes, and next you will spout off what they have all been saying all the way down the coast. Canada will be ours because its armies number but six thousand, and they are not only drunken fools but spread out to boot! It won't fadge, Jim," said Jules hotly. "For in spite of all that, they have Major General Brock! He is not only energetic and ambitious, but he has the wit to carry him through this war victorious. Not only does he have control of the waters, but he is fighting an inept American army!"

"Jules!" said his son-in-law in shocked accents.

Lance smiled ruefully. "Jim, my father is in part quite right. We have gone about this thing all wrong. Detroit is in danger of going to the British. And why? Simply because we allowed the British to gain control of the Great Lakes and the St. Lawrence. Our forces have to take wilderness trails to get their supplies through, while the British have the run of all the water routes! Our only chance is on the Atlantic." He turned to his father. "Which brings me to the subject I have been meaning to discuss with you, Father."

"Eh?" said Jules, diverted from his purpose, for there was that in his son's tone that he recognized. Egad, he thought, looking deep at him. Lance was so much his mother. Irene had suffered much in Ireland, and the wariness had ever remained in the recesses of her blue eyes. Lance had the same eyes, the same will, and even his tone was more often than not styled after his mother's. He sighed at her memory. Izzy never had the power to evoke so strongly her mother's memory, she was so much more himself.

"I went to New York specifically to see Rodgers . . . I know, I know you thought I went after that sale, and I did, but it was not the main reason I went there. Father, I have been commissioned by the American Admiralty. My men and I leave late in August on a special mission. We will be using the *Sea Hawk*."

"What?" cried Jules. "Are you mad? You are my only son . . . my heir! I won't allow it. Lance, Lance . . . wasn't it enough . . . what you went through in Barbados . . . didn't that teach you that they are not playing games any more, Lance?"

"Dad," he said affectionately, quietly, "do you really believe that I have promised my help to my government because I wish to engage in . . . games?"

"Lance," said Jim tentatively in the short silence that followed, "your father is right. You are his heir . . . you owe—"

"I owe him everything! My life, though, is still my own, and I don't intend to give it to the British. Look here . . . I am an excellent sailor, and you don't for a moment think I am going to engage in actual combat? My *Sea Hawk* would never stand a chance. The British are devastating the American market with their seizure of our ships. Our privateers are fighting back by doing the same. My vessel is not outfitted for privateering . . . but I can help the cause by reconnaissance. I know the seas well . . . I know the West Indies and what routes the British are fond of taking. Yes, we should do very well."

Jules moved away from both young men. There was no arguing with either of them. Each needed to carve his own path in the world, just as he had done. He kept silent, but a part of him was struggling beneath the strain. Lance moved behind him and put a hand on his shoulder. "Och now, sir," he said with an Irish brogue, "you don't mean you have no faith in yer only son now?"

Jules turned to his son and smiled in spite of his concern. "Faith! You will give them Hell, and well I know it!"

At Brabant, Windmera's entire world was disintegrating before her eyes, and she was helpless to prevent the process. The massive decay breaking down her walls had started with Louise and Jokai, and had continued on, for now she was losing Brabant as well.

She sat staring at the ocean breaking viciously against the reef. Here approach from the sea was impossible . . . how she wished she had the same protective reef on land. Oh, God . . . how had it all happened? She closed her eyes, for it was still all too vivid, still all too close. Jokai!

She and Roderick had arrived at Brabant that fateful afternoon only to discover that Jokai had heard about Louise's marriage and had run off. There was time. He'd been gone only some fifteen minutes. He was on foot. They would take horses, fresh horses! How wonderful Roderick had been. He didn't waste precious time making objections, asking questions. No, he had simply followed her lead, left the curricle and saddled a Brabant gelding as she saddled her roan.

Brayward House was in sight, but all the while Windmera had a sense of doom and still she prayed. Let everything be all right. Let me be in time to take Jokai away unharmed. Poor Jokai.

She knew Jokai had run not to injure Lord Brayward but to confront Louise. She knew it in her heart, and she knew too he would be in danger. He was a slave, he could be severely punished, but even so she never dreamed that more than that could occur. She imagined him beaten, she imagined scandal, but never his death.

She was too late. He lay among the exotic blooms, Louise bent sobbing over him. Louise stained with her black lover's blood. Lord Brayward was not there. He had withdrawn to another part of the house, and Windmera didn't care to find him.

How frightening that scene had been, how shattering. Her youth, her ideals, had not prepared her for such violence, and still she was strong. It was the fighter in her. She turned first to Roderick.

"Go and find Brayward . . . calm him if you can. We must protect my aunt . . . she will be ruined if this gets out to the tattle-mongers!"

Roderick squeezed her hand. "I cannot leave you . . . with this . . ."

"You can and you must. I have to get her away from this room."

He frowned but left her, and Windy turned back to her aunt. She took a long heavy breath of air, for her head felt strangely light; she felt oddly dizzy and her knees felt like so much jelly. Faint? No, no . . . what a miserable thing to do. Faint, indeed. She bucked herself up and went to her aunt, touching her in an attempt to get her attention.

Louise looked up sharply, ready to do battle lest anyone try to pry her from Jokai, and then she saw Windmera for the first time. Windy's face came in hazy, but she could see the violet eyes full with their pity. "They killed him . . . *I* killed him . . ."

207

"Shhh, Tante, no, don't talk like that. Come, come with me," said Windy assuagingly, taking her aunt's arm firmly.

"No. They will take him away . . . bury him where he does not belong . . ."

"No, they shall not do that. I will see to it that Jokai is taken to Brabant. I will give orders that he be cleaned and dressed in a fine suit and buried beside my father and mother in the family plot."

Louise looked up again, her eyes bright. "You . . . you will do that? No, they won't let you."

"They cannot stop me, beloved. It is Brabant land."

"They will say it is illegal to bury a slave in a white man's plot . . . they—"

"They can do naught. Believe me. Trust me, darling . . . I will see to him." She helped her aunt rise up, "Now come, come . . . you must come away from here."

Louise allowed her niece to lead her upstairs. She allowed Windmera to remove the bloodstained clothing from her. She sat quietly in shock as Windy put a washcloth to her face and neck, as a nightdress was slipped over her head. She said nothing as Windy spoke soothingly, leading her to the large satin-covered bed.

Windy was frightened. Her aunt was suffering the trauma of a guilt too large for such a woman to bear. She needed sleep. She sat on the bed with her a few moments and waited for Louise to close her eyes. After a time, certain that Louise had drifted off, she gingerly left the room. She had to see to Jokai. She met Roderick on the stairs.

"I have sent for the doctor. I am told he is not far off, seeing to patients nearby, so he should be here soon, darling," said Rod, taking her hand. "How is she?"

"I . . . I don't know. Oh, Rod . . . we have so much to do. Jokai . . . he must be taken quickly to Brabant . . . before Brayward gets it into his head to do something awful."

Roderick snorted derisively. "Brayward, my dear, is in his cups. He won't be up to anything for some time. I will have a carriage prepared."

"Yes, yes . . . and I will get some of the servants to—"

"No! You will go to the sitting room. I have asked that tea be brought to you there. I will see to everything," said Roderick firmly.

"But—"

"Windmera . . . please do as I ask. Allow me to help in this regard."

He was so strong, so good. She sighed. "Thank you, Rod . . . but should I perhaps go and sit with my aunt?"

"No. You might disturb her. She probably needs to be alone. Now do as I say. I will join you as soon as possible." He pushed her toward the sitting room down the hall.

Louise heard the door creak shut and sat bolt upright. She had fooled Windmera. Good. She knew what she had to do. Windy had nearly provided the answer, though she thought she knew the moment she held Jokai's dead body in her arms. She would join him. But Windy, her darling niece, had made it all perfect. Now, now she would know at least that she and Jokai would be near one another in death. They would be buried side by side!

She went to her nightstand. Ah, good, her laudanum, just as she had instructed her maid, her things all in place, even her china mug. She emptied the jar into the mug, poured the fresh water from the pitcher and brought it to her lips. In strength its odor was repugnant. She sipped it. Oh, God . . . how can I get all this down? I must! With some determination she downed it, choking as she came up for air. Vile! Oh, Jokai . . . forgive me. Let there be a merciful God . . let Him bring Jokai and me together in death . . . let us at last be one! She lay down, a hopeful smile upon her lips.

The time dragged for Windy alone, and then Roderick was there. She had never realized how strong he was. Not once had he questioned her about this affair. He just saw what needed to be done and did it. She went to him and put her arms around his waist, and in silence did he hold her. She needed to be held. She needed to get the sight of her aunt bending over Jokai's dead body out of her mind. She had to get the sound of her aunt's sobs out of her senses. She just wanted to stand there holding someone stronger than herself and be held.

He stroked her black silk curls. The feel of her against him, needing him, moved him to admit an emotion that frightened him. She was his! She must be his. He would do anything to keep her, have her. She was strong, as strong as Godwin's daughter would be.

A knock sounded at the door, and the doctor's arrival was announced. "Good," said Roderick, "Show him upstairs to Lady Brayward's chamber."

"No . . . I shall go with him," said Windy, going forward.

"Are you well enough, darling?"

She smiled at his concern, "Yes, yes, quite well enough . . . thanks to you."

Windy shuddered as she remembered what had happened next. It was like a nightmare. The memory haunted her wickedly. It repeated itself over and over again, making her relive those moments. How quietly she had spoken with the doctor, making some nonsensical excuse for her aunt's state as they entered her chamber. How still, how lovely her aunt looked . . . how strangely blissful. The doctor frowned immediately and sniffed the air. "Your aunt is not in the habit of taking opium, is she, my dear?"

"Certainly not!" Windy spied the laudanum bottle on the nightstand. Her delicate brow went up. Evidently Louise had not been asleep as she had thought when she had left her. She must have taken a dose . . . just to get to sleep. "But . . . she does take a drop of laudanum now and then . . just to help her sleep."

"Tch, tch, very bad," said the doctor. "Not a good idea to depend on that stuff. Don't approve of it, myself. It's derived from opium, you know . . . habit-forming! Now, let's see."

He approached Louise and touched her lightly. "Lady Brayward?" he stared at her a moment. She was in a strange state . . . her smile . . .? And then a dawning hit him. "Dear God!" He turned from her to the dark bottle and held it up to the candlelight. It was empty! He picked up the china mug and sniffed it, recoiling from the pungent aroma. He scanned the nightstand, hoping it had merely spilled, but only specks of the dark-red powder were evident. Hastily he took up her wrist, dropped it. It fell limp, lifeless.

"What is it? What is wrong?" cried Windy in some distress.

He didn't bother to answer but took out his stethoscope quickly and applied it to Louise's heart. Nothing. Still he waited . . . but there was nothing. The woman was not yet cold, but she was quite dead. He straightened and looked sadly at Windmera. Shaking his head, he made his attempt. He so hated this part of doctoring. Especially when such concerned, such caring eyes asked, begged him to make all well . . . and he couldn't.

He hated having to say, "I am sorry, Miss de Brabant."

"Sorry? What do you mean?" Windy was frightened beyond thinking. She pushed past him. She took up her aunt's limp heavy shoulders.

"Tante . . . wake up. Tante Louise . . . wake up. Speak to me! Don't . . . please don't leave me . . . Tante . . . please . . ."

The doctor took hold of Windmera's arm, but she screamed and shrugged him off. "Tante Louise! Tante Louise! Wake up . . . wake up wake up wake up!"

The doctor rushed to the door and found Roderick already coming down the hall toward him. He was relieved. Perhaps this young man might be able to calm her. It was tragic, so tragic. "Her aunt . . . I am sorry, Mr. Ravensbury . . . but I am afraid the woman has overdosed. Miss de Brabant . . ."

Roderick didn't need any more. He swept past the doctor almost roughly in his haste to reach Windmera. He went to her and pried her hands away from Louise's shoulders. She beat at him to let her go.

"Stop it! Stop it! I must wake her . . . she must walk . . . she must! It will help! I remember once . . . she must walk!"

"No my darling." His words were soft, scarcely audible. "It is over for her." He stood ready, ready for her. He wanted to shield her, make himself all-important to her. Fate had aided him. At last . . . fate had come to his cause!

No! No! No!" She was weeping, pushing him away. And then she looked at her aunt. Windmera saw, she understood, and she fell into convulsive racking sobs on Roderick of Ravensbury's chest.

The breakers came once again into Windy's view. It was over, had been over for a week now. July was coming to a close in this year of 1812. God! What a year. Her father and Louise both gone from her, and now Brabant! What had Mr. Willes said? Oh yes, Brabant was no longer able to sustain itself. They would need a buyer . . . a buyer willing to pour ready cash into the estate. She was losing everything. Only Roderick was left to her now, for even Bunky was no longer about. He had taken it into his head to take a party of young men sailing about the West Indies. Oh, thank Heaven for Roderick!

Seventeen

September 1, 1812 — Boston, Massachusetts

The American frigate President *was docked in Boston Harbor,* as was the schooner *Sea Hawk*. The captains of both vessels sat over an elegantly laid dining table discussing the recent turn of events that had brought them hither. The *President* was an impressive ship, carrying forty-four guns, and it had just returned from a chase that had nearly taken it into the English Channel.

"Damnation and Hell!" said its captain, Commodore John Rodgers, with some self-contempt. "I should have had the *Belvedera*. Lord, Landon . . . she was within our grasp, and what a coup that would have been." He sighed gustily and shook his head. "My mistake was not taking them broadside. No, we had to sail ahead instead of yawing . . . we had to be too damned smart . . ."

Lance Landon smiled and his blue eyes twinkled, for he liked Rodgers and admired him as a man's man. "Commodore . . . need I remind you that not only have you captured seven English vessels in these last few weeks, but you have also done quite a job of diverting the British all the while. Our privateers have had virtually free run on the British merchants. Jesus, have you seen some of the prizes they have hauled in?" He made a rueful snort. "I would say we are doing a far better job on the sea than our army does on land!"

"Yes, but William Hull had no choice but to surrender Detroit. The British had control of the Great Lakes . . . it was just a matter of time!" returned Commodore Rodgers gravely.

"Aye . . . thank God his nephew bears up the name! What a feat that was for Captain Hull. Imagine one of *our* frigates devastating a British frigate! I smiled to read nearly side by side in the *Times* the surrender of Detroit by William Hull and the victory of his nephew on the *Constitution* over the British *Guerrière*."

"Yes, but we must remember that the *Constitution* has the force of a ship of the line." He grinned broadly. "Damn, but

I should have liked to see the captain of the *Guerrière* when he realized he was being beaten! Finished by an American frigate! I'll warrant they won't take our frigates or our captains lightly from here on in!" He smiled amiably at the uniformed man laying a covered dish of freshly cooked lobster before him. "So that brings us to you, Lance. When do you intend to unfurl?"

"We set sail in the morning, sir. I hope to reach the coast of Virginia by the end of this week, and from there do a tour of the Bermudian and West Indian waters. We've got quite a few privateers in that area that might be able to use a handy scout!"

Commodore Rodgers smiled. "Indeed, I have a strong notion we shall be hearing great things about you, Lance."

"You are too generous, sir," said Lance almost flushing.

"No, I have never been called that! But never mind. We've had enough of war. Let's get to our lobsters, eh?"

November 1812 — Barbados

It was midday at Brayward. Roderick was already tired, though, for he had been quite busy. First thing he had done was to ride over to Brabant Plantation to see Windmera, to again beg her to marry him, sail with him as his wife to Cornwall. He was ready to leave. Brayward had kept to himself since Louise's death, and the life at the plantation was duller than he had ever dreamed possible. Then too Godwin's letters were becoming all too insistent, and in Godwin's last missive there was the hint that he might come to Barbados himself. No! He wouldn't be so humiliated. Windmera was nearly his. Why, why must she hold out?

Since her aunt's death in July, Windmera had been leaning toward him. He knew her too well to believe she would ever allow herself to become dependent on him, but she did need him. She cared for him, appreciated him. He was sure her feelings for him were steady, secure. Then why did she say him nay? Well, his visit this afternoon to her solicitors would change all that. Now she would have no choice. He dropped off his waistcoat and turned away from his mirror to look at the alluringly feminine black form occupying his large high bed.

Gildy would have to do for now, but soon, soon he'd be tossing Windmera. The thought excited him, but still he did not move any closer to his bed. Windy still held his thoughts too strongly for him to approach another woman. It had been a stroke of pure genius to write to Godwin and ask for permission to purchase Brabant. He knew the answer would be in the affirmative, but it had not come until this morning. He had wasted no time. Off he went to Bridgetown, and there the matter was settled. He smiled to himself. Later he would ride out to Brabant, for he was expected, and there he would advise Windmera, as innocently as he could, how he had rushed to her aid. She would have no choice but to marry him now. She was destitute. What were principles when one was in dire straits? No, ideals and principles were for those who were powerful enough, fat enough, to enjoy them!

He looked toward his bed again. At the black woman waiting, her eyes bright. She was certainly handsome enough, but she was not Windmera. He sighed audibly. More and more all he could think of, dream of, was mounting Windmera. Less and less did other women satisfy him. But Windy excited his desire and then left him hungry. He had to banish his physical needs, now! Even so, there was a lack of excitement as he approached the bed, as he slipped in and felt the warm, smooth, youthful flesh next to him.

"What's the matter . . . don't youse want your keep-miss no mores?" she asked, attempting to entice him further with a winsome movement. She didn't mind being with Roderick. He was a skillful lover and generous as well. She liked displaying the gew-gaws he would drop her way. The other girls, Lord, they had to sleep with their white masters and none came off with half as fine things as she!

"Keep-miss?" The term amused him. "Yes, I want your pretty little body. But in truth . . . I'd give a fortune if you were another."

"Huh! Youse want that Mistress de Brabant, I knows! Lordy . . . but that one is said to be cold as the north winds! You won't get her in the ordinary way. No, you'll have to go to the *morphy!*"

"Morphy? What the devil is that?" he asked, his brows drawn in puzzlement.

Gildy smirked. Jest look at me, she thought, s'plaining to a white man! "A morphy be both man and woman! She brews potions, strong potions!"

He laughed. "A hermaphrodite, eh . . . and something of

a witch doctor as well. What sort of potion do you think such a creature can offer me?" He wasn't serious.

Gildy's voice became hushed. "The morphy's potions work. They come from Afrique. Youse want to bed that Brabant woman . . . youse best go see the morphy!" She smiled. "Then you'll remember Gildy kindly?"

He smiled wickedly. "Yes, my pretty black keep-miss . . . I'll remember Gildy kindly." With which he mounted her well.

"Insufferable!" shouted Windy at her four walls. Mr. Willes was a miserable excuse for a man! She had raged at him a few moments ago, pleaded with him . . . but nothing, nothing had worked. He had already sold Brabant that very afternoon and would not renege from the sale. He had the authority to do it, for his firm had been empowered by the terms of the will to do whatever was necessary with regard to the plantation. The firm of Willes & Willes believed the only way the plantation could survive was to bring in a buyer. Under the terms of the sale, Windmera de Brabant would be provided with an income for the remainder of her life, or so long as the plantation was profitable under its new management.

She paced, she hugged herself, she fumed. "And Roderick . . . you? You have done this to me!" That was it. She had made up her mind. She would go to Brayward House and see Roderick. She didn't want to. She hadn't been there since her aunt's death . . . but she couldn't wait till this evening. Talk? Yes, there would be talk. There already was talk, about her aunt, about Jokai, about Roderick's many visits to her with only her black duenna in attendance! Talk! What was such fustian stuff? What did she care any longer?

Off went her day slippers and on went her riding boots. She took time out to brush her hair into a semblance of order, piled it on top of her head, dropped on a bonnet to shade her face from the sun and off she went.

A knock sounded on Roderick's door. He sighed gustily but called out, "What is it?"

"Sorry, Master Ravensbury," called the black lackey. "But you got a visitor. Mistress de Brabant be waiting in the sitting room."

Roderick jumped as though the bed had been suddenly filled with red-hot coals. Gildy lay resting, but she turned and

215

cocked a brow at him, wanting to say something until she saw his expression. Lord, but he did have it bad for that white woman, she thought, looking at him.

"Tell Mistress de Brabant I shall be down in a moment . . . and serve her some refreshments in the meantime!" he called as he rushed to get into his clothes.

"You want I should wait for you?" said Gildy.

"What? No . . . no . . . go on, Gildy . . . I'll call you when next I want you!"

"Yes, massa," she said, slipping out of bed. She slithered up to him and took his hand, putting it to her breast. "Youse don't want any more this afternoon?"

He pushed her away roughly. "Damn it, Gildy! Get out of here now. I've got to hurry."

She laughed. "Lordy, but you do have it bad! Best be going to the morphy."

However, he was already at the door, shrugging himself into his superfine as he made his way down the hall to the great staircase.

Gildy stood in the open doorframe and sighed. He was some fine hard man, was Roderick. She had liked being his keep-miss, but something told her he would soon be turning away.

Windmera stood in the open garden doors of the sitting room. Outside a gentle breeze played with the roses and brought their aroma into the room. Her gown of fine silk was damp from the humidity, and its folds from the high-waisted bodice clung to her lovely body. Roderick was struck with her beauty the moment he entered the room. She had her back to him as she attempted to control her emotions. She stood gazing outdoors, watching the black hummingbirds do their work, watching a mongoose scurry across the lawns.

He stared at her black glistening ringlets, at the style in which they fell cascadingly from the top of her head. He looked at the neck, perfectly shaped as it curved into shoulders too alluring. Her profile caught his senses, the nose with its pertness, the high cheekbone, the full warm lips. He wanted her! "Windmera," he said coming into the room. "Is something wrong?"

"Wrong? Roderick . . . everything is wrong! What have you done? How can you call yourself friend after this morning's work?"

216

"Windmera . . . what do you mean?" he asked, frowning, though he knew full well what she meant.

"Roderick!" She stamped her foot. "I am not a dunce! Don't think you can spin a round tale and I will believe it. You have purchased Brabant right from under me!"

"Windmera . . . my darling . . . how can you so accuse me?"

"Do you deny it? Oh, my God, I shall go mad! Do you deny it?"

"Of course not, but I deny doing it to hurt you. Windmera, you don't understand—"

"No, it is you who do not understand. I had only to hold out until the crop was reaped . . . only until February! I would have managed to scrape enough together to keep Brabant. How can you have done this to me?"

"Windmera . . . Brabant was bankrupt. Your creditors would have seen you in debtor's prison long before February brought in a harvest. I bought Brabant to help you, not hurt you. I bought Brabant for you . . . as a wedding present."

She stopped her frenzied movement and stared at him. "Oh no, Roderick. What have you done? A bribe? You offer me such a bribe?"

He went toward her, but she backed away sharply, and he pulled himself up short. "What is this? What foolishness have you in mind? A bribe indeed. I have been asking you to marry me all these many months. In this last month together . . . I thought perhaps you had come to a decision. I thought perhaps you would accept . . . and when you did, I meant to present you with Brabant."

"Roderick," she wailed, "don't you see? You will now never be certain whether I accepted you for Brabant or yourself! How can I hold my head up and accept you?"

He went to her this time and took her shoulders tightly in his grasp, for he was in earnest now. "Hell! It is you who don't see! Do you think I care why you accept me as long as you do? I want you more than I want my miserable life! I want you with every beat of my being, with every movement I take! I want you to say, yes Roderick, I will be yours, and so long as you are mine and mine alone nothing else will matter to me! I want to bed you, love you, give you my seed, watch you carry my babe. I want you in every way a man can want a woman! Do you think anything else matters to me?"

She looked up and deep into his eyes. Yes, she believed

him, but there was something there in the recesses of his bright eyes. Something in the gold flecks that spoke of an obsession that almost frightened her. He loved her, but she sensed there was more, more to Roderick, more to his courting than desire.

"You may not care, Roderick, how you get me into your bed . . . but I . . . I do care . . . very much!"

His mouth suddenly without warning found her own. His kiss was hungry, demanding, all-consuming. He was fevered, and he wanted to prove a point, he wanted to show her that she was not cold to him.

He took her by surprise, and she could not reject him. Perhaps pity, perhaps gratitude, for he had been there when she needed him, perhaps both. At any rate, she did not push him away, but allowed him the kiss. He came up for air, he came up to tell her she was his. "Windmera, don't you see . . . we were meant for one another! Come with me . . . come with me as my wife and we will go to England."

"I . . . I don't know, Roderick. I . . . I can't answer you today."

"Tomorrow, then! There is a ship leaving for Cornwall next month. I shall be on it, Windmera . . . and so will you, as my wife!"

"No . . . I can't . . . it is too soon. Perhaps . . . perhaps . . . if I do accept you . . . we could sail for Cornwall . . . and be married there, with your family present." Oh, God, what was she saying? She couldn't marry out of pity! But was it pity? Didn't she need Roderick? Yes, she did. Didn't she want him? How many nights had she lain awake thinking of his kiss, his touch? Yes, she wanted him. But did she love him? She didn't know, she didn't know!

He held her tightly. Finally, "Very well, Windmera . . . we shall be married in Cornwall!"

Eighteen

Hobart's. It was the name of the grayed wood sign swinging before the chemist's shop in Bridgetown. Not unusual, since the owner's name was Hobart. A relatively happy man of some fifty years. He had come to Barbados as a young lad. He soon discovered a woman, married her and produced five daughters. He'd always wanted a son, but no matter, he was pleased enough as he was. He was getting old, though, and there wasn't a tremendous amount of money in his business. Just enough to pay a young clerk a weekly salary. He needed more help around the shop, cleaning up, taking care of the customers, while he attended to the books and took a little more time off to be with his family. That's why two years ago when Seana came up for sale he had been pleased to buy her.

She came cheaply, for she was too old to work in the fields. Sixty if she was a day. No one else seemed to want her, because they knew what she was. He knew too, but it didn't bother him in the least. Yes, Seana was a hermaphrodite. She had the distinction of carrying sex organs of both genders, though the female was the dominant sex. Hobart wasn't bothered by such nonsense. In fact, he rather pitied her. So it was she came to live in a wood hut some hundred feet behind the shop, well hidden by the shrubs and trees she had planted there herself.

Hobart allowed her much privacy. She was a good worker, she appreciated what kindness he showed her, and he was often amused by her scraps of philosophy. Yes, she was a morphy, and as such used her power over her fellow slaves. He knew too that the herbs and plants she grew were for a purpose. She was learned in the arts of black magic. Well, he was a practical man. He didn't believe in such things, but if it gave Seana some sense of importance, why not allow it, after all; perhaps it made up in part for the trial of her life. A freak among mankind, she was held in awe by her people. He indulged her, and Seana continued her arts, arts she had learned as a youth in Southwest Africa from her mother before her.

Evening had settled. Hobart had gone home to his family, his young clerk to his friends and Seana to her hut. She waited. Someone would come tonight. She felt it, sensed it. She was not surprised when the flimsy material she used as a door between her one-room shack and the outside world parted and there stood a tall and elegant Englishman.

"Seana?" said Roderick. He was nervous lest anyone spy him there, and he wished she wouldn't stare so. What a strange creature, what odd short hair . . . what huge eyes.

Seana was buxom, broad. He was a white man, but he was here at her hut. He would want no fuss. She didn't bother to get up.

"I is Seana. Come. Come in."

"I . . . I was told by Gildy that you might be able to help me," said Roderick, attempting to gain control of the situation.

Seana smiled wide, showing cracked, blackened teeth. "I's do what I can." She moved a plate across the table, indicating that he should fill it.

Roderick dropped two gold coins, heard them clatter and then looked up and across at those large strange eyes. "What I should like is . . . something to help my fiancée feel more at ease . . . on our wedding night."

"Wedding night, eh? A little wine is all you need, honey," said Seana. She was enjoying this. She liked to make them squirm first.

Roderick lost his temper, and his voice came harsh, rough. "Look! I am not going to stand here and discuss this with you. I have just given you more than enough for what I need. Can you or can you not supply it?"

The smile never left her face. "I can. Surely I can." She reached up for a jar and took out a plump handful of brownish-green dried leaves. These she deposited into a smaller jar, put a lid on it and shoved it across at Roderick. "Now listen good so you'll know. That there is a Bantu drug. Yohimbe, they call it, and it be powerful strong. You got to boil it like tea . . . give it like tea. You add some honey to it . . . to cut the bitter, you know. Look now, suh . . . it takes a full hour to work . . . and your bride, she might feel a little sick at first. Don't worry . . . coz in the end it'll work jest fine. If *you* was to take it . . . lordy but it would harden that staff of yours for three, maybe four hours. So use it sparsely on her . . . less'n you wants to kill her wit love!"

"But . . . it will make her . . . want to . . . ?" He was doubtful, wondering if this old freak was playing a May game with him.

"Yes, yes . . . yohimbe will make her want to very much. She will be climbing all over you. You'll be pleased enough . . . and come back for more, I'd mark."

He didn't tell her he was leaving the island on the morrow. "It had better work, Seana . . . or I will come back!"

The *Sea Hawk* cut through the deep blue. Four months! They had been at this business for four months now, using Norfolk as their home port. Commodore Rodgers was correct in assuming that Lance Landon would wear the hero's halo. He was soon becoming a legend in his own time. He had assisted in the sightings of at least one hundred British vessels, enabling ninety-two to be captured. He attributed his successes to timing and a crew worth their salt. The American fleet of privateers . . . now they were something too! He smiled to himself, musing over the knowledge that while the New Englanders had deprecated the war at its outset, more than two hundred privateers out of some five hundred were New Englanders!

He sighed. Yes . . . and the navy was doing fairly well too. What morale they were losing in Canada was certainly picked up on the Atlantic. Success and action . . . a good combination. And still, Captain Lance Landon could not claim any contentment.

His restlessness plagued him. Why couldn't he get her out of his mind? That dratted female! It was nearly Christmas, six months since he had last seen her, touched her. He had done everything to banish her memory. Taken other women, gone into daily activity on board his schooner . . . everything, and nothing had worked! Time! He told himself time was the answer. Time would make him forget. What he explained to himself in such moments was this. He had taken a taste of an enticing piece of cake, putting only the pretty fluffy icing to his lips. It left him hungry for the whole cake, and not getting it, well, it left him with a wistful yearning. This is what he told himself. This was how he explained away his unusal state of emotions. Still, when he looked out on the deep mysterious blue, saw it churn into darker almost purple depths, he was reminded of her lush violet eyes, and he ached sorely.

The violet eyes he wanted to forget looked at the docks of Bridgetown and nearly overflowed with their sadness. Windmera stood on the merchant vessel *Southsea's* upper deck, silently saying goodbye to Barbados. Christmas had come and gone, December would soon be over, the New Year would bring her into 1813, but she would no longer be in Barbados. A Bajan always, but displaced.

Windmera had always wanted to go to England, but not like this, not in defeat! Her pride railed against her. What was she doing? Running like a scared bunny, running away, hiding behind Roderick's kindness. But perhaps, perhaps it would be better for Roderick and her in England . . . away from the nightmare of the last six months. Roderick had mentioned his parents recently so much, saying how pleased they would be to have her at Ravensbury. How much his father looked to their marriage. Marriage? Marriage to Roderick? Again her mother's voice haunted her. Stop! She had to stop thinking. She had said her goodbyes. She had left Bunky blinking in the sunlight on the *Liberté*. She would go to England, and if she loved Roderick as much as she thought, she would marry him and go to his bed.

This thought numbed her. But why? He was so good, so patient. He was handsome, desirable. He wanted her, yet he never forced her the way that miserable Lance Landon had tried to do . . . Lance Landon! No! She wouldn't think of Lance Landon. He was a demon not to be fancied.

It was Roderick she wanted. Roderick. Why are you torturing yourself, Windy? She asked herself this several times while she stood there in the sun on board the *Southsea*. You are doing the right thing, the only thing.

Then all thought fled, for Rod was beside her, touching her, sensing her need for silence and allowing her the time. So in stillness they watched as Barbados shrank out of view and the world she knew was swallowed by the varying shades of aquamarine. And then there was only water all around.

The *Sea Hawk* had put out of Norfolk directly after the Christmas festivities. They sailed the coast and came up with nothing, and then there was the British frigate bearing down on them! They didn't stand a chance, for the *Southampton* carried two hundred and eighty men and some thirty-eight guns. But she was a heavy lady, unable to tack with the swiftness of the nimble *Sea Hawk*. They received a blow that fell short, merely shaking up the men to move faster and splintering their stern.

Captain Lance was quick-witted. The frigate was between him and the American coast. He had Bermudian waters to the other side and couldn't take the chance of finding himself sandwiched by yet another British vessel. He tacked and set his course south, losing the *Southampton* as the wind took him full sail.

"Hold her steady, lads! We'll take her south and bring her back up tomorrow closer to the coastline!" He stood high on the rigging, working with his men, but he stopped a moment to gaze southward toward the West Indies, toward Barbados, and he saw in the sky, on a white cloud, dark masses of rippling black hair, cherry lips parted in a merry laugh and eyes the color of spring violets. "Damn!" he cursed softly to himself.

Roderick paced nervously in his cabin. The evening had fallen upon them swiftly. He had meant to serve Windmera the yohimbe tea at six, but something had stopped him. That old witch Seana! What if it wasn't an aphrodisiac? What if it was something that might hurt Windy? He would try again tonight to get her into his bed, but with seduction, not drugs! He had to seduce her, take her maidenhead, ensure their marriage. Perhaps even marry her on board the *Southsea*. Much better to marry her before they reached Cornwall and Godwin . . . just in case!

He went to her cabin door and knocked softly. Windy was a good sailor, she already had her sea legs from all her trips on the *Liberté*, but being out this far was a new experience for her. She was excited, and her eyes were bright as she opened the door wide. Rod stood there, very virile in a short brocade dressing gown over his pantaloons. He wore no shirt, and the dark auburn curls at his chest showed at the neckline. She stopped and cocked her head adorably.

He wanted to take her then and there, whether she allowed him or not, and so he walked in without waiting for an invitation. She put up a brow, surprised at him.

"Close the door, Windmera," he said softly.

"I don't think so, Rod."

"Close it!" he snapped, losing his temper.

For answer she stomped out of the room and started making her way to the captain's cabin, where they were invited to dine. Rod's exasperation was audible as he chased after her, caught her in the companionway and held her arm in a hard grip. "Where in Hell do you think you are going?"

"To dine with the captain, and if, sir, you intend to join us, you had best don your jacket and shirt, don't you think?"

He stared at her for a long defiant moment, but he couldn't very well make a fuss there in the companionway. He let go of her arm. "You would try the patience of a saint, my dear . . . and I have never been accounted such."

She smiled amiably. "Oh, Rod. I know . . . but you must not ever try to force me to do anything. It so nettles me that even if it is something I want . . . I immediately balk. I don't know why . . . but there it is."

"I know why, my dear. It is because you are a spoiled child. If you are to become my wife, my lady, you will have to control that little compunction of yours . . . you will have to consider *my* needs as well as your own." His words were measured. He knew enough of her now to know what would make her contrite.

It worked beautifully. She flushed vivid pink, and a sense of guilt nearly overwhelmed her. "Oh. I . . . I . . . know you are right, Rod. Forgive me."

He touched her lips with his finger. "Forgive you?" He sighed. "Go on . . . I shall join you presently." He watched her go, watched the sway of her hips. Lovely . . . but her temper . . . he would have to tame it!

Perhaps it was that contriteness, that sense of guilt, that later put the invitation on her lips. It was wrong, she knew, to entertain a man in her cabin even for a moment. But this was no ordinary man. This was Roderick . . . soon to be her husband. He came in, a confident curl to his lips, and he watched her as she fidgeted about the small quarters. His eyes met hers and took her gaze to the bed. All conversation was lost. She couldn't think. He was exciting, and there was a womanly need in her loins. She had turned twenty in December . . . yes, she was twenty, and desire was well within her.

He saw the passion in her eyes and came forward hungrily. Now, at last he would have her, by his own means, and to hell with Seana! His hands went to her waist and drew her close, his lips murmured against her own, sweetly, gently, tenderly disguising his lust. He couldn't chance frightening her off. She responded to his kiss, pressing herself against his taut body, inciting his passion to ravenous proportions. "Do you feel it, Windy? Do you feel what I feel . . . need what I need? Give it to me . . . to us . . ." he whispered in her ears.

"I . . . I want to," she breathed and gasped as she felt his hand cup her breast, fondle it through the cambric she wore. She felt now, perhaps now, she should submit to him, allow herself to relax and enjoy what they could share together. His kisses made her heady, dizzy, but as he attempted to undo the buttons at her back, she stiffened. Not without marriage. Her mother had wanted her to save herself for marriage . . . save marriage for love. These words kept shouting at her, cooling her heat. "But I can't! I just can't. It . . . it isn't right, Rod . . . not until our wedding night." She gave him this last.

He pulled himself up and stared hotly down at her. She was shivering. Damn it then, Windmera, he thought angrily, you have brought it on yourself! We will have to use the yohimbe! He said, his voice a mixture of bitterness, anger, frustration, all controlled, "Very well my little general . . . as you wish."

She watched him withdraw. Her body ached all over. She felt a warm tingling sensation between her legs. She wanted to be taken. She was hungry for it. Then why? Why did she stop him?

Lance Landon's startling blue eyes twinkled as they steered the *Sea Hawk* north along the coast. He called to Jackie, who was in the watch atop the mast, "Eh, lad, anything?"

"Not a sign!"

At Landon's back one of his crew grumbled. "Whot I says is that we oughta be catching us a prize, that's whot! We been letting all our privateers take them hauls and not a one of them for us."

Landon laughed. "Very well! Why not? Let's put it to the vote, men." He watched most of his men gather around. "How many are for taking the next merchant vessel we sight?"

"Aye!" It was nearly unanimous.

He looked up to the watch where Jackie stood. "And you, my bucko, what say you?"

"I say let the next merchant we sight be fat!"

This enjoined an outbreak of merry conversation that carried them through the morning. However, the afternoon brought a threatening sky. On the sea there is little warning, save the suddenness of bright into gray, blue into black. Dark swirling clouds smothered the blue, the sea as though in contention swelled, puffing up in consequence, and a hard misting beat the air, cooling it.

"Whot's this, capt'n?" called one of his men. "A squall, you think?"

"If it is, we are not in its heart. Best start trimming! Keep clewing, lads—we've got to start reaching if we're to avoid the storm!" shouted Lance at his men.

He took on the job at the bridge, relieving his man there. They had to sail across, abeam the wind; this would enable them to pick up speed, as it would hinder the pitching and send them quickly planing the sea. It would also put them closer to Bermuda than he cared to be, during the storm, but there was no help for it.

The *Southsea* was not so lucky as to catch only the edge of the squall. The small vessel was tossed mercilessly, and its captain, not half as experienced as Lance Landon, was in a frenzy to simply keep afloat.

Windmera went above for only a moment and was told to return to her cabin at once. Indeed, she heard the creaking masts and was very happy to comply. By midafternoon the yawl had lost its jib and was hopelessly off course. Their destination was Bermuda, where the captain had a small shipment he had intended taking up.

Roderick, to give him credit, was not backward in lending a hand on deck. He worked well into the afternoon, and when Windy next thought to take a peek at the damage above, he was coming down the companionway, soaked through.

"Oh, Rod . . . you will catch your death," she said, running a hand over his wet sleeves.

"Never mind. I'll be dried out in a few moments. The worst of it is over. It's too dark to do any repairs and the men are just simply too exhausted, but at least we have outlived the storm."

"Well, come to my cabin after you have changed. I'll make you some hot tea."

"I tell you what," he said thoughtfully. "You get a pot of boiling water from the galley and some honey . . . I'll bring my own mixture of tea."

"Oh . . . fine . . . I'll get some biscuits, too . . . you must be starving!" she said, smiling warmly and going off toward the galley.

He watched her and smirked to himself. "Starving," he repeated softly, "but not for long . . . damn, not for long!"

A beautiful white moon, round in its brightness, sat in the sky holding court with its twinkling minions. The sea was

226

still, pleasant now that its temper was spent. It lapped against the hull of the *Sea Hawk* approvingly, almost lovingly.

Landon was on deck, dressed in shirt sleeves and a leather jerkin. It was nearly January, but the weather in those parts was fair enough and he often underdressed. He was staring, thinking of a million things, and then he saw it.

A silhouette against the blue-black sky. A sad thing she appeared with her jib split and bent, her sails wracked, unclewed; she floated as though almost dead. He put up his spyglass and looked at the flag, torn, beaten by the storm. He couldn't make out the colors in the dark, but the Union Jack was unmistakable. Next, he looked for a watch. Incredible, there was none. Of course . . . the storm, they had been caught in the heart of the storm, blown off course. Her crew was probably below getting a bite to eat before returning to the deck. Her captain was probably trying to figure out just where he was.

Landon laughed softly and called quietly to Jackie, who had just appeared from the hatch. "Well, lad . . . we have our merchant. Get the men up here quickly . . . we'll have to be fast if we are to do this well. Get the flag down and put the Union Jack up. Come on, Jackie, step lively!" he ordered on a laugh.

"Aye, aye, sir!" said the first mate of the *Sea Hawk,* moving to gather the crew together.

Roderick took a huge portion of the biscuit into his mouth and watched Windmera sip her tea, her yohimbe tea. He had heavily laced it with honey, lest it be too bitter, and she wrinkled her nose.

"Your mixture is strange . . . and, oh, Rod . . . I do not take so much honey in my tea."

"Never mind. Drink it down, the next will be better. You have to start teaching me what you like and what you don't like."

To be polite, she continued to sip at her cup until it was nearly gone. She wondered at Roderick, for he didn't touch his own. "Rod . . . why don't you drink your tea? You'll be the better for it."

"No, no . . . I think instead I'll get a glass of brandy," said, getting up and stretching.

Windy got up from her chair and went to her porthole. She was feeling a little warm and thought to open it.

"What are you doing?" he asked, his eyes narrowing, watching her closely.

"I . . . I thought I would get some air."

"Don't you feel well?" He remembered the old witch had said this would happen.

"I . . . no . . . no . . . actually I don't think your tea agreed with me," she said, dropping onto her bed. "Oh . . . Rod . . . my insides are in a turmoil."

"Keep your head down in your lap. I know from experience that it helps a weak stomach. Go on," he said, pushing her head downward. "I'll be right back. I just want to dip my handkerchief in some of your water."

He returned a moment later from the washstand with the cloth and put it on the back of her neck. "There . . . is that better?"

"I . . . think so . . ."

"Here . . . lie down . . . don't worry, my dear . . . that's right . . . just lie there quietly." He stood watching her. "How do you feel now?"

"Not very well."

He sat beside her and stroked her hair. "Don't worry, love . . . you will feel better soon." He almost wanted to tell her, to gloat over it, but fear kept him from mouthing the words. Fear that if she became angry it might reduce the effects, fear that she might try to spite him afterward. No, he would have to keep his secret. He bent and gently kissed her forehead. His hand went to her heart, over her breast, his thumb pressed her nipple through the material of her yellow day gown.

"Rod . . . don't, please . . ." she whispered, for her stomach churned still.

He frowned. How long . . . oh yes, Seana had said it might take an hour. Damn! How could he wait? Well, he had waited this long; a few more minutes were nothing to the months of torture she had put him through!

The *Sea Hawk* needn't have bothered putting up its fraudulent flag. The men of the *Southsea* had done more than eat below deck. It had been a rough hard day, and they all suffered now from various injuries and aches. Rum went around as a solution to their groans, while the captain looked the other way. In the end, he retired to his cabin to plot the next day's course and sent only one man to the bridge . . . a lad well foxed from the rum who was barely able to hold the wheel. He saw a sleek schooner coming abeam and screwed his eyes on it. He never heard the lap of oars from a long-boat. He never heard the five men scrambling up the sides or the one who came up behind him. He never knew what happened as the butt of a pistol came down upon his already groggy head.

"Good," said Lance to Jackie, and then ruefully, "Something tells me you have a natural vocation for putting poor souls out! Now, down with you into the galley . . . I'm for the captain!"

Captain Saunders was no more than twenty-five. He was inexperienced at sailing and at command; however, he had the good fortune to have a wealthy merchant for a father, and upon his expressing the wish to command a merchant yawl, the *Southsea* was bestowed upon him. He had bought a load of sugar and rum from the West Indies and meant to make a killing with it in England. It never entered his head, in spite of all the talk, that a privateer, an American privateer, might dare to attack his vessel and make off with it!

Captain Landon didn't bother to knock at the captain's quarters, he simply broke the door down by a forceful rushing kick. At his desk sat young Saunders. "What . . . what is the meaning of this?"

"A reasonable question, I am sure. So I'll answer it quickly and to the point!" Captain Landon bowed. "I am Captain Landon of the *Sea Hawk* . . . Americans, you see . . . and we are about to relieve you of your rather worn but I am certain fatly laden yawl!"

Saunders looked down the barrel of Captain Landon's pistol and gulped. "You . . . cannot mean that." He couldn't think of anything else to say.

Landon laughed. "But I do. Now tell me . . . have you any passengers?"

"Yes, yes I do . . . a young woman . . . and an Englishman."

"Damn . . . oh well . . . it can't be helped." He moved his head as Jackie and another *Sea Hawk* crewman came up alongside. "All secure?"

"Aye, the crew of the *Southsea* is waiting on their captain in their own longboat. We're lowering it already."

"Excellent. Now kindly escort the captain to his men and then come back. I am afraid the *Southsea* carries passengers. They will have to go too." He sighed again. He didn't like involving civilians . . . but if he was going to play at privateering, that was just one of its disadvantages.

He made his way down the companionway and opened the door to the first stateroom. Empty. He moved farther down and across and opened the door wide. He saw a familiar male form leaning over a familiar female form, and suddenly the sight burned in his eyes. This, this was Roderick, leaning over Windmera! He saw them on the bed together and tensed. His heart's beat picked up substantially. How, how could the sight of her, even thusly, still have such an effect over him?

He stepped into the room and said, his voice full of contempt, "It appears I intrude?"

Roderick spun around and jumped to his feet. Windy, still dizzy, still nauseous, knew the voice, and with a violent sensation grabbing her heart she propped herself onto her elbows to see Lance Landon. He stood, his bronzed face framed in his glorious black hair. His body firm, his legs apart, and in his hand a gun! What did it mean? Oh, God . . . he was here . . . here . . .

"Lance . . ." she said. It was scarcely audible, but he heard it, looked past Roderick and drank in her face. Was she pale . . . or was that his imagination? Were her eyes strangely dilated?

Roderick didn't know what was going on, but he understood the gun in Lance's hand. He used that moment to dive, but Lance was too quick for him. His fist rounded and planted itself in Roderick's belly, and then followed by delivering another to his jaw, sending him backward.

Jackie was there, gun in hand, another crewman at his back carrying a long-bladed knife. Together they descended on Rod and pulled him to his feet.

"Into the longboat with him," snapped Landon.

"Wait . . . Landon . . . Miss de Brabant is ill. I implore you to let her be."

"Are you asking me to spare her the hardships of a trip to Bermuda in an open boat?"

Roderick's eyes nearly burst from his head. So that was it, Landon was a privateer. What to do? The drug would soon begin to work . . . and she would be in Landon's hands. "No! Just . . . give her into my charge."

"Well?" said Jackie. "Should we take the lady?"

"No." He smiled at Roderick. "I am not such a villain as to send a lady of Miss de Brabant's qualities onto the open sea. No, I think we shall keep her." He signed to Jackie to take Roderick off.

"No!" cried Roderick, and then to Windmera, "Don't fear, darling, no matter what happens . . . I shall come for you . . . *I swear it!"*

"Rod . . . ?" cried Windy. She was feeling strangely euphoric and warm shivers moved up and down her spine. She turned to Landon. "What . . . what do you mean to do with me?"

"Why, pretty moonflower . . . you are a prize of war!"

3

Every night and every morn
Some to misery are born;
Every morn to every night
Some are born to sweet delight;
Some are born to sweet delight,
Some are born to endless night.
Joy and woe are woven fine,
A clothing for the soul divine:

—William Blake, Auguries of Innocence

One

Captain Landon did not go above; he knew his men would handle the affair well. They knew the way of it. The *Southsea* would first be put in tow, and then they would set a course for Norfolk as soon as possible, but first, first he would speak with his prisoner. There was a strange tangy smell to the air. He sniffed it and frowned, for it reminded him of something, but never mind, here she was, his frosty cake, the one that had for so long bothered his memory!

"You do get around, Miss de Brabant," he said as he came closer to the bed.

She ignored it. The nearness of him was driving her mad. Her limbs felt weak, and her blood, it singed her flesh, her muscles. "I . . . asked you what you intend to do with me."

"I have already told you, my beauty, you are a prize of war! I can do anything I wish with you."

She should tell him, tell him her place was with Roderick, her intended husband, but something stopped her. "You . . . spared me once. Why undo one of the only good things you have ever done for me?"

He laughed derisively. "You are a baggage! One minute you are cuddling up with some aging sailor, now you are going across the Atlantic with a popinjay. How many, Windy . . . how many have clambered into your bed? Why are you so afraid to add *me* to the lists?"

She couldn't believe the words she heard. Never, never, had anyone ever accused her of such a thing. She sat propped on her elbows staring in disbelief, unable to answer such an outrageous question. He took her silence to mean something else altogether.

He made her a bow. "My men will show you to my quarters on the *Sea Hawk*, madam . . . I hope you will be comfortable until I can . . . keep you company. For the time being I am needed elsewhere."

He wouldn't let her rule his mind this way! So he told himself as he poured into the work on deck. And then, she was there, led by Jackie into the longboat in the brine. He wanted to rush . . . to go to her side, carry her over to the boat himself, but he held himself in check and allowed the honor to go to his first mate. The various members of his crew watched the mood flicker over their captain's face. They remembered Windmera too. She was the same one that drove him in Barbados! Odd how life's turns brought them together again. The tow rope was secure, and swiftly, nimbly did the captain take it to his own vessel. The thought of being with Windmera, even just talking to her, was manipulating every fiber in his being.

In Captain Landon's cabin, Windy's warm shivers had worked into a wild crescendo. An intoxicated feeling took hold of her fancies, and suddenly she couldn't bear the clothes she was wearing. They itched, they burned, she had to have them off! She nearly tore them in her frenzy to be free, and then she stood naked in the candlelight Jackie had lit for her. Naked! She stared at herself in the long looking glass on the wardrobe door. She pulled at the ribbon, and her long black hair fell and tumbled down her back to her waist. She played with its long strands, pulling them down her front to shade in part her full supple breasts. And then she was overcome with a series of sharp pelvic tingling sensations. Oh, oh, God! She was in need. She wanted Lance . . . Lance with his blue eyes, his rugged face, his broad shoulders and bold hands! She wanted him!

Lance opened his cabin door, saw in the candlelight the heady vision of Windmera and quickly slammed his door shut. She spun around and faced him, and he sucked in his breath.

"My God," he breathed as he gazed on her long thick black hair, at the full round breasts pointing at him seductively, at the small waist and the alluring slender hips. He felt his rod hard and pulsating, demanding release, and he worked quickly at his breeches, loosening the buttons. His vest was thrown off almost viciously as he closed the space between them. A tumultuous stampede on his nerves had taken over, riotously in command of his every move, as he took hold of her and brought her to him.

The touch! The feel of her was enchantment, exhilarating, inebriating. She was more than satin-smooth, firm, flawless. She was more than beauty, more than woman. She was the being he had wanted, the only one he had craved, and there was a strange wild contentment in that first contact. He had been a man parched in the desert, and she was his first long draft of cool sweet wine.

His kiss nearly drowned them both in fever. His hands found the youthful swelling breasts, teased the nipples already taut, already hungry for his mouth. His head bent as she threw her own back, and he kissed a line down her neck to the sweet cleavage, pushing the swells up with his hands and suckling first one and then the other. Was it possible that such ecstasy could exist between a man and woman? He had never known this before . . . not quite this!

Windy's knees buckled. She couldn't take it any more. The drug had worked its black sorcery. All inhibitions were lost. She didn't know anything but sensation, didn't want to know anything but the wonder of this virile man's touch. She was on fire, and there was a persistent need in her pelvic region driving her mad with desire. She haunched herself, found his bent knee and pressed her bare crotch upon its hard roundness. Ah, that was good, more, more, she thought ravenously as she pushed down harder, wild with the tingling sensation of its snug fit.

"Windy, Windy . . . you hungry little bird . . . come, love . . . come," he said, picking her up cradlelike in his arms to take her to the bed.

"Lance . . . Lance . . . I . . ." She didn't know what to say, what she wanted to express. She only knew she craved more of him. His kisses were spellbinding, wrenching an ardor she could not control, but there was something else she needed, something more substantial.

"I know, my little bird, I know what you want," he said, for he had already laid her upon the bed, divested himself of his loose breeches. He was parting her thighs, taking in breath over her beauty. She was perfection! He mounted her, positioning himself just so, holding his staff against her. One hand took hold of her black silken tresses near her neck and brought her mouth to meet his, and even as his tongue sought to enter did he plunge his tumid muscle into her readied womb.

The yohimbe had done its work. Her passion was at a height, but even so, Windmera felt the splitting of her vestal shield, and a small cry escaped her lips. Ready as she was, sweetly honeyed to receive him, all tenseness gone, still did she stiffen.

Lance nearly stopped in mid-movement. More than the whimper, more than the sudden rigidity came through. He felt himself tear through her maidenhead! She had only stiffened for a moment and her cry was barely audible, for she was in the grips of inordinate desire, and she moved intemperately, contorting her body in a manner that complemented his lunges, but still he was aware, and it came as something of a shock. A virgin! But there was no time to question, he could only whisper in her ear, "You surprise me, my moonflower . . . every time I turn around . . . you surprise me . . . but here . . ." he said, his voice low with his passion, his hands going to her hips, "this is the way of it," he said, rotating her into a steady energetic movement.

His staff was enough to pleasure her, as was his dexterity with his hands. He touched her in ways that brought out and worked the effects of the drug within her to its fullest potential. She thrust herself into his increasingly propelled drives. The sweat on his brow glistened as he held himself in check, waiting until he had satisfied her, and then she was holding onto him as though she were suddenly sinking. The tenseness in her groin eased with a rush, and she relaxed in some part. He smiled, kissed her eyes, her ears, her neck, and then allowed himself one final series of powered contortions before he knew he was ready to climax, and then quickly, swiftly and with wondrous control he pulled himself out to give his seeds to the mattress.

He sighed and gazed at her. God, it had been good, better than any woman he had ever had. She was flushed, but he wanted to go on holding her. Slowly, easily, he took her up, and lying on his back he brought her on top of him. She made no objection. Windy was unaware of what she did. She was still totally intoxicated, but the sweetness of his kisses on her face pleased her into a smile. "Windy . . . you were a virgin. Why didn't you tell me?"

"I . . . told you once," she said, still smiling. She was pressing her body against his. He had such a wonderful body. So hard, so muscular. Her movements inflamed him, and then suddenly she was taking up his hand, putting it to her breast.

Damn! There was no one like her. No woman had ever enchanted him quite this way. He had wanted to lie with her, study her, dissect this being that was Windmera and see what it was about her that so tantalized him. Having the cake had not contented him. It had not satiated him, he wanted her still! He bit at her lip and he whispered on a smile, "Oh, lady . . . you will be sore when I am through with you!"

Morning came and took hold of Lance's consciousness with

a shake. He came blinkingly to life and found beside him nestled on her tummy a bewitching creature. Windmera. How he had possessed her! More times than he thought himself capable of had he taken her, ridden out her hunger. He frowned. There was something about that, something in the manner she took him to her, that bothered him in the cold light of day, and he remembered the tangy aroma in her room. He wondered. But no time, no time. He had to rush to get topside, for they should be along the American coastline soon. Norfolk would be reached by the end of the day, though with a yawl in tow it would be slower going than usual.

As he dressed he glanced several times in Windmera's direction. She lay there covered with the sheet to her naked shoulders, and watching her he felt the desire swell within him again. What to do with her? The thought of parting with her irritated him. No, he would keep her awhile longer . . . but she would need her things. He'd just go over to her cabin on the *Southsea* and fetch them. By then she would be awake and they would take breakfast together. He smiled, enjoying the notion.

Windmera awoke with a start. She sat bolt upright, noted her naked state and gasped as she pulled the covers to her neck. She moved and was visited with an inner soreness along the inside of her thighs, and then she remembered something. She remembered staring at herself in Lance's long mirror, she remembered Lance coming across the room, sweeping her up, taking her to this bed. "Huh!" she gasped and jumped away from the bed as though it were filled with poison ivy. And in spite of her aching head she stood with the sheet to her chin, staring down at the blood on the covered mattress.

Lance came into the room. She didn't notice him, so much in shock was she over her sudden dawning. Heaven help me, she thought as it came into her consciousness what had occurred. Sudden flashes of the night's wantonness flooded her cheeks with color.

Lance caught the line of her vision, saw the bloodstains on the bed, and his own mobile brow moved expressively. So, more proof. She had been a virgin. It was almost an accusing finger and one he had tried to forget. A sudden feeling of pity, compassion for her situation, made him drop the garments he held in his hands on a nearby chair and go toward her, saying gently, "Good morning, moonflower. I've brought you some of your things." He was standing so near. "I'll have one of my men bring in your trunks later." He was taking her easily into his arms as though it were the most natural thing to do.

But it wasn't, not for Windmera, not on this morning. She had been standing nearly frozen with shock. His touch awakened her spirit, and she pushed at his chest, jumping back out of his way. "Don't, don't you come near me!" she shouted.

He stiffened. He was already troubled, for his visit to her room had put a notion in his head. The tangy aroma . . . had it been that alone? He knew such potions as yohimbe worked in conjunction with one's natural desires, not against them. But still . . . it could have been due to the potion alone. He made a second attempt to comfort her. "Windmera . . . you have nothing to fear in me."

She stared at him with something of disbelief. She had stayed in the same bed with this man. She couldn't recall it all . . . but pieces came blazing into her mind. His hands on her . . . his naked . . . Oh, God! He had made her vulnerable somehow. He had given her something to drink . . . must have given her something to drink. She couldn't remember. Her pride overcame her fear, and she put up her chin.

"Afraid? I am not afraid of you. I simply loathe the nearness of you. Evidently you think to make me a slave. But it shall not be so easy, captain."

He was taken aback. Nothing in her behavior last night had prepared him for this. His own conscience pricked him in accord with her words. A question loomed. Hadn't he taken her on board his ship with but one purpose in mind? If she had not come to him as she did, would he have forced her? He couldn't be sure, and the uncertainty of the answer plagued his temper. Still did he retort sharply, "A slave? My lass, you were no slave last night, nor are you now! You will note how freely you speak to me. No slave would dare!"

"No, of course not . . . not a slave," she returned sardonically. "What was the word? Oh yes, a prize. I am your prize of war!" She hugged the sheet closer to her body, all too aware of his probing eyes, and she moved farther back, nearly coming in contact with the cabin wall. "Well, sir . . . this prize won't perform, not for you! Never for you!"

"No? Your performance last night was superb," he said half-baitingly, half in earnest anger.

"Oh! You are insufferable. You . . . you . . . you know

very well you ill-used me . . . like so much chattel. You know what you did to me!"

"I did exactly what you wished me to do!" he snapped.

She blushed, and had she been a lesser maid she might have collapsed beneath the strain of unspeakable flashes of memory and unthinkable flashes of the future. But she was Windmera, and so she fought. "You must have made me drunk! It is the only answer." She was saying this as much to herself as accusing him.

His face clouded over. He had of course realized on his visit to her cabin this morning what the tangy aroma had been. An aphrodisiac. Yohimbe by name. Quite potent. He had encountered it as a youth in New Orleans and had never quite forgotten its power. He hadn't been sure, however, whether she had taken it with intent or whether it had been administered to her without her knowledge. So, Roderick of Ravensbury had drugged her. And then he smiled to himself, for it had not been Roderick who had won the spoils of his efforts! It was too funny. Suddenly the entire situation became all too funny, and he began to shake with mirth.

Windmera's jaw dropped. "How . . . how dare you! So then you admit it? You did get me drunk."

He looked up at her piquant accusing face, this woman-child who had had him jailed in Barbados, this woman who had taunted his dreams, who had finally satisfied them in a way he had never thought possible, and who would now be his enemy once again. "I?" He chuckled still. "No, my lass, I gave you no such thing, but your popinjay . . . he did. Not drink, however . . . something far more effective. He gave you an aphrodisiac, but then was not able to stay to enjoy its effects!" He went toward her then, for all this talk, all this hot conversation, was getting up his appetite.

"No! He couldn't . . ." She could see he meant to touch her, and she already had her back against the wall. "Don't you come near me. I don't believe you. Roderick couldn't . . ." But already her mind was going back to the bitter-tasting tea.

He saw the moment of recall light in her violet eyes. Such eyes. Such a body, just within his grasp, naked beneath the sheet, and his. Yes, his. For no other man had ever had her. The thought excited him still further. With one movement she was pressed against his hard lean body, and he was gasping at the sensation her flesh aroused within him. Her hand did not strike him; instead she took her fingers and pinched his belly fiercely. He was surprised as well as pained and moved back slightly. She used the moment to win her freedom and scurried off, but there was nowhere to go except across the bed to the other side of the cabin. He reached out and caught the sheet. A swift hard pull left her naked to his hungry vision. She went down for the quilt, but the delay found her wrapped neatly in his arms, and so they were sprawled on his bed.

"Let me go, you blackguard!"

"Would you have preferred to be set on the open waters with your popinjay and a pack of sailors? Would you have? I had no choice but to take you." He tried to assuage her temper, win her approval, but his excuse sounded lame even to him.

"I loathe you!" she hissed. "Let me go! Or is rape one of your intentions as well?"

"Ah, then you admit I did not rape you last night?"

Suddenly she wanted to cry, but she held herself in check. Not here, not now, not in front of him. Her want of tears kept him hard against her. Had she known she might not have maintained such stoic control. No matter; they were interrupted by a knock.

"What is it?" asked the captain irritably as she struggled against him. This was not how he imagined the morning after would be for them. This was not how he wanted her, fighting, always fighting him.

"Its Jackie, capt'n. Cook has sent up a fine breakfast for you and . . . the lady." He blushed on the word, didn't know where he would look when he brought the tray in, but the men had all insisted he be the one since he was the favorite.

Lance released Windy, threw the quilt over her and went to the door. Without letting his youthful first mate into the room he took the tray and thanked him curtly, displaying his ill temper. Jackie stood on the other side a moment shaking his head. Earlier that morning his captain looked in a fine fettle . . . but now? *Women!* They would drive a man mad if he let them. He surely hoped such would not be the case for his captain.

Lance brought the tray into the room. It was set for two. He put it down on his round dining table and turned to her, his face set in a cold hard line. "I will leave you to your breakfast, Miss de Brabant. I find my hunger . . . has flown." With which he turned and left her to herself.

She watched him go, staring after him for some time.

What was she to do? She had lost her virginity to this dreadful buccaneer! And he was that . . . a pirate! And American to boot, at war with her country! How unfeeling he was. What did he mean to do with her? And Roderick . . . what had happened to Roderick?

Thinking of Roderick, however, brought a crease to her forehead. He had doubtless drugged her just as Captain Landon had said. He had wanted her enough to do that. But oh, Rod, she thought, how deceitful you can be. She had never seen him in such a light. What would become of her . . . what had become of Rod? How could she be reunited with him? Too many questions loomed, and she found she had no appetite for food either. Cook's excellent breakfast grew cold and was left untouched.

Captain Landon stood on the bridge, apparently studying charts, gazing now and then at his binnacle, but his mind mused on other things than the current, the tides, the winds or the compass. So, Lance concluded to himself, you have had your very fine way with her, but she is still very much in your blood. A problem, for she is right, you know—you don't have the power to take her against her wishes. Something would be lost. She won't give herself freely. So what to do?

He sighed. He should have put her in the longboat with Ravensbury. Ravensbury? What was she doing with him in the first place? What was she doing going to England? For he had seen the charts of the *Southsea* and their final destination was England, which the logbook noted as Windmera and Roderick's destination. Was she going as his mistress? No, she was a virgin. But there was no maid in attendance. Mysterious . . . nearly as mysterious as Windmera herself. Here she was, from her point of view virtually raped, and yet she did not dissolve into tears or hysterics. A strong lass, and in spite of himself he felt a wave of admiration for the being in his cabin.

What to do? Now, now it was for Norfolk, for the *Sea Hawk* was in need of repairs. There they would discharge the *Southsea*, divide the booty with the Admiralty, see to his vessel . . . and then . . . God only knew!

Two

Dark indigo blue rolled, danced, played out its contentment, peaking with white foam, teasing, hinting at its depths. A dangerous beauty was the ocean around the men of the *Southsea*. They huddled together beneath the scudding clouds, and they grumbled.

"Damn them pirates' eyes!" said one.

"Aye, but it could've been worse. Hell . . . we're at war with the Americans. Thank merciful God they seen fit to leave us fresh water and food enough for two days."

"Deuce take ye for a dimwit clod! Water for two days!" retorted another sailor irritably. "Ye think we can reach Bermuda by tomorrow? For, my mate, that's when our food and water will run out!"

"Shut yer tallow face, you twiddle poop!" returned his friend. "We been rowing all night and me arms are near to breaking off! I don't need you telling me it's for nothing!"

"Take heart, men," said their youthful captain. "We are in English waters, I am certain of it. Even if we don't reach Bermuda by tomorrow, we shall be spotted by an English vessel."

They had been rowing in turns with the two sets of oars given to them by the Americans. Sleep had come in shifts and had not been enough. Their arms ached from the work of rowing, from their previous exertions during the storm. They were beaten with fatigue and in no mood to have the young captain attempt to hail their morale. Some grumbled audibly at him, accusing him of ineptness, and an argument ensued.

All this went on around his head, but Roderick paid little heed. He would survive this. By God or the devil he would survive, and he would get his revenge! He rowed harder than the others, did not sleep and took water only when the round of provisions went by. The weather had turned chilly, and though his coat was damp from the saltwater spray, he needed no blanket, for Roderick burned from within.

Over and over his mind formed a picture. A picture of Windmera sweetly, sweetly under the spell of yohimbe, and there before him standing in the way was Lance Landon! He would have the man's blood. Windmera was his. She was Godwin's daughter and she would be his bride. No matter that Lance had her now. No matter that Lance might have taken her to his bed. In the end Windmera would be his. He swore it silently through the night, he swore it now to the gray heavens above. He would survive this. He would find a way to wherever Windmera was, and he would take her away from Lance Landon and then with his own hands he would erase Lance Landon from the earth. It was the only way to cleanse Windmera. And thus was he tortured!

Another night came upon them with still no land in sight. It seemed as though they were the only ones left in the world. There was nothing but deep-blue ocean and sky. Their mouths were parched with dryness and they were weak, for the biscuits were hardly enough to sustain them, and they were losing all heart, except for Roderick—he knew he would survive this! So it was with no great surprise the next early dawn that he sighted a yawl. He stared at its lines and then at the flag flapping in the wind. British!

"English . . . an English . . . vessel . . . straight ahead," he called hoarsely.

Windmera sat on the bed and contemplated her situation. The enormity of it suddenly welled and overflowed. She curled up into a corner of the bed and with the quilt tightly held began to cry. A knock sounded, and again a young male voice announced his name.

"Sorry, ma'am . . . it's me, Jackie . . . first mate . . . I come to take the tray and straighten up for the capt'n." For Lance Landon had asked his trusted second-in-command to play this humble role while Windemera shared his quarters, and the faithful Jackie had obliged.

She jumped off the bed, wrapped the quilt around her and retreated to a dark corner of the room between the wardrobe and a tall dresser.

Jackie entered blushing and noted her position. God, but she was pretty. He heard her sniff and felt a sudden sympathy for her. Poor little thing. He saw the untouched breakfast tray and shook his head. He went to the closet and pulled out some fresh linen and went to the bed. Blood!

He stood stupefied for a moment, and then it lit in his head. Well, dang if the wench hadn't been a virgin! Sweet life, but that wasn't like the capt'n to be raping virgins! He went beet-red, stripped off the sheet hastily and worked quickly to recover the bed. He turned to pick up the break-fast tray and saw out of the corner of his eye Windy's bent head. Poor thing, she looked shamed, and he sought to comfort her. He went toward her instead of the tray. "Ma'am?"

She didn't look at him, "Yes?"

"I'm . . . real sorry . . . I mean . . . that you had to be involved in all this. It's the war, you know," he said lamely.

He was sweet, she thought. She turned her violet eyes toward him, and he gasped audibly. Pretty? Damn, the wench was the most beautiful woman he had ever beheld. "Yes . . . I know . . . at any rate, it isn't your fault. If only I could figure out just how I shall get home."

He went closer, drawn by her loveliness, by the softness of her voice, by the need in her eyes. "Don't worry . . . capt'n will know the way of it."

She wanted to retort, but just then her eyes flew to the door, which was opened by Lance Landon's hand. He stood there, his shirt open at the neck, his bright-blue eyes taking in the scene and a sudden sneer pulling his mouth.

"I see you have managed to find someone to entertain you, Miss de Brabant," he said dryly and then glanced at Jackie, his eyes bright with anger.

He said nothing to the lad, but Jackie was quick to scoop up the sheets. "I'll just leave the tray in case either of you decides to pick at it." With which he rushed out of the cabin, breathing with some relief as he escaped.

The captain closed the door at his back and leaned against it, his arms folded, "Get dressed, Miss de Brabant . . . or are you trying to get an encore of last night?"

She gasped. "I intend to get dressed . . . as soon as you leave the room."

"I had left the room, thinking you would be quick about it. I found instead that you were using the time to seduce my first mate!"

"How dare you! Get out!"

"No, I am afraid not." He motioned with his jaw, and she noted its set lines. "There is the gown I fetched for you . . . and what toiletries you may need."

"Very well, captain. I should like to do just as you bid in this instance, but cannot possibly attend to it with you standing there!"

He remembered a night, it seemed years ago, when he stood on a beach and watched her struggle into a shift. "We are no strangers in that respect, lass. You've dressed before

246

me on a beach, you've lain naked in my bed. No, I think I'll just remain and make sure you don't get into mischief." He knew he was being obstinate but didn't know why.

She nodded angrily. "You think I care whether you watch or not? You are an animal. I don't give a fig for your presence!" Still, when she went to the washbasin and poured out her clean water, she held the quilt around herself with one hand. An awkward manner of washing, but this accomplished, she dried herself with the towel, again with one hand, and went to her gown. He had chosen a lovely gown of dark lavender velvet, but he had neglected to bring her small clothes, and as she searched she realized Jackie must have scooped them up with the linens. She sighed, sat on the bed and pulled her gown up and over her head, quite a struggle with one hand as the other still held the quilt. When the folds of the straight-lined skirt of the gown had fallen down around her, she dropped the quilt and this time had free use of both hands to pull the dress on. And then she sat, aware that she would need help to close it up, as the gown buttoned up the back. On the ship with Roderick she had always chosen gowns that laced or buttoned in the front. So she sat with her problem.

Lance had watched all her contortions with some amusement, and as she sat somewhat out of breath from her exertions he laughed out loud and went toward her. "Get up!"

She glanced at him for a defiant moment. "No."

"Would you prefer I called in Jackie to help you . . . the young man who was just here?" he said, his voice hard once again, his eyes losing their twinkle.

"No, no," she said, getting to her feet. What did he mean to expose her shame to every male on the ship? What a cad he was! She gave him her back, but turned to look at him as he did nothing to assist her. "Well?"

"Well what, ma'am?" he asked innocently.

"Oh, you are insensible," she cried in frustration. "What do you want from me, Captain Landon . . . blood?"

He softened at once. "No, Miss de Brabant, what I want from you is something you have already told me is not within my power to obtain." His voice was low, slightly charged. His fingers worked her buttons slowly, and his lips found the smoothness of her neck.

She closed her eyes. Why, why did his touch have the power to work her into such a state? His very nearness put her out of temper, for she hated her weakness. She was attracted to this devil, physically attracted to him. It had nothing to do with a joining of spirits, of souls. It had nothing to do with love. It was his touch, his rugged good looks, his eyes, his smile! Oh, she hated his power over her sensations.

She moved away from him and went to the mirrored dresser. There she picked up his brush. "May I use this? You neglected to bring mine."

"Of course. Your things will be brought to you later." He moved to the cabin door. "Why don't you come on deck when you are done? You will get a fine glimpse of the American coastline."

"Oh . . ." She was excited in spite of herself. American soil! She was about to see a brand-new land. "I . . . I should like that."

He smiled, said nothing and left her to arrange her hair. She stared in the mirror. No longer a virgin. Do I look different? she asked the reflection. Do I look tainted?

Three

January 1, 1813 — Norfolk, Virginia

The first thing Windmera noticed about her new environment was the water. The approach to Barbados was through pools of aqua, lime and minty blues. Not so to Norfolk. The sea changed in hue from indigo to a dark grayish green. She wrinkled her nose. Surely this water was not to swim in, not after the clear beauty of the sea at home. And the coastline . . . so different, so much sterner. No welcoming emerald isle this, but a cold and severe picture. She didn't know what she had anticipated but only knew her imagination had not prepared her for this. There was something beautiful to it all, in spite of its starkness in comparison to her island home. There was a promise of greatness about the land, a hint that all was not what she saw in view. No lush greens, yellows, aquas or reds to tantalize the eye, but something more.

The harbor teamed with life. So different than Bridgetown. Boats were anchored everywhere; larger vessels too were docked. Windmera stood fascinated by all the new sights and sounds. She was leaning over the bulwarks, her velvet shawl wrapped tightly around her shoulders, for it was cold, so much colder than she had imagined it could be. Thank goodness she had thought to have some warmer clothes made for her trip to England, she thought idly, and then frowned. England! Would she ever get there? Her long black hair was unhampered by ribbons. It waved in the breeze, dancing around her shoulders, as did the short curls around her face. Lance watched her provocative profile. The violet hue of her gown exactly matched her eyes, and he was hard put to tear his gaze away to the more necessary occupation of seeing to his vessel.

What to do with Windmera de Brabant? They were divided by rents he could not breech, did not know how to repair. He had acted on a whim taking her on board, without thought to the future. All he had known at the time was desire. He had seen her there on the bed in her cabin on board the *Southsea* and had known he couldn't let her go. He hated slavery. He was pinched by her accusation. She said he had taken her like so much chattel, and it was true. He was in discord with himself. He was a man's man living in a man's age. Women were things to be used, petted, some with respect, others with admiration, but all for the pleasure of a man. He was at war with her country and she was a prisoner of war . . . a prize, as he had so admirably put it to her the other night. He could do with her what he willed. All her possessions were now his. Her trunks, her coins, even the clothes on her back. It was no better than what she deserved for her treachery in Barbados!

Still, it irritated him. But he had made up his mind to it. He would let her make the decision. "Miss de Brabant?" he said, his jaw set in a hard line.

She turned a haughty look upon him. "Yes?"

"I should like a word with you in my cabin."

She frowned and looked toward his cabin door, whose overhanging roof was located topside. "If you insist."

"I do," he said taking her arm. She yanked out of his hold and went on ahead. He sighed and signed for Jackie to take over his post.

Once in the cabin, the closed door keeping them private, she turned and regarded him from her dark-violet eyes. He found her breathtaking, but controlled his feelings. "Sit down, Windmera."

"I prefer to stand," she answered coldly.

"Oh, very well, I like looking at you that way, but I think I'll sit," he said, dropping his large muscular body into a chair at his back. He folded his arms akimbo and studied her purposefully.

She went hot beneath his scrutiny and made an inarticulate sound before sitting on the edge of the bed. "What do you want?"

He smiled wide. "You."

"Uh . . . what do you mean?"

"Windmera . . . you know what I mean. What I propose is to make a bargain."

"A . . . bargain?"

"Indeed. I have brought you on board the *Sea Hawk* against your wishes, true, but it was either here or out there on the open sea with a pack of sailors gawking at you for days on end. Do you realize what that would have entailed? No matter, you will say you would have preferred it to my company. So be it. But what is done is done. I offer now a solution to our quandary."

250

"Which is?" She was frowning. There was something cock-sure about his smile.

"You are destitute. Everything you have is mine. Hear me out before you object. We took the *Southsea* and everything on it. Even the gown you wear is mine. However, I am not a mean-spirited man, Windmera. If you don't agree to my bargain . . . I will give you a way out. I want you . . . have already possessed you. I should like to continue to possess you." He was charmed by her blush, but continued to go on audaciously. "And in return I shall protect you, care for your needs while you remain with me. At the end of the war, I shall convey you back to Barbados."

She stared at him with disbelief. "You want me to become your mistress? I . . . a de Brabant? Don't you realize . . . I was on my way to England with Roderick to become his wife!"

He had sensed it in his heart. Why else would she have been on board with Ravensbury? "I am sorry for him . . . and if you love him, for you," he answered softly.

"If I love him? How dare you doubt it!" she ranted.

"It doesn't matter. What does is that you are no longer in his care but in mine. If my terms are not suitable, you may take your things and disembark in Norfolk. However, I feel it necessary to warn you regarding the dangers of such a move."

She knew what the dangers would be. She and her Aunt Louise had often spoken about the trials of a woman alone in the world. She would have not one man to contend with . . . but many from all walks of life. Oh no, she didn't want that road. "How generous of you," she said sarcastically.

"Windmera . . . I would frank you, of course . . ."

"I don't want your money!"

"In either case, you will be getting it. You have but to make up your mind."

"When must you have your answer?"

"I should like to have it by tonight." His meaning was clear. "But I think not . . . tomorrow . . . yes, tomorrow will be fine."

"You are . . . too good!" she said contemptuously.

"Come, let us call a truce in the interim. Come back on deck with me."

She didn't answer him but swept past. She needed air and nearly ran to get it. How could he be so inhuman, so un-feeling? In Barbados she had suspected him of a far gentler

nature. She had even at one time dreamed about him roman-
tically . . . and now here he was as wicked a villain as any
storybook character. Oh, she hated him for so humiliating
her. She was a de Brabant! Reduced to such a state, and all
because of his . . . lust! She would rather have sat ragged
and frozen with Roderick in the longboat than be in the state
she now found herself.

Sudden hooting cheers sprang up from the bustling docks.
Sailors, civilians, men, women and children were shouting felicitations to the *Sea Hawk*. The word had got around that
the *Sea Hawk* had returned with an English prize! Everyone
was waving, laughing, congratulating themselves and each
other for having known that Captain Landon was one of the
best on the seas. Always he came in victorious! He boosted
their morale, gave them hope, and they loved him for it.

Windmera was temporarily diverted by it all and stared at
them in wonder. Why . . . to them, Captain Landon was a
hero! She looked at the English yawl in tow. Yes, she supposed to the Americans he would be a hero, and then for the
first time it dawned on her. They were at war. Her country
and his were at war with one another. This is part of it . . .
taking each other's ships. He could have killed everyone on
board but didn't. She frowned, not liking to concede him
anything.

All the commotion made her unaware of the biting cold
wind that stung her cheeks and whipped up her color. She
was listening to everyone at once. They drawled. Their accents were so strange, so different from Lance's, but then
Lance's accent was a unique mixture of New England, English and Irish, the last two having been an inheritance from
his parents. She was musing on this when she first saw the
woman in the chocolate-brown coach.

Windy was struck by the blue upholstery that flashed as the
doors of the brown coach were swung open. She saw a
woman's blue slipper emerge, and then rows and rows of
frilly blue lace tightly fitting a tall and most elegant woman.
Ginger-brown curls hung beneath a fetching blue silk bonnet,
and light-blue eyes surveyed the *Sea Hawk* with something
more than mild interest. Windy's brow went up as she
watched the woman make her way to the gangplank with a
diminutive black maid in attendance. Without knowing why,
Windy turned to look at Landon and noted that he too had
marked this woman's arrival. She watched him, saw the

flicker of interest, of admiration, as he went forward to greet the newcomer.

He bent low over the lovely woman's gloved hand. "Mrs. Clayton," he said, his eyes going up to flirt with her over her hand.

She smiled warmly. "Congratulations, sir. I reckon you are mighty proud of yourself."

"You mean the *Southsea?*" he said, motioning over his shoulder at the yawl. "It was nothing . . . just a stroke of luck."

"Luck indeed. You are too modest, captain . . . though I shouldn't be here speaking with you at all after the shabby way you treated me."

"How so?" he bantered, but knew full well she was referring to his hasty departure during the Christmas holidays. The woman had been getting too close to the point. She wanted marriage, and he had no intention of marrying a woman like Stacy Clayton.

She gave his hand a rap. "Wretch! But you will make it up to me by coming to dinner tomorrow night." She suddenly saw Windmera and stiffened.

He noticed the direction of her glance and smiled. "I should be delighted to attend your dinner party."

"Who is she?" said Mrs. Clayton on a low drawl.

"My first mate's sister. We are conveying her home to her parents as soon as may be, as she had been staying with cousins in Florida for a time," he fabricated quickly. He had no intention of allowing a woman like Stacy Clayton to carry gossip about Windmera. It wouldn't be fair to her, and it irritated him to think anyone would think lowly of Windy, perhaps because it was his fault she was in such a predicament. No matter, Stacy Clayton accepted his explanation immediately. Again the hand to his lips, and then they were watching her glide off the schooner and back to her carriage.

"Why didn't you tell her the truth, captain? Ashamed?" hissed Windmera, infuriated beyond reason. "Your first mate's sister indeed! Why didn't you tell your sweetheart that I was part of your prize, or didn't the conquering hero dare? But then a man who would rape virgins and take other men's wives wouldn't know what the truth is!"

He went to her, his fists clenched at his side, for he wanted to shake that look off her face. "I didn't tell her what you are to me because I thought to spare you! And for your information, chit, Mrs. Clayton is a widow! I don't trifle with virgins or married women. You may have been a virgin, but may I remind you that when I entered my cabin last night, you gave no indication of the fact?"

He turned his back to her then and stomped off. She was left red-cheeked and miserable. She looked up and saw Jackie frowning at her in some concern. She couldn't face him and ran to the companionway stairs. What she needed was privacy and a good cry.

How to get through this first night? So different from the night before. Last night she had been insensible, but now, now she had all her wits about her. Every nerve end tingled with dreaded anticipation. What would he do? What would he say? She had taken her first meal of the day (for she had refused both breakfast and lunch) at Jackie's insistence, but the captain had been nowhere in sight. She hadn't asked about him, and Jackie had offered her no explanation of the captain's absence, he had merely put one serving place on the dining table in the captain's quarters.

Afterward she had thumbed through some books she found in the nightstand cabinet. She dozed off with one of these in hand and then awoke with a start. The cabin was shrouded in darkness, for the wax candle she had lit earlier had burned itself out. It was late, very late, and she was still fully clothed. What to do? Would he be coming? Perhaps not! Good. Then she could undress in peace and be comfortable for a time. She first lit a nightstand candle and then struggled with the buttons of her gown, managing to get the top undone and then twisting the gown partially to work on the others. She was finally able to shed her garments. She went through her trunks and brought forth a suitable white nightdress, slipped it on, took up her brush and worked at her hair. However she had scarcely done ten strokes when the cabin door opened at her back. She saw him first in her looking glass. His shirt was open to the waist beneath his cloak of dark wool, and his bronzed chest showed through with its silky smooth black curls. His blue eyes were strangely glassy, but she guessed why at once. More often than not in these last five years she had seen her father after a bout with the bottle. The captain was in his cups!

"What . . . what are you doing here?" she whispered on a harsh breath.

"I? May I remind you, lass, this is my cabin," he said, and his words had not the slur her father's had always had when he had been drinking. Nor did he sway, but still she knew the captain had been drinking heavily. It was in the air, it was in his mien. She was frightened, but she put up a brave front.

"And may I remind you that you said you would not bother me this night?" she returned. "You should not be here at all."

"No . . . I am not so foxed I don't remember what it was I said. No, my beauty. I said I would not trouble you for an answer, and so I shan't. I merely wish to get out of my clothes and into my bed. I shan't touch you, my dear!"

She stared with disbelief. "You can't mean to sleep in the same bed with me?"

"Why not?" He smiled roguishly. "We did last night . . . very comfortably."

"We won't tonight!" she retorted, her cheeks hot.

"I have no passenger accommodations. This is the only cabin . . . the only bed . . . I am afraid we shall have to share it this night. No matter, I have already given my word . . . which I might add is a sight surer than yours. I shan't touch you!"

She frowned. What was that supposed to mean? When had she ever broken her word to him? She knew he blamed her for his predicament in Barbados, and perhaps rightly so, but she had never lied to him. She assumed being in his cups he didn't realize what he said. She put up her chin, went to the bed, took up a pillow and the quilt and brought them to the floor. Here she laid out the quilt and set down the pillow. Thusly she planted herself, wrapped the quilt about her and shut her eyes tight. It was hard and uncomfortable, but it was better than sharing a bed with the scoundrel.

Captain Landon was a gentleman. It offended his sensibilities to allow her to so inconvenience herself. He was a man who had every good reason to both admire and respect womankind. His mother had been a light in his life. His sister he treasured as a spoiled but precious being. His experiences with the fairer sex had left him no scars, and although he had been hurt and infuriated with Windmera for her deceit and treachery against him on her island, he had no real wish to cause her harm. Still, in spite of all these factors and for reasons he could not explain, he lost his patience and temper with her and instead of offering to take the floor himself and give up the bed to her, which under ordinary circumstances he would have done, he said instead, "So be it! You wish to prove what you would rather do than be near me. Very well, experience what it is like, lass, know what you take on."

So saying, he dropped his cloak onto the chair against the wall, shrugged off his shirt and let it fall to the floor, where followed his boots and breeches. He climbed into bed with a sigh and lay there on his back. It was well she had kept herself aloof. It was well they were not in the same bed, for truth had it that he would have been hard put to it to keep his promise. He had gone drinking with some acquaintances in Norfolk, hoping the great quantity of gin he had consumed would dilute his virility. He thought he had had enough when more than one wench he had fondled failed to arouse him. There, safe to return and keep his promise to Windmera to let her be this night. However, one glance at her in her scanty nightdress had sent his manhood aloft, his passion to all-consuming heights, and he lay now frustrated in his bed wishing she was not so near, wishing she was nearer. Damn, but this was Hell! Windmera had brought him nothing but Hell!

Four

Stacy Clayton's town house sparkled. Her husband's family had amassed a fortune from his tobacco plantation. They owned it still, but her husband had also begun a bank which was located in the heart of Norfolk. It was here Stacy had preferred to live. Her husband had been good, gracious, kind, generous and old. Very old. He wanted a beautiful hostess. She wanted a rich life. She came from Southern aristocracy, but her family held no pretensions to financial independence any longer. She had been sold of her own free will to the highest bidder, and it had been Mr. George Clayton. She hadn't minded in the least. She had minded less when he had died a year before and left her free to enjoy her money and her beauty, for both brought her many suitors.

She was good Southern *ton,* and her house was inundated with Southern quality. Fashion abounded, champagne flowed freely, slaves scurried, everything was as she wanted, and to top it all, Lance Landon had returned from the sea. She watched him as he crossed the ballroom floor toward her. He was well dressed this night in the dark superfine coat and breeches Beau Brummell in London had made famous. His white ruffled shirt enhanced his bronze rugged cheeks. By God but he was a well-formed man. She remembered their lovemaking, and it sent shivers down her spine. He was already at her side, taking up her hand, smiling with those wonderful blue eyes of his.

"Mrs. Clayton," he was saying lightly, flirtatiously, "you look, as always, delectable."

She agreed with him. Her gown of gold silk exactly matched her elegant stature. Her ginger curls had been dressed just so, her topaz egret sparkled in her hair as did the matching set at her ears and throat. Yes, she knew how well she looked, and she knew he would have eyes for no one else at her house, though many a belle was looking his way.

"Let's show 'em how pretty we can look together, captain," she drawled coquettishly, "I do so love a waltz."

He smiled and led her out. This woman had managed to while away many enjoyable hours for him only weeks ago. For a time, he had thought she had even been successful in routing Windmera's image from his memory. But when he was away from Stacy he forgot about her. She was a shallow woman, unable to hold his interest, but nevertheless she certainly was a woman and one well worth holding, touching. He dived into the effort with some zeal, putting Windy's large violet eyes out of his mind. Last night had been torture. This morning they had bandied words, and then again that evening just before he left the *Sea Hawk* for Stacy's affair. Nevertheless, he would have his answer this very night upon his return, and so he had advised her! Damn the chit, even now with Stacy's voluptuous body so close to him he was thinking about Windmera!

Windmera sat on deck looking out onto the flickering town lights. He was impossible, cruel. He had given her the ultimatum, and she would have to give him her decision. Go out there . . . into the world alone . . . and find herself in perhaps worse straits than now, or continue with him until the war was over. He had said harshly that he had already taken her maidenhead, it no longer mattered . . . what did she hope to preserve?

She asked herself the same question now. Yes, what was left to preserve? Your dignity! She answered herself at once. Your pride, your faithfulness to Roderick, whom you must return to. Hadn't Rod called out that he would find you? He knew what Lance would do to you, but it didn't matter to him, that was love! What Lance offered was a coldblooded affair. There was only one answer. She would have to find a way to escape. Perhaps steal a boat and sail out to sea where an English vessel might find her . . . take her to Bermuda. With any luck she might make it on her own to Bermuda. But how, how? It was all too much for her, and she found herself unable to contain her tears. They flowed on one giant gulping sob.

A hand came down upon her shoulder, and she turned her tear-stained face around sharply. She saw Jackie, his fair hair in disarray about his youthful pleasant countenance. His light eyes were bright with concern.

"Don't cry, Miss de Brabant," he begged. He was sadly troubled by her agitation. She was a fine lady. A good person. Captain shouldn't have left her here so miserable. He should have taken her somewhere on the town, cheered her up. Truth to tell, Jackie was overwhelmed by Windmera. He had never known such a female before, and his heart was boyishly lost to her already.

She held his hand as a friend. "Jackie . . . oh, couldn't you help me?"

He brightened and sat down beside her at once. "How do you mean?"

"Couldn't you get a boat for me . . . help me escape . . . so that I can get to Bermuda. . . to my bethrothed?"

He grew grim. She was engaged to someone. It irked him strangely. His love for her was platonic, pure. His nature was not a jealous one, and had the captain been treating her properly he would have been satisfied to leave it at that. However, the captain had not been treating her in the manner she deserved, and he had found it necessary to step in to comfort her. But he knew his loyalties. He was the captain's man. He would not send her to some damn Englishman in Bermuda. "I am sorry," he answered.

She pouted. "I thought you were my friend. You seem to feel for my predicament, yet you won't help me. Is it that you are afraid of the consequences to yourself? I suppose I must understand that."

"Aw, no, Miss de Brabant. You've got it all wrong. You give the captain time to shake off his black mood and you'll be the better for it. I'm to guard you while he is away, you know . . . I've never broken with the captain, never . . . and I don't mean to, not for all the beauty in the world. He depends on me, and if it weren't for him . . . I'd be nothing today." It was his own affair, what Captain Landon had done for him so long ago. His alone. He didn't have to explain to anyone, but he wanted to banish the sadness from this girl's eyes. She was so lovely. He brightened on a thought. "Look here, I know what will set us up right and tight, Miss de Brabant. If you give me your word not to run away, I'll take you on the town, show you some of the sights. How's that?"

She opened her eyes wide. She liked the notion very much. It would do her good, and perhaps she might discover a way of escape for the future. "I should like that . . . very much. But won't your captain object?"

"Naw . . . he said to keep you safe . . . I can do that and give you a good time. . . if'n you promise not to run off?"

"I promise I won't run off . . . not tonight. All right?" she said, smiling.

"Good. Come on, then," he said, getting up and taking her hands to pull her to her feet.

"Oh, wait . . . just give me a moment to put up my hair."
She looked down at her simple gown and shawl. "And
change into something prettier."

"Hurry up, then." He grinned wide, watching her rush off,
pleased with himself for making her smile.

"Tch, tch, tch," said a gruff crewman at his back.

Jackie looked up to see one of his shipmates and pulled a
face at him. "What's got you all crusty, Ben?"

"Capt'n ain't gonna like you playing games with his piece
of skirt!"

"Don't call her that! I'm only taking her about town for a
spell. No harm in it. Capt'n won't mind."

"Whew! I tell you what, lad. I ain't gonna be within a
hundred feet of him when he gets back and finds the two of
you gone!"

"Well . . . maybe we'll get back before he does," said
Jackie, beginning to worry over the matter.

"Best be," said Ben, going off toward the gangplank. "Poor
Tubs, he's on watch tonight, and if you don't get back before
capt'n it'll be left to him to say you went off wit the wench!"
He shook his head as he made his way off the schooner, but
the frown was wiped off Jackie's face a moment later when
he looked up to see Windmera, a vision in white cambric,
coming toward him, a dark cloak over her arm.

Captain Lance Landon stepped out of his hack, paid the
driver and made his way to his schooner. It had not been an
easy thing to tear himself away from Stacy. She had been
very tempting, and he had not wanted to insult her, but he
found himself restless to quit her company and return to his
vessel. He wanted his answer from Windmera. He wanted to
know what to expect. Hell, what if she decided to leave?

It was this that plagued him most. Would he let her? She
was such a obstinate little creature, full of pride. She would
hate to give in to him on principle alone, and he admired her
spirit, but would he let her step off his schooner and enter the
great open world with all its dangers?—and it surely held
dangers for someone like Windmera. With all her fight, with
all her bravado, she was an innocent. She didn't dream how
people would use her if they had the chance. Without a male
to protect her she was so much pickings. No, he didn't think
he would let her walk off his ship . . . but then what about
his word? Would he have to keep her with him untouched
until the end of the war? Hell and fire!

He nodded to Tubs, who winced when he reported that all was well. Where the devil was Jackie with the capt'n's skirt? Damn, but there was going to be an explosion tonight, and he waited at his post for the inevitable.

The captain went to his cabin, opened its door, lit a candle and found it empty. On his bed a gown had been tossed. It was the gown Windmera had worn that day. He frowned and went back into the companionway and up the short flight of stairs to the deck and called, "Tubs?"

"Aye, capt'n?"

That was all Tubs said, but Lance Landon caught something in the tone that further creased his brow. "You know what I am going to ask next, don't you, Tubs?" he said dangerously, walking toward the small round man.

"Aye, capt'n," said the man with resignation.

"Well then, my man?"

"Aw now, capt'n . . . the lad didn't mean no harm by it. She was looking like a wilted flower . . . setting out here crying . . . and the boy, why . . . he thought to take her for a drink maybe . . . that's all. Get her mind off her troubles . . . there be naught to it."

Captain Landon's sensual mouth went hard. His blue eyes grew cold. "I see." He moved away toward the flickering lights of the town and attempted to gain control of his emotions. How dare that young scalawag presume to interfere? He would have the boy's hide for this. But damn, it wasn't Jackie's fault. He was ever a soft-hearted thing, bringing stray cats onto the vessel, throwing coins to the beggars! No. It was Windmera's fault. Windmera with those big eyes had done this. What was her game? Why Jackie?

He heard the sound of a musical giggle, and in the rays of a street torch made out Windmera's face as she rounded the corner with Jackie at her side. Her hand was linked in the crook of his bent arm. Her dark cloak was open wide to show the low décolletage of her white gown. He could see how well she looked, with her long black hair piled high upon her head, some strands allowed to fall low, long over her shoulder. She was enticing, and she was on the arm of his first mate!

Windmera had enjoyed herself. He had taken her to the town hall, where a winter concert was in progress. He had purchased tickets, and they had enjoyed an hour of music before he took her to the fashionable hotel in the town square. Here they had enjoyed coffee and cake in the restaurant before taking the long walk home. They laughed over silly things, finding conversation easy because neither expected more than that from the other. However, Jackie got a good look at his captain's stern face before he helped Windmera up the gangway, and all laughter was drowned in a new concern. Ben had been right. The captain was very upset.

"Where the devil have you been, Mr. Wyburn!" snapped the captain, not deigning to look at Windmera.

Jackie blanched. Landon had never been so curt with him, had never called him by his family name. He stuttered on his reply, "We . . . I . . . I . . . you . . ."

Windmera was furious. How dare Lance treat the boy so shabbily? She stamped her foot. "I asked him to show me around town!"

"But I asked him to make sure you didn't get into mischief!" retorted the captain hotly, his eyes raking her. "Go to your cabin!"

She wanted to stand and fight, would have sooner died than comply, but more than her pride was at stake here. She feared for Jackie. She had no way of knowing the captain's anger against his youthful first mate was a temporary thing, that it was she who would in the end experience its full potency, not Jackie. She glanced worriedly from Jackie to the captain.

Jackie whispered, implored with his eyes, for he was already aware of Windmera's contrariness. "Please . . . go on . . ."

"Very well," she said putting up her chin and stalking off.

The captain glared after her and turned his stern eyes back upon the lad. "Explain yourself."

Jackie's fair face was flushed with color. Did the captain really think he would try to undermine his position with Miss de Brabant, try to make love to her? It was mortifying, and he was near to tears.

"Captain . . . she seemed so . . . unhappy . . . I thought to keep her occupied. I took her to the concert at the town hall . . . we went for cake afterward . . . I never meant to . . . would never . . ."

The captain had already softened. He put his hand on Jackie's shoulder. "I know, lad . . . forget it. Did it take all your money, entertaining my guest?"

The boy flushed with pleasure, for the twinkle was back in Lance's eye. He was ever sensitive to his captain's moods. "Naw," he said gruffly. But as he saw the captain was about to go, he stayed him with a word. "Capt'n . . . she is only a child, you know . . . in many ways . . ."

Captain Landon glanced sharply at Jackie, for he sounded so worldly-wise. He smiled in some amusement. "I shall try to keep that in mind. Now go on and get some sleep."

Windmera threw down her cloak onto her trunk with some force. He was a brute. He was cruel and pitiless. How could he have so humiliated Jackie? How dare he treat Jackie so badly? How she wished she could serve him a settler! If he thought to dress her down as he had Jackie, he had quite another think coming. So violent were her emotions that she trembled beneath their force, and then there he was . . . smiling!

He dropped off his dress coat, hung it carelessly on the knob of his cabin door. He undid his vest, pulled off his neckcloth and undid his shirt buttons and then sat down upon his chair, putting his booted feet up on his bed. "There. Now, Miss de Brabant. Your answer, if you please. Do you remain with me or go abroad?"

Oh, he was so cold. So arrogant. She wanted to give him a setdown, tell him she would rather die than lie in his arms, but tonight had done many things for her. She had seen how impossible it would be for her to manage and maintain what respectability she had left to herself if she took on life alone in America. But even this had not decided her. It was on her way home. She had seen many small sailboats docked. They looked unused, and when she asked about them, Jackie had replied they belonged to the plantation owners who enjoyed sailing from time to time. They were left virtually unguarded!

Well, she had lost her virginity to Lance Landon. She had nothing more to lose. What was one more or even two more nights to her? She would endure them until she could escape from his dreadful vessel and snatch up a boat, and then, then it was freedom! She faced him squarely, and her violet eyes were unreadable in their depths.

"Why . . . Captain Landon . . . did you have any doubt? Of course I will be your . . . mistress . . . share your bed . . . sell you my body. What else could I possibly do?" She would do it, but she would if she could make him miserable all the while. She saw the dissatisfaction in his eyes. Good. Her words had found their mark. He had *some* feelings after all. Good. He sat there frowning, so she braced herself and started working the front lacings of her gown. These undone, she dropped the gown off her shoulders, exposing her full luscious breasts, but before she could lower it any further, he muttered a curse beneath his breath and stalked out of the room. She had meant to needle him with her remark, but had never dreamed it would have that much effect. Odd. Everything about Lance Landon was so unpredictable.

He paced on deck. Damn, but her decision was something that should have sent hot blood surging through his veins. Instead it left him shaky. He was a cad. He knew himself a blackguard. Her words had left him sore with himself. Damn, but she was a woman to defy the devil himself. It was, of course, her eyes again that tortured him, reminding him that she had been a virgin, that she had been a promised bride. Well, that was done. It could not be undone. He called to Tubs and sent him below for a bottle of whiskey. But a few swigs of this left him no better off, and at last he returned to his cabin.

She had put out the candles. He feared to stumble over her in the dark, for in all probability she was again sleeping on the floor. But she was not. He could just make out her form in the bed. He lit a single candle and left it in its holder on his dresser as he shed his garments. He slipped into the bed, and she gave the first sign that she was awake.

"Aren't you going to snuff the candle?" she asked on a hush, for in spite of her act she was terrified.

He smiled warmly. "No, my beauty . . . I'm not ready to sleep yet. Your remark was nicely calculated to turn me off, and it worked for a time. But only for a time. I soon knew your game."

She sighed. He was a hard-hearted man. However had he become that way? "One thing, Captain Landon. What will happen if you . . . if I become pregnant?"

He touched her nose. "You won't."

"I . . . I won't? I don't understand."

"You will," he said, bending low, taking her mouth. Oh God, it was so good. The feel of her body next to his. That sweet mouth opening to receive his exploring tongue. He had wondered whether the satisfaction he had received when taking her what seemed that long-ago night had been intensified in imagination, but no, this, this building fever, was real! His hand went to her breast, fondled, found the nipple. His lips traced a road to it, sucked first, then teased with his tongue. Then he moved his body down the length of hers so that he was kissing her midriff, her waist, her belly, lower still to the tuft of soft hair. He came back up again, but this time took her hand. "Feel this, my love," he said, taking her hand to his rod, forcing her fingers round its hugeness. He moved her hand in the manner he wanted, and then as she worked him his hand parted her thigh, touched, explored, found the berth he sought, inserted a finger, teased audaciously until he felt her haunch her body in wanton abandonment.

Windy couldn't believe she could behave this way. His kiss had excited her beyond belief, and then his touch, his hand fondling. It was wrong. All so wrong. She shouldn't feel this way. When Rod had touched her she had never felt this way. Lance's hands were arousing an erotic sensation in her groin. She could not plead any form of drunkenness this time. No, the only thing she had imbibed was coffee, and she was fully aware . . . all too aware. She was shocked when he placed her hand around his manhood. It was wonderous how the male was formed. She was curious and thrilled all at once. Thrilled because she suddenly knew she was the one who had caused this passion in him, that she was capable of maintaining it. But she wanted to hold herself aloof. Yes, she had made this bargain and would keep it, but she wanted to keep a part of herself from him. Her mind, her heart, her soul. She must. She would utter no words of endearment even though he spoke enchantment to her ears. She would not respond even though her body moved with a will of its own! And then his fingers discovered the place between her legs and proved her false to herself. Was it possible? Could she be thrusting herself into his touch, calling his name, begging for more? It was her voice, her voice saying, "Oh Lance, Lance . . . please . . . take me . . . now . . . now . . ."

"No, my beauty, not yet, not yet, there is more, so much more." He had positioned his rod between the lips of her vagina, but he did not thrust. He moved his staff first in a circular motion just at the opening, then a little deeper he went, moving it back and forth, driving her to frenzy.

She grabbed hold of his body and haunched herself roughly, hungrily, into him, but still he did not penetrate farther. He was enjoying her, every inch of her. He would go on this way, it was so good, but he was losing control. She was a sensual, passionate woman, and her wild movements were disintegrating his control. He groaned and dived deep within her.

They were as one. She felt his hard lean body against her

265

own as he moved. His hands were all over her, raising her rump to receive his thrusts, touching her ardently in places she hadn't known were alive with nerve ends. His words held her in the spell, incited her responses.

"Windy, Windy . . . you are so perfect . . . oh, God, how you move me." He would touch her hips, rotate her, but she discovered movements all her own, discovered their power over him and used them well. He groaned with pleasure, "Ah, babe, my sweet babe, that's right, keep it up, keep it up . . ."

This couldn't be her, not Windmera de Brabant, daughter of quality. She couldn't believe the heights he took her to, resisted every now and then as sudden realization played with her mind. She would go rigid beneath him, and then he would work on her again, using his expert knowledge with a force that left her breathless for more, and then she knew total satisfaction. She slumped with the release that came, but he chuckled in her ear, whispered something about bringing her to it again and began his voracious pumping. "Do you like this, love?" And as he changed movements, "And this?" His lips caressed her skin, found pressure points and bit gently, tenderly. His fingers frenzied her until once again she wanted him to plunge himself into her fully, she wanted to retrieve his manhood, hold it with her womb.

He brought her to yet another climax, and then he knew he could remain within her no longer, not without making her pregnant. With a gasp he yanked himself out and completed his shooting safely without.

She closed her eyes. She was so ashamed of herself. It hadn't happened the way she had planned, and she had planned it all so well. She was going to lie there rigidly unmoving beneath him, cold, aloof, unresponsive to his manipulations. How had he obtained her lustful answers to his exertions? She had never dreamed it was possible to be excited that way . . . not without loving the man! Love? It was impossible. They hated one another. Or did they?

When she was in his arms, in the circle of intimacy, she felt one with him, she felt their souls meet and smile. Was that love or passion? Oh, God, she could remember still her begging him to complete the act, giving her the sexual gratification he had worked her into wanting, needing. She had behaved like a strumpet and had enjoyed every moment. There was no use pretending otherwise. And now she knew more than ever before the need to escape him as soon as possible.

Lance was lost in the afterglow of pleasure. He had pulled her into his arms so that her back rested neatly against his chest, her rump against his drawn-up thighs. She had taken him to Hell and then to Heaven all in one night. What was she? What was it about her that made their lovemaking better than he had ever had with any other woman? Yes, she was beautiful, but so was Stacy and so many others he had taken to his bed. What made this one so different? He kissed the back of her neck, felt the roundness of her voluptuous butt smoothly against his resting staff, and without even realizing it began a slow, willful cadent beat against her satin roundness. Oh, God, she felt so good, so good. A moment later he felt his manhood begin to rise, felt her sweet rump push back against his hardness and knew himself on fire all over again. Was that push on purpose? Was she responding? No matter, he would have her now!

Windy felt him against her, felt the muscle that had joined him to her so hedonistically resting flaccid now against her, and wanted him to know she was no longer as susceptible. She would not be held any longer. She pushed back in an effort to stop his insidious movements against her. And then she felt the sudden change come over him. She was caught up in a new wonder. All she had done was push . . . yet, he was responding as though she had invited him to dine. She was startled by her power, amazed at his sexual strength, for she had been versed over the years by her flighty Tante Louise. A piece of knowledge gained here, another there. Louise had told her many things about men and women, haphazardly, but facts all the same. There was something exciting in knowing she was able to arouse Lance Landon. In spite of her contention with him, she knew him a virile, attractive man. She knew that he could have any number of women, and here he was . . . wanting her! It thrilled her in spite of herself.

Suddenly, secretly, for she couldn't admit it yet to herself, her body began to react. Yes, she wanted him, hated herself for her weakness but knew herself again caught up in his passion. There was no use objecting, no use hiding behind a look of innocence; she knew herself jaded. She was an unmarried woman in bed with this man; she could claim innocence no more. There was a sadness in the knowledge, but there was also a strange tingling sensation now coursing through her. He was touching her thighs, massaging them suggestively, allowing his fingers to stray between, higher, just coming near her opening but not quite getting there.

Then, with a groan that sent tantalizing shivers racing through her body, he pulled her up by the waist onto her knees. He got to his knees as well directly behind her and bent her over. His hands came from beneath and cupped her dangling breasts, and with an expression of ecstasy he guided his hard pulsating penis to the opening he sought just as she gasped, "What . . . what are you doing?"

"What you teased me to do." He chuckled, pleased with her confusion, slightly heady with happiness, for she was his. He was her tutor. No other!

She felt his thrust, heard his words of bliss at her ears, and suddenly could remain aloof no longer. She had meant this time to maintain stoic control of herself. This time, she would not move for him, not respond for him, but oh, as he teased and played at her womb she did so want him to go deeper, and finally with a groan of resignation she thrust back into his dive and gave over to the fever of their union.

Five

Sara of Ravensbury sat in the wheelchair that had long ago become both her refuge and her prison. Her hair was no longer that bright shade of gold, but a faded hue of tired yellow. Strands of silky white were seen in its folds, for she wore it braided at the top of her still quite regal head. The years had been cruel to Sara, but she had retained some of her former beauty, and she sat nearly at peace with herself as she gazed out of her long window on the frosted lawns of Ravensbury.

Flashes of her youth passed sharply, strangely vivid after all these years. She could almost see herself running through the fields to her dark gypsy, but his face was vague, his features muted with time. It was gone. All of it was gone. She glanced sharply at her lap. Beneath her ivory satin gown were legs, useless legs, shrunken things. Time had not eased the pain of losing their power. She ached still to get up and cross her room to her door. She longed still to move them beneath a man. A man . . . she had not had a man in two years, not since Dr. William Evans had departed Cornwall for a new practice and a bride in London. Thinking of William now was only a dull ache. If she had had the use of her legs he would be hers still. But she didn't and he wasn't and it no longer mattered.

Sara was forty-seven. She had endured the unendurable, and she had at last come to terms with herself, her past and her future, for Sara of Ravensbury was dying.

She sighed and looked back into her room toward the door. She had sent for Godwin. Odd. She had never thought she would do that, but it was necessary now. The new doctor imported from Penzance had been very kind, but he was incapable of ceasing the onslaught of her consumption. It did come, sapping her life's vitality, wreaking havoc with her lungs so that at times she thought she would walk from the sheer force of her coughing. The new doctor . . . how ill at ease he had been when he told her she had not long to live. He didn't have to tell her, she already knew, though hearing her fears confirmed made it all the more real. Odd. How many times she had wanted to die, and now, now that finally her wish had been granted, she wanted only to live.

Godwin had been told, yet he had not come. They lived in different worlds, and he rarely came to hers. She was no longer strong enough to go to his. She had not seen him since Roderick's departure ten months ago. Yes, ten months ago he had paid one of his rare visits to her room and had told her that Heather was dead. He had told her that he had a daughter and that he had arranged for Roderick to marry the girl. She had been furious. She had called for Roderick. She had forbidden it, but neither one paid her any heed. And now she was dying and she had sent him a plea. She knew Godwin hated her still. He was unforgiving still, but the knowledge no longer had the might to make her bitter. She was dying, and she wanted one thing, her son. Only Godwin had the power to give him to her.

She knew Godwin. He did hate her but he had never given her reason to believe he would not come when she called. He would not deny her an interview. A knock sounded at her chamber door, and she called out quietly.

"Come in, my lord."

He opened the door and stood a moment to consider her, for the sight of Sara in a wheelchair had always a disquieting effect on him. He had always believed that the accident that had made her a cripple was a judgment of God, that it was justice, and still he could not fight the sense of pity, of regret, that overcame his hardened heart when he saw her thus. But he had learned not to display his feelings. He had learned the trick of shielding himself. "You sent for me, Sara?"

"Yes, Godwin. Do come in and close the door, please. There is something I should like to ask of you . . . beg of you if I must."

He frowned. She was not the same Sara he had known twenty years ago. She was not even the same Sara who had wielded her power from her chair. Something had gone out of her. She was a broken woman. He had seen her even in her crippled state capable of reducing the servants to tears, of getting the household in order, of tooling her son when he would do other than her bidding. This woman was not Sara. Where was that avaricious gleam in her eyes? My God, the thought struck, could the knowledge that one was dying do such a thing, create such a change? He was taken aback by her sudden helplessness. She had never appeared so impotent to him before.

"What is it, Sara?"

"It is Roderick. I am aware that we both know I have not long. I have . . . reviewed my life and have seen what I have done, to you . . . to myself . . . but worst of all to Roderick. Godwin, I have done so much to Roderick. I need him to be here . . . to come home . . . I must make it up to him."

Godwin snorted. He did not wish to be cruel to this sick dying woman, but when she spoke of making it up to Roderick, it was almost more than he could bear, "Do you really think you can make up a lifetime of torment with a few inadequate gestures? Roderick despises you. Make no mistake, you have not enough time to make it up to him!" He saw her wince beneath the blow of his words, and he felt a swell of pity. He fought it down. She deserved no pity! He faced the wall, put his hands in one another at his back and began to pace. He stopped and looked at her. "I don't know what you hope to do. Ask for forgiveness?"

"No . . . no . . . not forgiveness. It is not for myself, Godwin. I swear it. I know you find it hard to believe . . . but it is not for myself. I have done worse than neglect Roderick. I have turned away from him, blamed him for . . . for our division. He needs to know that I loved him, love him so very much. Every child . . . needs to know he is loved."

He took an angry step toward her, "Sara . . . Roderick is a child no more! What he needed is past. He is a man . . . already formed. You can do nothing to alleviate the hurts he suffered as a boy. A scar is a scar. It cannot be erased."

"But it can be balmed . . . I can try . . ."

"Then you may do so. Roderick will be here any day now . . . with his bride. You may extend your sudden benevolence to them both. You may make it up to Roderick . . . and to Heather as well," he said, watching her closely.

She closed her eyes. "He is marrying Heather's daughter. There is nothing I can say that will prohibit either of you from going through with it?"

"No, Sara, there is nothing you can say. In fact, I couldn't be more pleased, for I take it from Roderick's letters that he has formed a lasting attachment for my daughter." He beamed at the thought. What could be better? His adopted son and his natural daughter? Perfect.

Sara felt stung by the thought of such a union. Her son to Heather's daughter! She would see Heather in the girl. "So . . . you have won at last," she said quietly.

"Yes, by God! What you cheated me out of in my youth

you won't cheat me out of in my waning years! You are dying, but I . . . I am not, and I will see my flesh and blood and have at last my family." He spat these words at her, for his memory had worked him again into bitterness.

She winced, shrank away with his words, with the picture this evoked of the future. She would be no more. Her son would belong to Heather's daughter. She was nothing to anyone. "But . . . he does return soon . . . he will be here . . . before . . ."

"Yes. He should be here within a week. He is on the *Southsea,* together with my daughter. Now, if you have nothing more . . . ?"

"No, Godwin . . . I have nothing more," she said quietly and turned away from him. She heard his retreating footsteps. She heard the door close at his back. No, she had nothing more.

Roderick stood on his balcony in the Governor's Mansion in Bermuda and looked out to sea. The water was full with the foam of crashing waves against coral reefs. The water was that translucent shade of aqua, with purple blotches marking more mysterious depths. It was breathtaking, but it held no spell for Roderick.

His thoughts were bent on one thing. Revenge! To that end, he had sent off a letter to Godwin. He would need his own vessel, with a captain well seasoned. He would need arms and he would need funds. His plan? To sail to Canada and thereby make his way through the wilds to Mystic, Connecticut. He would need to disguise himself as an American. So be it. No matter the odds, he would do it, for he intended to find Windmera and he meant to destroy Lance Landon. Both were equally important.

He thought of Landon. Fiend seize the man's eyes for having looked Windmera's way. A plague take Landon's manhood for having dared to touch her . . . and Roderick was certain that by now Landon had taken his bride to his bed. No idle threats hung in his fantasy. He meant to kill Landon, with his own hand if he could.

To this end he would work, but he would need patience. It would take time for the letter to reach Godwin, for Godwin to send him what he needed. In the meantime, the governor had been very generous with his loan, for the man was acquainted with the name of Ravensbury. He would have to make do with the pleasures this small island had to offer. He set his jaw. Pride? It would be his again when Lance Landon was dead!

Pride? Windmera de Brabant awoke in Landon's bed and wondered if she could ever hold her head up again. She wondered how she would face him when he too had awakened. She had been vanquished. How does one hand over one's sword to the enemy and still hold chin well up? Last night had shattered all pretensions to the thing called pride. She had found his touch, his lovemaking, all-absorbing, and had given herself without restraint. There was only one answer. She must escape him, and soon . . . soon, before she found herself in the grip of an emotion from which there was no escape. Love? No! Don't think it! Not to someone like him. He is a heartless libertine. He has used you. You were a source of pleasure . . . nothing more, she told herself sharply, lest she lose her sense of purpose.

He stirred beside her, and without meaning to, without wanting to, she recalled the previous night. She had lost count of how many times he had taken her. She remembered how tired she had been that last. She had been sleeping in his hold, strangely secure in the strength of his arms, when suddenly she felt a pleasurable sigh escape her lips and realized it was due to his touch. His touch! Omnipresent and potent, charging her madly with desire, until finally they lay enervated in a quiet embrace.

Now. Yes, now was the morning after. She had made her bargain last night and she had kept it . . . all too well. How would he treat her on this morning after? She was terrified.

Lance's lids fluttered open and felt the softness of her silken locks. His face was nearly buried in the sweet scent of her hair. Oh, God, she had been good! Better than that first night when she had been wild with the effects of the yohimbe . . . and still he felt a certain part of her was held aside. She had given him her body, responding because she was a hot-blooded creature, but he knew she had not committed her soul. Did he want her soul! Damn it, yes! He wanted all of her. He moved his hand and found her lush full breast. Damn if he wouldn't take her again. "How about some breakfast, love?" he whispered, simultaneously letting her know just exactly what he meant.

She gasped and jumped off the bed, grabbing the quilt with her as she went. This left him naked, and she stared for a moment before averting her gaze. He was a beautiful man.

She had noted it last night as he made love to her by candle-light, but the light of day showed her just how beautiful.

He chuckled. "No?" He started to get up. "I could change your mind . . ."

She was determined to keep herself aloof. "Stop it, Lance. It is broad daylight!"

"All the better, my love," he said, already coming hear her. "You cannot mean to play the prude . . . not after last night."

She blushed hotly and lowered her eyes. "Please, Lance . . . my . . . I have such a soreness . . ." It was the truth.

He stopped his advances immediately, and his hand went instead to her head. He stroked, and his eyes softened. "Yes, of course . . . I was forgetting . . . how very new you are at this." He pushed her toward the bed. "Go on, love . . . relax while I get dressed."

She acquiesced silently, propping herself up to watch him at his labors. She was struck by the mien of the man, and observed him with sudden avid interest. He poured the fresh water into a basin and began scrubbing his face, neck and shoulders with a washcloth. He then toweled himself and shrugged into a fresh pair of breeches, pulled on a shirt, socks and Hessians and then quickly, carelessly, put a brush through his long black hair. As he buttoned his shirt, Windmera interrupted his whistling.

"When you were in Barbados, you mentioned a sister . . . have you any others . . . a brother?" She didn't know why, but she was curious about him.

He smiled, pleased with her curiosity. "No, I have only Izzy . . . and my new nephew. They live in Buffalo, though my father will not be satisfied until he has got them in Mystic." He was amused with the memory this evoked.

She tilted his head. "You are fond of them . . . your sister, her son . . . your father. I can see that. What makes you leave them . . . take to the sea?"

"The need for excitement, I suppose. What made you leave your plantation, your aunt?" He thought immediately of Roderick, and it creased his brow even before he heard her answer.

She sighed. "That question has a long, long answer, and I don't know if I can . . . talk about it," she said quietly.

He stopped his ministrations and turned to stare at her. "You mean you didn't leave to get married to Roderick . . . go to England and enjoy the fashionable life?" There was something of scorn in his tone. How could she claim to love

274

Roderick? She couldn't have given herself so sensually if her heart was pledged elsewhere.

She fired up at once. "You throw your insults around aimlessly, Captain Landon. Quite a lot happened after you made off with your shipment. Yes, it was yours, and you had every right to it, but Brayward was right—we had sold at a terrible loss and were not able to . . . absorb such a loss. Tante Louise meant to enlist Brayward's help . . . she married him, and then Jokai was killed . . . and she . . . killed herself." This last on a whisper. She turned her face away. She wanted to cry, for suddenly she felt lost, but she was made of sturdier stuff.

He was surprised by this last, and his voice was sympathetic. "I am sorry, Windmera . . . I know you loved your aunt. Do you want to talk about it?"

"No, no . . . I want to forget it," she said, shaking her head vehemently.

"And Roderick . . . he was helping you to forget it?" Again the edge to his voice. His couldn't think of her with Ravensbury and not feel a tenseness enshroud his temper.

"Yes. Roderick was there when I needed him. Roderick loves me." She glanced away from him. "Could we not . . . speak of something else? Please."

He frowned, but there was a different style to his countenance this time. It was somehow disquieting to see her hurting. The last few months had done much to the beauty who had first captured his eye in Bridgetown. She was older in more than years. Still, his tone was colder than he meant it to be as he moved toward his cabin door. "Get dressed, Windmera. I have some business to attend to this morning, but I rather think I will take you with me. Afterward I trust I may entertain you as well as my first mate managed to do last night."

Six

A dark troubled figure silently, swiftly made a straight path toward the gangplank of the *Sea Hawk* and scurried down its length to the shadowed emptied docks below. There was no watch this night, because its captain had ordered the crew to get a solid night's sleep before they set sail at dawn. And Windmera had seen her chance!

It was all too perfect, this opportunity, and even Lance was not about to deter her from her purpose. She scowled over this, for she was certain the sudden decision to set sail tomorrow morning was due to the note Lance had received just before they sat down to dine. Humph! More war business, no doubt! How serious he had been while he perused its contents. He had gone off to his men, returning with the news that they were off for New York in the morning, and how would she like that? Like it? She hated it! If she allowed him to sail off from Norfolk she would be too far to make tracks to Bermuda! However, a plan had formulated in her desperation. A hasty plan to be sure, for it had come to her while they dined.

They dined. Still, she could not forget this their final meal of the day together, though she would oust its memory if she could. Lance had been strangely sullen, so much in contrast with his heady mood of the day. It was Stacy, of course. Stacy, whom he had probably gone to this evening to . . . make his farewells. Stacy, whom he was probably holding . . . kissing . . . even now. Stop it! What do you care as long as it is not you he is mauling? To perdition with them both! Soon, soon she would be out of Stacy's and Lance Landon's way!

She pulled her hood lower over her eyes. Her other hand held tight the napkin sack which held a loaf of bread and a small half-finished bottle of wine. Provisions. She kept her features averted from the high street torches. It was a cold night and the wind whipped at her cloak, demanding admittance, but she didn't feel it, so intense was her purpose, and yet even so the thoughts of the day penetrated, forcing her to relive hours she would have rather forgotten.

It had started with Lance telling her he could give her as

pleasant a time as Jackie had the other night. She had not thought it possible, but he had. He rented a phaeton, saw a rug over her knees and proceeded to show her the city. It was fascinating, and then they stopped at an inn just on the outskirts. Such a quaint and rugged place it was, unlike any in Barbados, but the fare was excellent and she was well disposed to it all, for Lance had been at pains all morning to set her at her ease.

She felt all the bitterness, all the tenseness leave her body. She felt young again and laughed easily, almost girlishly, at his amusing anecdotes. For a time, she even imagined she liked him a great deal. Oh, how they talked. It was as though no barrier ever stood between them, and she nearly forgot that there was still a barrier. An intangible one, but a strong one all the same. He had made of her a mistress, not a wife, and in so doing he had slashed her pride. It was on their way back to the *Sea Hawk* that she was mercilessly reminded just what she had become and the pleasantness of the day departed in the face of reality.

"Lance?" drawled a pretty voice at their back. "Lance, darling?"

Captain Landon turned around. He was not pleased to find Stacy enmeshed in bright-blue velvet coming toward him. Damnation, he thought, she was bound to make a fuss and set up Windmera's bristles, for no man wants a former mistress facing a present one.

"Mrs. Clayton." His voice was soft, amused, as he bent over her fashionable glove.

Stacy Clayton's eyes appraised Windmera with something akin to scorn. This was that fancy piece he had named as his first mate's sister. No one's sister this, but a slut! He kept a woman on board his ship to serve his needs. That's why he hadn't come to her the other night. She loathed Windmera immediately.

"Lance . . ." She drawled his name, allowed her finger to wander up his chest. "I do so want a word with you, love . . ." she said sweetly.

"Perhaps later, Stacy . . . as you can see, I am otherwise engaged at the moment," said Lance. His hand had already taken Windmera's arm, while his right hand tipped his hat to the tall irate beauty before him. Truth was, he sensed danger, had an instinct for it, and hoped to get Windmera away before the woman unleashed her tongue.

"Lance Landon!" snapped Stacy, not to be put off. "How dare you!"

"But Stacy . . . you cannot really expect me to desert my charge? I will gladly give you my time . . . later." He tried to assuage her ruffled temper with a warm smile, but it was useless. She was in a rage of jealous and slighted pride.

"Later? I'm supposed to sit around and wait on you while you amuse yourself with this trollop?" Her words carried, and many heads turned around to stare.

Windmera had been rather enjoying the exchange until now. She saw the curious glances aimed her way and shrank from the word "trollop" as though she had been publicly slapped. Ordinarily she would have been quick to slap back. She was a fighter, a spirited thing, yet she took a step back and withdrew within herself. The woman's accusation rang true, and the truth slashed across her pride.

Lance saw this in a flash. His Windy, subjugated by such a creature as Stacy Clayton? He grew unreasonably angry. "If you were a man, Stacy, you would have been felled. However, I feel I must tell you that I see only one trollop, and she is standing in our path!" With this he had pulled Windmera along, sweeping past the aghast creature in his wake.

Stacy's astonishment ebbed into quiet fury. She stared well, as though to outline Windmera's form. She would do the chit an injury if she could. She would hurt them both, and she was well able to bide her time and search out the right moment, the right place.

The incident had proved a damper to the day. Remembering it now brought a tear to Windy's violet eye. That she, a de Brabant, should have to stand and take such an insult, be unable to deny it! The worst of it all was its truth! Lance had brought her to it . . . no other. A small voice named another, but she answered it immediately. Roderick had given the potion to her, yes, but he meant her for wife, not mistress!

No matter! All of it would not signify, for she would make good her escape and put it all behind her. And then, finally, she saw what she needed. She gave silent thanks to the Lord, for there was the sloop, the *Penguin*!

She had picked this out as the simplest and yet sturdiest to abscond with to Bermuda, and now, at last, she would see it through, and to the devil with Lance Landon! She picked up her skirts, wrapped them around with one hand and bent to tug at the rope, bringing the boat in closer. It was a Marconi-rigged sloop with a mast at the middle and two sails, a mainsail and a jib. She had long ago learned the knack of sailing from Bunky, but even so, it was no easy job to take a sloop, even this rather small one, out to open ocean all by oneself.

Nimbly she was in the waist and throwing off her cloak to better work the sails. She then began the necessary job of clewing to the boom. She broke her nails on the rough spars, swore beneath her breath, and was at last ready to pull up anchor and store it in its locker at the bow. This done, she released the ropes keeping the boat to the docks and took up a position at the stern. Tiller in hand, she pointed the *Penguin* toward the open harbor. Her stomach did flip-flops and something deep inside her wanted to burst, but she sat staunch to her purpose, catching the wind and keeping her rudder moving with a close deftness. "Bless you, Bunky, for putting me through my paces," she said in a whisper, for the harbor was a crowded and narrow channel and she had but the aid of a halfmoon to see her through.

It was some time before she allowed herself to relax, but she felt secure once the harbor was at her back. She took out the compass she had taken from Lance's desk and squinted until she was able to make out the direction of its needle. Ah . . . a little tacking should put her on the right course. She set the boat at a forty-five-degree angle at the wind. It occurred to her that the war had drawn her neatly into its net, for here she was a common thief. She had stolen the sloop, the compass, the loose coins she had found in one of Landon's coats, and not one bit did her conscience hurt. After all, it was war!

Captain Landon closed the door softly and stared through the darkness at the form of Windmera in his bed. It was a strangely satisfying sensation, knowing she was there waiting even in sleep. He hadn't wanted to leave her after dinner . . . she seemed so withdrawn, depressed . . . but the note he had received from Commodore Rodgers needed immediate attention, and he had gone to meet with him. He shrugged off his many-tiered black cloak and dropped it onto a chair. His buckskin shortcoat followed, but it was to the corner of the bed that he went to pull himself out of his Hessians. However, first he would plant a kiss upon her nose. He stretched out beside the covered form, and his hand went around it and stopped. He sat bolt upright, pulling away the cover sharply,

279

and the pillows that met his astonished gaze set him to cursing. "Hell and brimstone, Windy!" He jumped off the bed and went to a candle, lit it and looked about the room. Assimilating that she had taken little more than what was on her back, he moved into action. "Where, damn it, girl . . . where would you go?"

He did another quick appraisal. Women were dramatic creatures; she might have left a note. But no, nothing on his desk. Nothing but the charts he had worked earlier. He would have to disturb his men and search the docks. If she took it into her head to run off on her own . . . ?

Captain Landon found such a thought more terrifying than facing a well-armed brig. The docks at night were no place for an innocent like Windmera. It came hard that in spite of the two nights they had spent in each other's arms, Windy was still an innocent. His beautiful woman-child . . . all starry-eyed, all hot and fire, yet sometimes cool and softly sweet, a perfect blend of exciting contradictions. She had run from him . . . why? Why, Windy, why? Stacy, came the reply. It was Stacy.

Damn, but he would find Windmera . . . had to find her. It was the sole thought that drove him below to wake his men. It was the driving force that kept his fears from his heart.

A dockside tavern rolled and bumped with the lively crowd it contained. Beer, rum and mountain-grown whiskey abounded, and boisterous parties rollicked. One group in particular had imbibed more than was their wont, for they were young men on the town together, two locals and two who carried the name of the Patterson Cotton Plantation. An interesting foursome, much in their heyday and ready for sport even at one another's expense.

"Hell, but I say we can do it in six hours!" cried Wiley Patterson, the younger of the two Patterson boys. His eyes were already glassy, and his mop of brown hair was in wild disarray.

His friends, in no better shape, appraised him and put it forth as their considered opinion that he was in fact crazy. Wiley took instant umbrage and called on his older brother to defend his stand.

"Well, John! Tell them."

"Hell no . . . can't be done," said his older brother disloyally. "That is, not in six hours . . . that ain't the record, Wiley. Six hours and fifty-five minutes to Onancock, that's

the record. Reckon we could beat the record. In fact . . .
tide's up . . . wind's up . . . let's prove it!"

"Eh, that's the spirit! Come on then, John," said Wiley,
jumping to his feet.

John, the more serious of the two, was twenty-one. He was
in his cups but not foxed enough to be ignorant of the danger. "Pa will likely break our heads when he hears."

"That for broken heads!" said Wiley, snapping his fingers
in the air to indicate the paltriness of such a consideration.

John sighed, turned to their friends. "Well then?"

"Ten dollars says you can't do it!" put in one of these two
individuals bravely.

"Ten it is!" snapped John enthusiastically.

Some fifteen minutes later found them wharfside at their
point of mooring, but search as they did, scratch their heads
over the problem as they did, nothing turned up their missing
sloop.

"What?" exclaimed John, taking a tour of their slip.
"Where can the *Penguin* be?"

"She's been twigged, John, that's what!" returned his
brother in wonder. "Someone has made off with her!"

"Here . . . best be calling for the constable," suggested
one of their friends. "I'll fetch him if you want."

"Reckon you'd better!" said John gravely. "Damn, but
what are we coming to when anybody can just sail off with
your own boat . . . and Hell . . . what is Pa ever going to
say?"

Jackie's face was drawn in concern. Whatever would make
her run off in the middle of the night? Where could she have
gone? He did a tour of the various slips, checking each mooring. Women were temperamental creatures. Perhaps she had
run off in a fit of anger, had then lost her way and taken refuge in a catboat?

He pushed aside the memory of Windmera asking him to
help her escape. Escape? Where to? And besides, she and the
capt'n had seemed to be getting on famously this afternoon.
In the purity of Jackie's love, he dreamed of marriage. He
saw a wonderful white gown with Windmera shading all others as she took the captain's hand. Yes, he dreamed they
would marry and live happily ever after. Thus her name
would be protected from the scandal that was sure to follow
if the captain did not do the right thing by her. He sighed.

But now she was making it all very difficult! Where had she gone?

A bevy of angry voices filtered through his thoughts and he saw two linkboys holding their torches high. There lit the badge of a night constable, who seemed overcome with irritation, and four young well-dressed men just about his own age. Everyone seemed to be speaking at the same time. It caught his interest, and he sidled near, but just as he was about to move on he heard his name at his back and looked around. "Aye, capt'n . . . over here," he answered.

Captain Landon had turned up nothing at the nearby inns. He had thought perhaps she had taken refuge in one of the better hostelries, but upon thorough consideration decided this was probably an addle-brained notion. He then stopped two patrolling men on citizen watch, but they had shaken their heads gravely. He was at his wits' end when he saw Jackie's back. He went toward him, but even as he asked he could see from his first mate's face that no word of her had been acquired.

"Nothing?" he asked, hoping all the same.

Jackie shook his head. "Not a sign."

"I am not drunk, sir!" snapped John Patterson. "I admit to being a trifle in my cups . . . but I know my own slip when I see it, and I am telling you the *Penguin* is missing!"

"You sure you didn't jest take it out and lose it somewhere . . . and come up with this round whopper to throw your daddy off the scent?" asked the constable suspiciously, for the young men standing, or rather swaying, before him didn't have the look of respectability. They'd been up to mischief, he'd swear.

Wiley took a menacing step toward the officer. "Shall I strike him down, John?"

"Hold just a moment," said a firm authoritative voice.

All attention turned toward Captain Landon, and he proceeded before further bickering began, "Am I to understand that a boat belonging to you is thought to be missing?" He was frowning, for he had suddenly remembered what it was that had bothered him about his desk. The compass he had prepared was no longer there. Everything else had been in place, but that had been missing.

"That's right," said John Patterson. "But . . . who are you?"

For answer, the captain whipped out his card and placed it

in his hand. "Now . . . can you give me its description and whether or not it had any provisions on board?"

"Provisions . . . no . . . I don't think so . . . and the *Penguin* is a Marconi-rigged sloop. What more can I tell you?"

"Is she sturdy enough to make a trip to Bermuda?" said the captain sharply.

"Bermuda?" said John, scratching his head.

"Why?" demanded Wiley. "What's it to you?"

"I don't know yet. But please . . . answer my question."

"I suppose . . . though Pa never tried it . . . and not we certainly. But wait on there . . . we are at war with England. Who would want to sail to an English colony?"

"Who indeed," said the captain quietly to himself. "But tell me one other thing. How do you know your boat was not taken this afternoon . . . yesterday . . . the day before?"

"Oh, Lord . . . as to that, we sailed her up to Chincoteague this morning to have a look at the wild ponies," said Wiley.

"Probably lost her there, too . . . and too afeared to tell your pa, so you're up to making tales!" grumbled the constable.

"Let me hit him," begged Wiley. "Please, John . . ." But his brother held his arm in tow.

"Thank you, gentlemen. If my suspicions prove correct, your sloop will be returned to you within the next few days. Where may I get in touch with you?"

John Patterson took out his card and handed it over. "We'll be staying at the White Horse Inn until Tuesday next."

The captain started to take his leave, but one other thing popped into his mind. "Boys? I would appreciate it if you wouldn't file a formal complaint just yet . . . but give me the week."

John Patterson scratched his head. "I dunno . . . but sure . . . sure . . . we'll wait out the week."

Captain Landon took up Jackie's arm and led him off. His first mate turned horrified eyes to his captain's face.

"You don't mean you think Miss de Brabant . . . has set sail . . . all by herself . . . for Bermuda?"

"I am afraid so, Jack . . . and we'll have to find her, before the storms of January do!"

Seven

How many hours had been swallowed up, Windmera couldn't be certain. However, the excitement of her undertaking had been lost in the discomforts of her situation. She hadn't been on the open ocean more than an hour before she noticed that the little moonlight she had was shaded by a hovering cloud. She stared into its depths, trying to determine for herself just how foreboding this cloud might be, when it opened up and gave her its contents. Cold! She had never known such cold. The rain wet her through, and then the wind iced it over. She rubbed her gloved hands together, gave up and yanked the sodden things off her fingers. She rubbed her velvet-covered arms beneath the cloak now heavy with its hold of water. Her cheeks seemed frozen and her mouth stiff, but she had to work the bilge pump and empty the bottom of the boat. However, the rain had given her some fresh water, in a container of tin she had found and set out. She would need, it for she calculated a journey of some four days to Bermuda.

Lance Landon! She would never see him again . . . her escape this night had set them finally, forever apart. He would have no way of knowing where she had gone. For no reason at all, she suddenly felt irritated. It was the wet, the cold, the constant vigil at the tiller, she told herself, nothing more. She was glad . . . glad to be rid of the one man who had set out to bring her down, the one man whose only proposal had been degrading. He had only brought trouble to her, this Lance Landon.

She sighed and checked her compass in the dimness of nearing dawn. Southeast was her direction. There she would find the string of isles known as the Bermudas. She had been there only once, on a short holiday with her parents. It was lovely, but its beauty was not what she sought. Roderick would be there, had to be there. Surely he and the men of the *Southsea* had made it within range of English waters. She was certain that Roderick would be there. How pleased he would be with her for escaping. How proud. Roderick . . . and then she thought of Lance Landon, of the two nights she had spent in his arms. The first, she scarcely recollected. The second, however, was still vivid enough to bring the fire into her blood, and her body flushed beneath the weight of the memory.

What would Roderick say? But she knew he would still want her; an instinct told her he would still want her. He would be angry, and in his cold and calculating way he would be vengeful, but he would be unable to seek Landon out and exact his ounce of blood. The war kept Landon safe. Oddly enough she admitted to herself a grave relief over this fact. Why? She answered her question simply: because. Just because. Oh, you are being ridiculous, Windmera! she snapped at herself. Why should you care whether or not Landon goes free for his crime against you? in fact, you should rather wish he wouldn't . . . you should hope that Roderick finds him and runs him through . . . you should . . . oh hang it! What's the use . . . just mind you don't fall asleep at the tiller!

She would have to devise something to hold the tiller on course and allow herself some naps during the day, but she would need daylight to work the ropes and the sails . . . and now, now she must pray that no American vessel would find her. Oh, my God! The danger loomed before her eyes . . . another American? No! God wouldn't do that . . . not again. He had a reason for putting her in Landon's way, she was sure of it . . . though she couldn't fathom it. Perhaps it was well that Landon had taken her, awakened the woman in her . . . readied her for Roderick. That was terrible. How could she think such a thing? She was at odds with herself, and it suddenly occurred to her that Rod had never aroused her to wantonness. She slapped all these thoughts away. Not now! Stop it, Windmera. Think of something else. But try as she did, Landon's eyes flashed and twinkled before her own, Lanon's touch seemed still moving along her flesh, kindling fires that had no business starting then, starting now. She closed her eyes and gritted her teeth. She hated him! She hated the power he had over her.

Landon moved, paced on his bridge like a panther caged. Too many thoughts, too many vituperations plagued his heart. Guilt took him on a private journey and brought pictures before his eyes. He saw too clearly the faults that were his. He had taken an innocent. For Windmera had been that. Lust had moved him to forsake all finer principles. He had suffered in those six months away from her. Windy had filled his dreams, had taunted his waking hours, had prevented him from enjoying other women, and then she had been there, miraculously within his grasp, and he had known only one thing, that he couldn't let her go, and he had taken her.

His conscience did battle with himself. What else could he have done? Allowed her to accompany Roderick in the longboat? No! She was a woman, and to allow her the hardships of the open ocean would have been inhuman. Liar! His heart called him liar. Had she been another woman, she would have been given freedom of choice! And then, having spared her the rigors of the sea . . . did you, Lance Landon, did you take her to a place of safety? No . . . but she came to me . . . yes, in a drugged state . . . is that how you choose to win a woman? No . . . but I had no way of knowing.

Really? But you knew afterward, and what did you offer the girl? Was it something she could refuse, were the alternatives less reprehensible? He shuddered as he remembered. He had given her a way out, oh yes, a purse and the freedom to disembark from his ship. Clearly he had outlined what lay ahead of her on the streets. She had understood. He recalled how coldly he had presented her future. A choice. His bed and safe passage home at the end of the war . . . or the streets! Windmera de Brabant was an innocent, and what he should have offered was his name!

No! She does not love me. It doesn't matter . . . you owe her your name.

Such were his silent arguments with himself, and as the dawn began to light on the horizon he made himself a promise before God, asking only that he find her to carry it out.

The sun was up, but it gave off little warmth, for the winds bore its rays off in great harsh swirls. Windmera was still dreadfully damp from her soaking earlier that morning, and her head was beginning to ache. She found the bread she had safely tucked away and took a chunk of it. She needed sleep, but the anchor line was not long enough to reach the depths, and she dared not take a chance on drifting. She estimated Bermuda to be some five hundred miles off.

She shifted in her discomfort, but something was wrong. She felt chilled to the bone, yet her ears, her neck, her forehead were burning. Her stomach began to churn, but she set her mind against it, telling herself she was only tired, refusing to be ill, mentally willing away all symptoms, and for a time it worked and she was able to continue to man the tiller skillfully and tend her sails. However, as noon approached and she again bent for bread, she felt not only a queasiness but a dizzy sensation as well. She had had nothing to drink since the night before. She was trying to conserve the rainwater she had captured in the tin can. Perhaps now was the time to take a swallow? She lifted it to her lips, but no sooner had she sipped than she knew she could fight nature no longer. All her being seemed to heave in that one moment as she gave up the night's dinner to the sea. Afterward she took up a piece of her underskirt, tore it, dipped it in the water and spread it over her face to cleanse herself. She felt no better. She should feel better . . . but she didn't.

Was it becoming foggy, misty . . . or was her eyesight blurring the sky . . . the sea . . . into one? The tiller . . . I must work the tiller . . .

She set herself in place, took up the anchor rope, bunched it around herself to keep her from moving too far off course. She was afraid she would slip off, faint. She wrapped her arm round the tiller with the rope, keeping the compass at hand. Oh, please, God . . . don't let me be ill . . . not yet . . . please, not yet . . .

"She can't have more than three hours on us, Jackie! We should have caught up by now," said Lance. There was a strained line about his mouth, in his eyes.

"Aye . . . but if you figure she fell off . . . to sleep, I mean . . . she may have drifted some, out of our line of vision," offered Jackie.

Captain Landon examined the sky. Nightfall was about to descend, and there would be little chance of finding her in the dark, for the skys were clouded and no moon would shine their way. "Hell! The wind's been coming from the north all day . . . could be she drifted.

"All right then . . . no use guessing . . . let the wind take us for a spell before holding her on course. Let's see if we can pick up her sails before nightfall!"

He gave off his orders and stood alone on his bridge. The wind whipped angrily at his short dark-blue coat. He put up its collar, but still it slapped his cheeks, swirled his hair turbulently. He worried about Windmera. Had she encountered any rains? She was in an open sailboat, by herself, attempting a voyage of some seven hundred miles. Gallant-hearted was his Windmera. Never was there a woman like her . . . never would there be again . . . but she loved another, she loved Roderick of Ravensbury!

Night came and went slowly for all concerned in Windmera's flight. The sun came up with the morning. A bright-blue sky with scarcely a cloud to hint at the previous day's grayness, but Windy was unaware of the weather. She was fighting the effects of her first night's chill. A high fever scurried through her veins. Her throat was as red as her flushed cheeks. She had spent much time hanging over the side disgorging what little her stomach held, gagging over her own saliva when she had no more to give. She was left dehydrated and suffering from something very near pneumonia. Each cough seemed more intense than the last; try as she did to subdue them, they wracked through her body. Windy's will ebbed even as her fever mounted. Why had she done this to herself? Why had she run from him? He hadn't ill-treated her. She would die now. . . . Her spirit fought such paltry wailings; even in her fever, her soul doubled its fists.

She tried to focus on the compass in her hand. Was she off course? She checked her rope . . . was she secure? Yes . . . she must be. She had fainted, blanked out, several times. Each time her sheer force of will had brought her to . . . but she knew if she was not soon found by an English ship she would be lost. She knew well the potency of the fever.

Lance Landon had not slept. The bright sky found him once again on his deck, pacing hard. They were at full sail, for the wind was with them. They would gain on her . . . had to, for his vessel was designed for speed, his men trained to work with the wind. Then why, why hadn't he seen her sails? She was but one girl, working a sloop . . . she couldn't possibly work at full sail twenty-four hours. She would have had to take in sail at night.

He watched the deep indigo part before the strength of his bow and clasped his railing to look farther, and then he saw it. A sail! Up went his spyglass, his hand trembling over its neck and then clearly did he read, *"Penguin."*

"There, lads! The *Penguin!* Get ready to furl . . . but steady now, steady as she goes!" he shouted in some jubilation. At last. He imagined her chagrin. She would be fighting mad, his Windmera, but no matter, he would deal with it.

Eight

"Clara!" Roderick could not believe his eyes as he looked up at the all too familiar profile in the curricle across the street. Clara, here? How? Hurriedly he crossed busy Hamilton Street, uncertain what he felt, for he hadn't seen her since the day he had asked her to marry him. He hadn't been able to face her and had sent her a note instead, saying simply that his father had not approved the match.

The profile moved, but not enough to see him, and he called again, "Clara?" She would be angry with him, but even so, he had to see her now, talk with her, touch her. He put out his hand and touched her arm.

The lady jumped, and her silk shawl fell off her dainty shoulders, covering his hand. She turned full face upon him, and though her eyes were deep-blue and her face heart-shaped and lovely, she was not Clara Boswell. She was so much younger, finer, sweeter. She flushed bright-pink. "You . . . you mistake, sir," she said in some confusion, for Roderick's hand still rested far too near her own.

Roderick stepped back, and she was better able to see that beneath his cream-colored top hat sat auburn curls. His lean height carried well the creamy short-tailed coat he had just purchased and charged to the governor. His Hessians shone brightly, as did his smile. She had never been approached by any man so sophisticated, so polished in style, and she was quite intimidated. He found himself amused by her blushes and with a flourishing bow determined he would enjoy making the chit's acquaintance, "So sorry, Miss . . ." He waited for her to supply the rest.

She thought him rather forward, but her shyness forbade rudeness, and she faltered but replied that she was Miss Delia Hopkins.

He took his time over her name. "Miss Hopkins. I thought you someone I knew very well in Cornwall."

"England? Oh . . . have you come from England?" said the girl naively.

"In a manner of speaking," he answered, sidling up closer.

Delia's large blue eyes moved away from him and found a large woman coming toward her. She could see that her aunt

289

was out of temper and assumed correctly that it was due to the fact that she was in conversation on the open street with a strange man. Her agitation showed in the nervous picking of her fingers at her soft blue skirt. He caught it, frowned and turned to find the source of the girl's nervousness. "Ah . . . your governess, no doubt?"

She giggled. "No . . . my aunt. You had better go."

"Not at all, my dear. I don't mean to let you slip away so easily." He smiled now toward the husky and rather staid older woman, tipping his hat as she came to a halt before him. "Madam. Please forgive my impudence toward your niece. I thought her someone I knew . . . and upon discovering I was wrong, wished to stay to make my apologies to you." He withdrew his card, of which he had but a few left, and offered it to the matronly woman.

She took it, perused it with some hauteur and pursed her lips. "I see. And are you on business in Bermuda, sir?"

"Alas, no. I was on my way home to Cornwall when our merchant ship was attacked by American privateers. We were allowed to escape in a longboat. I am now awaiting word from my father. The governor has been good enough to put me up in the interim."

Miss Julia Hopkins had long been a spinster and had forgotten what it was to be courted by a handsome blade, but she had no real objection to men. Hers had been a sad tale, not a tragic one, and she wondered whether or not there was a catch here for her niece. Her smile warmed. "Well, Mr. Ravensbury, I hope you find your stay in Bermuda an enjoyable one. I shall send you an invitation to tea." It was her way to be curt and to the point, and she was pleased to see he took no offense by her dismissal. Instead he lent her his arm as she hoisted herself into the curricle and took up the reins. She nodded, but her niece stole a glance back at Roderick.

Such large innocent eyes, quite taking, he thought, and mentally he made a decision to seek out the wench and further his acquaintance. She was far too delectable a morsel to pass by untouched. And then he thought of Windmera. He gritted his teeth, because thinking of Windmera these days also brought to mind Lance Landon. He could never think of one without the other, and inwardly he did battle. But he would erase Lance Landon, and then Windmera would be solely his. And . . . in the meantime, he was the governor's guest, and there was this pretty little Delia. . . .

Lance was in the waist of the sloop almost before they were in close enough to board. "Windmera?" he called, then frowned, for she lay wedged in beside the tiller, her head fallen to one side.

He approached in long hard strides and bent to touch her. "Oh, my God . . . Windmera . . . you are burning up!" Hurriedly he worked free the rope she had knotted about herself, cursing it for slowing him down. She began a series of wild coughs that sent a gripping fear to his heart. Finally he had freed her of her device and picked her up. Her cloak was still heavy with the wet, but he paid it no heed as he hurried to get her on board his vessel.

She was still unconscious as he slung her over his shoulder and managed the feat of clambering onto his own ship. "Jackie!" he called sharply. "Bring the *Penguin* in tow and then go to cook and see what he has for a high fever . . . sage tea, if he has any on board."

"Aye, aye, capt'n," said Jackie, his fair face paling as he took in Windy's countenance.

The captain's brain buzzed with a fever all his own as he made his way to his cabin. The door flew open in his hand, but when he laid Windy down upon the bed they had shared, it was gently, tenderly. He untied her damp cloak, clicking his tongue. "Windy, Windy . . ." He went to his door, closed it and returned to the task of undressing her. This done, he put her beneath the cool quilt.

What to do? What to do? When Izzy had come home from playing at the pond that winter so long ago . . . the time she had fallen in . . . what had been done? A light lit in his eyes . . . rubbing alcohol! That was it! It helped to bring down the fever! That and a small dash of laudanum. Quickly he rushed at his supply cabinet, brought out the rubbing alcohol and a washcloth and poured the alcohol into a basin. To it he added some clean water, and dipping the cloth in the mixture he went to Windy. He dabbed at her forehead, her cheeks, he gently rolled her onto her tummy and wet her neck, her shoulders, her back. Then he repeated everything all over again.

A knock sounded at his door. He covered her and called out irritably, "Yes!"

"It's me, Jackie, capt'n. I brung you some soda water and crackers. Cook says to get her to hold this for a time. He's got the sage, but it takes time to prepare."

"Right! Bring the tray over here. And then, Jackie . . . I depend on you . . . we've lost valuable time already. We've got to head first for Norfolk, all speed, drop that dratted sloop off and then head for New York."

"Aye, aye, sir!"

The door had closed, leaving him alone with her once more. He shook his head, slid his arm beneath her naked shoulders and propped her up. Even in her stupor she was thirsty and would have gulped at the soda water he put to her lips, but he did not allow it. Some of it spilled as she frantically tried to take the glass in her hands, but in her weak struggle he managed to control her. The crackers she would not take. She set her teeth so that they only mashed against them, and at length he gave up this effort and returned to bathing her in the alcohol.

The hours wandered by, and Windmera's fever had not abated. Lance could not be certain, but he felt instead that it had mounted. She had fallen into delirium, and her sobs were wrenching his heart. Continually she called for Louise, now and then for her parents, but the trauma of Louise was the more recent and had her still tightly within its grip.

"Louise . . . no! Please . . . don't marry him . . . what of Jokai? But it *is* my business . . . I care . . ." All these words on the edge of a sob. "I knew it! Mama told me . . . never marry for anything but love, Mama told me. You mustn't do it . . . Tante . . . Tante . . ."

Lance sat watching her toss, and the tears rolled down as he imagined her suffering during the last six months. So much had happened to her but as he attempted to stem the flow and soothe her even in her delirium, she called out another's name, and he stiffened.

"Rod! Oh, Rod . . . how can I bear it without Tante Louise? Oh, Rod . . . away? Away . . . to Cornwall . . . not sure . . . not . . . Brabant . . . bankrupt . . . yours . . . no! I won't be bribed! No . . . yes . . . love you . . but . . . but . . . oh, Rod . . ."

"Please, Windmera," begged the captain of the *Sea Hawk*, "get well . . . only get well and I shall do all I can to make it up to you. I swear it!"

Oddly enough Windy stopped her wild tossing and lay still, as though his words, his voice, had gotten through the haze that hung between her and reality. Softly she said another name. "Lance . . . ?" But even in so saying it built up a new fire, a new torturous thought. Lance was the name of the

292

man who had made of her a mistress. Her convulsive movements took on power. "No . . . no . . . a trollop . . . I am . . . no . . . get away . . . get away."

That night was a nightmare for the two beings in Captain Landon's quarters. She suffered with her maze of ghouls and he with the entity of truths. He never wavered from her side, never abated his war against the fever. The sage tea he forced down her throat, praying she would hold it. The soda water too he would put to her parched lips. The alcohol he used almost continuously, and then suddenly she lay still, her tossings at an end. He took up a watchful position from a chair, pulling it up close, raising his feet to the bed so that any movement of hers would wake him, and so it was that the morning found them.

He had dozed off, and his head lay limp against the chairback, for he had slumped during the night. There was a tiredness around his closed lids, but it came more from fatigue of mind than physical weariness. Windy's lids fluttered and then snapped open. Where am I? Oh, God . . . the fever . . . I had a fever . . . I tied myself . . . but this bed . . . all too familiar . . .

She attempted to get up, but her arms would not hold her, and still she moved, and in so doing saw a pair of boots propped up near her legs. Her eyes shot up their well-built length and found Lance Landon's face.

Strange was that moment! All conflicting emotions fused into one, and that one at variance with her will. Relief! Relief flooded her before she could think, before she could speak. She realized it, because Windy knew herself well and seldom held the truth from her eyes, from her ears. She knew relief and told herself it came because she thought she might have died out there on the ocean. Even so, this reason brought her shame. You should want to die, yes, you should want to die, rather than live as his mistress!

Landon sensed something. It came through his drowsiness like a shot, sending him bolt upright. He rubbed his eyes and could not disguise the look of animation at finding her awake and apparently in her right senses. "Windy . . . thank the Lord!" he breathed, bending to take her hand. He put it to his lips and closed his eyes. "Such a night . . . I was so worried . . ."

She scowled, but a glance about the room put off the frown and sent a thoughtful look to her dark-violet eyes. He had nursed her?

"How . . . how long?"

"We found you yesterday morning. You were delirious all day . . . all night," he said softly.

She stiffened. "Delirious? What did I say?"

He smiled. "You gave away no secrets. Now hush . . . you need your rest if you are going to get well enough for the wedding!"

"Wedding?"

"Indeed."

"Whose wedding?" she cut him off sharply.

"Why . . . our own, love," he said amiably, just slightly trembling beneath the gravity of the words.

What was it she felt? Something was stirring up her insides. Exuding from her blood were bubbles full with fresh air, exploding in her gut, in her veins. What was he saying? Did he love her? Was Lance Landon saying he loved her? She calmed herself. *"Our* wedding?"

"Of course. Oh, Windmera . . . I want to make it all up to you. I owe you that at—"

"Owe me?" she cut in harshly. Even in her weakened condition she managed with the fury his words aroused to prop herself up onto her hands. Her violet eyes flashed a storm of lightning, her words were like the cry of a wounded animal. "Owe me? Oh, by God, you are beneath . . . I . . . I loathe you! Were I able . . . I would slap your face! I wouldn't marry you to save my life . . . *or my honor!*" She sank back onto her pillows nearly exhausted by her wrath. She was hurting, but it was hidden in her anger, and still did a tear form. She turned her head away quickly. She couldn't let him see.

He had made a mess of the moment. Why were words with this woman such a difficult thing? He had never any trouble with words before, but then he had never proposed to a woman before. Everything seemed to come out wrong. But there . . . even as he was about to explain, disclaim his clumsy words and exchange them for better, she had cut him off with words of her own. She would rather forsake her honor than marry him. She wanted only Roderick. She wanted to retain her freedom so that she might give it to Ravensbury!

He controlled his own rising anger, but could not keep the cold from permeating his sentences. "Madam, I have come to see that my treatment of you . . . was not in keeping with the respect due to your station . . . to your family name. I want only to set things to rights."

"Then return me to Roderick!" she snapped unthinkingly. Something deep inside her knew this would gall him. She said it for that purpose.

He stiffened. "Would that I could, madam . . . but unfortunately the war makes that impossible. Perhaps you will reconsider my offer when you are feeling more the thing." He was insanely furious now, but he was well able to pull the reins on his temper. He wanted to shake the memory of Roderick out of her. He wanted her to want him, not Roderick. So he curbed his rage. He got to his feet and stretched, indicating that her decision was of little matter to him. He touched his roughened beard and further made light sport of it all. "I see what it is! Most improper of me to have proposed in such a condition. Your popinjay never would have done so. Well, I'll shave . . . and we'll have a go at it later," he said, picking up his toiletries and bowing himself out.

Windy watched his retreating form from the corner of her eye. Fool, she called herself. To imagine for a moment that he loved you . . . *fool!* But she was tired, far too tired to cry, so she brushed the tears away. I won't cry because of him . . . I just won't!

What is this new game he plays? asked Windmera of herself as she sat staring at her reflection in the looking glass, her hairbrush poised over a long black curl. She stroked the silky lock over her ear and threw it backward to join the rich mass at her back.

They were on the sea again, though they seemed to hug the coastline on their trip north. The captain had entered Norfolk Harbor only long enough to return the *Penguin.* During that time he had looked in on her often, as had Jackie, but his tender loving care was accompanied by clipped sentences and dark scowls. What was this man Lance Landon? What moved him? What did he want from her? He made no attempt to enter his cabin on that first night, nor had he attempted her bed since. From Jackie she learned that he had actually taken a bunk below with the crew, astounding everyone, including himself, with his chivalry, so it was natural that Windmera should be thrown into confusion.

A knock at her door disturbed her musings, and with a trace of eagerness she looked its way. "Come in."

Oh, he was a handsome man, in every way, strong, sensual,

provocative and yet winningly boyish. He had just such a grin lighting his features, twinkling his deep-blue eyes. She felt herself drawn to him in a flash, felt her knees jell, felt her pulse rate increase. He came into the room and his eyes scanned her. Suddenly they lost the twinkle and the grin vanished. She was scarcely dressed in her thin nightgown of white batiste, and her all too alluring form brazenly invited admiration. "You didn't know who was at the door, madam. Don't you think you should have covered up first?" His tone was contemptuous.

Oh! He was infuriating. How could one man so frighten, so excite and so anger her? "Captain, Jackie knocked earlier and said you would be dining with me. I assumed, correctly, that you had come for that purpose."

He inclined his head, for the cabin door was already closed behind him. "Then I am flattered. However, as I have resolved to keep my hands off you until you are my wife, I rather think you had better don your wrapper." He had relaxed some, but there was still an underlining of winter to his words.

She felt her cheeks go white and then red. Why hadn't she slipped into her wrapper when he knocked? Had she wanted him to see her thus? She couldn't think. She had no retort and so put up her chin and swiftly put her arms through her satin sleeves and tied the belt tightly about her small waist.

The captain watched her. Even her covering did nothing to abate his desire. He wanted her so badly he could taste her flesh against his lips. Her scent was fresh, her own, like a flower just opening its buds in the start of the day, dewy and fragrantly bewitching.

"You will marry me, Windmera," he said softly, his voice low with restraint.

"Never!" Her rebuttal was sharp, almost spiteful.

He scowled. "I don't understand your stubbornness. Windy . . . don't you realize your position? I am trying to make it up to you."

"Yes, I know! Do you really think I will marry you to ease your conscience? You are making the great, the supreme sacrifice, aren't you? Here stands a great man! He gives his freedom to spare the honor of a lowly woman! Well, I don't need your condescending gallantry, and I am not deceived by your feeble attempts at chivalry! You were from the first moment I met you a . . . a boor . . . without honor. You are still!"

296

"And you, madam, a traitorous bitch without principles. You lack them still!" He turned on his heel and opened the door wide. Jackie stood with a tray in hand, and he nodded curtly, "You are free to serve the lady. I shall be taking my meal with the crew!"

Jackie stood helpless, looking from Windmera to the retreating form of his captain. God love them, they sure were making life Hell for one another!

Nine

"Please, Aunt Julia . . . send him a card today," pleaded Delia, her blue eyes round. It was always so when she wanted something. She would hound both her father and her aunt until finally from weariness or guilt they would give in.

Julia Hopkins regarded her niece. She was very fond of Delia, for the child was good and kind-hearted and so very obedient in most matters. "My dear . . . it would not do for you to form any . . . attachment for this gentleman. You are but sixteen, and he quite near thirty I am certain," she said gravely.

"Oh pooh!" She giggled and put her hand over her mouth, a most adorable gesture, "Do forgive me, aunt, but what I meant to say was, Mother was just sixteen when she met Father . . . and I am certain not much older when they married."

"That is quite another matter, child. Things were different then, and your mother . . . well, she was exceptionally mature for her age. You are still so much an innocent."

"Auntie Julia, do invite him, please, and I shall strive not to throw myself at his feet." Again the dimples were there, making it quite useless for her aunt to say her nay.

"Oh, very well. But only to tea, mind . . . don't expect me to extend the invitation to dinner."

Her niece was already flying out of the room. "You are a darling, and how can I expect anything from you now?" She giggled and was off, leaving her aunt smiling and then sighing.

Delia ran out onto the veranda. From there she could see the little horseshoe-shaped cove she had been wont to swim in when she was younger. She so rarely got the opportunity now. She clasped her hands around herself in jubilation. She couldn't wait for Roderick of Ravensbury to accept the invitation. She couldn't wait to look upon his face, hear his voice, for Delia had been smitten on first sight. At sixteen one always knows what one wants, for youth lives but for the moment.

She saw her father coming up the garden path on his way back from the greenhouse. He loved his green island home, though they had come here but four years ago. He had found after Delia's mother's death a need to get away from the house they had so happily shared, and Bermuda won his heart.

She waved enthusiastically, and he smiled as he put up an answering hand. It wasn't really fair to his daughter. She was such a ravishing beauty. She deserved a London season, but he just hadn't it in him to return.

"Papa . . . Papa . . . I am so excited. We met the most interesting man in Hamilton today. Only fancy, he was attacked by American pirates on his way home to England, and is now staying at the Governor's Mansion. You can imagine his consequence . . . his address . . . oh, Papa . . . he is wonderful . . . and we are going to have him to tea . . . *today!*"

He had taken her hand and slipped it through his arm. He patted it now. "He sounds a remarkable young man. What does your aunt say to all this?"

"Oh . . . she thinks him too old for me. Do you, Papa?"

He laughed. "How can I say when I don't know his age?"

"Aha! Then you don't think I am too young to get married?"

He laughed out loud and shook his graying head. She was in her ingenuous style totally captivating. "You are playing games with your old papa." He beat her small upturned nose with his finger. "And you are very good at it. We'll see . . . we'll see."

"Then you will be here for tea?" she said hopefully.

"Of course I will."

She sighed her relief. "Oh, Papa, I am so glad . . . for though I love Aunt Julia dearly, you know how staid she can be with strangers. It would have been a dull affair without you."

He laughed. "Oh, I am persuaded, my dear, that your young man will, if he is all you say, keep it from being that! But to ensure your tea party's success, I shall be on hand and keep Julia from scowling all the fun out of it. Satisfied, puss?"

"Oh, yes, Papa." She hugged him fiercely. "I do love you so much!"

New York! Its candlelights and torches beckoned, but Windmera was a prisoner on board the *Sea Hawk* and had no way to answer its call. She nearly stomped her foot with exasperation as she stood huddled in her cloak on deck and stared out at the snow-covered docks. There was so much out there she wanted to explore, but would that beast take her?

Oh no . . . off he went without a word. No doubt he had a woman in every port. The thought turned down her mouth. A week had passed, and Lance Landon still had not come to her bed. A week she had used to throw every insult she could think of at his head, and still did he insist she marry him. The man was quite mad!

She watched the puff of her breathing form clouds in front of her face. This crisp sharp cold, so intoxicating, invigorating. That white snow . . . she had never seen it before. She wanted to play in its folds, feel its substance. She sighed, for Jackie stood unobtrusively at the stern and she knew he watched, as did the man above in the crow's nest.

A man came up the companionway stairs and mumbled something to Jackie, who then made his way toward her.

"Er . . . Miss de Brabant . . ." He blushed at the thoughts that intruded. "Your bath is ready. We had it prepared in captain's quarters, though he usually takes it in the galley . . . but thought you'd want your privacy."

"Thank you, yes, Jackie, I would." She smiled kindly at his youthful shyness. How odd . . . they were just about the same age; perhaps he had a year or two on her, had certainly seen more of the World, yet she felt infinitely more mature, older somehow. She moved past him and took the stairs far more lightly than her mood, which was downcast, confused. Somehow she would have to weather all this and come out whole, come out unwarped, come out still Windmera. But how? Every day taught her she would never be that carefree Bajan girl again!

Captain Landon was weary as he slowly took the gangplank to his deck. War talk at the table that night had been fast and furious after he had delivered to Captain William Bainbridge the note in his possession penned by Commodore Rodgers. The attacks on the seas were going well, so well that England was in an uproar over the American successes, but there was fear that such an uproar would convince the British Admiralty to divert some of their ships of the line from the French war and set them against the American coast. What to do? Opinions tonight at the long table had been widely different, with some namecalling, some heated politics, some overconfidence, and all furious. In spite of the fact that Captain Landon thrived on action, excitement, adventure, he was not one of the War Hawks. He wanted peace, strove for peace in his plans, and it fatigued him to find the men so indifferent to its requirements.

He signed to the crewman on watch, found Jackie, patted his shoulder absently and strolled leisurely toward his cabin. Jackie started forward, putting up a hand with which to detain him, and then stopped. A slow grin swept the youthful first mate's countenance. A catalyst was needed to close the rift between woman and man, and perhaps now was the time.

Captain Landon took the latch to his cabin door; he wanted only a change of clothing before retiring to his bunk with his men. He sighed to himself to think he'd be spending one more night on a hard cot when he could be in his own bed with Windmera.

A branch of candles met his gaze first, for their flames flickered with the rush of cool air. A gasp sounded in his well-trained ears. A vision replaced the candlelight in his eyes. Windmera . . . by God, she was tantalizing, sitting there with her hands crossed over her breasts, her eyes two pools of flaming violets.

"Can you not see I am bathing?" she snapped, giving him her back. Every inch of her trembled, but it was not with cold. A thrilling anticipation permeated her being, tickled her subconscious.

"I can see very well. Most improper of me to intrude. I am certain your popinjay would have instantly retreated . . . but then he is a fool, I am not!"

"No? I don't know what you are!" she said, wanting to maintain her composure, not knowing how.

"I thought I told you once. I am a taker, Windmera." He was already on his knees beside the wood tub; he had already picked up the sponge from the water, put it to her back. "Here, let me . . ."

She went rigid, but she couldn't stop him, his touch sent hot spears through her. Her mind tried to maintain control, and she breathed, her voice low yet burning, "Stop it . . . don't touch me."

"Ah . . . so soon we forget," he said lightly. He dropped a kiss on the nape of her neck, "Have you no principles, my dear? Did you not come to a bargain with me?"

"I recall you saying something about . . . wanting to set things right?" she returned sharply. "It is you who vacillate, not I!"

"No, my love . . . I shall not take you until you will it with every inch of your delectable body. I am asking you

301

again to be my wife." His tone belied the seriousness of his proposal.

It made her angry to hear the mockery in his voice. *"Never!"*

He sighed, and with every ounce of will power he possessed he pulled himself up. He wanted her more than ever before. He needed her beneath him. He thought of spreading those beautiful satiny legs and closed his eyes, knowing this would be one more agonizing night. He got to his feet. Silently he went to his wardrobe cabinet, pulled out what he needed and went to his door. There he stopped and had a moment's satisfaction, for the surprise on her face could not be concealed. It brought a smile to his lips.

"Goodnight, moonflower," he said softly.

He was gone. As quickly as he had come, he was gone. Oh, God! Am I going mad? I didn't want him to leave. I wanted him to lift me from this tub . . . I wanted him to carry me to that bed . . . and love me! Oh, sweet mercy! What is happening to me?

Mystic, Connecticut. Like a key its docks jutted out into the harbor. A tall white lighthouse pointed the way at the tip of the key. Masts of numerous vessels crisscrossed in the blue sky. Roofs covered with white clean snow littered the horizon, their red-tiled tops visible in sections the sun had burrowed through. The *Sea Hawk* had docked and was a part of this new scene.

"Come, Windmera," said Lance, taking up her arm. "I want you to meet someone." He could see his father, tall, distinguished, rising above the other men coming toward them.

Windmera felt a rush of fear. This was all so new . . . and her situation made her uncomfortable. She saw too the tall ruddy-cheeked man. He didn't look very much like Lance, and yet she knew at once this would be Lance's father. There was just something about him. She allowed Lance to lead her down the gangplank through the shoveled path, wet now beneath her boots from the sun's work, and stopped as Mr. Landon's hands took his son's shoulders. It was fascinating watching two such large strong beings give over to even stronger emotions. It had been three months since they had last seen one another, but it might have been three years, so great was their pleasure at being reunited. Lance remembered his purpose and turned toward Windmera, taking her arm beneath her cloak and pulling her up to his father's gaze.

"Father . . . I want you to meet Miss Windmera de Brabant."

Mr. Jules Landon's light eyes showed some astonishment. What was this? How the devil? However, good breeding forbade putting these questions to the air. He smiled kindly and bowed over the lady's gloved hand.

"Miss de Brabant . . . what a charming surprise." He turned toward his waiting coach. "However, it is far too cold to stand here talking. Shall we . . . ?"

Windmera was put at her ease at once. She liked Lance's father, and wondered how such an admirable man had such a cur for a son. And then her sixth sense, her need for truth, wagged a finger at her. Was Lance Landon such a brute? Had he not let her be once he found himself guilty of bad conduct? How he set her at odds with herself! For she didn't want to find anything good about him, she wanted to go on despising him.

In sudden desperation she looked out onto mounds of snow. Its drifts lifted in the air some five and six feet in spots, and she was intrigued with it. Wistfully she edged near to its soft whiteness, for she longed to touch it . . . to play with it, know its substance. She slipped off her glove, dove out of Lance's hold and scooped up a mound in her hand. Its cold surprised her, though she expected it, and she made a childlike discovery. "Why . . . it is so wet."

Lance's amusement exploded. Everything she did enchanted him. She was so different from any woman he had ever known. "What the deuce did you expect, Miss de Brabant?" Even in his amusement his tone was coldly mocking. He was hurt by her stubborn refusal to marry him, and his hurt brought out the sardonic side of him, pushing it always forward.

She put up her chin. He was always so rude! "I didn't know what to expect," she said in her defense, though it was not entirely true. She had never seen snow, but she had read about it. However, she could not allow him to mock her. "You forget, it does not snow in Barbados!"

His smile vanished. He remembered the May Dust, the Savannah prison hole, her treachery. "No, it does not snow in Barbados," he said, and his tone was hard, hinting at things she did not quite understand.

Jules Landon had listened and watched during this interchange. He was amazed by the restrained passions of both his son and this lovely woman. There was more here than met the eye, but that he knew the moment he had heard the name de Brabant. A frown took residence over his face. How had Lance got this enchanting chit? What was it all about? What did Lance intend for her? He would have his answers, and soon!

Ten

Jules Landon had been waiting for this moment. He was alone with his son in his study. They held each a glass of French brandy in their hands. Their guest was resting abovestairs in the comfortable and elegantly styled colonial house. He studied his son for a long moment as Lance sipped the brandy, and then he made up his mind. Straight talking was needed now.

"Well, Lance, I want to know what Miss de Brabant is doing in your keeping."

Lance had been waiting for this. He was a man fully grown, but he had no wish to displease his father. However, he was aware that he was about to bring down severe censure upon his head. Even worse, he was going to bring disappointment to his father. His confession could do nothing else.

"Father . . . please sit down. I will tell you everything, but I don't want to be interrupted, no matter how shocked you become, until I have said everything I need to say. It is a long, complicated story."

Jules took up his leather chair, set down his glass on a walnut table and folded his hands. "Agreed."

Lance eyed him a moment, "Well, then . . . on Barbados I met Windmera de Brabant. I thought her . . . honest in her intentions toward me. I believed her when she said she wanted to help me get my shipment and be off. I was wrong. She betrayed me, and we were put into prison. You did not know the circumstances before . . . I didn't feel it necessary then . . . but it will explain to you in some part my recent reprehensible behavior toward Miss de Brabant."

He sighed before proceeding. "You have seen her . . . you will not be surprised to learn that in spite of her treachery, I found her attractive. When we escaped, she was on board her vessel. I used it, and for a time there . . . in my anger . . . nearly raped her." He saw his father's shock and put up his hand. "I said 'nearly.' The circumstances . . ." He shook his head, not knowing how to explain. "You see, I believed that she led me . . . never mind, I spared her and we set sail." He looked away as though he were looking back in time, seeing it all pass before his eyes.

Sudden dawning came to Jules Landon. So! All those months after his son had returned from Barbados, all those black moods, and silent retreats . . . for a woman? He had wondered if a woman had entered his son's life. He had now that answer. "Go on, Lance."

"Yes. As you know, we have been playing at scouting on the high seas. We had just come back from spotting the *Java*, which as you know Bainbridge was successful in taking. The men were in good spirits and ready for some sport. We made a bargain to take the next English merchant ship as our own and sponsor the costs of these past few months. We spotted the *Southsea*." He got to his feet and took a tour of the room, eyeing the well-lined bookshelves without really seeing them.

"She was on the *Southsea*. I saw her and knew I couldn't put her in the longboat with the others. I didn't think. I only knew I couldn't let her go this time. I had her put in my cabin on the *Sea Hawk* . . . while the crew of the *Southsea* were set on open waters with just enough provisions to see them through a couple of days."

He came closer to his father, put his hand through his silken black locks and fell into his chair. How was he going to say this without bringing censure to Windmera? For some unexplainable reason, he couldn't have his father thinking ill of her. He leaned forward in his chair. "I went to my cabin with every intention of taking her this time . . . and I did. She was, of course, a virgin. There is no excuse for my conduct, and only one thing I can do to make up for it. I must marry her."

Jules did not at first speak. He played with his lower lip a moment. "I see. You are telling me you raped her?" He couldn't believe it. His son could not rape a woman! He wasn't made of that sort of stuff.

Lance frowned. He was certainly in a pickle. "I . . . seduced her. Oh, Father . . . it might as well have been rape. Yes . . . there is no other word for it. I gave her no choice. It was submit to me or walk the streets!"

Again the quiet "I see," the thoughtful silence afterward, the penetration of eye. He would read his son's mind if he could, but Lance had put up a shield. "Do you love her?"

Lance stopped suddenly, caught up by this question. Love? He had never once asked himself if he loved her. He wanted her above all others, wanted, needed her as he had never wanted or needed before. But love? "I . . . don't know. I only know I must marry her."

"And she?"

"She won't have me!" He said it desperately, once again on his feet, once again pacing in his agitation.

Jules Landon was surprised. "But . . . you have compromised her. I don't understand. Does she so dislike you?"

"She despises me . . . and loves another."

"How is this?" Jules was taken aback, "What other?"

"You see . . . she was traveling on board the *Southsea* with her fiancé. They were on their way to Cornwall to be married there."

Jules shook his head sadly, "You plucked this woman away from her betrothed? You seduced her? Lance . . . Lance . . . I cannot believe it of you."

"Believe it, for it is the truth!" Lance's tone was bitter. He was angry with himself, with the situation. "Look, father . . . it is no use going over it. I don't know what possessed me that night. I don't know how to explain it . . . whether it can be explained. I only know that she must marry me . . . or be ruined."

"Yes, of course. Well, women are unpredictable and change their minds often. She may do that."

"No, I don't think so. She waits out the war to be reunited with Ravensbury."

"Ravensbury?"

"Her fiancé." Suddenly his face grew grim, "But I swear it, Father, I intend to have her! She is wasted on Ravensbury."

"You know this Ravensbury? The name sounds familiar," he said thoughtfully, wondering where he had heard it.

"He is a scoundrel with a jackal's heart. He had us put in prison, and he is not good enough for Windy!"

"I see . . . but you are?" His father's brow was up questioningly. He did see, though he was quite certain Lance did not.

Lance was thrown into confusion at the starkness of the question. "I can understand, after all I have told you, that you now believe I am not . . . but I would try to be worthy of her."

They were interrupted by a manservant who knocked at their door. Jules called out and the door opened. "Miss Barker to see the captain, sir," said the butler, smiling easily at Lance.

"Ah, Miss Barker," said Lance's father. "We were forgetting about your Miss Barker. She has a stake in all this!"

Lance Landon shot his father a helpless look, but Jules smiled at the elderly butler. "Yes, Vern, bring Miss Barker in and have cook send us some tea and biscuits at once."

The rustle of skirts over the well-polished oak floor, a whisk of scented air, and she stood on the threshold. The hood of her fur-lined cloak she had already thrown back, exhibiting a cluster of orderly russet curls piled at the peak of her well-shaped head. A smile curved her thin but shapely lips. A graceful movement dropped her heavy dark cloak into the arms of her neat large black maid. The Barkers were among the few Northerners who maintained slaves. Quietly she ordered the older woman to retreat to a chair in the corner of the room, and on that note she went forward, hand extended, toward Jules Landon.

"Mr. Landon . . . Papa and Mama send their best, though they want me to tell you how put out they are that you and Lance"—she smiled toward the object of her visit—"are not coming to dinner tonight."

Lance's bright-blue eyes surveyed her. Her height and figure were good and neatly displayed in the pale-green velvet she wore. Ivory lace trimmed her low neckline and the cuffs of her long tight sleeves. There had been a time when he had been interested in Eleanor Barker. He went forward and took her hands, neatly whisking off her kid gloves and putting them both to his sensual lips. The action thrilled her, and her hazel eyes lit up seductively in response.

"I must take the blame for that, Elly," he said, his voice low, bantering.

Twenty-two years old was Elly Barker. A beauty and an heiress. She had her pick, but she wanted only Lance Landon. He was her ideal. Handsome, witty, rugged, virile and heir to a minor empire. She was used to getting her own way, and it had looked as though she might get it with Lance . . . and then he had gone off to Barbados . . . and then the dratted war took him off again. But now, now she would exert all effort into her project, for surely he was home now for a while.

She gave his hand a slight rap. "All right, then, you must make it up to us!" She smiled, but she was in earnest. "I don't know why you won't come tonight . . . but I won't press you. However, tomorrow night you must be free?"

Lance chuckled and Jules answered, "My dear . . . Lance

has only just put in this afternoon. How your family got the news so fast is beyond me . . . but as they did, they must also know that we have staying with us a houseguest."

"Oh?" she said, frowning suddenly, wondering who the houseguest could be and why the grapevine news had left out this bit of information.

"Yes, Lance has brought home with him . . . the daughter of a dear and very old friend," said Jules, glibly prevaricating.

She gave Lance a sharp look. "Really?"

The study door opened and a bright musical voice rang out.

"Mr. Landon . . . only look what I found on my window ledge . . . the poor thing is nearly frozen to death." Windmera saw Miss Barker and stopped short in some embarrassment, a small blackbird held tightly in her grasp.

She felt all eyes on her and stood, a perfect harmony of youth and beauty. She was wrapped in a dainty ivory silk, her long black hair shining all about her shoulders as it cascaded to her waist. Excited with her find, she hadn't bothered to put up her hair after its brushing. She was flushed, and her eyes of violets were warm in their bright roundness.

Lance saw her and nearly gasped, such was her effect on him. No other woman held a candle beside her. It was more than beauty, more than desire. Its intangible cable held them united. He saw only Windmera. All others were forgotten as he was drawn irresistibly toward her. "Here, let me see . . ." He was already beside her, taking the bird in his firm hold. "Ah . . . he must be kept quiet . . . and fed, for he is half-starved." He turned to his father and Miss Barker.

"Excuse us, please . . . but I think this poor creature needs immediate attention." So saying, he took charge of both Windmera and the bird and was gone a moment later.

Jules stood a moment, a slow smile spreading across his face before he turned to the outraged Miss Barker. "My dear . . . I am so sorry, in the commotion of the bird, we have neglected to introduce you to our houseguest, Miss de Brabant. Perhaps when they have settled the blackbird, you will have a chance to meet."

"No doubt." She fought to regain her composure. Miss de Brabant, it would appear, was a worthy opponent!

"Ah . . . here is the tea," said Jules thankfully. "Will you pour, my dear?"

Once again a smile lit her lips. "Why, of course, Mr. Landon, with the greatest pleasure." She had no intention of leaving until she had had further conversation with Lance.

"Here . . . let me do it," said Lance as he watched Windmera try to put some bread into the bird's mouth. They had found a hat box, deposited the weak blackbird and gone off after ready food.

"He won't open his mouth," she said in some concern.

"Oh . . . won't he, by God." Lance laughed. He had the bird in a firm hold, the bread held in a tweezer. He forced the beak open, deposited the bread. "Now, to get you to swallow it, my little friend." Then to Windy, "The glass of water . . . pour the water in his beak while it is wedged open with the bread."

She frowned, fearing the bird would choke, but silently obeyed and watched with fascination as Lance massaged the bird's neck. The bread was swallowed with the water and the procedure repeated until they felt the blackbird had taken quantity enough to sustain it for a time.

"Well done, Lance!" said Windmera, forgetting her grievances against him.

He smiled as he saw the bird safely in the hat box and punched air holes into its lid. Getting up, he brushed away whatever dust he might have gathered onto his velvet coat and then reached down for her hand. He pulled her light weight up with force enough to bring her into his arms, and there he held her, his eyes hungry. Tenderly did his lips brush her ears, her neck, as his hand moved in the folds of her long bedroom-tousled hair.

She was mesmerized by his touch. It was startling to realize the heat he aroused in her, and for a moment she was lost to him, to his embrace, his wandering kisses and then finally to his mouth as it closed on hers. Rockets of lightning flashed before her eyes. A veritable spectrum of colors followed. Was it possible? Could she so despise a man and yet be driven to such soaring heights in his arms . . . at his kiss?

"No . . . stop it . . . Lance . . " she whispered feebly, making some halfhearted effort to pull out of his hold.

He didn't believe her. Why must she pretend? "You don't want me to stop . . . do you, Windmera? *Do you?* Hell, woman! You want me . . . you may loathe me for reasons all your own . . . but at the same time, you want me as I want you . . . *I feel it!*"

He shouldn't have said that. If she had wanted to melt in

his arms and give over to the call of her body, that desire was replaced by a new one. Her pride came before all else. She gave his lower leg a sharp kick and stepped back to view her handiwork. She stood, hand on hip, her cheeks scarlet with anger, her eyes trembling storms of violet fury. "You would have better luck with another . . . perhaps that woman downstairs. She looks ready for your sport, but I, sir, *am not!*"

"You needn't direct me, Windmera. If and when I want another woman, I shall know well how and where to get one! It may interest you to know . . . that for some unexplainable reason I apparently . . . want only you. Don't you see, love . . . I want you to marry me . . . not just bed me . . . and my patience is wearing raw!"

"Is it? Your patience is raw? How sad. What of mine? You pluck me from all nearer ties . . . and then have the effrontery to cry about your discomfort!"

He sighed with some exasperation. "Windmera . . . yes, I plucked you off the *Southsea.* You know very well that at the time I had but two choices, to take you with us or send you into the longboat. That left me no chioce! But . . . and my love, I do regret bringing your memory back to this, for I am certain you look back on it with disquiet . . . when I came to my cabin afterward . . . you were willing . . . most willing . . . Hell, Windy, you were eager!" He put up his hand to still her ready retort. "I had no way then of knowing that you were a virgin . . . or that your eagerness was precipitated by yohimbe! However, for the bargain I forced upon you I take full blame . . . and that is why I have brought you here to my father. I am trying to make amends . . . do what I should have done from the start."

She was furious with him, though she couldn't say why, for in truth his little speech seemed rational, well thought-out. She was in a state, though, for his words left her hot and cold and wanting to slap him. "You can't make amends now, Lance . . . unless you have thought of a way to return me to Roderick."

"Even if I knew where Roderick was . . . and I don't, I can't . . . nay, girl, I won't return you to him. He isn't worthy of you." He was serious, his eyes sought hers in earnest, pleading with her to relent, to compromise.

"Not . . . worthy of . . . ?" She couldn't believe his arrogance. "And I suppose that means you are?" She directed a look of contempt at him.

He took up her shoulders and shook her. "You drive me insane. One moment all I want is to hold you . . . touch you . . . the next I want to break you . . . bring you beneath my hand." He tossed her viciously away from him. He had never roughly handled a woman before. He remembered that night on board the *Liberté* when he had nearly raped her. What was it about Windmera that brought out the savage in him? He was shaking from the experience, glaring at her in his fury.

"Get out of here and leave me alone. Why do you hound me? You have women enough . . . in fact, one awaits you this very moment in your own parlor!"

He reassembled his mind, coordinated it with his nerves and held himself in check, and in control once more he gave her a long thoughtful glance. Why was she always so angry with him? Why? What had he said earlier to turn her soft yielding body into jumping flames that would not be held? Why did she harp on Elly Barker? Was she jealous? An interesting thought. Could it be possible? She hated him . . . why would she be jealous? He put it to a subtle test. "My woman downstairs?" he said glibly, as though he had forgotten.

She nearly blustered, "Now, don't tell me you have forgotten the pretty girl with the russet curls you were so intent upon when I entered with my poor blackbird? Really, captain . . . you are even more reprehensible than I thought possible."

"Oh . . . *that* woman," he said, well pleased with the results of his little game. "I had quite forgotten Miss Barker. Wants me to make her Mrs. Landon . . . yes, perhaps I had better go below . . . and do her up brown. Quite a lovely girl, Elly," he said blandly as he went toward the door.

She stood open-mouthed, and a new look came into her eyes. He was quick to note it, and he smiled, tipped his hand to his forehead and bade her good afternoon. He was pleased enough to see her eyes flicker. So then what had this last proved? Was she jealous? If so, what did it mean? By God, his mind was in a whirlwind. What was this woman who so held his thoughts?

She watched him go, and then with a thump fell heavily upon Isabelle's pretty bed. She folded her arms across her middle and sighed. He was impossible. And then, in some agitation, she wondered what he would be saying to this Elly Barker. What would they be doing . . . and would they be alone?

312

Eleven

Mr. Hopkins watched Delia and Roderick conversing in low tones as his sister poured the tea. This Ravensbury was certainly all Delia had said. He smiled to himself. Here now was a match for his jewel. Roderick was heir to both title and fortune . . . no treasure hunter here! That was important, for his Delia was such an innocent. He didn't want her hurt. She was a romantic, and so many young men today could hurt her, but not Roderick, he had no need of Delia's money. Good. He liked too Roderick's style and address . . . polished! He had learned his way around London. That was excellent, for he wanted Delia to be taken to London and shown the kind of life she was entitled to enjoy. Yes, here was a match for his daughter.

He waited for a lull in the conversation, for the tea to have been properly sipped, before saying, his eyes twinkling, "If you are going to show Mr. Ravensbury our gardens, Delia, I think you had better fetch your spencer, for I noted a chill in the air earlier this afternoon."

Julia turned startled and reproachful eyes upon her brother. What was he thinking of, sending them off alone? "Francis . . ." she said in a low voice, intending her tone to speak her mind.

He patted her shoulder and smiled benevolently as his daughter skipped toward him, planted a kiss upon his cheek and turned childlike toward Roderick. "I have a spencer in the hall . . . we can take it up on our way out."

Roderick made a bow toward Julia Hopkins, smiled at Mr. Hopkins and followed leisurely as Delia glided out of the room. Julia rounded on her brother. "Francis! What can you be thinking of?"

"I am thinking that if Father had not so curtailed your movements you would not now be tending house for us, but for your own family."

She bit her lip. It was painful remembering. She wished he wouldn't speak to her of it. "My . . . my case was different. Times were different."

"Times were different? My dear girl . . . our father destroyed all your chances of happiness because he was selfish

313

enough to want you with him. He loved you . . . but selfishly, for he couldn't bear to be parted with you. And you? You gave away your future to tend to his whims . . . you would be tending to them still if he hadn't died. Well, I have no intention of hurting my child in that manner! Here is a man for her, Julia. They will make a match of it, if we leave them to themselves!"

She frowned. "But he is so worldly . . . she is . . ."

He patted her hand. "Never mind. You can't think such a gentleman would take unfair advantage? Posh! He will be coming to me for her hand before the month is out . . . see if he don't!"

Roderick had already sought Delia's hand. They stood framed in exotic greenery, a breeze playing with them gently. She was frozen by his sudden touch, by the intensity of feeling it aroused, and her blue eyes looked long into his as he pressed his lips to her fingers and then to her palm. "You . . . you shouldn't do . . . that," she whispered.

He chuckled. "Shouldn't I? Tell me why."

"I . . . don't know . . . exactly. I mean . . . I do . . . but I can't explain it. We don't know each other well enough," she said lamely.

"And when we get to know one another better"—he was teasing, for he found her enchanting—"then I may proceed?"

She blushed furiously. He was so wonderful. He was a prince and she a sleeping princess. Would he wake her with his kiss?

"Perhaps." And so saying she laughed, a naughty sound taken by the wind and her sudden flight, for she raced toward her house, towards safety, security. She wanted to keep Roderick there, with her, but she was too frightened to give in to her desires. He watched her a moment before taking chase. She would be his, he was sure of it. He would have no problem bedding this one, but oddly enough the thought did not leave him exhilarated.

More snow! It had started during the night, and Windmera sat in her cushioned window seat looking at the crystals as they fell still. It was all too beautiful. There was a hushed quality as though everything outside had just been painted in place. The trees were heavily laden; their drippings looked like strings of diamonds in the gray morning light. Bushes took on shapes in the snow, here a thorny hog, there a crane

314

on stilts. The stables in the distance set among the fir trees ... all of it had a fairy-tale quality. A horse's whinny as the grooms gave them their feed in their stalls. She sighed. It all seemed so peaceful.

A fire glowed in her marble-framed hearth. She glanced at it now, wondering if she should add another log. What a nice room this was. Bright and cozy. Lance's sister must have been very happy here. How odd, thinking of Lance as a small boy ... followed by a younger female version of himself, for so the painting on the parlor wall appeared to be. Such had been her first thought yesterday when she had seen it. Again, a heavy sigh. What time was it? Should she get dressed? In Brabant a black slave always came up with a tray. Would a servant come with morning tea here? She was hungry. She hadn't eaten much yesterday ... and dinner she hadn't touched at all.

This bedroom had become her sanctuary. She took refuge there and begged off coming down for dinner. A tray had been sent up, but though she tried picking at it, she gave up the effort and set it on the hall table outside her door. What was to become of her? Lance's father was kind ... but this was no household for a single girl. If only Lance's sister were here she would have someone to talk with ... someone who would understand her predicament. How would she ever get away? How would Roderick ever find her?

"Git on up with that, Sam," said Sam's mother. She was the cook, had been the cook for the Landons going on twenty-five years. The kitchen was her domain, and all the household servants eventually came to its warm embrace. She knew them all, listened to their woes, plied them with sound advice and heartening meals. Sam's duties were clear. He was Mr. Landon's man. Taking up trays to female guests was not within the bounds of his jurisdiction, and so he expostulated strongly.

"Never you mind, you old croaker! That little girl ain't had a bite to eat all yesterday. More'n likely she's got a case of homesickness ... coming from all that heat into all this cold. Now, my boy"—Sam was forty if he was a day—"git on up with it, for Gilly is over to the barn and won't be back for a spell."

Sam took up the tray. "Aw, Ma ... when you gonna treat me full-grown?"

"Maybe tomorrow. Now hurry up before those biscuits I

made get cold." She was grinning wide, her hands on her ample hips, as she watched him take up the tray and grumble loudly as he left the room. He was a good man was Sam. Dependable. She had seen to that after his father died, but he had a smidgen too much pride.

Lance was on his way down to the study. His father had been up for hours, he had been told upon waking, and he thought he'd have a quick word with him before making tracks to town. On the stairs he encountered the disgruntled Sam. "What is this, Sam? I am told father is in the study."

"It ain't for your pa, Mr. Lance. Ma says miss hasn't eaten . . . says I got to bring her this pronto . . . and you know what Ma is when she gets a notion on."

Lance knew well what cook was, and he chuckled. "Here then . . . give the tray to me. I'll take it in to Miss de Brabant. Blame it all on me."

"Ma won't like it," said Sam, shaking his head.

"Won't she?" He bit his lip in fear. "Then God help me later." Again the deep chuckle. He waited for Sam to turn himself about before managing the tray back up the stairs and down the hall to Miss de Brabant's chamber. At her door, he balanced the heavily laden tray between hand and hip and without knocking opened the door.

Windmera saw the door flash open and jumped. "What do you want?"

He glanced over her. Damn, but she was lovely. "What I want is . . ." He hesitated intentionally. ". . . is for you to relax and enjoy this tea cook has sent up to you." He set the tray down on a nearby table.

She noted his line of vision and turned pink. Hastily she ran toward the bed and scrambled with quilts and linens in her search for her wrapper. Lance marked the crumpled heap, moved, bent and held it up for her inspection. "Is this what you want?"

She saw the dance in his blue eyes, held her head up as well as she might and went forward. Extending her hand toward the flimsy, however, found her in his arms. He was so quick, so deft, that it nearly took her breath away. He held her a moment, wanting to kiss her, and his voice was soft, low and provocative. "Do you know how ravishing you are? Do you realize how much I want you?" He then quite suddenly released her and withdrew a step. His voice was now

316

grave. "I understand you did not eat your dinner last evening. I hope this morning finds you with a better appetite."

He was moving toward the door, but stopped and turned back. "Be a good girl, Windmera . . . eat, and if you do justice to your meal I will take you on a tour of Mystic this morning."

She forgot the wrapper, she forgot her blushes at finding herself first in his arms and then free of him. She clapped her hands together like a child, and her violet eyes were bright with excitement, "Oh . . . I should like that above all . . ." She caught herself. "That would be very nice. I shan't be above thirty minutes."

He found his tongue in his cheek. "Of course, Miss de Brabant . . . as the lady wishes." He backed off and let himself out. By God, she put him through all the emotions. Never before had he been so alive!

He was surprised to find that at the end of thirty minutes Windmera stood at the top of the stairs, smiling! The lady was punctual, but in spite of the pleasantness of this surprise, he frowned. She glided over the wide darkly printed carpet toward him. Her cloak hung gracefully in soft brown folds over her shoulders. A gown of fawn-colored velvet peeped at its center opening, and Windmera looked thoroughly enticing, but Lance frowned.

"Don't you have anything more serviceable to wear?" was his remark.

Windy had been quite pleased with the results of her hasty efforts. Her hair she had brushed and tied at the top of her head, neatly and prettily. Her gown she had chosen with care and coordinated with her boots and cloak. This was not the reaction she expected from him, though why she should seek Lance's approval was not a question she asked herself at that moment. "What is wrong with what I am wearing?" She glared at him defiantly.

"Wrong? Naught . . . for visiting someone's parlor. But my dear, we will be visiting the shipyard. At any rate, there is nothing we can do about it now. Come along," he said, taking up her gloved hand.

She pulled it out of his hold and walked in front of him as he opened the door to the front drive. There she stopped short and ejaculated with childlike glee, "That . . . that is a sleigh! A horse-drawn sleigh! I have never seen one . . . really seen one . . . oh . . ." She ran through the high snow toward it and touched its runners. With face upturned toward

Lance, she told him breathlessly how she had read about them . . . how her mother had often told of her own youth, of riding in them through the snow, and how excited she was now about the entire thing.

He laughed, lifted her and set her down in its well-cushioned leather upholstery. Setting a clean and heavy blanket over her knees, he then proceeded to nimbly jump in beside her. Reins in hand, he urged the matched bays at his head forward, and Windmera felt the sleigh slide into motion.

"I hope you won't be too cold," he said, smiling at her bright face.

"Cold? Oh, I don't mind it . . . I rather like it," she said, for nothing could dull her excitement.

He beamed and sent the team off at a heady pace. They took the bend in the road at high speed, and he was amused at the squeaks of delight that emitted from Windmera. She felt bubbles tickle her tummy and giggled, feeling much like a schoolgirl on an adventure.

He wanted to hold her. She was a wild young thing, full of fire, full of warmth and gentleness . . . and a treachery that had once sent him to prison. How could such a thing be? "Windmera?"

"Yes?"

"What made you do it?"

"What made me do what?" she answered, smiling at the passing scenes.

"What made you turn me in to Brayward? Why did you trick me into believing you really wanted me to have my shipment? Why did you serve me false?"

She rounded on him, her eyes wide with her astonishment. "Is that what you think?"

"It is what I know," he said quietly.

She put up her chin. "Really! It is what you know, is it? Very well, if you are smart enough to . . . know it, why can you not figure out the reason?"

"I . . . I want to hear it from you," he said gravely. He did desperately hope she had some excuse that would make it all right.

How dare he think such a thing of her? He was always misjudging her. How could he? Well, she wasn't about to explain anything to him. Defend herself? Why should she? Let him think what he wanted.

"As I said, Captain Landon, if you were clever enough to
318

draw your own conclusions, formulate your own opinions . . . then answer your own question!" She turned from him.

He studied her a moment. She was angry again. Why? He was the one who should be angry . . . and wasn't. She was driving him mad.

A weather vane in the distance marked the beginnings of the town, for it stood atop the shipyard building. Lance pointed it out. "Look there, love . . . for as the future Mrs. Landon, this is the heart of your empire!"

She ignored the reference to her being the future Mrs. Landon, though in truth for no discernible reason the words thrilled her.

"What, do you mean? What is that building? It is so large."

"That is the Landon Shipyard. To its left are our lumber sheds . . . to the far right is the paint shop . . . the machine shop . . . and there . . . see those sloping docks . . . they are the construction ways."

"Oh, Lance . . . how exciting. Will you give me a tour of it all before we see the town?"

He smiled warmly at her. "You really are interested?"

"Of course I am. I have never actually seen how a ship is constructed," she said lightly, curbing her enthusiasm lest he misunderstand.

He pulled up his horses outside the enormous building marked with his family name. A young lad came running outdoors and welcomed him.

"Walk the horses a bit," said Lance as he gave the reins into the boy's hands. He turned and received Windmera tightly, firmly, in his grasp. Their eyes discovered each other in a manner that bludgeoned unspoken resolves. He felt a tremble shake his body. She felt a heat melt her bones. He set her down, and his voice was gruff.

"Watch your step now . . . and I'll take you to see a vessel in the process of construction." He led her down a shoveled path toward the ways where a skeleton schooner was in works. Proudly he began her lesson. "First, we have to know what route the ship will normally take . . . how it will be used . . . what cabins and speed requirements the purchaser has in mind. Then we draw a draft . . . design the ship on paper . . . then a small-scale model." He pointed. "See here . . . this is the keel . . . the very backbone of the ship. This in the middle, these are called the ribs. It is framed out so that the hull is supported by these . . . they are called bilge cradles."

"How do you get it into the water?" she asked, her mouth agape at the superstructure.

He smiled. "After the ship is completed, a process worked deck by deck, we get her ready for launching. Usually she is about eighty percent completed at the time of launching. We lay ground ways on either side of the keel blocks . . . these here supporting the hull . . . these are greased heavily, you see. The ground ways extend to the water. Then the launching timbers are used. They are set on the ground ways and built up to the bottom of the ship. It is rather complicated . . . but imagine a cradle being built beneath the ship from bow to stern. The cradle takes the weight of the ship while it is on the ground ways, then the keel blocks are removed. We then slide her down the ways."

"What would happen if she got stuck . . . didn't slide?"

He smiled. "It happens. A ram at the bow gives her a push. She'll ride the cradle into the water until she floats . . . and if all is well she'll be seaworthy and do just that!"

"It must all be very thrilling, watching something you have designed take shape . . . fulfill your expectations."

He looked at her a long thoughtful moment. "Yes . . . I love this end of the business."

"But you love sailing more? You would rather be out there, fighting the billows?"

Again, the long thoughtful look. "Six months ago, yes . . . I preferred the sea, the excitement of finding my way through her canyons . . . never beating her, for no one but a fool could think he has conquered her." He hesitated, unsure he should go on.

"And now?"

"And now . . . I don't know . . . the land feels good beneath my feet. Being here in Mystic feels good . . . better than ever before. Why I don't know."

She shivered in the harsh inlet wind. A snow flurry caught her full in the face. She put up a hand to brush away the crystals from her face. He was before her, his gloved fingers flicking away the snowdrops from her nose, tracing her full cherry lips tenderly, lovingly. She was shaken by his gentle look, by his soft touch. She didn't think she could bear it, and then he was smiling and saying, "Come on, love . . . let's finish the tour in the sleigh, where I can bundle you up . . . and then we'll have hot cocoa in town."

"I think that an excellent notion, sir," she said, not un-

320

pleased with this new side of him. Suddenly she thought how easy it would be to like him . . . really like him . . . if he hadn't violated her. But he had, and she must not forget what that made him!

Twelve

"Fire and brimstone!" Godwin shook his fist toward the vaulted ceiling of his library. "Have the gods no justice? Am I to be thwarted at each turn?" He turned dark bright eyes on his friend and shook the letter he held in his fist. "John . . ."

Captain John frowned. "What is it, man? What is wrong?" He knew the letter was from Roderick, but whatever could the boy have done?

"John . . . pirates . . . American pirates . . . they have taken Windmera!" It was an anguished cry, for his fury was not unmixed with pain.

"And what of Roderick?"

"Roderick? Roderick sits in Bermuda . . . but he has a plan, a good one I think. Here . . . read." He shoved the notepaper at his friend.

John took its crumpled pages and smoothed them over, reading out loud when he could no longer contain his astonishment.

"'. . . her abductor an American we both knew in Barbados. This American savage may think he has reason to illtreat her, but I swear to you, sir, that for my sake as well as your own, I shall hunt him down and make him pay! I know him, I know where he may be found. It is my intention to go after them as soon as you forward me a banknote enough to purchase a vessel and man it well. I shall have your daughter for wife, Godwin—be sure of it! Nothing will stop me from that end.'" It was signed Roderick.

"Yes, yes . . . good lad!" said Godwin, his eyes bright with his growing madness. Again his hand tightened into a fist, again it shook heavenward. "You have set us a task . . . but my lad will see it done!"

"Godwin . . . you . . . he cannot be serious?" cried John in disbelief. "Roderick is no sailor. Our own well-seasoned men are having trouble raiding the American coast . . . how can he possibly steal into any American harbor?"

"He can't . . . not alone. You are right he is no sailor! But John, you are! There is none like you! You could take that swift yawl of yours in and out without being seen. You know the American coast—"

"Yes, I know the northern coasts . . . but what if this American's home port is in the South? I have never sailed there . . . my charts are inadequate . . . my men may be unwilling . . ."

"Hell, John! Would you deny me?"

"I have never denied you . . . but I have my men to think about. We could all be shot as spies."

"I shall make it worthwhile for your men. A prize worthy a king whether they are successful or not. Just for the attempt . . . if any of them are killed the prize money shall go to their families!"

John hesitated. "You would risk Roderick?"

"There will be no risk if you are with him. I would not risk either of you for anything . . . for anyone . . . but Windmera."

John didn't answer, for he was lost in thought. At last he gave his friend a long look. "Very well, Godwin . . . but we won't be able to use my yawl. We will need something sleeker . . . and more heavily armed!"

"Done!" He pulled on his bellrope, and when a lackey appeared he ordered curtly, "Have our horses brought up . . . we are riding for Penzance!"

A letter! A letter from Roderick had arrived. Not addressed to her. No, she and Roderick had not parted on good terms . . . but she would know his news. Why had a letter come? Why was he not here . . . with his bride? Sara yanked hard on her bellrope. A lackey appeared at her open door.

"Have his lordship attend me," she asked quietly as she attempted to collect her thoughts.

"I am sorry, madam," said the footman softly. He had always pitied Sara of Ravensbury. Whatever she had done, she had paid for it, he felt, and his lordship needn't treat her so coldly, so indifferently. "But his lordship . . . he has just called for his horses."

"He is going out?" She was worried. Something was wrong. Her son, something was wrong with her son. "Please . . . wheel my chair . . . to the stair landing."

He complied and stood back as Sara called Godwin's name sharply. He was in the large central hall below with Captain John. There was a plea in the tone. "Godwin . . . please . . . ?"

"What is it, Sara?" He was impatient to be off.

"I . . . I understand you received a letter today."

"Yes."

"Roderick . . . ?"

A look of scorn. "Your son is well but not able to return home yet."

She closed her eyes. She was so tired. "Godwin . . . have you told him . . . about me?" Why must he make her beg?

"About you?" He had almost forgotten. She was dying. She wanted her son home. He softened, chastised himself for it and returned to the nature time had made for him. "No, Sara . . . his priorities now are elsewhere."

He walked out then, but Captain John stared at her for a long moment. It was true, then. Sara was dying. He had suspected as much, though Godwin had never come out with it. Roderick should be told. He would take it upon himself to inform the lad before they set out for the States! He must have maggots floating about in his head to have allowed Godwin to talk him into this affair. Sail for the States? Only the very best English privateers were attempting to raid the American coastline, and not all of them were successful! Ah, bah! He was an old fool for giving in to Godwin's madness. A sigh, thick, heavy, giving no relief, ebbed out of him as he followed Godwin outdoors.

A warm night it was, though winter had hit Bermuda. Cool breezes shook the petals off the flowers and bent the palms. Whitecaps glistened in the moonlight as they crashed against coral reefs. Crabs slowly, purposefully trudged over the sands, over the roads, on a journey only instinct commanded. Quiet descended as plushly feathered birds settled for the night. Lovers met in coves, in garden mazes, but Roderick met Delia in her father's hothouse.

Orange blossoms and their fruit gave over their perfume between fronds of exotic blooms. The moonlight trickled through leafy branches and lit on Delia's face. It was not the first time she had agreed to meet with Roderick, it would not be the last. She loved him. He was more than a man, he was a god, her god! He was to be worshiped, followed, trusted.

"Delia . . . my love . . . how I have waited for this moment," whispered Roderick as he kissed a path from her ears to her lips. Tonight he would have her, all of her. She was ready to give over, he knew it.

"But . . . Roderick . . . it isn't right . . . you mustn't . . ." She mouthed words she didn't believe. If Roderick said

324

it was right, if it was what he wanted, then it was law. She would do whatever he asked.

"You were meant for me, Delia . . ." His hands undid the lacing of her bodice. He freed her small pert breasts, raised them in his large deft hands, bent his head, took the nipple with his mouth.

She arched beneath his touch, and her hand went to his hair. Was it possible for a woman to feel such pleasure beneath a man? "Oh, Roderick . . . I love you . . ."

"Show me Delia . . ." He felt almost savage as he raised her skirt. He didn't have time now to undress her, he had to have her now, quickly. "Show me, pretty woman . . ." He was spreading her legs, undoing his breeches, positioning himself. Damn, but he had to have this one. She was special. Really special. It thrilled him to touch her, more than any other woman he had ever known. Something about her always touched him. This was wrong. He shouldn't be taking her. She was a virgin. He was certain of it, and he . . . he shouldn't be using her . . . hurting her . . . for in the end he would be hurting her . . . but damn! He plunged into her tight sweetness.

She yelped, and his hand went over her mouth. "Hush, babe . . . there, it won't hurt any more . . . there . . ." He moved expertly, keeping her knees apart to get more of her. She whimpered now and then because she was so small and his drive was too hard. But she wouldn't stop him. If he felt he had to do this to make their love complete, she would let him. She loved him so . . . wanted to keep him . . . she must let him if she was going to keep him.

He was done. He lay exhausted beside her. She was good, though she would be better when he had finished with her. She was his.

He moved onto his elbow and looked down at her. She was blushing furiously in the dark. He could see the red glow to her cheeks, and suddenly it made him laugh. "Little innocent . . ." He stroked her cheek. What was it he felt for this girl? He was puzzled by it. He thought of Windmera. Damn . . . but he wanted Windmera . . . would always want her. She was something he had to have. Windmera was meant for him. No other could he take for wife, but this little bit of fluff, this elf of a woman with her round blue eyes, tugged at his heart.

"Oh, Delia . . ." he said without thinking.

"What . . . what is it? Have I displeased you?" She was

worried, there was such a sound to his words, as though he meant to impart a regret. She wanted no regrets.

"Displeased me? No, my girl . . . come." He got up and took her hands. "We had better get you back up your balcony to your room."

She stopped him, pulling like a child on his sleeve. "Roderick?"

"Yes, love?"

"Do you . . . do you still love me?"

He smiled. "Yes, Delia . . . I still love you." Easy words to say. They would do to comfort her now. But later, when he had gone from Bermuda . . . what then? Stop it! He controlled his conscience. She would find some sweet lad to marry her. Yes, probably . . . just as his mother had when his natural father had left her. Stop it! Stop it! He shut his eyes and his mind, but he found he could not look into Delia's eyes when they said goodnight.

A fire blazed in the hearth. Around it candlelight flickered iridescently in the veins of the black marble that made up its frame. Above its mantelshelf rested a painting of some obscure country scene. Stretched out before it at a long rectanular dining table sat the Barkers, the Landons and Windmera de Brabant.

Mr. and Mrs. Barker were situated at each end of the table. Jules Landon, Windmera and George, the Barkers' son, held an uneven advantage over Elly and Lance, who sat facing them. Conversation was by no means desultory, for not only had Jules and Steven Barker been friends for more than twenty-five years, but so had their sons been friends as well. Lance never allowed friends to pass that thin line he held up as shield, but George had always been right at its border. They loved one another nearly as much as brothers.

Elly was in a high fettle. She had her friendship through her brother to exploit over this little island rival of hers. She was spruced up in a gold silk that neatly showed her excellent figure, and she depended upon her brother to entertain Windmera. In this plan she found a willing ally, for George's gray eyes lit up the moment they found Windmera.

"Damn, but I don't agree, Jules!" said Mr. Barker, poking his fork in the air for emphasis. "We had every right to expect a victory in Canada. The British had but six thousand men . . . drunken fools . . . rejects of Wellington's! Spread out they were, too."

"We didn't stand a chance as long as the British maintained control of the St. Lawrence. They have a good man in Brock . . . Detroit was theirs the moment we had to depend on wilderness trails!"

"Gentlemen . . . really . . . all this talk of war . . . I am certain Miss de Brabant must be affected by it all. After all . . . she is British, isn't she?" said Elly sweetly.

Lance frowned at her. God, but he hated cattiness. However, before he could rush to Windmera's defense, she smiled and said quietly, "My father was French . . . though he was exiled on an English colony. My mother was English. My politics are my own."

Elly flushed, for the tone in Windmera's voice was not one on the defense. She changed the subject. "Mr. Landon . . . with all this talk about invasions and such, I wonder at Izzy choosing to remain in Buffalo."

"Unfortunately the snow makes it impossible for her to travel at this time. She is again with child." He was beaming quite proudly.

Felicitations were offered, and then Windmera felt her heart stop beating and involuntarily her eyes flew to Lance's face. George had winked across the table and asked in a jovial manner, "Well, Lance my man . . . did you have a chance to call on Stacy Clayton?"

Lance grinned and raised his glass. "I certainly did. She sends you her regards."

"I'll just bet she did, you old dog!"

"Stacy? Who is this Stacy?" asked Elly, pulling a sour face at her brother.

"A Southern belle . . . or should I say, the Southern belle of Norfolk." He grinned at his sister. "A friend of mine. I thought she might keep Lance from becoming too lonely."

"George!" objected George's mother.

"No, no . . . you misunderstand. She leads the social world down there. I was lucky enough to be introduced to her when you sent me down there on business last summer. I simply thought she would take Lance in hand . . . what I mean is—"

"I think we know what you mean," said his mother, glaring at him hard.

Lance was attempting to keep a straight face. Neither his father nor Mr. Barker were successful and fell into thick chuckles. Elly pouted, and Windmera suddenly thought the entire thing too funny to resist. She giggled and looked at

George. "Rest easy, Mr. Barker, I believe your friend Mrs. Clayton . . . took Captain Landon well in hand." It was a whisper meant only for George's ears, and therefore no other heard it.

George burst out laughing, and this time both Elly and Lance glared at him. Lance frowned. Whatever had Windmera said to him? And how had they managed to become so friendly in such a short span of time? Admittedly George was a fine-looking man, with a clump of unruly russet locks that somehow gave him an air of romance. He had charm, manners and address. But Hell . . . why should Windmera be so taken with him? For the first time in many years Lance felt out of sorts with his closest friend.

"Shall we retire, girls, and allow the men to enjoy their port and their talk of war?" This from Mrs. Barker.

It was not a suggestion but a command. The girls in her charge had no choice but to demurely follow, though both would have gladly remained. Windmera had always enjoyed the conversation of men better than that of women, and Elly wanted to work her charms on Lance. However, they gave in gracefully and left the room.

George watched Windmera go. She was breathtaking in her gown of dark blue. Sapphires glowed around her neck and in her ears. Long black curls cascaded from the top of her head, where a matching velvet ribbon held them. Her figure was sensuous and alluring, more so because of the way she walked, natural, lively, bouncing. Egad, but this was one beauty worth giving up his freedom for. Lance glared at Windmera and thought much the same. However, he then happened to see the look that came into his friend's eyes.

"George?"

"Hmmm . . . what?"

"I want a word with you in private," said Lance.

"Do you . . . ah . . . the Stacy wench! By Gad, she was a charmer," he said, getting to his feet, allowing Lance to push him along at the shoulder into a corner of the room, leaving their fathers to argue politics.

"Yes, she was . . . but—"

"Knew a few tricks too, that one," he continued along the same vein.

"Never mind her," said Lance impatiently. "George . . . look, there is no way to put this except bluntly. Miss de Brabant is mine!"

George turned surprised eyes to his friend's face. "Yours?

You mean . . . you are engaged?" He could not hide the disappointment from his tone.

"Not exactly . . . but we will be."

"Hell . . . what is that supposed to mean?"

"Look, George . . . what should it mean except the lady is mine?"

"Really? What makes her so?" George had an obstinate side to his nature.

"I make her so!" Lance was angry now, and it was with effort that he kept his voice low.

"Elly always had a notion you and she—"

"I cannot be responsible for your sister's notions. Until a year ago, she had a fancy for Thomas Corey!"

"Well . . . she don't want Corey any more. She wants you . . . and what's more, if you want Miss de Brabant, you have no business encouraging my sister the way you did tonight!" snapped George, on the defensive. He was attracted to Windmera, but in part it was spurred by Lance putting a fence around her. He and Lance had been friends nearly all their lives. Each would have died to save the other, but in spite of this they had always been rivals, in sports, in manner of dress, sophistication, studies, and especially with girls. But neither one had ever been seriously involved with a woman before; it was just another sport.

"You call my manner to your sister this evening encouraging?" He made a derisive sound. "Don't be a noddy!"

"Well . . . you didn't pay Miss de Brabant any mind. I call that damn odd."

"What I do in that respect is my own business," said Lance between clenched teeth. "All you have to know is that Miss de Brabant is on *my* shelf!"

"Lord, man, if that don't beat all! And I'll tell you another thing, the lady gave no indication of wanting to be on your shelf!" He glared defiantly. "I consider her fair game!"

Fists clenched at Lance's sides. "Don't you ever speak about her in such terms!"

"Hell, Lance, you know damn well what I meant!" He sighed, backing off some, for he could see Lance was in earnest. "Look . . . maybe I am overstepping. Tell me you are in love with her, and sure . . . I'll not raise an eye in her direction."

"Love?" That word again. Why did it always crop up? First his father asking, now George. It was a terrifying word . . . love. He had never committed his heart to any woman

before. Discounting his mother . . . and she died . . . his sister . . . and she left with a husband. Love? He answered with an exasperated note, *"That,* my man, is none of your business!"

"Isn't it? Well, then, you have to settle the matter right and tight, old friend, for I'll tell you what. Miss de Brabant is a fine woman, worthy of a man's heart. You! You have just come from bedding Stacy Clayton and God knows who else . . . you flirt roundly with m'own sister . . . and I'll tell you what else, Lance, Miss de Brabant don't seem to give a fig for you and your antics!"

"Shut up, George, before I break your jaw!" said Lance, his voice dangerously low. "You want Miss de Brabant . . . very well . . . I give you my leave to try your hand at her. She won't have you . . . devil is in it that she won't have either of us. But . . . by all means . . . try if you must!" He pulled himself up and moved away.

George watched him. What was wrong here? Why had the conversation turned ugly? Lance had never behaved this way over a woman before. They had taken bets over the wenches, they had shaken each other soundly over them. But never had it turned nasty! Laughter had always reigned over their arguments. He watched Lance a long moment before saying lightly he would join the women. He left the room, and Lance, cursing softly beneath his breath, was quick on his heels.

Windmera lay in her bed. A fire crackled in the hearth, and snow was falling quietly outside her window. Purposely she had left the drapes drawn so that she could watch the multifaceted crystals on their journey. The light outdoors had an eerie glow, fascinating in its twilight stillness. She stared through the darkness at her hall door, and something inside her yearned desperately to relive the moments past when Lance had bid her goodnight.

Jules had said goodnight in the central hall below, and she had turned toward the stairs.

"I'll take you up, Windy." It was Lance's voice, and it was full in its softness.

"That isn't necessary, captain . . . I know my way," she said coldly. She was peeved with him, with the way he had ignored her all evening, with the way he had dallied with Elly Barker, whom in spite of everything she liked.

"I know," he said and took her elbow. She wanted to yank out of his touch, but Jules was still there. She was fast learning to love Lance's father, so she pulled a face at Lance and allowed him the liberty.

Upstairs the hall was dark, as the servants had left only one candle lit on a wall table. She felt shaken with a tingling sensation. Suddenly he was stopping her, taking up her hands, looking into her eyes with an emotion she had never seen there before. She half expected him to kiss her, she half wanted him to try, but he didn't.

"Windy . . . George is the best of good men . . . but he is not for you!" He blurted it out before he could stop himself.

What was this? What new quirk? This man was unbelievable. This Lance Landon and his arrogance . . . his gall! Her eyes were bright with the challenge when she answered, "Is he not? Who then is for me? You say Roderick is not . . . George Barker is not . . . then who, my fine captain? *Only you?*" Her tone held mockery, and it drove him further into his rage.

He gripped her shoulders. "That's right, Windmera! Only me!" He did kiss her then, but it was cruel in its intensity. It was a sign of ownership, not desire, not affection, and even so there was a depth of feeling, a sudden crystallized perception that transmitted itself to her inner being, arousing an unbidden veracity within her breast. What was it? What was this sensory tingling he engendered in her? What did she feel for Lance Landon? It was the first time she had really asked her self this question. Before she had always known, or at least had thought she knew. She hated him, did she not? She could feel nothing for him but dislike . . . and yet . . .? No! It was only that he had bedded her . . . only that! She was tied to him emotionally because he had taken her virginity. No other emotion was involved. Love? No . . . impossible . . . never!

Still, in that moment when his grip savagely bent her to him, when his touch incited ferment within her veins, she wondered. She pulled away from him. She had to get away from him, from the doubts his touch instilled in her heart, in her mind.

"Let me go! I will marry whom I choose!" She fled to the safety of her room, half afraid he would follow and somehow sadly disappointed when he did not. Surely if he cared he would have followed? Care? He didn't care . . . and neither did she!

On this thought she shut her eyes, but instead of closing him out, he was brought vividly into focus, as was the day they had spent together. How his eyes had twinkled in their deep blueness over their mugs of hot cocoa. What an adorable little tea shop it had been, with the prettiest tablecloths and flowers from their own hothouse. How amusing he had been. She had laughed to hear him speak of his youth, his sister. They had trudged through the snow on their walking tour of Mystic. He had taken her to the Mystic Press, to the Oyster House, the weaver shop, the hoop shop, the general store and lastly to the lovely white church. How well liked he was! She sensed it immediately in people's smiles, in the way they reacted to his presence, and she began to wonder at this side of him.

And then all was ruined! At Elly Barker's he became so . . . rakish! Elly was a lovely girl, and Windmera found herself liking her, liking George. Conversation came easy after Elly's initial frostiness had thawed. George was very attentive, and Windy thought him sweet, and then she looked up to find Lance glaring at them. It tickled her, for at first she thought him jealous. Lance jealous? How exciting this was! However, this was shattered, for the very next thing he did was to encircle Elly's waist and whisper something in her ear! Brute! Libertine cad! She hated him! How could she have thought he was jealous? If he had been, surely he would have strived to get her attention, to amuse her even as George was doing, but no, he didn't care, for there he was paying her no mind as he flirted with Elly Barker!

She turned on her pillow, for her heart ached. Everything was in such a muddle. If only . . . But ifs were for children, as are wishes, and Windmera was beyond that.

Thirteen

Jules Landon's pale-blue eyes were alive. He thought of
Irene . . . would she approve of his methods? Indeed she
would. Yes, Windmera de Brabant was a girl Irene would
have wanted for their son. Well, the way things looked,
Windmera and Lance would never get together. They needed
guiding, and the first step toward this was separating them.
Allowing a little time to pass before they saw one another.
Amazing what time could accomplish, especially if properly
wielded! It was this that took him to his son's room early this
morning.

"Lance . . . I want you to ride for Boston, now."

"Boston . . . now? Why . . . I've only just come home!"
Consternation showed on his features. He was already thinking of Windy . . . of George.

"I am sorry, son. I would make the trip myself . . . but
my rheumatism has been acting up."

"Of course you can't make the trip! But . . . why in Hell
does either of us have to go?"

"You know that new firm we built the *Whaler* for? Alsace
and Company?"

"Yes."

"Well, they owe us a hefty sum on it still. The problem is
that I know they have ships laid up in port with goods. They
are afraid to make their deliveries for fear of British capture
. . . so they are waiting it out. For that reason, I don't wish
to make it difficult for them. However, at the same time, we
made a delivery in good faith, and I feel strongly that some
payment should be made toward their contract. I want it
handled delicately . . . but I want it handled!"

Lance frowned. It was an excellent reason for making the
trip, but damn, he didn't want to go just now. "Yes . . . I
understand."

"I thought you would. Do you take the coach?"

"No . . . I'll take my horse. But have word sent to Jackie.
I'd like him to accompany me if he can."

An hour later Jules Landon saw his son and Jackie off the
grounds. He was well pleased with himself, and now, here

333

was Windmera. What a beauty! What fire in her eyes . . . it was no wonder she was driving his son to distraction!

"Good morning my dear," he said as she stood hesitatingly in the doorway of his library. "Have you eaten?"

"No . . . I wasn't very hungry." She came into the room. She hadn't heard anything of Lance this morning, and she sensed something, she didn't quite know what. She looked about, wondering where he was.

"Well, you must eat. Sit down and join me. We have a fresh pot of tea and the most delicious tarts you have ever tasted." He was smiling reassuringly.

She responded. He put her at ease, so she dropped into a nearby wing chair and began pouring. "Mr. Landon . . ." she began.

He interrupted, "Jules. I should like it if you were to call me Jules."

She blushed. "I don't know if I can . . . but I'll try. Jules . . . I was wondering . . . I used to do a great deal of riding at home . . . I miss it terribly."

"You want a mount? Of course, my dear. Why don't you stroll down to the stables and take your pick?"

"Thank you . . . but I want to be sure I don't choose a favorite of yours . . . or Captain Lance's."

"If you can ride, you are welcome to ride my roan. He doesn't get enough exercise these days. As to Lance's horse, you needn't concern yourself. He is gone off with Lance," he said glibly.

Her reaction confirmed his intent. "Gone? Lance is gone? But where?" Her face had fallen ludicrously.

"We had business in Boston that needed his immediate attention. I don't expect he'll be back before the end of January, as we have friends in Boston he no doubt will visit while there. But . . ." He bent to pat her hand. "We shall strive to keep you amused in the two weeks of his absence."

She put up her chin. He didn't really think she would be lonely for Lance? "I don't care whether he is here or not!" She said it a bit too sharply and then relented. "Oh . . . how dreadful that must sound to you. He is your son . . . but he must have told you something about the circumstances that . . ."—she was blushing furiously—"that brought me to your home?"

Jules Landon looked grave as he nodded, but he stopped himself from saying anything. Better to let her talk, to get it out. She had no one really to talk to. He wanted to be her sounding board. It was necessary for her to air her grievances to someone other than Lance, who was responsible for them.

She couldn't look him in the face, meet his eyes. "You must not think that it was all Lance's fault. I wouldn't be honest if . . . I were to say such a thing. It was unfortunate that I happened to be on that ship . . . that Lance thought I had betrayed him on Barbados . . ."

"Excuse me . . . betrayed him in what way?"

"You mean he didn't tell you that he thought it was I who had him trapped in the warehouse . . . had him arrested?" She was surprised.

"He did not tell me the details of that particular experience, though I do recall his mentioning something about his having been wrong in trusting you."

Odd. He was such an unusual being, this Lance Landon, but then, so was she, for though she had not said a word in her defense when he had questioned her regarding her part in his imprisonment, she couldn't allow Jules Landon to think it of her. She rushed to assure him that she had had nothing to do with his capture at Jackson Warehouse.

"Sir . . . I planned it with your son . . . I got him the letterhead he would need . . . discovered the best time to act . . . but something went wrong. I don't know what. I don't know how Brayward found out, but I swear it, I did not betray Lance."

"Lance thinks you did?"

She nodded. "Yes, he asked me the other day why I had betrayed him."

"Your answer was?"

"I wouldn't honor his question with an answer," she said on a bitter note.

He touched his chin with his fist. "I see . . . then Lance still believes . . ."

"Yes! And I don't care! He has no right to think such a thing of me. I never gave him reason . . . but that doesn't matter . . . and I forbid you to tell him."

"You forbid me?" His brow was up.

She turned scarlet. "Please, sir . . ."

"I shall try to keep out of it. However, I must tell you that I don't approve of a lie remaining between two people who are to be married." Here now was the test.

"I won't marry him," she said quietly.

"I have reason to believe that it is in your interest to marry

335

my son." His answer was meant to pinch her to further confession.

"Well, it isn't! He doesn't love me!"

"Doesn't he?"

"No . . . and I don't love him."

"And you do love . . . this man . . . what was his name?"

"You mean my fiancé . . . Roderick of Ravensbury," she said softly. Roderick? How long now . . . three weeks? They had been apart three weeks. What did he look like? She tried to visualize him. What were the color of his eyes? Hazel? Brown? Did they laugh? Why was it so hard to remember him? All those months after Lance Landon had sailed out of sight, she had remembered Lance's face, his eyes, his touch! Why was it so hard to bring Roderick to life?

"Yes . . . that's it. Ravensbury. Good family name, that. You love him, of course . . . want to be reunited with him?"

"I . . . of course," she answered but there was a hint of doubt in her tone. The same doubt that kept her from wedding him in Barbados.

"I see." He was smiling. "You are very young, my dear, and Lance is confused, put on edge by untruths you refuse to set right, by emotions he has never before met and doesn't know how to deal with. He was very young when he lost his mother—"

She frowned, for a knock sounded at the door and there stood George and Elly Barker. Drat! She had wanted to hear what Jules Landon was about to say. She had wanted to hear it so badly. Of all the unsuitable moments for the Barkers to come calling! Jules had opened a road she wanted to travel; but she did the polite and smiled a welcome.

Jules was well satisfied and not unhappy about the interruption. It was good. Enough had been said for the time being. She would need space now to think everything over, to see Lance perhaps in a new, more glorious arena than before. He got to his feet and pulled the bellrope as he greeted his guests.

"George . . . Elly . . . what a pleasant surprise, and how neatly timed, for I was just wondering how best to entertain Windmera with Lance away."

"Away?" It was said in unison, with brother and sister exchanging glances. There was never any knowing what Lance Landon would be doing next!

Stacy Clayton's brother-in-law glanced at her from beneath

336

his shaggy brows. He was more than fifty-five now. His wife had given him eight children, six of whom had grown to adulthood. Stacy? He had wanted her from the first moment his older brother had brought her home. Two years! She had been a widow more than two years and still she refused him her bed!

It galled. Countless others he knew she entertained there . . . but not once had she even allowed him a kiss. Damn, but he wanted to bed her, especially at moments like this when she willfully teased him. Look at her, brazen in her black lace wrapper . . . purposely she allowed it to part down the center, exhibiting her nakedness as she moved across her boudoir, choosing her gown with total unconcern for his presence! But this latest escapade of hers was more than even he could take. He would not have the Clayton name dragged through the mud. He would not have her sleeping with his son!

"Damn it, woman, I am talking to you!" he snapped.

She dropped the gown she was holding up for inspection and gave him a long disdainful look. Look at him, with his paunch belly, his balding head, his protruding eyes and his sweaty hands! Did he really think she would ever let him near her? Fool! How had he ever managed to have such a fine-looking son? It tickled her a moment to think perhaps his son was another man's seed . . . but no, not that toady wife of his! "What do you want, Monty?" She saw him stare at her breasts, She loved it, having him pant over her, knowing she had such power over a man.

"I want you to leave my son be! Fiend seize it, Stacy . . . he is only twenty."

"Hmmmm . . . deliciously twenty!" she said, moving her hands over hips.

"Think of the scandal!" he roared. "Have you no scruples?"

"Scandal? I can weather it."

"But I can't and won't!"

She moved toward him. "Monty . . . you are making a fuss because it's not you. Isn't that true?" her voice was low, she was near, near enough . . .

He reached out and grabbed her arm, pulling her roughly into an embrace. His sweating palm closed over her breast, his wet lips pushed to find her mouth.

She yanked out of his hold. "Oh, God . . . you disgusting pig! I can't stand your touch! Lordy, your brother had ten years on you . . . but he knew how to please a woman. Reckon you are a Clayton, honey? Could be you are a by-blow!"

He slapped her then, hard, and she went reeling backward onto her bed. He was after her in a moment, but her foot came up sharply, kicking him in the groin. She was up in a moment and at her door, calling her male slaves. Two black tightly muscled manservants appeared, and she pointed at Monty Clayton. He was bent over his belly.

"Show my brother-in-law out!"

They went to him, but he shrugged off their hands viciously, and he snarled when he looked at his sister-in-law. "Stacy . . . I won't forget this! I am a vengeful man . . . expect my wrath! Expect it, Stacy!"

He was gone. She frowned. His words were frightening. Was he a vengeful man? She had seen that in the past five years work on others . . . but what could he do to her? Naught! He could rail, he could fuss, he could even cause her some social discomfort, but in the end . . . what could he do? Naught! He was a sniveling pig!

Delia stood on the crest of a hill. The ocean deep in its clear aquamarine was lit in her eyes. Breakers crashed against the reef; deafening was their sound. Creamy sands stretched below for miles. Palms swayed in the cool morning breeze. Everything was life, sweet and harmonious, for Delia was in love. January was drawing to a close. She had known him scarcely three weeks, but she was his, in mind, in spirit, in body. Her world was Roderick, and all other beings, even her father, were secondary to her now. She longed only for the moments that would see them together, alone.

Roderick spied her above him as he dismounted and dropped his reins. She was lovely. Her bright-yellow curls danced in the wind. Her profile was angelic. She was innocence and beauty fused into perfection. A longing came over him, for in some part he never wanted to leave her. She forced to the surface all finer emotions . . . but she was not Windmera. She was not of Godwin's blood, and she would never be his wife! Another would come to claim her after he had gone. . . .

It was a disquieting thought. He shivered beneath its weight, pulled up his shoulders and moved up the hill. When he reached her he couldn't speak. His hands took her face, his eyes spoke quietly, intensely, and his mouth cherished.

"Oh, Delia . . ." He was already lowering her to the earth . . . lowering her . . .

She couldn't speak. She was filled with a need to please him. She wanted only to please him, love him, be everything he desired. If now and then she wondered why he never spoke of marriage, she pushed it aside. He would . . . at the right moment. Perhaps when the ship arrived from Cornwall with his funds. She couldn't think of that now. Now, she had to love him . . . keep him. . . .

"Damn it, capt'n . . . this has been one helluva trip you put me through. I wouldn't do it again for love or money!" complained Jackie as he held his gelding in check.

Lance grinned. "Thanks, sport! But really, Jack . . . thank you. I really needed you this time."

"Oh, yeah? I don't know what fer! Hell . . . you ain't been talkative going in or coming out . . . and as to foolin' around Boston . . . well, capt'n, you were deader than a doornail!"

"Was I? Aye . . . I suppose I was."

"Hmmm. You can say that again."

"Well, don't! Go on . . . get into town with you and get some rest. It's been a long day, and God knows I've pushed you as hard as I have our poor horses!"

"Aye, capt'n . . . will I be seeing you over the tavern later?"

"No . . . I don't think so." He watched Jackie urge his horse into a trot toward Mystic. Two weeks! He'd been away two weeks, for the trip going in had taken three days and then it had taken another five settling up amicably with Alsace and Company. Then just as he'd meant to start out for home he'd bumped into some of his father's friends. There was no getting away from them . . . or his mood. Jackie had tried desperately to even his temper, taking him first to a cockfight, dragging him later to a disreputable tavern that in the past would have enormously delighted him, but left him flat. His appetite for women, food and wine had flown, and he returned to Mystic hungry for something he could not name.

He patted his horse's neck. "Good boy . . . good Prancer . . . I'm proud of you, love." He had made the three-day journey home in two, for once on the road, he couldn't get home fast enough. What had Windmera been doing in these past two weeks? What had George been up to? Stealing a march on him? He would have been very much relieved to know that George had thought it unfair to take advantage of his absence and had for the most part kept his flirting superficial, a condition that exactly suited Windmera's mood.

Lance picked up the pace of his trot, rolling evenly with his horse's gait, his hands light on the reins yet fully in control. A tingle ran throughout his veins and he felt warm in spite of the biting cold at his cheeks. The stables were a welcome sight, but he had not the patience to stop there as he ordinarily did, saving his groom the walk to the house. This time he rode straight up to his front door.

Sam saw him coming and slipped on a wool shawl before opening the door wide and going out to take charge of Prancer's reins.

"Have him walked . . . I don't want him working up a sweat, as he had been rode hard, Sam. Tell 'em to give him water and then his feed . . . and thanks, Sam." With that he took off his cloak, throwing it negligently onto a hall chair he passed on his way to the library. He was excited beyond belief. Why? He didn't know, but he did know he wanted to see Windmera . . . now, now!

Jules Landon moved his queen across the board. He was frowning all the while, stealing a glance at Windmera's studious expression. A chuckle lit in his pale-blue eyes. She had fallen for the bait, he could see it in her own violet orbs. Such vividness they contained, her eyes!

She was sitting on the floor, her calves tucked in under her blue velvet skirt, her long black hair streaming down her back. Pert black curls framed her piquant face, and a victorious smile lit her lips. She clapped her hands together and got to her knees to make her move. "There! I have your queen, Jules!"

"So you have, little girl . . . so you have," he said in mock defeat. "But of course"—he moved his knight as he spoke—"you realize that this is checkmate!" He grinned boyishly across the board at her.

She gasped as she stared at the board. Her king was surrounded by rook, pawn and knight. She couldn't move him from without that stronghold. How had she fallen for his trick? "Oh . . . you horrible man! You tricked me . . . you let me think I was pulling a coup by offering up your queen."

Jules chuckled, and to his mirth was added that of his son's.

"So, Father has outfoxed you, eh, Windmera?" Lance had watched the whole from the doorway. It had been strangely satisfying to see Windmera at his father's feet, playful, happy . . . he almost wished it was he, not his father, enjoying a game of chess with her.

"Lance, my boy!" said Jules, getting up and going across the room to take his son's shoulders. "Devil! You are frozen through!" he exclaimed, touching him. "Come over here . . . by the fire."

"So I shall . . . in a moment." He moved away, toward Windmera, who had gone rigid upon her knees. Her heart's beat forgot its proper timing. She heard his name, and chaos ruled her body. She couldn't move, couldn't speak, and when he approached and took up her hand, there was nothing she could do but allow him to draw her up to her feet.

"Windmera . . ." It was a whispered sound. His lips brushed first her fingers and then higher upon her wrist. He drew himself up but retained his hold on her hand. He had forgotten his father's presence. Indeed, Jules made that easy, for he wandered over to the sideboard table to pour a glass of brandy for his son. "Windy . . . I've missed you . . ."

How should she respond to this? She felt a wild inexplicable tremor shake her. It was physical . . . only physical . . . meaningless.

"Why, captain . . . I find that hard to believe. I am sure Boston offered you diversions enough," she answered at last, avoiding his eyes, averting her own.

"And you . . . I imagine you had diversions enough while I was gone?"

"Oh, yes," answered his father, putting the glass in his son's hand. "George and Elly were here nearly every day. Just yesterday the three of them rode over to Seamen's Inn. Met some other of your friends there for lunch. So you see, we have managed to make certain Windy would not be lonely for you."

Lance stared hard at his father's benign expression. What was this? Was the entire world mad? What was he up against? "Thank you, Father." His voice was dry.

Windy pulled her hand out of Lance's grip and moved slightly away. This was all too much for her. The suddenness of his return had shaken her more than she could bear. She wanted to flee but couldn't leave, couldn't take her eyes from his face. And he? He wanted to take her in his arms, touch her face, caress her lips, but they stood divided.

Such was Lance Landon's homecoming! His father observed them and smiled. Each was near the breaking point. They needed now to laugh together. They needed to be alone, untroubled by the designs of outsiders. They needed to drop their defenses to call an end to the game. But the moment was not yet!

"Windmera . . . I have some matters I must speak to Lance about." His tone was suggestive.

"Oh, of course. I was supposed to work on my embroidery. Elly did make me promise to have it done by the end of the week." She laughed. "She means to make a proper lady of me!"

"You are lady enough without Elly's toils!" snapped Lance.

She blushed, not unpleased with this. "Thank you, captain, but your Elly says I am a sad hoyden."

"She is not *my* Elly . . . and if that is what she says, she is sadly mistaken," he said, more softly this time, his eyes holding hers.

She smiled and glided past him. He wanted to reach out and detain her, but his father called his attention away. "Lance, now come sit by the fire and tell me what news you have!"

"What? Oh . . . yes," said Lance, sighing. This was not exactly what he had in mind, but there was nothing for it. So he sat.

Fourteen

Much later they were alone. The fire in the hearth was in a roaring blaze, the candlelight flickered warmly in the coziness of the mellow room, and Lance's blue eyes were boring through the electricity in the air, vanquishing Windmera in one single swoop. He was coming toward her. She knew he would take her in his arms. How had Jules left them like this? Why could he not have had Sam show the new arrival in . . . why had he gone?

She stood riveted by her own sensations, by his eyes . . . by the need she had to be touched by him. He whispered her name.

"Windmera . . . I . . ." His hands had already taken her waist, had already crushed her to him.

She heard a sound. Jules was returning. She pulled away. "Your . . . your father . . ."

The heat was in Lance's cheeks. The excitement had melted his eyes into blue water. How could he let her go? He was craving her in a way that left him breathless . . . starving. But she was right, someone was at the door . . . opening it. He released her and turned at her side, his brows drawn in a frown.

Jules opened the door and stepped aside to allow a small leathery-faced man to enter before him. He was telling the man to warm himself by the fire, he was looking meaningfully at his son and he was saying in a voice tinged with portentousness, "Lance . . . Mr. Cooper here has come from New York. He has some rather bad news for us . . . regarding Commander in Chief Harrison's attempt at Detroit!"

Lance was alert, tense, all at once. What was this? Had Harrison already tried to retake Fort Malden? He wasn't supposed to make the attempt until their supplies were secure! "Hell and damnation!" He stepped forward. "Nothing could have gone wrong. Harrison is the best, and from what I heard . . . his plans were perfect!"

Mr. Cooper's sharp round eyes darted toward Windmera. Evidently he didn't feel that what he had to impart was meant for a woman's ears. He indicated this by making a series of deprecatory coughs.

Jules smiled patronizingly, "Sorry, Mr. Cooper. Whatever you have to tell us, you will have to do so with Miss de Brabant present. She is my son's intended bride, and we Landons don't believe in keeping our women in the dark on matters that affect their lives as much as our own!"

Windmera declined to refute his reference to her status. He thought enough of her to trust her. She sent him a winning smile that froze on her face, for she saw the doubt on Lance's countenance. *He* didn't trust her! He didn't want her here. She felt her heart constrict within her chest. She bit her lip, and because she couldn't speak she started to move toward the library doors.

Jules sent his son a meaningful glance, but Lance didn't need it, he was already reaching for Windmera's arm. He caught it in his firm grip, and his eyes no longer held doubt. "Stay, Windmera . . ." It was a whisper, but it thundered through her mind, her soul. *Stay, Windmera, stay, Windmera!* She wanted suddenly to hold onto him, draw strength from him, for her own limbs felt weak, devoid of power.

He sensed it and put his arm about her, leading her to a chair, setting her there and then turning on Mr. Cooper. "All right, then, let's have it. Who has sent you here . . . with what and to what end?"

"As you already know, the name is Cooper . . . Samuel. I'm a courier for the Admiralty." He withdrew from his inner dark wool coat an ivory-colored envelope seealed with red wax. He handed it to Lance Landon. "This is for you . . . to be perused in private and then burned, if you please. The rest, I've been empowered to tell you and your family beforehand, if you will." He waited, received a nod from Lance, who held the envelope in two hands but stood rigidly, still fearing the worst. He wasn't ready for another voyage! Undoubtedly that was the meaning of the envelope. He wanted to stay here in Mystic . . . he wanted to . . . what? What did he want? Windmera. He wanted Windmera.

"Right, then," continued Samuel Cooper, moving to sit heavily upon a cushioned wing chair. He sighed. "There ain't a better man on land than Brigadier Harrison . . . so I wants it clear that I ain't about to pull him down. He and Winchester were the men for the job . . . but something went wrong. Harrison, he was set up with ten thousand men under him., and all fired up to win Detroit back. Them Kentuckians . . . brave lads every one! Hell bent to get Detroit after Hull lost it back in August. But Harrison, he saw it couldn't be done until the river iced over. Yep, said, he'd advance his army with sleds across the Detroit River and attack Fort Malden, but they needed supplies, you know." He grunted before proceeding. "Damn fools . . . trusted word got to them that there were unguarded supplies at Frenchtown, you know . . . so Winchester took his command . . . split 'em and sent seven hundred of 'em to River Raisin, where the supply depot was.

"Well now, surprised they were to find the redcoats there putting up a fight. Beat 'em back and took command of Frenchtown. Now here is where Winchester pulled a boner! Underestimated his man! Proctor is no fool, but Winchester now he must have thought so, for damn if he didn't take our men into an open field and camp 'em. Proctor, now, he got word about his soldiers and the loss of Frenchtown and he meant to get it back. Over the Detroit River on ice they came. You would have thought Winchester would have set up guards . . . scouts . . . but Hell . . . nothing. So the redcoats and their Injuns come over the ice. Snuck up on us with their howitzers, and we didn't see 'em till they was on us!" He sighed again, picturing it all in his mind He hadn't been in battle since he was a boy in '76, but it was all very vivid, very alive to him. He winced with the pain of failure before proceeding.

"Well now . . . nobody could've been more surprised then Winchester when up he looks to find the British surrounding their camp! Lord, but even so our lads put up a brave fight . . . some two hundred of 'em going down under fire until Winchester surrendered!"

Jules shook his head and moved to his window. This was a blow. He wanted to collect his thoughts, but Cooper at his back had risen to his feet, pleased to see the depths of emotion on both Landons' faces. "Hell . . . and that ain't all of it! Bloody redcoats . . . may they rot . . . you know what they did with our wounded? Left them to the Injuns! Fiend seize their bloody souls! To the Injuns . . . to be scalped and tomahawked every last one. Those Kentuckians of ours, they're in one hell of a rage . . . and who can blame them?"

Lance looked grim. He put his hand on his father's shoulder. "There is now only one solution. We must get control of at least one of the Great Lakes!"

"I . . . I was thinking of your sister," said Jules Landon. Buffalo, it was far too close to Canada . . . to Frenchtown . . . to the British! Odd, he had been born and raised an Englishman . . . but for too long now he was one no more. He was an American. His children were American.

Lance's expression was grave. "Write to her . . . convince her she must come home until this thing is over."

"I will try."

Windmera had been quietly listening to all of this. She was involved. She didn't want to be, but she was. Here she was, herself half English, worried about the Americans . . . about Izzy, whom she had never met, about Lance, and the meaning of the envelope he held still in his hands. She got up without realizing it and moved to him, touching his hand, not knowing what to say. "Lance . . . I am . . . sorry."

He looked long into her eyes. Such speaking, such innocent eyes. How could he ever have doubted her? He had trusted her once. But now, now she had no reason to lie. He stroked her cheek, one lingering, cherished touch, and then suddenly he was excusing himself. She watched him leave the room, and then she was turning to Jules, running to him, going into his open arms. "Jules . . . what does it mean? He will be leaving, won't he? Won't he?"

"I am afraid so, my dear." He was patting her back, because Lance would indeed be leaving and there was no doubt in either one's mind about the danger he would be meeting. Mr. Cooper shook his head sadly. Too many good young men had been lost already, but war, now, it had to be. This country of theirs . . . it was derived out of war, had to be protected, even by war. They couldn't let the British ride roughshod over them, now could they? War! It was the only answer . . . wasn't it? He shook his head. But so many young men. . . ?

Windmera made no attempt to get into her bed or to question her motives. She sat scantily clothed in a flimsy pink nightdress, curled up on the hearthrug and staring into the blaze. The radiance of her roaring fire flickered on darkened walls, and she hugged her knees to herself. A knock sounded.

She had known this would happen. She got up and moved almost eagerly toward her bedroom door. It would be Lance. Had to be Lance. She didn't know why she felt this way, but she hadn't seen him after the courier's talk with them earlier. He had called for his horse and then suddenly he was gone. This had to be him!

The door opened wide and then slid out of her hand. It was Lance. He hadn't bothered to remove his hat and cloak, and they were covered with the damp chill of the night. His cheeks were flushed, but his eyes were bright. "Windy . . . I . . . I wanted to see you before I left."

She managed to breathe, "But . . . you won't be leaving till tomorrow . . . ?" He smiled wryly. "I'll be gone long before you or Dad wakes up." He hesitated. "Windy . . . let me come in . . . just for a moment. You can leave the door open if you wish."

She nodded, stood aside and allowed him to stalk into the room, for stalk was the only description for the heaviness of his walk. He had so much on his mind. He stood with his back to her, his hands facing the flame, waiting for her to join him in the depths of her room, all too aware of her untouched bed . . . of the open door.

She was drawn to him. She didn't know what made her reach up and tenderly remove his hat. Perhaps Jules had softened her with all his talk of the little boy . . . perhaps she even saw that little boy now. She only knew her hands moved to assuage, her fingers went to the tie string of his cloak. He caught her hand suddenly, halting all movement. "Windy! I . . . I don't think I can stand any more." He stepped away. He paced, looking like a wild animal caged. "I came . . . to ask you again . . . will you marry me?"

Something inside of her suddenly said yes, but she heard her voice, distant, yet her voice, say, "Why . . . why do you want me to marry you, Lance?" And then before he could answer. "No! I know why. It's wrong . . . it's the wrong reason."

"It's not the only reason." His voice was low, moving. He was coming toward her, reaching for her waist. His eyes were hungry for her, they ravished her with one swoop. "I want you. Windy . . . so much . . ."

"That is not enough. A marriage is not . . . my taking your name . . . your taking my body! A marriage is a creation unto itself, a work of art. It needs some very special ingredients to work, to take shape. Lance . . . you should love the woman you marry . . . love her beyond all reason . . . beyond all else. She should love you."

"Love?" he scoffed "What is it but the joining of two people who want each other?" He had her waist in his grasp, he was pressing her against himself. "You want me . . . even now. Windmera. *Admit it!*"

"Yes . . . yes . . . part of me does want you. But Lance . . . it isn't enough!"

"What then? Shall I vow my undying passion? Isn't that what all women want to hear? You want the word? So be it! I love the sight of you, the grace of you, the way you walk, talk. You fill my dreams, Windy . . . all my desires are centered in you . . . I ache for you." His mouth was on hers now, taking, taking, demanding more than his words would let her give.

Oh, God! She wanted to lose herself in his kiss. But he still had not said he loved her. He still talked of lust. That wasn't enough for her. She wanted more . . . so much more. She pulled away.

"No, Lance . . . even that is not love. If I were to accept you on such a basis, every time you saw a new woman, you would be hotfooting it in her direction. You are talking about pleasures . . . they can be found with any woman you find attractive. I don't want to be just another pleasure in your life."

He threw up his hands. "And you will let me go . . ." It was almost a plea.

"I will let you go because you give me no choice . . . you have never given me any choice." She remembered earlier this evening, the quick dart of pain she had experienced when she realized Lance was mistrustful of her presence in the room with the courier. He still did not trust her. A marriage needed trust.

He picked up his hat, his pride showing, and even so, he said her name. "Windmera . . ." But he could say no more. He stomped toward the open doorway, and there he stopped. "Windmera . . . ?"

"Yes?"

"Is it still Roderick?"

"I . . . I don't know." She smiled disarmingly, melting in part his hurt pride. "At least . . . I don't think it is George." She was giving him hope. She was inviting him to try again.

He smiled and then frowned, vacillating between thoughts. He wished he weren't leaving. It was the wrong time . . . the wrong time. But he could do naught about it.

She stopped him as he began to pass through the doorway. "Lance!"

He turned again. "Yes?"

"How long . . . ?"

"I don't know." His eyes gazed long at her face, at the violet warmth of her eyes, at the long shining black hair spilling over the lushness of her ripe young body, and he sighed. "Damn . . . I just don't know!"

Fifteen

"Armstrong has the right idea, Perry . . . but your ships won't be ready before summer!" Lance paced as he spoke. He was irritable these cold days in February. He was far from home, and he was disgusted with the war effort in Canada. He had been brought first to Pennsylvania, to Presque Isle, to inspect the plans the American Admiralty, headed by the newly appointed Secretary of War, John Armstrong, had envisioned. He moved to the long window and looked out on snow-covered lawns. All he could think of, even now, was Windmera. But his orders were to proceed to Norfolk. . . .

Oliver Hazard Perry frowned. He moved to Lance's back and put a hand on his shoulder. "More than our naval deficiencies are eating at you, Lance. Can I help?"

Lance turned around sharply. Did it show? He smiled ruefully at his friend. Perry was as young as himself, but he had just been given the entire command of the New Erie Fleet! He had enough to worry about without thinking of his problems. "No, old friend, you can't help. The trouble is I was supposed to help you . . . but after my meeting this afternoon with the shipbuilders at Presque, all I can do is to tell the Admiralty and you that those ships will not be ready for you this spring."

"You are certain? There is nothing they can do to cut back on the time factor . . . hire more men?"

"Damn it, Perry!" Lance stood on no ceremony with the young commander, they had been friends too long. "They are straining at their guts . . . but they can't work miracles! Those designs—which we do need, by the way—well . . . they just can't be worked any faster!"

"Lance . . . word has it that England is planning to send a man well known for his competence . . . Sir James Yeo. We expect he'll have over four hundred men, and these will include equally competent officers. They will be sent in to take command of the Canadian lake navy."

"When?"

"Our sources seem to be quite certain that he will arrive some time in May. So you see . . ."

"Lord love you, Oliver Hazard Perry! Not afraid of an Englishman, are you?" teased Lance.

Perry smiled. The burden of command had already put lines about his eyes, hardened his mouth. He smiled so rarely these days.

"No . . . we have reason to believe our forces can hold their own, but we want to do more than hold our own!" He sighed heavily. "Don't you see . . . they are bound to organize in Lake Ontario . . ."

"Then look for an alternate plan, because if the devil himself were to head the Canadian lake navy, we couldn't get those ships any faster!" returned Lance grimly.

February blew its gales over Bermuda. Palms bent beneath their might. Spanish pikes lapped their stalks against one another. Sand shifted in swirls along the beaches. Fishermen rubbed their hands before their fires and grumbled. A storm was not unexpected at this time of year, and Delia had been through winter gales before, but this time she fretted, she pined and she gave her aunt and father cause to wonder.

"What is it, dear? Surely you are not afraid of the storm?" asked Mr. Hopkins in some concern. He had come up behind her as she watched out her window.

She jumped at his touch, made a futile attempt to smile and moved agitatedly away. "Of course not . . . but the wind at the shutters . . . the trees slapping each other . . . it's nerve-wracking."

Her aunt eyed her suspiciously. Delia had been behaving oddly of late. For one thing, she was becoming moody, secretive. She wasn't like that. She had always been such an open, honest girl.

"Delia . . ."

"Oh, Auntie, please," she interrupted roughly before her aunt had the opportunity to finish her query. "I . . . I am tired. I just think I'll go up and lie down." She scurried out of the room, not bothering, not daring to look back.

Her aunt and her father exchanged glances, and though Mr. Hopkins would have dropped it there, his sister could not.

"Francis . . . there is something wrong! I don't know what it can be . . . but there is something wrong with Delia!"

It wasn't in his nature to prod his daughter. If something was wrong and she didn't want to speak of it, then so be it. She was entitled to her privacy. "Julia, you are letting your imagination harbor all sorts of nonsense. Delia is in love. We both know that. The storm simply means she will not get to see Roderick this evening for dinner. That is all."

Julia Hopkins frowned over this. That could be it, of course. Delia was ever radiant when Roderick was expected, dull and sluggish when he was not. Perhaps she was making too much of it? She sighed and allowed the subject to end there.

Delia sat among her satin pillows on her cushioned window seat overlooking the front drive. It was cold here, drafty. She should sit nearer the fire . . . it was stupid, sitting here . . . watching! What could she hope to see? Naught! Roderick was out there, in the storm, and it was all her fault!

They had been together in the hothouse that afternoon when the gale hit. She had pretended to go out for a walk along the beach, he had secreted his horse on the grounds, and then they had gone to each other. It had been wonderful. More and more she was learning to enjoy his touch, to enjoy the things he did to her. At first, she had allowed it all for him, to please him . . . but now . . . now she yearned for him as ardently as he did her! So there, hidden among the hothouse blooms on a blanket he had provided, they had made love. As she watched him dress afterward, she heard the first clatter of rain. She frowned and went to a foggy window and peered out.

"Roderick . . . it's raining, heavily . . . and a wind seems to have picked up."

He let go his waistcoat and went to her. His arms went around her, pressing her back into his chest, thinking how good it was when they were together. His lips nibbled at her neck. "A soaking is naught after I've been with you, love. I shan't even feel it."

She snuggled up against him. He always said the right things. He always made her feel whole and beautiful. But the wind outdoors worried her. Resolutely she pulled away. "Nevertheless, Roderick you must leave . . . *now!*" She frowned at the lackadaisical manner he fell into. She hurried him, buttoning his coat, plopping his hat on his head, laughing with him during it all and then pushing him toward the door. "Please, Rod . . . do hurry . . ."

"I strongly suspect, Miss Delia, that you are trying to be rid of me." he teased, plopping a kiss upon her nose.

She smiled, not bothering to answer him. He loved her. His

eyes said it, his touch said it. She had grown so much in these past few weeks. She had blossomed from girl into woman. She was supremely happy, and it was all because of Roderick of Ravensbury. She watched him vanish in the woods bordering her estate and then ran to the house.

She would have gone to her room had her father not chosen to open the library door and peep out. "Ah, there you are, Delia! Your aunt and I were just about to send out after you. Come in here, child . . . you are wet!" He ushered her into the room, simultaneously motioning the footman. "Have tea brought in at once."

Her love was right! She told this to herself and managed to subdue the blush rising to her cheeks. She hated having to face her father after she had been with Roderick. She told herself there was nothing wrong with what they did, for they would marry . . . and soon!

She heard her aunt mumble something about the weather, but she was too engrossed in reliving the pleasurable moments she had just spent in Roderick's arms to really pay attention. And then there was a thunderous sound! She felt the ground rumble with the resonant thud. It wasn't the first time she had heard such a sound. It was the unmistakable cry of a tree, a great tree when it has been brutally uprooted. She jumped and ran to the closest window and there saw a huge old cedar, beautiful, great even in its woe. It lay on its side, its roots exposed to the rain and wind, its earth gorged, its branches broken.

"My God . . ." she breathed, suddenly realizing. Roderick . . . he was riding out there. "*It's a gale.*"

"Of course it's a gale," said her aunt on a frown. "I said that when you first came in here."

They would have questioned her further had she not run from them a few moments later. And now? Now she sat staring at the fury of the storm. And Roderick?

"Please . . . let him be safe!" she prayed out loud. Oh, God . . . he has to be safe . . . I cannot live without him!

Monty Clayton's protruding eyes appraised his son. The boy was only just twenty. There he stood, a reed of a man . . . yet he had managed to possess Stacy! He was fairly certain the boy was still sneaking off to see her, though he had expressly forbidden it.

"Don . . . do you remember the discussion we had in January . . . about your Aunt Stacy?"

Don Clayton stood some inches over his father. He had his grandmother's bright flaxen hair and gray eyes. His face was lean, as was his body. He was considered by every belle in Norfolk to be the marriage prize of the season. This was, in fact, one of the reasons that had sent him to Stacy in the first place. She invited him, and he had figured out for himself that here was a pleasure without the danger. After all, even if Stacy were to get pregnant she would not expect him to marry her. How could he? 'Twould be incest! Such was his reasoning, which proved him his father's son. "I remember, Father . . . but . . ."

"Then you have still been . . . visiting your aunt . . . in private?"

"Well . . ."

"Have you or have you not?" thundered Monty.

"I have," admitted his son, managing a blush. "But Hell . . ."

"That is enough! Do you know what kind of scandal you are providing for the tattlemongers of Norfolk?"

"But . . . they don't know."

"*I* know . . . why wouldn't they? Dammit, Don . . . you are tossing your own aunt!"

"She isn't though . . . I mean, not by blood."

"That is not the point! Never mind . . . you will leave immediately for your Uncle Jasper's home in Georgia! I trust you will find his wife a bit too wrinkled to screw! Now . . . *get out of my sight!*"

Truth was, Don was getting a little bored with Stacy. It had been pleasant enough while it lasted, but he was ready for a change. His father held the purse strings, so there was no sense in antagonizing him any further. "Yes, Father," he said formally, just cold enough to exhibit his pride. He turned and left Monty Clayton to work out the remainder of his plans, for he still had Stacy to deal with. He hadn't forgotten his threat, and it had not been an idle one. He was a patient man, well able to wait for the right time. First, he had to get Don away, for he wanted no suspicious fingers pointed in their direction. That's right, Don . . . you'll go to Jasper . . . and leave Stacy to me, he thought, smiling to himself in the solitude of his room. Damn, but she had it coming!

A blizzard blew outdoors, but the library in the Landon home was bright with candlelight, a blazing fire and merry laughter. Elly and George Barker had arrived earlier that afternoon and were now forced because of the weather to remain overnight. So they made a party of it.

They were playing at games on the floor and Elly was pouting over her loss, pleading with her brother to share his winnings with her. Windmera laughed gleefully. "Oh, Elly . . . what a little scrubber you are!" she teased.

"A *what?*" returned Elly, eyeing her doubtfully.

Windy giggled. "A scrubber . . . it's Bajan for . . . er . . . beggar!" She dodged an oncoming blow "No . . . no . . . not quite that bad. It's what we call strolling musicians, actually. They come about usually in the holiday season. There is a ditty they have for wheedling the coins out of our pockets when they are through. Let's see, ah, it goes like this.

"As I was passing through Joe's River
My tender heart began to shiver
So if you are a cheerful giver,
Please give me something to warm m'liver!"

She ended the chant by dropping her hands into her lap and laughing happily. A look at Elly's expression and a meeting glance with George then sent them into whoops.

It was thus that Jules Landon entered upon the scene,

"It grieves me to disturb you, children . . . sad rattles that you all are, sitting on the floor." He shook his head with mock sternness over their lapse in conduct. "But cook tells me dinner is served."

He offered his arm to Elly, who took it gladly, put up her chin and a smile to Windy and said, "Scrubber indeed! I keep forgetting you come from that heathen island. One of these days you will have to explain to me just how Lance managed to sail in and out to get you without being captured by the British." She had a curious twinkle in her eye.

"Oh dear, I'm afraid I could never think of anything good enough to mollify you, Elly," teased Windy, evading the subject. "We shall just have to leave it to Lance to tell!"

"Speaking of Lance," put in George, neatly slipping a hand beneath Windy's arm and helping her off the floor, "where the devil is the man?"

Jules's expression was thoughtful. "From what I gleaned from Lance before he left, he should be heading for Norfolk . . . just about now."

Windmera's delicate brows met. Norfolk . . . Stacy Clayton. He would be going to Norfolk? She hadn't thought of that. Always she had pictured him at sea . . . sailing the *Sea Hawk* . . . with no other woman about to take his attention, catch his eye. A sudden wave swept her insides, bringing an ache to her heart.

"Norfolk, eh?" George chuckled. "The devil you say! Lord, and I thought he was off on national security." He made clucking noises and glanced toward his sister. "Too bad, Elly . . . it seems our Lance has designs on one Stacy Clayton!"

Elly shot him a dangerous look. "As if I care! I don't give a fig, as well you know! I told you yesterday I mean to accept Thomas Corey!" She glanced sideways at Windmera and bit her lip. She had fast learned to love the lively little island girl. Her manners were open, disarming, her wit warm, spontaneous. She knew that Windmera, though she would not admit it, was very much in love with Lance. She saw it there in Windmera's violet eyes. Her brother's ploy was cruel! Mentally she made a note to give him a good stiff kick to his shin later.

Jules too had seen the sudden haunted look come to Windy's face, and he gave her a steadying look. His tone indicated that he was not pleased with George Barker's tactics. "I think you mistake your man, George. You know very well that Lance's business is with the Admiralty housed in Norfolk and not with the young woman you so carelessly name!"

A quick glance told George that he was now in the suds. He could see his sister's angry gleam. Jules's tone had told him much the same, and there too he had never meant to put *such* a look on Windmera's face. He wanted her . . . but not at the expense of hurting her. "Oh . . . may I end in Hades . . . I didn't mean . . . look . . . can't a fellow make a jest?"

"Idiot!" snapped his sister before giving him her back.

Sixteen

The snow was gone. The lawns were yellowed from the long winter, tipped with the haze of frost. The trees stood stark and dreary, no longer bejeweled with their ice pendants. Gusts of wind tore through them, crying out against the end of their season. March had come in roaring as usual!

Windmera was fascinated by the changing seasons. Each new phase was something to watch, to wonder at. She was at the long library window, touching its brown velvet hanging, staring into the woods for signs of early-morning stirring. Jules sat in his wing chair near the fire, perusing his morning paper, now and then grumbling impatiently with its information.

Sam entered, cleared his throat and came forward, letter in hand.

"Excuse me, sir . . ." said Sam apologetically. "This just came by special post . . . from your son-in-law?" Sam was worried. Isabelle was a favorite not only with his mother but with him as well.

Jules dropped his paper and reached up, looking over his reading spectacles but a moment at his retainer to say thank you. Because he knew Sam was concerned, he added, "You may go now Sam . . . I will let you know later what's to do."

"Thank you, sir," said Sam.

Windmera's brow was up. She watched the changing expressions flit over Jules Landon's face as he perused the long epistle. Jim Foster had a difficult hand to follow, and Jules had several times to study the context before he understood the words. Then suddenly he felt the tears well up. His Izzy . . . his poor babe.

"What? Oh, Jules . . . what is it?" cried Windmera.

"Isabelle . . . my Izzy . . . she has suffered a miscarriage," he said quietly, keeping himself in check. "It seems . . . Jim says . . . she is greatly depressed. Windmera . . . I think she needs me."

"Of course she does," said Windmera, going to him with an affectionate hug.

"I must go to her at once. But . . . how can I leave you?"

"You needn't leave me, Jules. I have had an itching to meet your daughter. Now is my chance." She was smiling at him, but deep inside she knew this would mean her separation from Lance would be extended. He would arrive home in Mystic and they would be gone.

He frowned. "It is not an easy journey at this time of year. The roads are bad."

She snapped her fingers in the air. "That for rotten roads! Shall I go up and start packing?"

He brightened and then frowned. "Lance . . . I must get word to Lance."

"But . . . how can you?"

He puzzled over this and finally answered, "Never mind . . . I have the solution. Now up with you . . . though I daresay we shan't be ready to leave for some three days yet."

Roderick gave his horse's reins into the hands of a black linkboy and quietly ordered the horse watered and walked. He was frowning. He should have been pleased, because there, right before his eyes, was the *Conrad*. In it was Captain John Pearson, his father's closest friend, with funds and abilities enough to see him through his self-made mandate. Indeed, there before him was the way to Windmera, was the way to put a stake through Lance Landon's heart, was the way to regain his pride, retain Ravensbury, please Godwin . . . but something inside of him cracked.

He shook off the tension from his shoulders, straightened himself out. Here was the way . . . the only way! He stepped onto the gangplank and took it quickly to the well-polished deck of the merchant schooner Godwin and Captain John had purchased for this mission. Delia's image when last he saw her floated before his eyes. How adorable she had been, how concerned after the gale . . . she had run her tiny fingers over him looking for injuries, she had breathed a sigh of relief, and then she had cried because they had been apart two weeks. Two weeks . . . now they would be apart a lifetime. It brought an ache to his hardened heart. He felt it move within his bosom, but his steely will set it back in place.

Captain John had come out of the companionway onto the deck and spotted Roderick. His captain's hat was pulled low over his eyes, shading his expression, but Roderick's countenance was lit by the cool March morning sun. Captain John's brow went up. There was a change in Roderick. He could see it etched well around the eyes, about the mouth.

"Rod, my boy . . ." he said, going forward, reaching out for both of Roderick's gloved hands, shaking them vigorously.

Roderick smiled warmly. "How is he . . . how is my mother?"

"Godwin is well. Very upset over this business . . . but pleased with your plan, very pleased," said Captain John on a short breath. He hesitated.

Roderick noted it. "And my mother?"

"I am sorry, Roderick . . . she is not well."

Roderick was taken aback. He knew, of course, that she suffered bouts of protracted illnesses . . . but Sara not well? It was impossible. She was so strong . . . so determined . . . in everything.

"Nonsense!" It was his spontaneous answer. It came without thought. "Sara not well? You don't know my mother." He chuckled.

"Perhaps not."

"Now, come in and show me this splendid boat."

"It isn't a boat, Roderick . . . it is—"

Roderick laughed. "Never mind my shortcomings regarding nautical terms, just show me about. I see you are equipped with guns?"

"Eighteen guns, lad. Your father insisted upon it. We don't enter the States as merchants, you know."

"No indeed we don't . . . but this is not exactly . . . well, come on, Captain John . . . let's go below and discuss what I have in mind and see if it matches your own schemes, eh?"

"Good enough!" approved Captain John. The boy wasn't wanting in sense, at least.

Delia felt her belly. Inside her grew another Roderick. How wondrous was the thought. Effervescent bubbles of delight tickled her, and she giggled to herself. A child, their child, formed in love, to be nurtured in love . . . how all too beautiful. That very first time back in January . . . ? She wondered to herself regarding its conception. She had missed her period a week after their first time together. Then February had come and gone and now they were well into March. She was certain she was carrying Roderick's child. She should tell him. A doubt? No, of course not! It was only that he was about to ask her to be his wife. She just knew he would ask her now. His father had sent a vessel for him. He would leave and he would take her with him.

She imagined his face. How thrilled he would be to learn

she carried his son. It was his son . . . a boy . . . she knew it, just knew it . . . but she wouldn't tell him just yet. No, that would spoil it all. First, first she wanted to hear him ask her to be his wife.

She sighed, not unhappily, but a sigh all the same, for marrying Roderick would mean leaving Bermuda. How sad. Leaving her aunt and father. That would be difficult . . . almost impossible. But perhaps they would follow. Oh yes. She would nag her papa until he agreed. Of course he would.

She hugged her knees to herself. Yes, they would follow, and she would have her family all around her. She would have Roderick, their baby and her family. Such a lovely dream.

A knock sounded at her door, and she looked up to find her father's eyes peeping at her. He was so cute, she thought, so sweet.

"Papa?"

"Delia, come walk with me. It is so lovely outside."

"Of course, Papa!" she said brightly, scampering to her feet.

He pulled her hand through his arm. His precious babe. He didn't know what he would have done without her all these years. She was such a lively consolation. He sighed, for soon Roderick would be taking her away . . . but he must not be selfish.

Irascible winds whipped at Captain Landon's cloak, sending it flapping at his back. His long black hair was blown freely about his ruggedly handsome face. He stood looking out to sea on the topdeck of the *Sea Hawk*. The sun was descending, marbling the sky with veins of bright white, grays and dull blues. He scarcely noticed the cold beauty, for all he could see were violet pools, warm, alive, laughing!

He had much to consider. The past few weeks had brought him and his men into danger, and it was when they were under attack that he suddenly realized how much he wanted to live, how much he wanted to return to Windmera. They had been out on patrol when a British brig sighted them and leveled fire. They took a ball and suddenly the mizzenmast was coming down. Lance stood seeing it and nothing else except Jackie . . . right in its path. He didn't think, there wasn't time. He reacted! He must have flown from his perch, there was no other explanation for the speed he attained, and then Jackie was flung clear. He caught a good section of the mast on his knee, but miracously came through with only a damaged tendon. No breaks, no fractures.

This brought them back to Norfolk for repairs, but he was itching to leave, to return to Windmera. He ached for her in every conceivable way. He fancied at times he could almost feel her. Hell! What did she want of him . . . his soul? It was hers for the taking, certainly he commanded it no more. This protracted separation of theirs had infected him with nagging sensations forcing him to face buried truths. Love? Beyond all reason, she had said. Yes, then he loved, for there was no reason in it at all! Love . . . beyond all else? Yes . . . he wanted her barring all others. His body called for a woman . . . nightly it called, reminding him how long he had been without. Yet when he tried, the thought blemished what he had shared with Windmera and he found himself unable to perform. He left barmaids in a quiz, turning to his cups for comfort, and that left him aching in deeper waters. Windmera . . . Windmera . . . how he yearned for her.

There was Stacy, of course. She was no barmaid to be scorned. She had a skill. Perhaps he should answer one of her many notes? And then as though Heaven meant to play, he heard a feminine voice at his back.

"Lance . . . you devil!" she purred. Lord, but he was a handsome stud, and she needed one. With Don Clayton gone and the wives of Norfolk keeping her at a distance, she had been lonely these past two weeks. "They tell me you are a hero . . . so I thought I'd come by and congratulate you . . . since you haven't found the time to come to me."

He was surprised. In spite of her invitations he thought she might still be put out with him for his behavior back in January. Evidently all the notoriety he had received for successful sightings had bought her forgiveness. "Why, Stacy . . ." He looked her over audaciously. Her cloak parted down the center to display the provocative curves of her body in her gold silk gown. Her ginger locks framed her lovely face, and her lips pursed invitingly. Suddenly he had to hold her, feel her, rid himself of Windmera's image. Stacy could do it . . . she had the skills!

She felt warm, responsive, exciting in his arms. He was a man, wasn't he? Then he should feel something other than this cold. He worked himself by running his hand beneath her cloak, groping deftly for her breasts, finding, touching, fondling, raising her blood so that she pressed herself into his kiss.

"Oh, Lance . . ." she breathed at last, for a moment really forgetting that she owed him still for his insults. She could always work that off later, but now . . . "Let's go down to your cabin."

"Hmmm . . . that's a good idea." He could definitely respond to Stacy. He needed to. He put his hand on her butt and began to lead her to his stairway, and then Jackie's voice halted him.

"Captain . . . Captain . . ." He was out of breath from running. He waved a letter in his hand. "This . . . it jest come . . it's from Mystic!"

His blood went cold and he felt a shiver shoot up his back. He grabbed for the envelope and ripped it open, thinking, Windmera . . . something has happened to Windmera. Instead he read:

Lance:
Your sister miscarried. Jim didn't write just how bad she is and I am probably foolish, but I feel I must go to her. Windmera and I leave in the morning for Buffalo.
Get word to us as soon as you return home.

Love,
Father

"They've gone to Buffalo, Jackie." He had forgotten Stacy's presence. "Izzy . . . she's ill . . . Father and Windmera have gone to Buffalo."

"Windmera? Who is Windmera?" asked Stacy on an irritated note.

"His fiancée," offered Jackie glibly. He wanted her off the schooner. He had never liked Stacy Clayton . . . she was trouble.

Lance frowned at him but made no verbal objection to this, and when Stacy rounded on him for an explanation, he would say only, "Mrs. Clayton . . . I am so sorry to treat you so shabbily . . . but you will understand. My men and I must get ready to put underway immediately. I have to travel to Buffalo, as my sister is ill and may need me."

"I don't care if you travel to Hell, Captain Landon," said Mrs. Clayton sweetly before giving him her back in a huff and stiffly, swiftly making her exit.

"Good riddance," muttered Jackie.

Lance's brow went up, but a rueful smile informed his

first mate that he was not really upset with him. "Jack, we have to set sail . . . now. Have we enough supplies?"

"Aye . . . but the repairs ain't completed."

"The major ones are . . . the rest we can do en route."

"Then do we set a course for home, Capt'n?"

"No, my lad, for New York. We are going to sail up the Hudson."

"The Hudson?" repeated Jackie, surprised.

"I believe it's thawed by now."

"Aye, but—"

"We will sail up the Hudson, Jack . . . to Kingston. From there I can hire a horse and ride for Buffalo. With any luck and if m'father is in the coach, which he must be if Windmera goes with him, I just might meet up with them on the road! You lads can sail down the Hudson . . . and return to Mystic."

"Aye, Capt'n," said Jackie, smiling to himself. All this hurry . . . was it for Miss Isabelle . . . or Miss Windmera?

Golden turrets turned back in the space of a moment. Pinnacles of silver tarnished, stone columns crumbled. Delia's world was suddenly disintegrating!

"Try to understand, my love . . ." It was Roderick's voice. She could hear Roderick's voice. She could see Roderick's face . . . etched in pain, but it couldn't be Roderick. Roderick wouldn't say such things.

"How . . . how can I understand? You . . . you are leaving me? You are sailing away? You . . . you don't want me?" Was she still standing? She felt her knees weaken, felt herself falling forward. Strong arms held her up by her elbows, pressed her body close. "Roderick!" It was a desperate cry.

"Oh, my darling. My Delia . . . you will forget me. Someone far better than I . . . more deserving of you . . . will come along and snap you up!" He set her from him. This ordeal was almost more than he could bear. He was giving her away . . . to another man . . . telling her to find another man! Would he survive this moment? His mind splintered. He had to hold himself together or he would go mad! He loved Delia . . . yet here he was breaking her heart . . . breaking his own.

"You . . . don't want . . . me?" Scarcely audible, it met the air.

"Not want you? With all my soul I have wanted you . . .

want you still . . . will go on wanting you for eternity. But Delia . . . I am pledged to another woman!" There, it was out. He had told her at last. He had told her too late.

"Another . . . woman?" She was sobbing now. She should tell him. Keep him with the child. Tell him tell him tell him tell him.

"Forgive me," he begged, and then suddenly gave her his back. He could sustain no more. He had to get away from her face, from her eyes, before he did something stupid, before he threw away his future, before he snapped her up and begged her to be his wife! He couldn't do that. Windmera was his wife. He always thought of Windmera as his wife. Windmera was the key, was the answer to eliminate all this pain. Delia would get over him. As much as this hurt, it was what he believed.

She saw his outline recede, and she crumpled to the ground, to her knees. She wanted to call him, to say, Roderick, I carry your son . . . but Roderick had become a stranger. Roderick didn't want her, didn't want their child. He was pledged to another woman, a woman he would not give up. He was leaving . . . today. He would be gone. Suddenly the enormity of it all weighed too heavy and she sank into a heap, burying her face in her arms and sobbing as though every inch of her was on fire.

At first she didn't think, her sorrow overcame all thought but one, that he was going. Over and over this single thought slashed through her body like a sharp blade of truth. And then, insidiously, reality came with a voice louder than all the rest. "Scarlet woman!" it taunted. "You have shamed your father . . . your aunt! You bring a bastard to the world . . . for shame, Delia!"

She answered, warding off the voices with her upraised arm, "No . . . it wasn't like that . . . I loved him . . . he loved me . . "

"Not true! He leaves you!" It laughed over and over. "Not true, he leaves you. You are nothing but a strumpet! Your child will be a bastard, your father will be shamed!"

"No!"

She got to her feet, her small fists clenched at the warped faces, the vicious voices. Delia was breaking, and there was no one about to heal her. She ran as does many a wounded creature. She ran and found herself at the cliff's edge. Perhaps it was then that the terrible thing came into her mind, perhaps it had been there the moment she saw him walk away. She looked down and saw the white foam cuddling the reefs. Beyond lay the coolness of what seemed gentle aqua-blue waters.

Not menacing, these reefs . . . they stretched out on either side of her like welcoming arms. Such a long way down, though . . . but they wanted her, they did. Oh, yes . . . how soothing it would be to lie in their white foam. The crash of the surf seemed to speak to her quietly, beckoning her. "Come, Delia . . . we shall save you . . . come, Delia . . . we shall cleanse you . . . come . . . come . . . come . . .

She opened her arms wide as though to embrace them. She dove, and then as she flew downward she opened her eyes. Closer, closer . . . no . . . the reefs were not loving! No . . . they were evil . . . grinning . . . pointed and harsh . . . no! No . . . no . . . no . . . *Roderick* . . .

Seventeen

Stacy Clayton quivered with irritation as she stepped out of her carriage and started forward for the large double doors of her gracious town house. She never reached the knocker. The wheels of her carriage rumbled forward as a dark hand came from out of the bush and seized her around her mouth. A large cloth was stuffed partially into her mouth as she was dragged backward into the shadows. She saw the flash of a black hood with slits for eyes, nose and mouth just before another cloth was drapped over her eyes and tied at the back of her head. Her cloak was stripped viciously away from her shoulders, and she heard a man's voice, not the one who was holding her, laugh. He reached down, and she felt his hand fondle her breast beneath the bodice of her gown.

"Eh, for the love of . . . not now, you fool! We's got to hurry."

His partner shrugged but straightened up. "Now what?" he asked with a sigh.

"The blanket, idiot! Can't you do anything?"

Stacy felt a blanket made of horsehair scrape her skin as they wrapped her in its folds. Who were these men? What did they want with her? Why? Suddenly she was lifted off the ground and carried a short distance. When she was dropped it was into a pile of straw. Wheels rolled beneath her, and she fell against what seemed to be the sideboard of a wagon. Where were they taking her? Her heart beat furiously. She had never been so badly treated. Stacy Clayton was Virginia blood! She came from a family who boasted their surname, she had married high . . . how dare anyone treat her in this manner? And she was frightened to the very core of her being!

They had robbed her of her senses. She couldn't see, couldn't smell and could scarcely hear. Still . . . certain sounds filtered through. Tavern sounds. Ribald jests of . . . sailors. She was sure she could hear the revelry of sailors. Where . . . where were they taking her?

Once again she was being lifted, carried. If only she could see. If only they had not draped the blanket around her. Oh,

365

God . . . she thought she would suffocate, and the gag was choking her. And then, a familiar voice.

"That's it boys. Lay her down . . . right there . . . I want her hands tied to the bedpost . . . then you may leave . . . and by the way, there is a bonus for each of you over there on the table."

She heard the men thank him as they flung off her blanket. She struggled as they pulled at her white arms and tied her wrists tightly to the brass headboard. *Damn Monty!* Damn him! She waited. Did he really think he would get away with this? Did he? Fool! She would have him hung! Scandal? She would drown him in it! So, he wanted his piece of flesh? He meant to rape her. Very well, then . . . there was little she could do about it. But later . . . by God, she would make him pay!

He waited for the cabin door to close and then chuckled softly as he moved toward her and removed the cloth covering her eyes.

"Hello, my dear . . ." His voice was soft, but his hand had already grabbed hold of her bodice and with one savage movement he had ripped it down the length of her body. "There, that's better."

Her eyes glared hotly at him but she lay very still. She wasn't going to fight. Oh no . . . that would give him too much satisfaction.

The light was dim in the small room. He moved into the shadows to remove his brocade dressing gown. She watched him in disgust. Fat and old . . . pig! She hated him. He came toward the bed dressed only in his breeches. He reached down for a breast, and in spite of her resolve to bear him without fighting she jerked uselessly in an effort to escape him. He laughed without humor. "No? We'll see." He bent his head, and squeezing her breast roughly he brought the nipple to his lips as if to suckle but instead he bit, hard.

She nearly choked on her scream, and tears started to her eyes. "Did I hurt you, my dear? So sorry . . . but if you behave, I won't have to hurt you any more." He was straddling her now, reaching for the cloth that hindered her mouth. He pulled it out. "There, is that better?"

"Swine!" She spat at him. "I hate you!"

"But you will perform for me . . . if you want to be returned to your pretty little home in the morning," he said evenly.

Fear lit in her eyes, "Where . . . where am I?"

"A slave ship, my dear . . . you are on a slave ship."

"No!"

"Oh yes . . . and I promised the captain that if you didn't cooperate . . . he might have you. He knows so much about training unruly women. It seems there is quite a demand for bright-haired creatures like yourself . . . in certain parts of the world."

"No, Monty . . . you wouldn't . . . please, Monty . . ."

He was unbuttoning his breeches, taking out the swollen muscle, pointing it at her. "Please me, Stacy . . . as you please so many others . . . and perhaps I may decide to let you stay in Norfolk."

"For pity's sake . . . Monty . . . think what you are doing."

He laid his penis on her flat white belly. His hands moved to clutch her breasts and then to tear away at the remaining material at her gown. "Spread your legs, Stacy . . . spread them for me."

"I can't, you fool, you are sitting on them!" she snapped. How inept he was, even in rape!

He made an inarticulate sound but shifted. He was on top of her now. He ran his hands over her body. Oh, God! His hands were made of sweat. He was disgusting . . . his mouth was too near . . . please, she prayed, if he must violate me . . . let him do it without kissing me. She was frightened. Not of the moment. No, the moment sickened her, but she was concerned for the morrow. And then his lips suckled her own. She was going to be sick!

"Don't kiss me, Monty! I swear I . . . will be sick if you do," she threatened.

She wasn't making it easy, the lousy whore! He hated her, wanted to hurt her for all she had put him through. Damn, but he would hurt her, for his probing fingers told him she was dry, unready for his entrance. He plunged then, hard. She withdrew, stiffened beneath him, and he started plummeting in wild hedonistic fury. Damn, why didn't she respond? Why for everyone else and not for him? "Move, Stacy . . . damn you . . . move!"

She did as he asked, but only because of her fear, and then suddenly he was finished, he was pulling out, moving away. He looked down at her with contempt. "You are something of a disappointment, Stacy!"

"Am I, Monty? Or is it you?" As soon as she said it, she regretted it. Damn her sharp tongue, she thought, for he was raising his hand, bringing it across her soft cheek, leaving a stinging red mark in its wake. She would kill him for this. She swore it to herself. With her own gun she would kill him!

She watched him as he moved about the room picking up his things, dressing. She listened to his heavy breathing. She looked down at her naked body, wondering what he would do now. "Monty . . . would you please untie me now? My wrists are raw."

"Untie you? No . . . I think not," he said.

"You think not! Monty, untie me at once!" She felt a trickle of fear slide up her back. What now?

"No, my dear. You are staying here. Did you think it would end with that little toss in bed? No . . . if I had wanted just that, I could have had it these many months ago. No, I told you that I would be revenged for your insolence, your degrading behavior, your insults . . . and I shall be revenged." He was at the door, grinning.

"Monty!" It was a desperate scream. "You can't get away with this. I will be missed . . ."

"Will you? Then I shall have to find a note . . . in which you explain to the family that you have run off with a man . . . an inferior sort whom we would not have approved of. Sad isn't it?"

"Monty!" She was crying now . . . he couldn't leave, but he was already out the door. She began to scream his name, and then the door opened. She stopped her struggles and stared at the bearded grotesque figure of a man with a captain's hat set rakishly on his head. He stood for a moment leering at her before he entered and closed the door at his back. "Oh, God . . ." she breathed and then closed her eyes.

Fascinating is the deep indigo blue. Mysterious are its depths. One stares at its rolls, at its foam of salt, at its life forces, but not even the best of sailors ever knows it. Roderick made no attempt to glean an understanding of its might as he stared out to sea. He stood at the bow of the *Conrad*, alone with his thoughts. They were heading with the wind in their sails for a course that would take them to Canada. It had been decided between them that docking in Canada and then slinking in across the border on horse would be easier, less conspicuous, than trying to blow their way into Mystic. It held its dangers, but Captain John conceded that it might work.

Yet even as he sailed for Windmera, it was of Delia he

thought. What was she doing now? Would she be crying? Would she soon forget? Night was upon them, and in the dark-blue velvet sky he could see her flaxen locks, her corn-flower-blue eyes, her innocent smile. Oh, Delia . . .

Another ached for Delia. Her father. His white hands gripped the box that held her tattered body, his own shook with the weight of her loss. His Delia, his bright jewel. Why? When they had come to him . . . told him . . . he couldn't believe. He had to look for himself, and when he did, he collapsed. There was no comfort. She was his child. God had no right taking her before him, taking her before she had really lived . . . no . . . his Delia . . . dead? No . . . no . . .

Julia knelt beside him, silent tears rushing her cheeks. She couldn't bear to look at the torn child lying in the ornate box beside her. All glory was over on this side of the earth. Their Delia was gone. But why? And then she thought of Roderick.

She thought of Roderick of Ravensbury and had her answer . . . but what good was the knowledge? There was no consolation in it. She had warned her brother about Roderick . . . she had felt from the start that he would hurt their Delia, and he had. Delia lay, her body broken, her spirit fled . . . and he, this Roderick of Ravensbury? He was free!

Connecticut had not yet been left behind. Five days of travel and they had still to reach the New York border. A weary thought indeed as Windmera put down the jar of liniment and unbent her tired muscles. She stretched her arms high and sighed. "I think that should do nicely, Jules."

"My word, child! Wherever did you learn to doctor a horse like that? That's the neatest job ever I clapped eyes on."

She smild. "Papa often scolded me for loitering in our stables, but stay I would, and I picked up all sorts of useful knowledge there." She was grinning naughtily now.

He put up a brow. "I'll just bet you did. Is that the sort of thing you tease Lance with? For if it is I'll swear he itches to take you over his knee."

She sighed. "He does seem to get angry with me more often than not . . . so I imagine there is some truth in what you say. But *you* did not get angry . . . Papa never did . . . and why should you? I meant nothing by it."

"Your papa realized that, as I do, but Lance aspires to a different place in your esteem. A chance remark hinting at

. . . shall we say, a past indiscretion is bound to pucker him. Haven't you noticed, girl . . . my son is daft about you!"

She sighed heavily. "I wish that were true, Jules . . . but I am afraid your son is daft on half the pretty women along the American coast!"

He chuckled deeply. "No, really, Windmera . . . Lance a womanizer?" He shook his head. "You have a very odd picture of him, my dear. Certainly he has had his fair share of pretty women. How could he not . . . being what he is?"

"Well . . . I don't want such a man for my husband!"

"And this Roderick of yours . . . he has been a monk, I suppose?" teased Jules.

She hesitated. "Oh . . . I am sure he has not . . . but he has never flirted with another woman in my presence . . . as your son has done!"

"Ah, unpardonable of him, I quite agree," said Jules gravely. However, Windmera looked further than his tone and noted well the twinkle in his eye. She cocked her head.

"You really don't. I am not fooled by you, Jules Landon . . . and I am not fooled by your son!"

"I don't imagine for a moment that you are, my dear. Now, I am finding a hollow in my stomach that needs repair. What say you to dinner?"

She eyed him suspiciously, but agreed readily. "Yes, I'm hungry too."

"Hmmm, and I daresay that maid of yours would like to see us done with our meal so that she can tuck you safely into bed before laying her weary head down and forgetting the trials of broken wheels and sad roads!"

"Poor thing. I don't know why you engaged a maid to accompany us. I am well able to care for myself, you know."

"My dear child . . . you may not have noticed that I am not quite in my dotage. However, I am pleased to think that others might note upon it. Your reputation would have suffered if I had taken you unchaperoned across two states with me."

She blushed. "I . . . I see . . . of course."

He laughed and took up her arm, breaking the uneasiness of the moment with his simple idle chatter. Her mind wandered, for it was so easy to see Lance's face when she looked at Jules Landon. Lance? Where was he now? When would she see him again? What would their first meeting after so many months apart be like? And . . . but she was being foolish. What did she care?

The *Sea Baron* was a slaver. The war was getting in its way, causing delays. Now, for example, they were having to give Bermuda a wide berth, and still they would be in danger of attack on their route to Africa. Three days. They'd been on the sea for three days without a sign of trouble, and then all at once the *Conrad* was upon them!

Captain John had already spotted the American slaver and sized her up. They were about equal in long eighteens and nines, but he felt the *Sea Baron* was inferior in strength. She was unused to war, while Godwin and he had outfitted the *Conrad* for tight action. What he needed now was to bring her under short-range attack. His men moved quickly under his orders, and just as the morning mist lifted he ordered the first shot.

The *Sea Baron* lost her main topmast. It plunged into the sea, taking some four men with her, knocking the wind out of them so that they met the water unconscious. Her captain, still groggy from drink and a sleepless night, scurried into his clothes as Stacy propped herself up and watched him from her bed. Hateful animal! He hadn't listened. She had begged, promised to pay him a great sum of money, but he had set sail with her anyway. How could such men exist?

He was jolted to the floor as the next cannon hit. Thunderous was the explosion in the quiet morning air. It dawned on her slowly. They were under attack. That was what all the fuss, the bells, the shouting were about. That was the sound she had heard earlier . . . the crashing report of splitting wood as the topmast heaved into the sea. She began to laugh. It was almost too good to be true. She saw him get to his feet. How she hated him . . . almost as much as Monty. "I hope you get a cannonball in your belly! I hope it burns your sick little cock!"

He didn't bother to turn around, to spit back at her. His men were ill equipped for battle. He was himself not ready to exchange with the British. He had to get on deck and salvage—Something rammed into his gut and he nearly keeled over.

Stacy jumped to her feet and ran across to the wardrobe cabinet. There was nothing for it but to drape one of his wool coats over her nakedness. She saw him grapple with his pain as he made his way down the companionway to the stairs. Water! They were taking in water. She had to get topside!

371

Deafening was the crack of the eighteen longs. Cannonades rattled the air. The *Conrad* was taking no chances on being reported; she placed herself in the *Sea Baron's* lee, pouring in heavy fire all the while. The hold was taking in more and more water. The tiller, foreyard and main boom were shot away, making the *Sea Baron* a lost cause.

Stacy stood at the opening of the companionway looking at the topdeck. It was covered with blood and wounded men. Screaming cries of pain echoed amongst creaking beams. The sails were cut to pieces, as were the crew. She stifled a sob and held her hand to her mouth, backing away instinctively. Then she saw the longboat. She had to get to it. It looked as though some of the men had already tried to lower it . . . but they had all been shot, or caught beneath the spars and rigging of the falling masts. She made a wild dash.

The *Conrad* made one last round of fire. They wanted no witnesses. This was war, and killing was what war was all about! Stacy felt the impact, and then suddenly she was thrown. She hit the water hard and went down, down, down. She struggled, she kicked, and when at last she reached surface she gasped for air. But she was being pulled down still. It was the weight . . . the weight of the wool coat. She slipped out of it and began to swim for some of the floating wreckage.

Roderick frowned. Some flash of something in the sea caught his eye. He picked up the spyglass and scanned the water. Bobbing wreckage, dead bodies, blood. Soon the sharks would visit. And then he saw what it was that had caught his attention. A swimmer! A female! By God . . . a female! "Dammit, Captain John . . . there was a woman on board that slaver . . . a white woman!"

"What? Let me have that," said Captain John, reaching for the glass. He leveled it and breathed his confirmation. "By damn, there she is!" He moved quickly, calling to his crew, "Get the longboat over at once!"

Roderick moved his spyglass. She was nude. His brow went up. Like a mermaid, floating to him. This should prove interesting indeed! An American mermaid.

Eighteen

Don't you want me to go with you?" offered Jackie.

"No thanks, Jackie. I am going to be riding hard as I go, and it will be easier to buy and sell one horse at a time, for I mean to have a fresh steed and ride into the night. With any luck I will catch up with them by tomorrow night."

"Aye . . . but they have a week on you, Capt'n," said Jackie dubiously. "Do you really think . . ."

"That I do, lad, for they had all of Connecticut to cross." He was grinning. "Damn, but my legs are twitching to get started. Did you strap my pack to the horse?"

"Aye . . . and a flask of whiskey to keep your insides warm." Jackie beamed brightly.

"Then take care of the *Sea Hawk* and those roughnecks of mine." He was waving himself off, moving toward the stables, toward the dark gelding he had purchased. It was already midafternoon and he didn't have much of daylight. By his reckoning his father would have made Kingston some days ago, though inquiries at the local inns had not told him anything. Perhaps they had bypassed Kingston, taken the Catskill mountain pass on their route. Usually when he traveled with Jules to Buffalo that is what they did. Very well, then, he would have to ride.

He walked his horse for a few moments, getting the feel of him, letting the animal stretch his legs, work off its spiders, before urging him into a canter. He had a comfortable gait, and Lance found himself enjoying the first hour's run. He was excited. Every inch of him seemed alive, tingling with anticipation. All he could think of was seeing Windmera, hearing Windmera, touching Windmera!

He was closer to them than he realized, for the coach had suffered a minor accident just before Kingston the morning before and they had stopped overnight at a roadside inn while Jules and his manservants repaired the damage. Dusk was descending, and Jules did not like the feel of the suspension.

"Curse this luck of ours!" he said out loud to Windmera, ignoring the shocked expression of the elderly maid he had

373

hired. "Drat it all, but I fear we shall have to pull up at the next posting house, my dear, and see to it. We might as well stay the night there as well."

"Whatever you think is best," said Windmera. "I saw a sign for an inn down that road. We can stop there. Who knows when next we will come upon one? This road does not seem a particularly traveled one."

He sighed. "I suppose you are right." He leaned out his window and called an order to his driver to turn back and seek the road they had just passed. This done, he sat back and contemplated the inn's approach. It was not quite to his liking. Off the road by some four hundred yards, with only a weathered sign carelessly displayed. "How ever did you see that sign, my dear? It appears to me that they are at pains to conceal it," he teased, but as they drew closer, he was beginning to have his doubts.

"Humph!" Windy laughed. "You Americans . . . leading me to believe that you are virtual pioneers, able to stand all the rigors of the natural life. What are a few overgrown shrubs . . . a building in need of paint?"

He scanned the place, noting that the ostler coming toward them seemed as anxious as anyone looking for a gratuity. The stables looked rundown, but then . . . they were off the beaten path. "My dear child," he bantered, "I was only concerned for the comfort of poor Pringle and yourself."

"Oh? I thought you might be pining after another inn like the one we were at last night. Revelry until the wee hours. Fie on you, Jules Landon!"

He blushed, remembering the enjoyable evening he had had after he had sent Windmera and her maid off to their room. Yes, he had looked forward to another, but that was not the reason that his skin prickled now. There was just something about this place. But no matter. "Pringle . . . what say you?"

She was peeping out of the window, where she sat beside Windmera. She was well pleased to be serving as a combined maid/chaperon and companion. However, the length of the journey was beginning to try her nerves. All she ever wanted at this hour was to get washed, eat her dinner and curl up in bed. It was all she wanted now. "Oh . . . I don't mind the place, sir."

"So be it, ladies. It is on your head if your linens are damp, your wash water cold and your food only passing!" pronounced Jules Landon with a smile. He alighted, called out orders to his driver and then helped the ladies out. He looked around absently, and for no reason at all it occurred to him that he would have done well to have brought a couple of outriders on this long trip to Buffalo. He had never thought of it before because he had always taken the trip with Lance at his side. Well, never mind. He sighed and led the women toward the inn door, where the innkeeper had just appeared.

Windmera looked the man over and for the first time wondered if Jules was right for not wanting to spend the night here. The man seemed pleasant enough, clean enough . . . yet there was something about him that sent a shiver up her back.

"Ho there, sir . . . what can I be doing fer you?" asked the innkeeper in friendly enough tones.

"We shall want two rooms. One for the ladies, one for myself."

"Very good," said the innkeeper, giving them a wide grin. "If you like, I can have refreshments sent to you in our parlor . . . while your rooms are readied."

"Fine," said Jules Landon. However, as Windmera linked her arm through his and entered the old building, she suddenly had a feeling of dread. She was being silly and missish, she told herself, and she repressed any chance comment. How stupid she would appear after all the teasing she had subjected Jules to regarding the place.

She dined convivially with Jules and still could find no cause for her sudden change of heart. Yet fear gripped her all the same, and when Jules bid her goodnight outside her door she clutched his arm. "Jules . . . just in case . . . bolt your door."

He frowned. "Very well. Now, don't let anything I chanced to remark bother your sleep, child."

"No, no, of course I shall not," she said, going into her room. Pringle had fallen asleep with the candle lit. She smiled to see her maid sprawled out, uncovered and snoring. She had never heard Pringle snore before. She undressed and slipped into her nightgown, accidentally brushing against one of her perfume jars. It fell to the wood floor with a crash, making a resounding clatter. Windy jumped and then glanced quickly toward Pringle, who had not budged.

For no reason at all she left the mess on the floor and moved toward Pringle's nightstand, where a cup of hot cocoa had been partially consumed. She picked it up, sniffed it.

375

Nothing. She could smell nothing odd. She put her finger into it . . . tasted it. Nothing . . . but wait . . . its aftertaste? Was there something wrong with it . . . or had the milk simply started to turn? She had to wake Pringle. Perhaps she was being foolish . . . but . . . ? She bent and shook the elderly woman. Pringle stopped snoring, but she would not, could not, wake. Windy worked at her some five minutes, but nothing, not even water on the face, served to wake her maid. Drugged? But why?

Windmera had not taken her hot cocoa tonight. She had left it on her stand untouched . . . but Jules had . . . he had added a shot of whisky to it . . . and had drunk it down! Oh, my God!

She slipped on her wrapper and slowly opened her door. The dark hall was empty. She glided across it to Jules's room and lifted her hand to knock, but the small crack in his doorway halted her. Instinct sent her hand to her mouth, seized her breath and held it suspended in her throat. She peered through the slitlike opening into the dimly lit room and found there two men. One the innkeeper, the other man a stranger. They hovered over Jules; the innkeeper was lifting Jules's eyelids, grunting in satisfaction, "Eh then, he'll keep!"

The stranger, a lumbering stocky man with a shock of gray hair, went toward Jules's portmanteau. Windmera didn't wait for more. There was no time. She had to get out of this place and find help. *A thieves' den!* They had stumbled right into a thieves' den! She had read that such places existed in America's wild West, but she never imagined they existed in a civilized territory. She found a window opposite the stair landing and carefully, slowly opened it enough to squeeze through. The first story of the inn extended some eight feet farther than the second story. She climbed onto the first story's roofing. It was slippery, and she had to grip to keep from falling. At its edge she looked to the ground and grimaced, for it was still quite a jump, but there was an evergreen bush whose tip she could just reach.

She used the bush to help break the distance of her jump, but she still landed hard, hurting her ankles, snagging her robe and tearing a goodly portion of it away. She began her run. She had to hurry before they guessed she was gone. Later if they found her missing they would know she had gone after help, and they wouldn't dare hurt Jules or Pringle . . . they would run . . . wouldn't they? She was so engrossed with this, with the effort of making for the open road, that she never noticed the ostler of the afternoon. He came out of the stables after trussing up the Landon driver and saw a fluff of white shoot past him. He frowned, and because he was slow-witted it took a moment for him to understand. However, when he did, he shot out after her in heady pursuit.

Windmera's ears picked up the sound of heavy boots at her back, and she turned round. A scream died in her throat. No . . . her lungs were already bursting . . . she had to keep running . . . had to make the road . . . perhaps hide in the woods for a time? She had to escape the big oaf at her back. The partial moon was for the most part obscured by dark clouds and there was little to light her way, to tell her how much farther lay the road. Her legs ached and she was sure her heart would stop pumping if she had to keep up this pace any longer.

He was gaining on her, his hand was reaching for her. She dodged, tripped on a rock, lost her balance and came up to find him towering over her.

"Got ya!" he exclaimed gleefully, much as though he were playing at hide and seek.

She screamed. Useless, she told herself, but it was an un-thinking reaction to the burly man's attack. He held her firm by her arm, his hand making an imprint as he shook her. "Shut up!"

For answer she kicked him in the shin. He howled and she had a moment to break free. Windy ran. With everything in her she ran!

Lance was tired. He'd been riding now for some seven hours, discounting the few minutes he had stopped to water his horse and take a quick meal. It was slow going now, with but a partial moon to light his way. He was contemplating the possibility of finding a posting inn up farther when he was halted by the sound of a terrified scream.

"Whoa there, boy . . ." He soothed his horse to a stand-still. Was he going mad . . . or had that sounded like Wind-mera? Impossible!

It was getting so bad that everywhere he went he heard her! But damn! Someone screamed . . . and it was a woman. From which direction? He moved his horse to the side of the road, slowly walking it, and then he spotted an offshoot, a narrow track through the woods. He fondled his horse pistol near his saddle and undid the catch of the holster, and then he moved his horse onto the wooded trail.

The ostler made a dive into the air and caught at Windmera's gown. It ripped in his hands, but he had managed to bring her down. She was winded with the force of her fall onto her belly.

He was laughing as he pulled her by her ankles. She kicked at him and found his hands shifted to her arms. He was yanking her to her feet. "You got to come with me!" he ordered in slurred accents. "They won't like you running around out here."

"Let me go, you fool!" she snapped.

He held her with one hand, and slapped her across her cheek with the other, causing her to cry with pain, and then suddenly he found a boot at his hip. Viciously he was kicked backward, felt himself picked up by the scruff of his collar, discovered an iron fist in his belly and then quick across his jaw, and then mercifully, just as he thought he would see and feel no more, he was dropped.

"I'll have your soul for this!" seethed Lance as he ripped the man's cord belt off his waist and used it to tie the ostler's hands behind his back. He then swished off his own neckcloth and stuffed it in the ostler's mouth. He picked up the man by one arm and shoved him toward his horse, and then he turned and found Windmera's eyes.

She had seen him approach just as she received the ostler's slap. She had seen the fury on his face and had watched as though in a dream as Lance laid the man low. Lance . . . here? He had come! Her eyes filled and then he was coming toward her, reaching for her.

"Lance . . ." It was a whimper as she dove into his embrace. He held her tightly and she repeated his name as though afraid he might vanish, and then she remembered. "Lance . . . your father . . . my maid, they have been drugged . . ."

He held her shoulders still, and the nearness of her made him melt. A moment ago, seeing her manhandled had made him go into a convulsion of rage, and now what was she telling him?

"What? Why?"

"They are thieves . . . oh, Lance . . . they are up in your father's room right now!"

"I see. Very well . . . we shall have to act quickly." He moved away from her, smiled to see her wrap what was left of her nightgown around herself. He took off his cloak and

378

draped it round her shoulders. "Moonflower . . ." he whispered, stroking her cheek.

He turned and went to the dazed ostler and pushed him forward. Windmera followed, tugging at his hand. "What are you going to do?"

"First, get this one out of the way . . . and then see to the others!" he said grimly.

"But . . . how?"

"Trust me, love, and promise me you will do as I ask."

"I promise," she said at once, too grateful to demur.

A few moments later, having seen the ostler tied to a post in the stable, he led Windmera around the inn to a pile of firewood.

"Stay here!" he ordered softly.

"I will not!" said the lady indignantly.

He raised a brow. "Windy . . . there is no time to argue. If something goes wrong, you will be free to run for help." He touched her chin, dropped a kiss upon her lips.

She agreed reluctantly and dropped to her knees. He undid the safety catch of his pistol and moved around the building. She watched until he was out of sight.

"Where the devil is Tom? Ain't he trussed up that damn driver yet? We's got to move if we're to get rid of the bodies and the carriage by morning!" said the innkeeper. He held in his hands a fat wad of Jules Landon's money.

"Yeah . . . I'll go to see what's keeping him. You go check out the ladies' bags . . . that pretty one . . . now I'll jest bet she's loaded with jewels."

The innkeeper grinned wickedly. "Yeah . . . she'll be good for some jewels . . . and what's more . . . you know, Harry . . . there is two of 'em. We could really sport this night!"

His partner's eyes gleamed appreciatively. "That's so, friend. That's so!" He skipped heavily down the stairs and out the front doors, where the butt of a pistol found his head. He crumpled into a heap at Lance Landon's feet. Lance grinned, got the man's ankles and dragged him quietly out of sight. He tied him up with the rope he had prepared from the stables before going toward the front doors again.

The innkeeper was more than a little irritated, and though he had no suspicions of foul play, he was a cautious man by nature. A few moments later, he came in search of his partners, but he carried a pistol in hand.

Lance stood flat against the wall, waiting, but when the

379

innkeeper came out into the cool night air, something made him spin round.

"Damn!" he shouted and let off a bullet.

Lance caught it somewhere in the upper region of his left arm. He winced, but his own gun was aimed, and far better than the innkeeper did he make his mark. Windmera started stampeding toward him the moment the first shot cracked the still night air. She came around the corner and found the innkeeper dead on his front steps. She found Lance holding his arm and looking grim.

She reached out and touched him, but there was blood staining his dark coat, dripping onto his fingers. She felt it and cried, "Lance . . . you've been shot . . . oh . . . my Lance!"

"What do you mean, charging here like that? It might have been me lying there, and then you would have been in a pickle, my girl!" he raged at her.

"Stop it! You are hurt," she cried.

He softened and smiled warmly at her. "Am I? Then come and tend me, my love."

Much had been done. Windy had helped Lance see to the bound men, dubbing them the unholy three. They lay now in the stables, two unconscious but tightly roped, the other dead, all three awaiting the morning.

Jules, Pringle, and the Landon driver proved to be too deeply drugged to rouse, so Lance agreed at last to allow Windy to see to his wound.

She found some basilicon powder in the kitchen cupboard, some clean rags and fresh water. These Lance helped her to haul upstairs, where they found one last empty room at the end of the narrow corridor off the stair landing. He stopped on the threshold of the door, staring quietly, disarmingly, first at the bed and then at Windmera. She put up a brow and gave him a shove ahead of her.

"Go on, Lance . . . your arm must be seen to at once!"

He put up his one good arm in surrender. "Done! My, but you are a pushy wench!" he teased, his eyes alive.

She checked a giggle and shooed him toward the high four-poster bed. "Sit!"

He grinned but obeyed, watching her covetingly as she bent to start a fire. How long had he dreamed of her? How long? All his life?

She still wore the cloak around her shoulders, but as the

fire began its blaze, she thought to take it off. Then she remembered the state of her nightdress and kept it on. Quickly she dipped her hands in the wash water, toweled them and brought the tray to the bed. Lance had already removed his dark coat and linen shirt. The shirt lay bloodied on the oak floor, and she frowned to see it. She bade him hold the candle as she wet a rag and brought it to his arm.

"Oh, Lance . . . your arm . . ." she cried in some dismay. "It's caked with blood," She was washing it down, trying to find the point of the bullet entry. She clicked her tongue. "However did you manage all this while . . . just look at this . . . 'tis so swollen beneath the blood . . . and . . . oh, Lance . . ."

He kissed her hand. "Yes, I am in terrible pain," he said, his eyes brimful.

She cast him a quick doubtful look before returning her attention to his arm. "Hold the candle steady!" she commanded, and then with some relief, "I . . . I don't think the bullet has lodged itself. Why, it seems only to have grazed you," she said in some surprise.

"Too bad . . . all your attention for naught," he teased, his voice mocking.

She pulled a face at him. "Well, it isn't for naught. You could get a very severe infection if I don't tend to it . . . so mind your manners, sir!" She held her smile in check and applied the basilicon powder before wrapping up the wound. "There, my hero, I think that should hold you for the night," she said, hands on hips.

His free hand went to her waist. "Windy . . ." He was rising, pulling gently at the strings of her cloak, letting it fall to the ground, and she stood riveted by his touch, unable to pull away, unsure of herself, of him.

"I . . . I had better say goodnight to you, Lance . . ." she said on a whisper. Oh, she wanted him to make her stay, but she never expected he would do so with his next words. His face transformed before her eyes. His lips moved across her cheek to her ears. "Windy . . . don't go . . . please . . . don't you realize? Windy, Windy . . . I was whole, at least I thought I was . . . before you . . . and then you came along . . . and . . . oh, Windy . . . make me whole again . . ."

He sounded like a lost boy she could not resist. Her arms went around him at once, her lips parted to meet his own, she was responding with every beat of her pulsating heart. Want him? She adored him. It was a sudden dawning, an

381

overwhelming revelation. She moved onto the bed, and he followed, his arms still wrapped around her as she guided him onto his back.

"Windy . . . Windy . . . will you marry me?" It was a plea. He wanted her answer in the affirmative even more than he wanted her now in his bed.

"Yes, Lance . . ." she whispered softly.

He went wild suddenly, caressing, cherishing, touching, engendering a passion within her, sending her out of control. She didn't even know how the remnants of her gown were removed, she didn't know how he managed to shed his breeches. All at once she was lying beside him and they were both naked. She felt the hardness of his manhood pulsate against her thigh, and her hand reached down, stroked, held. He made a low seductive growl as he pulled her on top of him.

He nibbled at her ear, positioned himself, and as he plunged into her sweetness, groaned her name not once but over and over again as though it were a symbol of all he felt. She gave herself freely, unreservedly, touching his heart with her own, melting into his embrace, thrusting even as he thrust, and as her ardor mounted she led him into frenzy. She sat up wantonly, and he opened his eyes, hungry for her, his hands raised to her full breasts as he moved within, as she changed the fever of their dance, hardening its beat, slowing its rhythm, tightening its steps. And then all at once she could contain herself no more. She had her release and sank onto his chest, her voice low, sweetly supple. "I . . . I love you, Lance . . ."

His response was almost savage. Love? It wasn't enough, no one word was enough to describe what they shared. Joy! She had once said something about pleasures, but this was more. It was a joy, a creation, a thing apart from all others. She had worked her fingers into his heart, into his soul, infested his spirit, she had become his earth. His voice was untamed in its intensity. "I worship you, Windmera . . . my own moonflower . . ." He was rolling her onto her side, maintaining his throbbing manhood within her, slipping her onto her back. She had climaxed, he knew that, and he was still holding himself in check. Not yet, he thought, not quite yet . . . he would bring her to another.

His lips traveled over her throat as his body contorted within her. She was so good, so tight, he could feel the pull of her. "My God, Windy . . . you are delicious . . ." he

382

groaned in ecstasy. He excited her to new soaring peaks of delight. She wrapped her arms around him hungrily, moving perfectly to his tune, until they lay spent in each other's arms.

He sighed, kissed her earlobes and then tenderly her mouth. "In the morning, my moonflower, I intend to make you an honest woman!"

"Hmm. In the morning . . ." she said sleepily, rolling onto her side, giving him her back.

His hand smoothed over her butt, his fingers explored, and all at once he had to have her again. He couldn't get enough of her. He dropped a kiss on her shoulder, plumped her on her belly, and as she began to frown, he mounted her, raising her hips to meet his offering.

"Lance . . . no . . . oh . . . no . . . Lance . . ."

"Oh, yes, my love . . ." he whispered, finding her body far more pliable than her words!

Nineteen

Emptiness! *Roderick was sick with it, with the hollowness,* the inanity of his existence. How long would it take for Delia to leave his mind? When would the craving, the restlessness, the uncertainty of life without her . . . when would these feelings leave? Windmera! Yes, he would think of Windmera; there was purpose in that . . . was there not? Of course. There was even nobility in it! Was he not dashing into danger to save Windmera from Lance Landon? Stubborn wench! It was all her fault. If she had married him in Barbados as he had wanted, Landon would not have taken her off . . . or would he? Landon had always wanted Windmera. Well, he wouldn't have her much longer! A sudden fear. What if Landon had disposed of Windmera? A certainty eliminated the thought. Landon wouldn't. Somehow he just knew that!

Very well then, he would think of Windmera, of possessing her, of her long black hair, her flashing violet eyes, her scampish wit, her smile . . . and then just as she formed in the darkness of his room she vanished and was replaced by hair of cornsilk beauty, and soft blue trusting eyes, dewy now . . . tears flowing on Delia's cheeks. Tears *he* had put there.

He blinked hard. No. He had never meant to care . . . Hell! Life had muddled up in his own hands. He was weighted with the obscurity of his life. His sense of purpose had withered, and he ached for a feeling he had left behind in Bermuda. How would he rid himself of the ache? How? Stacy Clayton. He should lose himself in Stacy. There was a woman to make a man forget all others. She was beautiful . . . willing . . . warm . . . but he couldn't work up his desires. He just couldn't. Something was wrong with him. They had been together on the sea for some five days now, and she had shown herself interested in him, but the response was just not in him. His manhood he had left behind on Bermuda in the eyes of an innocent. Oh, Delia . . .

Stacy lay awake on her small cabin bed. The bruises of her encounters on the slave ship had nearly vanished, and she was at ease with her present, secure about her future. The captain of the *Conrad* was a gentleman. Crusty, to be sure, and not well pleased to have her on board, but a gentleman all the same. He had promised her that he would escort her to safety on the American border and there give her enough cash to get herself back to Norfolk. Yes, both he and Roderick had shown themselves sympathetic to her recent trials. But from Roderick she wanted more than sympathy.

She shouldn't think of Roderick, of course. She should think of Norfolk, of Monty Clayton and how she would enjoy watching him die. That was the only thing she should allow to control her mind, but even as she told herself this, she ran her tongue over her lips and imagined Roderick near her . . . holding her. Oh yes, she wanted him. He was different from other men. He was quiet, brooding, with thoughts he would not share, passions he had refused to allow her to arouse. He was a man, this Roderick of Ravensbury . . . and she would have him . . . all of him. But first, she had to find out what drove him.

It had something to do with this trip of his to Canada. There was a woman in it somehow. She had to know. Tonight. She would go to him and discover the reason for his haunted eyes. Then she would make him forget all others. She would weave herself around him. The fancy thrilled her with anticipation as she wrapped the quilt around her naked body. She glided across the dark cold companionway to Roderick's door, and without bothering to knock she opened it and closed it quietly at her back.

He propped himself up on his elbows and stared through the darkness. She stood suddenly uncertain, almost shy, and he called out in a puzzled but calm voice, "Who is it?"

"It's Stacy," she said almost inaudibly. What if he rejected her? After the horror of her experience with Monty, with the slave ship's captain, she had lost some of her arrogance, some of her self-assurance. "Please, Rod . . . may I come in?" Her drawl was a whispered plea.

"Stacy? It's late . . . you shouldn't be here," he said gently. He didn't want to hurt her; not after what she'd been through.

"It's late, I know . . . but if you'd let me stay and talk . . . just for a while . . . I reckon I could get some sleep. Please, Rod . . . ?"

He smiled ruefully. There was no way he could send her back to her room. She sounded like a little girl lost. Her tone reminded him of Delia's stricken look the day he left her.

"Sure, pretty lady, come in and tell me what you have on your mind."

She sighed thankfully. Step one completed, now step two. She curled up on his bed. "All I have on my mind is that ugly brother-in-law of mine. I mean to have his heart cut out, you know . . . it's keeping me awake nights . . . just thinking on how I'll do it." She sighed again. "But . . . I've got to stop thinking on it, don't I? Aw . . . Rod . . . make me forget about it . . . talk to me . . ."

He gave her a long sad look. "Talk to you? About what, Stacy?"

"About yourself. Rod . . . there is a mystery here. What is an Englishman . . . heir to title and fortune, as Captain John says you are . . . what is such a man doing sailing off to Canada, risking the seas with privateers and American war brigs patroling the waters?"

He shook his head ruefully. "It's a good question. But I do have my reasons."

"I reckon you do, honey . . . but won't you tell them to me? What harm can it do? It might even help . . . to talk about it, I mean."

He gave her a long appraisal. "It might at that," he said quietly.

"Then . . . you'll tell me?" She was a little surprised. She had expected more resistance.

"Certainly, why not?" Why not indeed? Perhaps it would help . . . perhaps he would lose himself in Stacy Clayton and put Delia out of his mind . . . perhaps. It was worth the try. So he started telling Stacy about Windmera. Telling her that he met her on Barbados, that she agreed to travel to Cornwall with him and become Lady Ravensbury. At Stacy's insistence, he even described Windmera to her and smiled to himself to see Stacy frown, thinking it jealousy. And then he told her of the privateer, the *Sea Hawk,* and its captain, Lance Landon.

She sat bolt upright, clutching the quilt to her breast. "What? Lance . . . it was Lance that took her?"

"Why . . . yes . . . you say his name as though you know the man."

"That I do, Rod . . . I thought I knew him right well! So! That was the woman . . . now I remember the name. But Rod . . . he was in Norfolk, not Mystic!"

He leaned forward excitedly, taking her shoulders in his hands.

"Norfolk? Was Windmera with him?"

"No. She was with his father. Lance received a letter from his father in Mystic; I was with him when he read it. From what I saw over his shoulder . . . from what he said . . . oh dear . . ." She played the equivocator, the sophist, for she knew well this game. "It just didn't seem important at the time."

"You must remember! Where was Windmera? In Mystic with Landon's father, then?"

"No . . . Lance's father was leaving. That's right. Lance's sister was ill . . . and his father was off with Windmera to visit with her."

"Try to remember, Stacy! For my sake."

She liked this. He needed her. He would be grateful. It was a start. A good start. Perhaps then she would tell him what he wanted to know. "Well now . . . ah, yes, I remember . . . Isabelle lives in Buffalo! They were off to Buffalo . . . but I reckon they might be married by now, Roderick."

"Married! Confound it, woman, why would he marry her?" He was dubious rather than concerned.

"One of Lance's sailors called her Landon's fiancée . . . so I—"

He snorted. "It's all a fadge. Thinks to come off the gentleman with her, but it's nothing but a hum!"

"Rod . . . do you love her so much?" This in a small voice.

"I need her, Stacy! I need and want her. Buffalo, eh?" He put his arms around her. "Oh, Lord, Stacy . . . they have made it easy . . . too damn easy. Buffalo . . . I couldn't have asked for more!"

She let the quilt fall then, and as it slid to her waist she watched his eyes travel over her breasts. She closed her eyes as his hand came up to cup one, heard him whisper, "No strings, pretty lady . . . you understand?"

"No strings," she whispered as she lay back and received him. "No strings . . ."

It had not been an easy morning! Windmera surveyed her suffering crew and put a hand over her mouth to stifle a wayward giggle. Really, she shouldn't laugh, she told herself, but with last night well behind them, it all seemed too funny. Pringle! She would do naught but bewail their lot, whimper over their close call and praise Heaven that Master Lance had come to save them all.

"Thank God your son found us!" she repeated for the hundredth time. "What a marveleous . . . wonderful young man he is . . . so talented . . . so . . . oh . . . my head does ache desperately . . ."

"Drink your tea, Pringle. I promise you, you'll be the better for it," offered Windmera, giving the woman a gentle pat on the hand and taking up her own cup of tea. For her part she was ravenous and wished she had found more than the biscuits and jam in the larder.

"Tea? I can't swallow a thing after . . . after . . . those beasts . . . oh my word . . . drugged! We were drugged!" ejaculated the woman on a long wail.

Calker, the Landon driver, had been given his sleeping potion in his ale, resulting in his having come to with a head twice its normal size and throbbing quite pitifully. He held it now, for he was certain the old fidget had just screamed loud enough to blow what was left of it off into smithereens. "Lordy, woman . . . couldn't you hold it down some?" he complained.

Jules was in quiet agony and attempting to down a glass containing a mixture of his own making. His pain, he said, was beyond their capacity to understand, and more than that he would not say. However, she could see he was feeling more the thing, for she caught now a twinkle in his eye. She sighed. It was not an unhappy sound, for her thoughts were of Lance.

Oh, Lance. How sweetly he had kissed her into wakefulness. How his eyes had looked, how wondrous the moment had been for them both. She hadn't wanted to leave the bed, to move from his embrace, but he had patted her rump playfully and ordered her out.

"Ho there! You call a different tune this morning, sir," she teased, throwing her arms around his neck, pressing her naked body unreservedly against him.

He looked down into her violet eyes as they flashed up at him. How he moved her! "Because I want you for all time, my precious . . ." His eyes had melted into dark blue ponds of tenderness. They promised so much. His lips touched her cheek, burning her with suppressed passion, touching her with unspoken emotion. He picked up the linen from the bed and draped it around her. "You don't know how hard it is for me to leave you . . . but leave you I must." He was pulling away.

Then for the first time she saw that he was already fully

388

dressed. She looked him over. He must have been awake for a while. "Where . . . ?"

"I have already been to the barn. I managed to rouse Calker, but he is useless to me this morning. I have to go after the law, sweetheart, so that we may turn in those two devils . . . and have the other buried. I shan't be long . . . I promise." She was so beautiful, so perfect, and leaving her this morning was almost more than he could bear, but there was nothing for it. He went to the door and there stopped. "You, my little sweetheart, had best get to your room and wear something pretty for me. Muss your bed up some too . . . we don't want your maid getting the wrong idea."

"It wouldn't be the wrong idea," she bantered.

His brow went up. He wouldn't have anyone think badly of his Windmera. To him this was a serious subject. The smile left his eyes. "I am not jesting, Windy. Go at once to your room and do . . ." He stopped, for he saw the fire in her eyes, the defiance in the set of her mouth. He left the door and went to her. She turned away. "Please . . . ?"

She gave him a bright look. She would never be ordered, not even by him, but this now was something different. "Of course, Lance."

He kissed her long and sweetly, but her wandering hand melted the sweetness into lava, and suddenly he knew if he didn't release her they would be undone. He nearly jumped away in his effort to withhold himself. She looked startled but not displeased. He backed off till he reached the door, thanking providence she didn't choose to follow him, didn't choose to pursue her course, for his will seemed no longer his own. He smiled at her expression. "Later, love . . ."

Sweet musings! Ah, but then he was gone. She had done what he asked, and here it was nearly two hours later, and where was he? As though in answer a male voice at her back boomed and each occupant of the kitchen was shaken out of individual soulfulness.

"Good morning, everyone!" Lance's grin lit up the room. He went forward, going first to his father, who attempted to stand. He put a restraining hand on his parent's shoulder, bent and dropped a son's kiss upon Jules's soft gray head. "Father . . . in spite of last night, you are looking well . . . but I think you've put on a pound or two since last I saw you!" It was a tease and the laugh was in his blue eyes.

"A pound or two!" snapped Jules, ever sensitive about his weight, his hands going from his forehead to his belly. "No

389

such thing . . ." He stopped himself, suddenly aware of his son's ploy. "Scamp!"

Well, thought Windmera, perhaps now he will look at me. However, Lance still did not turn her way. Instead he went back toward the door he had just passed through. "Ah, there you are . . . got everything you need?" he was asking of someone, she couldn't see who.

"Yes, I believe so," said a small, thin, darkly clad gentleman at the doorway.

Lance turned to the company at large and motioned the little man into the kitchen. "Vicar Turnbell . . . my father, Jules Landon . . . my bride, Windmera de Brabant!" His smile blinded Windy, and she gasped. This morning? He meant to wed her this morning? She hadn't expected this. She had thought he would wait till they reached his sister's home.

"But . . . but . . . the men in the barn . . . ?" she said, for lack of anything better to say.

"The sheriff and his men are seeing to them already," answered Lance, finally going to her, taking up her hand, kissing it tenderly.

"Er . . . Lance ," said his father thoughtfully, "there is the matter of the license . . ."

"Have it! Had one drawn up in Mystic, you know . . . just in case," returned Lance, well pleased with himself.

Jules moved out of his seat and went to Windmera. He bent to a crouched position and looked into her violet eyes. They were soft with her emotion. "Is it your will, child? You mustn't let my son bully you . . ."

"He does not, Jules. It is my will as well as his own."

Jules got up. "Well, then, what are we waiting for?"

Twenty

The Conrad *carved an impressive path down the gray-blue* waters of the St. Lawrence River. The cool green shores of Quebec had been passed with only a short stopover for supplies. Roderick had taken Stacy ashore and purchased her a quantity of finery to replace the men's shirts and breeches she had been forced to wear. He didn't mind the expenditure. She was a lively, warm, willing companion, and she helped him over his rough edges. There was still a region she could never reach, the moments when Delia stole into his mind and would not leave. But Stacy was a help.

A change had come over Roderick, a softening of will, a softening of contact. The world appeared different somehow, and he didn't know exactly why. Women? What were these strange magical creatures? For man's pleasure. It was bred into him that women of all classes were in the end meant to serve man. What then? Why the doubts? However, he had not the time to philosophize, for his purpose lay clearly before him. He had to get Windmera, and getting her would mean downing Lance Landon. There was a certain satisfaction in the thought, and it made him smile to himself.

Stacy watched the passing expression flit over his face. She was in love! Not desperately, for that feeling had flown in early youth. However, in her fashion it was strong enough to make her care. She touched his lips. "You look as though you were about to swallow a mouse, honey," she drawled sweetly. "Whatever makes you look like that?"

He looked away from the gray river water and found her eyes. Cool and lovely, but not cornflower blue . . . never cornflower blue. What did it signify? They were lovely eyes. "It doesn't matter. Let's go below, pretty lady."

She was pleased. She had aroused him. Good . . . perhaps in time he would find he wanted her far more than this confounded Windmera woman! "I reckon that's just what you need, honey," she said softly.

Captain John watched them from his perch. He wasn't certain what he felt. Outrage? Shock? Here they were risking their lives to rescue and secure Godwin's daughter for Roderick's bride . . . and there he went making love to another woman! Sadness. Aye, that is what he felt overriding all else. This Roderick of Ravensbury was no fit husband for the little girl he had met in Barbados. But if she was the captive of this Captain Landon, this American pirate . . . well, then she was maid no more! Who was to say what was right? Godwin was entitled to his daughter . . . wasn't he? He shook his head sadly to himself, for there was no answer. Why had he allowed himself to be embroiled? Friendship? He was risking the lives of his men, Roderick's life . . . his own. Was it friendship? Aye, he thought. Godwin was entitled to receive it, and he honor-bound to give it.

Thus, the *Conrad* steadily sliced water, its aim, Fort Kingston, Canada, where they would dock, inform the Admiralty staff there of their mission and slip across Lake Ontario to the American side. There they would disguise themselves as Americans and ride for Buffalo. Tricky business at best, but necessary . . . and then, with the help of the fates, Godwin would finally have his daughter!

"Lance . . . oh, Lance . . ." cried Isabelle breathlessly. "We have been so worried about you . . . but my, I can see the excitement suits you, for I have never seen you look so wonderful!"

Lance stood aside and drew Windmera forward gently, pushing her toward his sister. "Izzy . . . I want you to meet my wife . . . Windmera." It was quietly, proudly said, and his sister was quick to see the tenderness in his eyes.

Her mouth open, she appraised Windmera. A beauty! Raven-haired, violet-eyed . . . such a face . . . a woman indeed for her brother. Isabelle had always been a warm and bubbly person, and she was no less so now.

"A sister at last!" Her arm went around Windmera. "You cannot imagine how dreadful it has been stuck between all these men. Even my child defied my will and was born a male!"

Windmera breathed a sigh of relief, and that hurdle over, the females of the house settled down to get to know one another while the men huddled to discuss the uppermost topic in their minds . . . the war.

"Dearborn feels that they might attack Sackets Harbor. Feels they've got some six thousand men to do it with!" said Jim Foster on a hushed note.

"Not a chance, Jim! Dearborn is behaving the fool. They don't have anywhere near that force, and what's more he has

Armstrong convinced now to delay our attack on Kingston! Hell, man . . . now is the time to strike . . . not later in the spring when Yeo arrives!" This from Lance, who shook his head with some disgust.

Jules sipped his brandy. "All this is very well, but it still brings me to one point and one point only. I want my daughter and my grandchild removed from the vicinity. Jim . . . you could have a marvelous practice in Mystic . . . we need a young doctor . . ."

"I know, Jules, and to tell you the truth, when the troops moved in last week, I began thinking that you were right. At least . . ."

"Now you're thinkin', lad! Don't muddle yourself up by putting 'at leasts' and 'ifs' into it!"

"It's Izzy mostly that has me moving to your way of thinking. After her miscarriage, she was lonely for you . . . for Lance . . . for Mystic. She has never really liked being up here in Buffalo. I want her to be happy . . . but—"

"But nothing!" This from Lance. "You don't belong here either, Jim. Your father wouldn't want you to carry on his practice if you weren't happy in it. You have your own life to live."

"So I do . . . which means I have to make the decision. Leave me to do that . . . eh?"

Jules and Lance exchanged glances, nodding quietly over it. Lance glanced over at his wife. She was curled up on the winged sofa, her legs tucked under her blue velvet gown, her black hair streaming thickly over her back. They hadn't had much opportunity to be alone these past eight days on the road to Buffalo. But their nights? Oh, God, their nights had been too perfect ever to forget. Thinking about them now infested him with a sudden urgency. He got to his feet, leaving Jim to his father's arguments.

"Izzy . . . Windmera must be tired," he said, taking his wife's hand, pulling her to her feet. "I know the way up. If it's all right with you, we'll use the guest room at the end of the hall."

Isabelle smiled. "Of course, Lance . . . I am sure you are both tired." Her eyes bantered with him. He was, of course, being outrageous, but never mind, so had Jim been when they had started out on their honeymoon.

Windmera excused herself, blushing all the while, but she made no protest. His touch sent rivulets of anticipation fluttering through her veins. She allowed him to throw remarks over his shoulder to his brother-in-law and meekly, quietly followed him as he pulled her along. How could she not when every nerve ending demanded she be alone with him?

Daylight flooded the room he had chosen, lighting up its floral design on the papered walls. The door was closed at his back. He moved quietly to the fireplace and added a log to the burning embers. He stirred it with one hand, undid his neckcloth with his other. She watched him from the velvet settee near the window. Sweet life, but she loved him! The sight of him, the sound, the scent! She watched him admiringly as he unbent and slipped off his cutaway coat, undid the buttons of his buckskin vest. His eyes met her own as he worked the shirt he was wearing, as he approached. He spoke not a word, but his eyes ravished her as he reached out for her waist, took her in firm command.

"Oh, woman . . . my woman . . ." he whispered tenderly against her ear. He had to close his eyes, for his emotions engulfed him. More than passion did he feel. He was complete. She had made his world whole, she had given it meaning. He called her his own, but it was not so, he was hers! His mouth opened to speak, but he could not find the words, and so he sought her lips.

His touch infused her with fire, with sweet expectation. She felt his soul caress and mingle with her own. His kiss vanquished all doubts, and because she wanted desperately to tell him how she felt, her lips moved against his, but all she could say was his name. She knew no fear when she was in his embrace, he knew no other want but to hold her, touch her, possess her. His fingers worked her gown, and it dropped between their legs. His shirt followed, as did her small clothes. His hand came up to fondle, caress, tease and seduce as he lowered her onto the floral-covered bed. The sunlight filtered through the heavy hangings of the four-poster, engulfing them in a warm reddish light. He lay beside her at full length, and his hand traveled over her nakedness, softly promising her pleasure, teasing her to ask for more.

She responded to his manipulations and pressed her body against him, but he pushed her back against the mattress. "No . . . not yet . . . I want to look at you . . . God, Windy . . . you are so beautiful . . ." Then almost savagely he nibbled at her lips before parting them, entering with his tongue. His hand took hers and lowered it to his hard throbbing manhood. He urged her to close her fingers around it, taught her how he would have her move. He smiled to see her blush, and then slowly, deftly, moved his mouth to her breasts, lightly kissing and then moving on to her belly, then lower still. He reversed his position and spread her legs, kissing first one inner thigh, the next, and then, gently, erotically, between the lips of her honeyed opening. She stiffened at first, frightened by the rate of her heartbeat, by the all-encompassing fever that threatened to overtake her. Her hand tightened on his pulsating manhood, and because she had to thrill him as he pleased and thrilled her, she began her manipulations with wild abandon, bringing her mouth first to kiss and then to take in his hard, beating rod.

"Oh, my Windy . . ." he groaned, coming around, sliding over her body, taking up her legs pushing them up and back, positioning himself. "My own hot-blooded moonflower . . . now give it to me, sweetings . . . now . . ."

"Oh, Lance . . ." She wanted him, but she wanted to tease him further, she was heady with the power she had to bring him to such ardor. "We are being wicked . . . 'tis the middle of the afternoon . . ."

"Wicked? Damn, but with what we feel for each other, it would be wicked not to in the middle of the afternoon." His voice was low, hungry. He would not be stayed. "Windy . . . Windy . . . I love you . . ." he asid, plunging in, dizzy with his need, wildly happy because she met his thrust, because her words echoed his own.

It was all she needed to know as she opened to receive him, and as they gave to one another, as their passion mounted and found release, she knew their love would find no limits. This was what her mother had meant, this was what Heather had wanted for the daughter she bore Godwin, Lord Ravensbury!

Shrouded windows. Everything clothed in darkness. Death. Death was near, she felt it, sensed its power creeping through her veins. No! Not yet . . . she had first to see her son. Her will fought her body, but it had no weapons, no chance to win. There was only defeat, darkness and death. Weeping? Why was there no weeping? No one to mourn her passing? No . . . there was only loneness and her ebbing spirit wandering through words that still retained enough force to beat her at last. Peace? Sara of Ravensbury prayed for it. Would it ever come? Numb . . . yes, numb was what she felt. The pain was at last easing, as was her breath.

Life? It would be over soon. She blinked and saw herself a

youth, a maiden . . . a girl shaken by the eyes of a gypsy lover. So long ago. So long had she suffered for the pleasures of a moment. So long had she suffered for the folly of a decision. A door opened, interrupting her dreams. Light. Hazed and far away. A man . . . such a big man standing in the path of its beam. Such brawny shoulders he had still . . . such red tousled hair. Godwin.

He had come at last, and he had come too late. All these years she had wanted him to . . . to what? To love her? No . . . he couldn't. He wasn't able. She had drawn an image of herself, framed it in roses and given it early to him to worship. Shattered. The image had curled in upon itself with the birth of Roderick, and all was shattered. He had never really loved her . . . Sara. No, he had loved an image. He had never really known her, and if he had . . . he would not have wanted her. She knew that now, but it was all too late. It didn't matter. But Roderick? Godwin had the power over Roderick.

"Sara . . . ?" It was Godwin's voice, but it held no pity. He felt none. He only knew suddenly that he could not let her die alone, so he had come to her room.

Her maid at his back dropped her face into her apron and wept softly. She had no great love for her mistress, but death was an overwhelming event, hard to deal with, leaving her insecure, and so she wept. It drew Godwin's attention. He frowned and quietly dismissed her from the room. This was a moment of truths, and he would be alone with Sara.

Sara's sunken eyes found his face. It blurred before her. Why did he blame her so for everything that had happened? He should have realized she couldn't stand by and let him humiliate her. She had to have Heather taken away. Why couldn't he see that? Divorce? He would have divorced her . . . married that . . . that woman. How could she have let him? Why didn't he understand?

"Sara . . . I don't know that we can make peace with one another . . . but—"

"But you would have your conscience clear?" Even in her weakness she was able to exhibit disdain, bitterness.

He shook his head. "You have never seen, have you? My conscience . . . clear? My life has been a Hell . . . because of you, Sara. My life has been meaningless! I have no conscience . . . you tore it from me long ago!"

"Have I done that? Could anyone do that to another being? No, Godwin. It was always in your power to set things right. Your life . . . my life . . . you had the power over both. But never mind . . . it is too late."

He closed his eyes. Some of what she said was true. An honest man would admit that he had had no right to love Heather Martin. An honest man would admit to himself that he had done an injustice to his wife in seeking to leave her for another woman. But he was more than an honest man, he was a human one. Sadly, he nodded. "Perhaps . . ."

"And now you would ruin Roderick's life as well." She had no strength. Her words were a whisper, an epitaph.

His fists clenched. "You deem his life ruined because he takes to himself a wife worthy of him?"

"I . . . deem it ruined because he follows your whims . . . *not his own.*" She was tired. She looked away and then back again into his dark-brown eyes. Such soft eyes. Why had they not loved her? "You should have allowed me my son . . . in this hour, Godwin . . . you should have."

A wave of guilt surged through his heart. He raged against it, but his words came out a plea. *"I could not, Sara!* Roderick had to win her . . . make her want him. How could I announce myself her father . . . wed her to Roderick? She does not know . . . must never know . . ."

Sara's eyes had closed, but her face was drawn in death. There was not the look of peace about her. Godwin stared, and for the first time in twenty years saw another's suffering. His voice was a whisper.

"Sara . . . I . . . I am sorry . . ." But it was, as she had said, too late.

A lovechild! Conceived in passion, nurtured in bitterness, but how odd . . . strangely disturbing that the thought should touch him now. Roderick shook his head. He had no way of knowing that the flitting words had come to him in the very moment of his mother's passing. It was as though some life force all her own spanned time and distance, spanned death just to touch him, to beg his understanding, to give him strength. He was a cold fortress of will, and he shrugged off the eerie sensation. What had he to do with such fancies?

He paced, covering the floorboards with irregular motion. Outside his quarters there was only darkness broken by the occasional torch of a passing sentry. The fort at Kingston was well maintained and his room not uncomfortable, yet Roderick was plagued with fears. Sara's face swam before his eyes. There in the fire's leaping arms, her lips moved, pleaded.

397

Sara! His mother. What was she doing here? Why should she intrude upon him now? What was it he felt for Sara . . . and why suddenly should he be distracted by her memory?

An answer, ready in its nature, came and thrust itself before him. Captain John, of course . . . it was because of Captain John. Back in Bermuda he had said Sara was unwell. He hadn't believed him, he hadn't wanted to believe him, it wasn't convenient to believe him. Sara was a strong woman. Just look at all she had wrought because of her will! Damnation! And then a voice deep within called his name. It was Delia's voice. Your mother loved a man . . . he left her . . . just as you left me . . . Roderick, just as you left me . . .

No! Oh, Delia . . . it wasn't like that . . . I love you, Delia . . .

A knock sounded at his door. It would be Stacy. He had arranged for different rooms at the fort, to keep up appearances. He called out welcomingly, for he couldn't bear to be alone with his silent rage any longer, "Come in, love . . ."

Captain John opened the door and walked in. His face was clouded over. "It is not Mrs. Clayton, Roderick . . . but don't worry, I shall only stay the moment."

"Here . . . Captain John . . . don't pull such a self-righteous face at me!" He was irritated with Captain John's attitude. The good captain made him feel like a wayward schoolboy. "What I do is my own affair." He relented, "Look . . . if you will promise not to read me a lecture, take off your coat and have a glass of brandy with me."

"I think not, Roderick. I came only because the plans have been set for the morning. We leave the *Conrad* in dock here at Kingston. We'll be hugging the shoreline of Ontario . . . guided by that Indian scout of theirs. When we reach the American side, we'll purchase horses—"

"I know all that. Have you exchanged the British currency?" said Roderick eagerly.

"Aye. That's why we leave in the morning . . . there is nothing left here to keep us." He sighed. "I trust you'll relay the message to Mrs. Clayton so she'll be ready—"

"I'll be ready, Captain John." It was Stacy at the door. She stood to one side, indicating that it was time for the captain to leave them.

"Yes, ma'am . . ." He hesitated, as though he would say more, then thought better of it and left them.

Stacy closed the door at the captain's back and turned to Roderick. "Well now, honey . . ."

Twenty-one

Lance strode into the Foster parlor. It was late afternoon and he was met by a cozy scene. His wife was curled up on the sofa determinedly working her embroidery. His sister was playing with her infant son. His father was lounging in a wing rocker, a copy of Cowper held up to the light, and Jim was working his accounts at his desk near the window. Windmera lifted her eyes and found him. He was looking as excited as a little boy whose team had just won a tournament. In his hand was the morning paper, which he had ridden to town to obtain. He slapped it vigorously and commanded attention.

"Look at this and learn just what sort of boys we have sailing the Atlantic!" He stepped merrily into the room, shoving the paper at his father. "Glory boys, every last one of 'em, on the *Neuchatel!* Chased the reds clear into their own Channel! Right smack dab into their own English Channel. Wouldn't give up until they had their prize! Hell boys . . . that's what they are!"

"I don't believe it," said Windmera, popping up and going to Jules's shoulder. She was joined by Jim, and they began reading excerpts of the daring exploit. " '. . . American privateer to be decorated . . . docked in Boston with a fortune in spices . . . outsailed, outwitted the British until they had them floundering in their own seas within sight of their own harbor!' " She turned up startled eyes, "I just can't believe it!"

"And why not? We aren't brought up on bread and butter, my girl!" returned her husband banteringly.

"What then . . . on buckshot?" she teased.

"On daring, my precious. We're raised on daring!" He was in a high fettle, pleased with his fellow countrymen and therefore pleased with himself.

"Here, Lance . . . let me see that," called out Isabelle, disentangling herself from her son, setting him on his blanket and advising him that if he didn't stay put she would have his father beat him soundly. He responded by gurgling gloriously and throwing in the air his favorite wooden toy. It came to earth with a crash, bringing the required attention. He heard the laughter go around and clapped his hands.

"Just look at young Jim. He is proud to be an American!" cried his uncle, going toward him and taking him up.

Windmera watched him play with the child. How good he looked with him, how right. She suddenly wished young Jim were theirs. Lance glanced up at that moment, saw the expression on her face and frowned. Immediately he put his nephew down onto the blanket again.

Isabelle was reading the article aloud, but Windmera was no longer interested. Why had Lance suddenly turned away from her? What was wrong with him? Isabelle sat down, finished now with the reading, and she let go a long breath. "My goodness, gentlemen, this certainly should do our men's morale some good."

"Hell, Izzy . . . it isn't our men who need boosting. It's Dearborn!" said Lance in some disgust.

"Lance is right. What with Dearborn skipping between one plan and then another, we'll never invade Canada . . . and Lord knows we must. We need Lake Ontario and we won't get it till we advance!" This from Jim.

"With the British controlling the St. Lawrence, I don't know how we can attack Canada and succeed," ventured Windmera doubtfully.

"Isolation. That's the trick. We need to isolate upper Canada by attacking Kingston. Defeat its garrison and we've got control of the harbor. The St. Lawrence would be cut off, you see," offered Lance enthusiastically.

"Yes, but Lance . . . Armstrong has still to attack York. Dearborn must give him the go-ahead, for we need to destroy the ships being built in York," said Jules on a frown.

"And so he will, just as soon as they hit Kingston!" retorted Lance almost merrily.

Isabelle sighed and whispered to Windmera as she moved to intercept her crawling son, "I'll just go up and put young Jim for a nap. It's not right that he should be listening to all this. It seems all we ever do is rear children on talk of war!"

Windy watched her leave. The men were arguing in earnest now, and it was no longer holding her interest. She needed to walk, to be alone with her thoughts. Quietly she left the room, took her cloak off its hook in the hall, pulled on her gloves and stepped outside through the kitchen door.

April breezes touched her, chilling the softness of her cheeks, pinching them into pinkness. Traces of snow lingered here and there like a patchwork quilt over the sloping land. She meandered slowly down the garden path thick with evergreen shrubs to the woods adjacent to the Foster estate. There was a stillness to the woods, majestic in their reviving season. Crocus shoots were tickled by the wind. Branches reddish with their prospering buds filled the sky, birds chirped in harmony, and it was good, for spring was pushing its way, demanding rebirth. Spring . . . and yet what were they talking of inside? War! Absurd.

However, it was more than the war that was troubling Windmera. A sudden realization this afternoon had sent her out to be alone, to pick at the new concern. It was the revelation that Lance did not want children. Why . . . oh why, Lance? Our love is so perfect . . . why would you not want to consummate it with a child? She had become a woman whose heart had mingled with his and returned to her changed, irrevocably changed. She was learning to know another being better than she knew herself. She was learning to love another being more than self. At times she thought their union so perfect that she feared the angels might in a fit of jealousy strike them down. He filled all her needs, he taught her truths and how to cope with them, and he left her feeling that she wanted to serve him . . . to bear him a son. But he didn't want one. Now it was all so clear. After those first few times of lovemaking he began withdrawing from her at the moment of his climax . . . giving his seed to the linens . . . and now she knew why.

She had been too happy, too satisfied in their love, to wonder about it earlier, but today when he saw her face as she watched him with young Jim, he had understood what she felt, what she wanted, and he had shown her clearly it was not what he wanted! But why?

Oh, Windy, Windy, she told herself, you are being foolish. You love each other. These past few weeks at Izzy's house, sharing family life with the Fosters and Landons, becoming a Landon, have been too wonderful to upset now with foolish doubts!

She was so chiding herself and had slowed her pace to lean up against a great oak when something caught her eye. Something dark, deep in the thicket of the woods. A chill suddenly gripped her spine and traveled its height to the nape of her neck. There was someone else in the woods with her! She heard the snap of a branch beneath a heavy boot and tried to locate its source. Why did they hide? Surely if she could detect their movement, they could see her. Why didn't they make themselves known instead of skulking about? And then perhaps instinct or common sense took over. She saw a cloak wave in the wind, nothing more, and she took a step backward, telling herself she had to return quickly to the house, telling herself this was no idle fear, that she was being stalked by someone.

"Windy!" It was Lance's voice. Lance calling from the mouth of the wooded path.

She turned and ran in his direction. She couldn't see him yet, but his call came to her ears again, and she ran hard toward his voice. She was frightened, really frightened, and when she saw him she dived headlong into his arms.

"Hey . . ." He chuckled. "What is this?"

"Lance . . . Lance . . . someone was in the woods . . ."

"Who?" He was frowning.

"Lance . . . I . . . I don't know . . . but whoever it was . . . oh, Lance . . . I know he was watching me . . ."

It troubled him. Windmera was not the sort to take fright easily, but he had to set her at ease. He touched her nose lightly. "And who wouldn't watch you, precious?"

"But . . ."

"Go into the house, Windy. I'll have a look out here." He was smiling still, but his tone was dead serious.

"No . . . you aren't armed . . . Lance, I have a terrible feeling about this . . ."

"Never mind. Just go into the house." He pushed her toward it and stalked off down the path. One could never be too careful. It could be that some lowlife had taken too much notice of either Windmera or Izzy when they went into town . . . it could be some brute with rape in mind. He would have to forbid the women the woods for a time. He moved stealthily, examining the ground for the obvious signs, listening for sounds uncommon. But as luck had it he passed by without taking the right turn, for not five feet from him was the print of a large man's boot imbedded in melting snow and wet dirt. Farther down he would have come across another set of prints, horseshoe prints of a lone rider, but Lance did not take that turn, and the tracks went undetected. He frowned. Perhaps Windy had seen some poor poacher hunting in the woods? It had been a hard winter, game was scarce. Perhaps someone had strayed onto their land? Still, it wouldn't hurt to keep the women near the house for a time.

Captain John rode into the wind. He had learned a lot to-day, but the choicest piece he had to bring to Roderick was not going to sit well! Of course there was a way around it . . . He gave his hack horse the right lead and bounded forward into a checked canter as he took the bend in the road. The inn where they had hidden themselves away was not far off; he could in fact see its red roof in the distance.

A moment later he was shrugging out of his many-tiered dark cloak and knocking at Roderick's door. Roderick's voice was anxious as he called out.

Captain John entered and cast a quick glance toward Stacy lounging on the bed, a glass of brandy in her hand. She sat up with his entrance.

"Captain? What news have you?" It was Roderick, speaking as he came forward, offering the captain a glass of brandy.

The captain took it and gulped down a long swig, for he was chilled to the bone. He had spent a long time outdoors watching the house after he had questioned one of the Foster servants on the road.

"Lad . . . I don't know how to tell you any other way but clean . . . and what Godwin will say I don't know . . . I just don't—"

"What are you talking about?" interjected Roderick sharply. "Speak up, man, and don't be giving me riddles!" He had been pacing the floor the better part of the afternoon. It was frustrating being this close, so close he could almost feel her.

Stacy moved forward. She was almost as anxious as Roderick to know the outcome of Captain John's sleuthing. After all, much of her future depended on it. She had pursuaded Roderick to allow her to remain in his company even though she should be on her way via stagecoach back to Norfolk. She hoped somehow he would want her to stay on even after they had located Windmera. She hoped . . .

"Lad . . . Windmera de Brabant . . . well . . . *she is a Landon!*" he blurted out at last. "Landon married her some weeks ago. Do you realize what this means, Roderick?" He was taking off his cloak, dropping it in a nearby chair, pacing as his hand shoved his hat away from his forehead, noting with a grimace the sly smile that crept onto Stacy Clayton's face.

Roderick felt a battering ram thrust into his belly. He was stunned by the blow. Married? Landon had married Windmera? Godwin's daughter . . . no longer available? *No!* It was impossible. Why had Lance married her? Was she . . . with child? *No!* The thought was horrendous. He couldn't speak, he couldn't move.

Captain John watched him closely. The man had received a flush hit. He attempted to assuage some of Roderick's pain. Gently he moved his hand, stretching to comfort Roderick with a touch, but Roderick whirled around viciously. "Damnation!"

"Aye . . . it wasn't meant to be . . . it never was, Roderick . . . never . . ." said the captain sadly.

"What? Do you think that I am stalled by this?" He made a derisive snort. "No, my good captain. Windmera may be married this day . . . but by the morrow . . . *she will be a widow!*"

The candlelight gave off a warm glow. The fire blazed in the hearth, and Lance felt softly tender as he watched his wife before her mirror. These moments were precious to him. He loved watching her, the manner in which her hands worked the brush over her shining hair, the expressions that would flit over her face in motion with her thoughts. She was light. She had the power to make him laugh when the elements tried his temper. She had the power to make him love when the world would ask of him otherwise. She had the power to work his passion even in his blackest moods, and always he had the need to touch, to stroke, to cherish her. There were times when she lay in his arms and he wanted to keep her there eternally, crushing her against his heart. She was love, and she had the power to give him true life.

He moved now to her side and bent to drop a kiss upon her shoulder. She stiffened, and his mobile brow went up. He was quickly learning sensitivity to her moods. "What is this? *Cold?* My hot-blooded wench is turning me up cold? I would know why?" He had swung her swivel chair around so that she was flanked by his arms, staring straight into his deep-blue eyes.

"It is naught," she said quietly.

"Naught?" He shook his head wisely. "Your eyes are sad and your mouth is drooping. Don't you trust me, Windmera? Isn't there the slightest chance that I could help?"

"You see . . . I know, Lance . . ." she attempted and flushed. It was such a delicate subject. How strange that she

404

could brazenly make love with him in bed, on the floor, in a coach, and yet be unable to speak about such things.

"You know? You know what?" He was puzzled.

"That you don't want me to bear you a child!" There, it was out, and she was biting her lip, for his expression frightened her.

He went rigid. He straightened and moved away from her, and his voice went cold, hard. "We don't need children."

She got up and touched his arm, but he would not turn her way, so she went to face him. "Lance . . . how can you? Are *you* making a decision for *us?* Don't I have any say in the matter?"

"No. As a matter of fact, you don't, my dear." He was so hard, unreachable.

"But . . ." She couldn't believe his attitude. "But . . . why?"

He frowned, and for a quick moment he glanced at her, relented and stroked her nose, "As I said, we don't need children. There is *us*, and it is perfect. Why spoil it?"

"Why would a child spoil it?"

"It might . . . and I won't take chances with our happiness . . . I won't take chances with your life!" He had voiced it. The fear. His mother had died in childbirth, and it had left its scar.

She stopped and stood a moment, searching his face, his eyes, and her arms went around him at once. "Oh, Lance . . . my darling . . . and I thought you didn't love me enough . . . how stupid of me not to see . . ."

He kissed her then almost desperately, and held her long and hard before sighing. "So then, the subject is closed," he said quietly.

She chuckled. "Is it? I think not, my darling . . . I think not."

"Windy!" he exclaimed, but already she was pushing him backward onto the bed. Already she was working up his blood with quick delectable movements of hand and body. Already all he could think was to get off her nightdress . . . spread wide her legs. "Oh, Windy . . ." he growled low in his throat.

Twenty-two

"Must you go, Lance?" Windmera was pulling on his neck, drawing him to join her among the pillows on the bed.

He attempted a feeble show of resistance. "Vixen! Trying to deter me from my duty?" He wrapped his arms around her, hugging her close, "Let go, I say! Unhand me, woman!" His lips nibbled at her ears, her neck, her mouth. "Seductress, enchantress . . ." His wandering hand pulled away the covers to display her full naked breasts, and the blood pulsated in his temples. "Ah, woman . . . woman . . ."

She laughed happily and pushed at his chest. "Do you stay, then?" Her eyes teased, her mouth tempted, her breath stopped hopefully.

He took a long good look and sighed sadly. "Devil is in it that I promised Perry I would meet him this morning. I gave my word, Windy . . . but damn if I won't be back here for lunch!" He flicked her nose. "And that, my girl . . . I intend to take right here in bed."

"You think so?" She put up a gay arched look. "That seems very single-minded indeed. What of *my* luncheon?" she bantered.

His hand went between her thighs and took strong hold. "I think . . ." His voice was low, husky at her ears, his manipulations were bringing her breath in short spurts. "I might find a way of appeasing your appetite at the same time, my love, but mind now, if I don't . . . you have to let me know, and we'll . . . hmm . . . have another go at it."

She laughed out loud and shoved him away. "Fiend! Cad! Get out of here at once!"

He smiled and moved to pick up his riding jacket. He shrugged into it as he crossed the width of their room to the hall door. There he stopped and cast his wife a long and tender look. "Until our lunch then, moonflower . . ."

Moonflower. Always it would cast up visions of that first night on the beach in Barbados. That wild night . . . it seemed an age ago. She blew him a kiss, and as the door closed on his back, she snuggled into her covers to relive their night. It was early yet, she had a while before morning tea would be brought up, before she must get ready for her daily ride on Izzy's mare. Life, she mused happily, was all too perfect!

Captain John stood near his tethered horse and watched Jules and Lance Landon recede down the pike. Good. The Landon men were gone! Now if only he could find out how long they would be away. He frowned and then quickly, resolutely made up his mind. He walked toward the Foster stables. Grooms. They would know, and for a coin or two there was no telling just how much he would find out.

Some time later when the good captain emerged from the Foster stables, his steps were quick and there was excitement lighting up his features. With any luck, they would be able to pull it off this very morning. The doctor would be gone on his morning rounds. The Landon men would be away until noon, and Windmera was in the habit of riding out on Mrs. Foster's mare at nine! All he had to do was to go back and get Roderick . . . all they had to do was to waylay her on the road! By God, it was almost too easy!

Roderick stood in the middle of his room. His marshy eyes were narrowed with thought as he listened to Captain John, as he seemed to comprehend that at last he would have Windmera within his grasp, but he was not well pleased. Lance Landon out of the way was not what he wanted, and it irritated him to no end. "Damnation, John! I won't leave until Lance Landon is dead."

"Roderick . . . don't be a fool. This morning she'll be out riding. We can get her and be off with no one to follow for hours. Roderick—think!"

"I am thinking. I want Windmera a *widow*."

"It isn't necessary!" interjected Captain John. "We discussed it. Your father will be able to have her marriage to Landon annulled. You know that is so. She is a British subject . . . Landon is an American . . . at war with us . . . it will be an easy matter!"

"I want their marriage erased not by documents but by death!" He pounded the satinwood table in the center of the room. "By death, John!"

"Dammit, man! Then you are on your own. I wash my hands of the entire affair."

"You can't do that," said Roderick, taking a step toward him.

"Oh . . . can't I? I told you last night I won't be a party to

407

murder." He sighed. "You want the girl. Godwin wants the girl. All right, then, I've given you a way to her . . . but if it's murder you have in mind for this American, then I'll be taking my leave of you . . . now." He started for the door.

"Captain John!" Roderick had taken hold of the large man's shoulders, had turned him roughly, and was for his efforts flung angrily away.

Stacy gasped. She went running to where Roderick had fallen and gave him a hand up. "Oh, Rod . . . can you not forget this Windmera?"

"She is right, Roderick. We could tell Godwin she can't be found. That's my advice to you. You and Mrs. Clayton . . . seem to have . . . feeling for each other. Why don't you—"

Roderick's rasping laugh cut him off. "Stacy is nothing to me!" He was beyond thought. Delia's image was alive before him. Windmera's pull was tearing him away. He was torn by two women, and Stacy was neither one. "Are you daft? Do you think I would forget Windmera for Stacy? Don't you realize what I have given up? Don't you know?" He shook his head. "No, of course you do not. All right . . . if I must do it your way . . . then so be it, for Windmera must be mine!"

Stacy is nothing to me! Stacy is nothing to me! She heard it over and over, the words reverberated between her ears, stunning her into evil. She stood erect beneath the blow. He had said no strings! He had promised her nothing, he owed her nothing . . . but oh, God, it hurt! Every inch of her hurt, and she wanted to lash out.

"You know, Roderick," she said smoothly in spite of her pain, "your sweet Windmera . . . she just might not go with you!"

He snorted. "You know nothing of the matter." And then because some memory jarred him, made him defensive, "You are quite wrong!"

"Am I? I saw Windmera with Lance in Norfolk . . . I saw the way she looked at him. She might wish to remain his wife!" She wanted to hurt him. Why? He had been honest with her. It didn't matter. She was bleeding and he didn't care. She had to hurt him.

Yes, he thought suddenly. In Barbados he too had seen a certain light in Windmera's eye . . . a light for Lance Landon. "You forget, Windmera had been on her way to Cornwall with me . . . to marry me!"

"Yet, my love, she is married to Lance Landon!" Stacy sneered.

"That is naught! Windmera is woman enough to make any man do what she wants. Do you think she would allow herself to be mistress to a man?" This he said with disdain, and for the first time in many years Stacy felt the flush steal into her cheeks. He could be cruel, this man she loved.

He pursued, "No, Windmera married him to protect her self-esteem, not her heart! It is me she loves!" He stopped, paced and then brought a careful eye to Stacy's face. "My dear, you will, I trust, get on that stagecoach in the morning and forget this conversation?"

"This and all others we have had," she said coldly. "That is what you want, isn't it? You want me to forget you?"

"Yes, my dear, I do . . . it is for the best," he said quietly.

She smiled. "Really, Roderick, do not imagine I shall fall all to pieces when you leave. I shan't."

"Then, my dear . . . I bid you farewell. The captain and I must leave if we are to proceed with our plans."

She inclined her head, for she could see he had no intention of taking her in his arms. Oh, cruel. He could have spared her a kiss. But damn . . . what was she? Some schoolgirl? No, she knew better than to expect anything from a man who promised nothing! She watched him pick up the bag he had been living out of these past few days. She watched him pass through the door without turning back. She licked at the dryness of her lips, and as her eyes met those of Captain John's she put up her chin. What? Would she allow this disdainful man to feel pity for her? No!

"You'll come up and float, ma'am . . . and you might want to remember but one thing, that he saved your life and left you in peace."

She wanted to rail at the good captain. Peace? Damn your eyes! Is that what you see? She said instead, "Of course I shall remember."

And then once again she was alone.

April winds tore at the hood of Windy's fur-lined cloak, unable to undo the tight strings keeping it securely on. Through the trees the sound of the wind came to her in spurts, causing her mare to prickle up worriedly. "There now . . ." soothed Windmera. She was well pleased she had chosen to wear her husband's old buckskin breeches and warm wool sweater. So much more comfortable to ride in than a hiked-up dress, for Windmera preferred riding astride to sidesaddle. A chipmunk scurried past the mare, and the horse took off unexpectedly. Quickly, deftly, Windmera gathered in rein, bringing up the mare's head, slowing the pace of the sudden canter, bringing her into a trot, using her shoulders to check the horse's pace as she pulled on the reins. It was good having control of such a fired-up horse, it was invigorating working as one with the beautiful animal. And then all at once the wind between the trees was forming her name.

"Windmera," it called softly, intensely, and she stopped to listen. "Windmera . . . Windmera . . . Windmera!"

But the voice . . . it was strangely familiar . . . strangely exciting. Who was it that called? She went close to the edge of the woods and peered. Again the call, distinct now as the voice came closer still.

"Windmera!" There was a pleasure in the sound, and then all at once she knew the owner of the voice. Roderick! It was Roderick.

She said his name in disbelief. "Rod? Rod . . . ?"

"Yes, my love . . . come!" he called, and she could see him now walking toward her. His dark cloak danced away from his lean tall frame. The curls at his forehead were swept around his handsome face by the force of the breeze.

Her reaction was very whole, very real pleasure. This was Roderick, and Roderick was her friend. He had been there during a very difficult time. He had been there when Jokai had been killed, when her Tante Louise had faced reality by joining her lover. Roderick had been there offering a friend's wine. And now he was here! He was safe. He had survived the ordeal on the *Southsea* and he was here and well. These were her only thoughts as she ran headlong into his arms.

It was natural, but Roderick misunderstood her joy, and such was his own that he immediately began showering her face with quick heartfelt kisses. Windmera at last! His bride! Godwin's daughter! And then his mouth *sought* and found her own.

Windmera stiffened. Suddenly she realized. Roderick was here to rescue her. Roderick was here to pick up where they had left off. He was here . . . oh, God! She pulled out of his embrace. "Rod . . . no . . . Rod . . . you don't understand . . ."

"But I do, and it doesn't matter. You mustn't allow yourself to think about it!" he said breathlessly.

"No . . . Roderick . . . I am married!"

"I know! Shall I keep you close and make you a widow?" He was laughing now, for finally, here was Windmera.

She was horrified. She shrank back from him. It was all too clear now. Roderick was here to rescue her! *Would he take no for an answer?* She had to make him understand. "Roderick . . . I am Lance Landon's wife! In every possible way . . . *I am his wife!*"

"It doesn't matter. The good captain assures me that we can have the marriage annulled in England. But my darling, if you prefer, I can rid you of your husband . . . in quite another fashion."

"No! Roderick . . ." She suddenly saw Captain John and recognized him. This was the man she had met on the beach so long ago. The man who had questioned her about her mother. She moved toward him. *"You!* How . . . what . . ."

Roderick had her arm. "There is no time now, Windmera. We must leave."

She pulled roughly out of his hold. "Listen to me! I am not going anywhere with you. *I love my husband!*"

"No!" It was an anguished cry, but he was furious as well. "Shut up! Do you think I care! Do you? After all we have been through? After a year of planning . . . courting . . . chasing you down?" He had her wrist and was dragging her now through the woods to the coach he and the captain had hired that morning. They had not anticipated Windmera would put up a struggle, but they had not wanted her seen riding through town after town. They wanted no one tracking them!

Captain John's brows were drawn together. This was wrong. The wench was in love with her husband. She didn't want Roderick. This put a new light on things. He stopped Roderick. "Lad . . ."

Windmera saw her opportunity. She broke away and made a dash for her horse. Roderick was on her in a moment, but in a last effort she threw up her hands and frightened the mare into a run. With some satisfaction she watched Izzy's mare take off for home. She felt Roderick grab her around the waist, and she kicked hard enough to put a dent in his leg. He dropped her, and she saw a flash of vivid color before sinking to the ground.

"Dammit, Roderick! What have you done?" cried Captain John, going to the woman slumped on the cold earth.

"I've taken the fight out of her. Now quickly, John, help me . . . open the coach doors so that I may attend her."

Captain John hesitated. If he refused now to help Roderick, the boy would attempt it on his own and probably end in

411

getting himself killed. There was nothing for it. He went to the coach and opened its doors, but as Roderick put her inside he said, his voice low and angry, "From here on in . . . the wench is my charge, Roderick. You touch her again . . . you'll answer to me!"

It had been a busy morning indeed. Perry had sent word the night before to Lance and Jules requesting their presence at a meeting of the shipbuilders he'd been having trouble with. He hoped that his old friends might help him solve some of his problems, and they had, but it had left Jules exhausted and Lance anxious to get back to his wife. They tooled their horses onto the front drive, and Jules remarked languidly that it was food and bed for him. Lance's blue eyes twinkled as he agreed, and his father gave him a jovial look. "Sly dog!"

However, Lance's attention had shifted. Something was wrong. The stables were in a state of disorder, and there was no one there to receive them. "Come on . . . let's ride the horses to the house and see what is afoot."

This they did at a quickened trot, to find Izzy at the open front door. Spotting them, she began to run in their direction. Lance's color drained. Windmera. Something was wrong with Windmera. He felt it, knew it. He jumped off his horse and went toward his sister. "Izzy . . . Izzy . . . what is it?"

She was out of breath. "Lance . . . oh . . . my mare . . . came back without her . . . some two hours ago. Everyone here has been combing the road, the woods, for her . . . Jim has just come home, and he says we must get the constable. Oh, Lance . . ."

Were his knees melting? He was Lance Landon. He was a man! He was used to shocks, to dangers . . . he was . . . oh, God . . . Windmera! What to do? What to do? "You say Jim has returned?" he managed.

"Yes . . . he was out tracking the woods along the road. He says if she was thrown, she might have attempted to walk . . . and then fainted."

"Izzy . . . have Jim send into town for a search party." This from Jules. "Go on, daughter. We must . . . all of us . . . keep our heads!" He turned to his son. "Come on, then . . . we'll take the north road. She told me once she likes the view from its crest."

Lance was at his horse immediately, but as he led the way

412

he turned a white face to his father. "Windmera was the best of superb horsewomen . . . she would no more be thrown—"

"Stop it, Lance!" interrupted his father. "Anyone can be thrown, and if she was, it could be as Izzy says. She may be lying in a faint or with a broken leg . . . nothing more!"

Yet Lance felt a very different fear grip his heart. Something had happened to Windmera, and she had not been thrown off her horse. It was something else. Something else. Oh, God . . . she had to be safe. Let it be anything . . . as long as she was alive!

The hours ticked by, long and hard to take. The men went in different directions, combing the area. Lance took to walking the woods. "Windmera!" he shouted over and over again, his voice hoarse with use, desperate with the passing of time.

"Lance . . ." A friend's voice. It was Jim, his brother-in-law. He felt Jim's hand on his shoulder. "Come away, Lance."

Lance got to his feet and moved away. "Let it go, Jim . . ."

"No. You haven't eaten all day. Come to the house . . . have something, just to keep your strength up."

"Are you insane? What are you bothering me about . . . *food?* Have you lost your reason? Don't you realize . . . I have to find her . . . Jim, I . . ."

"And you won't be able to if you don't take care of yourself!" snapped his brother-in-law.

"Jim . . . you mean well . . . but please . . . don't . . . not now . . ."

"Lance . . . Lance . . . *Jim!*" Jules was shouting for them. There was excitement in his voice.

Lance's eyes widened. "That is Father . . . Jim . . . something . . ." He ran toward his father's voice. Ran until his heart could pump no more, his brain could no longer sustain rational thought. He found him, took up his shoulders. "Father . . . ? Windy . . . Windy . . . ?"

Jules had a strange look about his face. "Lance . . . there is a woman, a Stacy Clayton, at the house . . ."

"Stacy Clayton?" He began to laugh. It was an ugly sound full of anguish, hate, disappointment. "Hell and brimstone, Father! What do I care about Stacy Clayton?"

"Lance . . . it seems she has information concerning Windmera!"

"What?" He was suddenly intense. What had she done? What had Stacy and her petty jealousies done? "Damn the woman! If she has hurt Windmera I swear I will wring her neck!"

Jules and Jim watched Lance stampede toward the house and exchanged wary glances. There was more to this than met the eye. More to it than Stacy Clayton, and they rushed after Lance, for if the Clayton woman had done something to Windmera, Lance was in a mood to kill her!

Twenty-three

Windy's head rolled. She felt it, and groaned. She could hear herself as though from far off. The interior of the wobbling coach blurred, but she could see something now other than darkness. She was in a coach. A voice. Someone was speaking. It was a man's voice, someone familiar. Yet . . .

"Mrs. Landon . . . Mrs. Landon . . ." Captain John pressed the wet handkerchief to her forehead. There was an ugly bruise already swelling around her eye.

Windy winced and attempted to speak, but something prevented her. She tried and tasted cloth. There was cloth in her mouth. She wanted to move her hand up, pull away at the cloth, but she couldn't raise her hands, they seemed stuck behind her back. And then she opened her eyes wide. Captain John came into focus, and with his face came recall. Roderick had hit her! Roderick meant to take her away! Lance . . . oh . . . Lance? Tears welled into her eyes and spilled silently down her cheek. And this man, her mother's friend . . . what did he have to do with it all?

"Oh no, lass . . . no . . ." soothed Captain John. "Don't be crying . . . you won't be hurt. I give you my word. You'll not be touched again . . . but it's to Cornwall we'll be taking you . . . to Ravensbury . . . where you belong."

She wanted to cry out. She didn't belong in Cornwall. She didn't belong with Roderick at Ravensbury. Her place was with Lance, with her husband. If only she could make this man see. The coach was pulling up to a stop. Who was driving it? Roderick, of course. He appeared at the window. "I've been driving for hours, John . . . it's time you relieved me!"

"No, lad . . . I'll not leave you in here with the lass. You're not to be trusted! If it's tired you are of driving, then take up a seat beside me and I'll handle the reins."

"Damn you, John!"

Captain John sighed. "Aye . . . for this day's work, I don't doubt I will be."

"All right, then. I'll take up a seat beside you, though you are making a fuss about naught. She'll be mine soon enough."

"Aye . . . as it happens you may be right, but until she be legally untied to Landon, you'll not be touching her."

415

Roderick said nothing to this. He had quite other plans in mind. There was the long voyage on board the *Conrad*, and Captain John wouldn't be able to watch him at all times, now would he? He only knew that with Windmera so near to him she drove him to madness. She was in his blood. It was not the same with Windmera as it had been with Delia. He felt no tenderness for Windmera. He felt instead an almost unspeakable lust. He wanted to tear at her with his hands, he wanted to bite her mouth, to taste her blood as he took her kisses, took her body. He wanted to subjugate her. She was no longer a virgin, but he would take her in a manner he was certain Landon had not yet thought to try. He would turn her on her belly and raise up the lovely rump and . . . oh, damn, he had to have her. She alone could save him from thoughts of Delia . . . Delia . . . no. He had to shut Delia away! Delia was gentleness and love . . . Delia was laughter and sun . . . Delia . . . stop! It was Windmera he needed to make him a Ravensbury . . . to unite him with Godwin! It was Windmera!

Stacy Clayton stood avoiding Isabelle Foster's inquiring eye. The darkness of a nearby corner had drawn her, for such was her mood. Torn between conflicting emotions, her restlessness won out, and she had come to the Foster home to seek out Landon. But now, she was filled with doubts.

Landon entered the room like a man demented. His clothing was askew and soiled. His long raven hair was windswept, tangled and wild. His blue eyes were dark with anguish, and there were lines about his mouth that terrified Stacy. One look at him told her she was wrong . . . she shouldn't be here. She was putting Roderick in danger. If she told Lance that it was Roderick who had taken Windmera . . . ? Oh, my God, she thought suddenly, he will kill Roderick!

Landon was upon her in a moment. He had seen that in her expression that convinced him she knew where Windmera was. He had her roughly in hand and was shaking her savagely. "Where is she? Damn you . . . where is she?"

Isabelle gasped in horror and made a grab for her brother's arm.

"Lance . . . Lance . . . stop it . . . you mustn't . . . Lance . . ."

He was beyond reason. He shook his sister off, and her husband entered the room in time to catch her from falling. "Stay out of it, Izzy!" He gripped Stacy by her arm and pulled her across the room to stand before a tall hardback chair. "Now, Stacy! Where is she? Speak up or I swear you'll not live to see morning!"

He meant it. She had no doubt that he meant it, for she could see the devil in his eyes. Lance Landon had become a madman!

"She is with Roderick."

"Roderick? Ravensbury?" he shouted, beside himself. "What the hell do you mean? Where has he taken her?"

"Oh, please, Lance . . . promise me you'll not harm him," she begged on a breathless note.

The man in the woods! It must have been Roderick . . . Windy had sensed it . . . and here was this slut asking him not to hurt Ravensbury! "Promise? I promise to put a knife through his black heart, you witch! You knew what he was about and you made no attempt to warn me? Dammit, Stacy, she is my wife!"

"I know . . . I know . . ." She was crying now. "And I am in love with him . . . but . . . he was obsessed with the notion of getting her . . . there was nothing I could do. He saved my life . . . I owed him my allegiance . . ."

He shoved her meanly into the hardback chair. "All right, then. Where is he headed with her?"

She wouldn't tell him. Lance would find him and kill him. She couldn't tell him. "No. I . . . I can't tell you."

His hand came across her face like a wide strap. He could hear the assembled company at his back object, come toward him, but he stalled them with his arms. He would brook no interference. "*Truth,* Stacy! I'll have the truth and I'll have it quickly, for I have no honor to share . . . not without my wife . . . you see I am quite capable of administering whatever it takes to find out what I need to know!"

She believed him. He might disfigure her, and no one in the room would even stop him. So she gave up Roderick on a sob: "He and Captain John are on their way to Fort Kingston . . . where they have the *Conrad* docked. From there . . . they go to Cornwall . . ."

"But . . . she is my wife? What does he mean to do . . . make her his mistress?" This on the edge of a sharp blade, it grated against his heart, but he had to know.

"No . . . he intends to have the marriage annulled once he is in England. He means to wed Windmera . . ."

"*I will see him dead first!*" whispered Lance, going toward the glass gun case.

"Lance . . . wait!" cried Jim. "We've got to think! By this hour . . ."

Lance wasn't listening. Once again he had turned back to Stacy, once again he was leaning menacingly toward her. "Another question, Mrs. Clayton. How were they traveling?"

"They had a hired carriage. They planned to . . . to change horses at the posting inns. Lance . . . I . . . I followed them . . . I saw . . . Roderick take Windmera into the coach. She . . . she wasn't conscious." She didn't know what made her tell him that. Perhaps because of her own experiences recently, perhaps because she wanted in some measure to prove herself better than she was. She didn't know, it had just come spilling out of her. She didn't dare tell him she had seen Roderick administer the blow that had sent Windmera to the ground.

Lance's face was white. He could visualize Windmera struggling, being brought low beneath Ravensbury's hand. He felt a pitchfork slide painfully into his gut. "I didn't think she went willingly with them, Stacy. You see . . . I know my wife." It was quietly spoken. He turned toward his father. "Right, then . . . we know that they will reach Lake Ontario before we can hope to catch up to them. Therefore they will reach their ship and be off . . . and the only way is to go after them with a ship of our own. That poses a problem, with the *Sea Hawk* in Mystic!" He was pacing like a caged animal.

"Hold a moment, son. Do you remember my family seals? I kept them sewn in the lining of my trunks during the Revolution . . . thought they might come in handy one day."

"Father . . . what . . ."

"Listen to me. Your only hope lies in chasing the *Conrad* . . . right into Cornwall if you have to! But as an American you wouldn't stand much of a chance. However, we are of English descent . . . proud English descent . . ."

Lance was gripping his father's shoulders in uncontrolled excitement. "Fiend seize me for not thinking of it! You are right. What we need is a swift schooner and an English flag to go with it."

"Not to mention a crew, and for that, my son, we are going to have to do some fast talking!" said Jules dryly. "But I imagine our compatriots will come up with both the Union Jack and the crew . . . what with the proper donations we intend to make to the cause!"

"We'll have to stake the *Sea Hawk* with Perry . . . offer it up to the War Hawks," said Lance, as though in warning of

418

what was to come, for he would have his father prepared for the worst.

"My boy, it is *your* vessel. If you are willing to risk it, I don't believe I have any say in the matter!"

"What in blazes . . . ?" cried Jim, all at sea. 'What are you going to do . . . sail into Cornwall with the *Sea Hawk?* That is crazy! You are—"

"No, no. I'm going to get Perry to lend me a schooner and put up the *Sea Hawk* in its stead. With the Union Jack, I'll just sail out the St. Lawrence with the British waving me on . . . and then, my friend, if I don't down the *Conrad* at sea I'll down them in dock. One way or the other . . . I'll have my wife before the month is out!"

Isabelle and Jim exchanged horrified glances as they saw Lance and Jules out. When they returned it was to find Stacy attempting to slip out of the house. Isabelle stepped in her path. There was no telling what this woman might do next, and she for one was not taking any chances. "Mrs. Clayton . . . we simply could not let you go out at this hour. You'll stay in our blue room upstairs . . . and in the morning one of our grooms will see you to town to catch the early stage. Now, do let me take you up." Her hand gently took Stacy's elbow.

Jim watched his wife maneuver. Really, these Landons were a spunky group, he thought musingly as he followed the women abovestairs. But . . . this chase to Cornwall? It was one thing for a privateer to chase an English merchant into the Channel . . . quite another for Americans to pose as English . . . and dock. Why, Lance could be shot as a spy! What was the alternative, though? Windmera was Lance's wife. Really . . . for a man like Lance Landon . . . just what was the alternative?

Was this really happening? This just couldn't be happening? It had to be a nightmare! Windmera stared at her four cabin walls, at the small cabin bed, out the high round window. Was she really on board the *Conrad?* Were they really heading down the St. Lawrence River? This was madness. She was Lance Landon's wife! How could this be happening? Her door opened, and Roderick stood in its fold. She stared at him a long moment. She wasn't afraid, not of Roderick, but she knew she would have to stall him somehow, for Captain John was at the helm.

"Roderick . . . what do you want?" she said, hoping she didn't sound nervous.

"Don't play the innocent any more, Windmera. We both know how Landon has used you. Mind, now . . . it bothers me . . . greatly, but perhaps you can make me forget . . ." He was coming toward her, closing the cabin door behind him.

"I don't want you to forget! I want you to think about it, remember it, know it at all moments. I was Landon's woman . . . his wife . . . I am still!"

"Are you?" He was grabbing at her arm, hurting her through the material of her shirt. She was wearing one of Roderick's, for the shirt and breeches she had donned three days ago had been torn during an earlier struggle with Roderick. Only then Captain John had been on hand.

"Roderick . . . how can I make you see? I love him. This is wrong."

"You wanted me once. You will again." He took her by both shoulders. "Windmera . . . my own Windmera . . . don't you realize what we are to each other . . . will always be to each other?" He was pleading now, for deep inside he was breaking. Everything was going wrong . . . everything.

Her hand moved imperceptibly to touch his cheek, but she halted herself lest he misunderstand. Her face was a mask of consternation.

"Rod . . . you say you love me. You were my friend. Don't you know what love really is?" He did not answer, and she shook her head. "No, you couldn't. If you did, you wouldn't be forcing me to accompany you. You would walk away."

He thought of Delia. He had walked away from Delia. She had wanted him to stay . . . and this one wanted him to go! Oh, spiteful Lucifer!

"Roderick?" It was Windy calling his mind back, forcing him to answer. He saw her face and it swam before his eyes. He loved Windmera. She was Godwin's daughter . . . there was something bewitching about her eyes, her lips, her body. He had to have her . . . he wanted to stroke her, own her. *He had to have her.*

"*Love?*" he answered at last, his voice a lesson in disdain. "Love is Hell! Windy . . . Windy . . . don't you know . . . you are damning me for taking you . . . he will damn me if I don't . . . and given the choice I'd rather be damned with you than without!"

420

What did he mean? Who would damn him? What was this all about?

"Roderick . . . what are you saying?" His words beat at her always like a sledge hammer. Too heavy to understand, yet there was meaning there if only she could trace it out. Roderick was driven by an obsession, a distortion . . . but how . . . what?

She didn't understand, but she could read the anguish in Roderick's face. This was Roderick. Not a stranger. This was the man who had held her when she needed to be held. This was the friend who had helped her in Barbados. Something she did not understand had controlled his hand, had forced him to make her pass the last seventy-two hours as his prisoner, but he was Roderick still. "Rod . . . please . . . let me help you," she cried. "Only . . . tell me . . . what is it that tortures you?"

"It is you!" It was the cry of a wounded stag as it faces its tormentor and makes one last effort at survival. "Oh, God . . . your eyes . . . you speak of love . . . you . . ." His words were coming in gasps now. "Love? Don't you see . . . love is why you must marry me . . . why I must bring you to Ravensbury!" He grabbed her shoulders and shook her. "Don't you understand? Why do you look like that? Haven't you ever wondered? Haven't you ever guessed? Has the name Ravensbury meant nothing to you? Did not your goddess mother never mention Godwin?"

"What . . . what do you mean? Why should . . . ?"

"Fiend seize your innocent eyes!" he screamed. "How dare you look as you do? How can you not know? How often I heard your mother's name! He would fall upon his bottle crying her name! Heather . . . Heather . . . Heather! Over and over again, and you say you never heard her mention Godwin?"

She took a step backward. He was jarring a memory. She didn't want to hear any more. She didn't want to remember, for the incident so long ago had disturbed her then and she had put it away, out of her mind, and still it came unbidden now! She had been fourteen and her mother was dying. She could see Heather's violet eyes, her own, go dark with pain. She could tell that Heather no longer saw what was before her, and then she had heard her mother speak quietly, softly, so softly that she couldn't be sure she heard, but now she knew that she did hear it.

"Godwin . . . shall we meet in death . . . my Godwin . . . ?"

Heather's voice, scarcely audible. Windy had cried and Heather remembered where she was. She had smiled and told her daughter to pay her no mind. So Windmera had shoved it away. It had not been a path she wanted to explore. However, Roderick had brought it back to her and formed a fear in her heart.

"Why . . . why would my mother mention Godwin's name? What has your father to do with us?"

He threw back his head. What sound was that he made? Was it the peal of anguish? Was it a pitiful laugh? He cast her a look, long and nearly filled with hate, contempt. "He has everything to do with you. Have you never wondered how you came to have such an unusual name? Windmera . . . it is out of the common, is it not?"

"My mother told me it was taken from a cliff's edge in Cornwall," she began defensively.

"It is a name indeed for a particular place in Cornwall, but you'll not find it on any map. No indeed. It is the name two lovers gave to their trysting spot."

"Stop it! I don't want to hear any more," cried Windmera, frightened now.

He took her wrist and pulled her against him. The blood was racing through his body, inciting fever. He was in a passion. He wanted to break her as he was breaking. He wanted to possess her as he was possessed. He wanted to find understanding in her eyes, but first, first he would have to make her see. "Don't you want to know the truth about Heather Martin and Godwin of Ravensbury?"

She cringed, for suddenly she thought she knew the truth. Godwin? Her mother must have been in love with this Godwin. That is why she had left Cornwall. But that didn't matter. She met and married Maurice de Brabant. Yes, that didn't hurt. She found her strength and squared up to Roderick. "I think I know what you are trying to tell me. Your father loved my mother . . . he was already married to your mother . . . so mine left Cornwall . . . and married the comte de Brabant, my father."

His laugh cut her off. "You little fool . . . you stupid little fool . . . is that what you think?"

The door was flung wide open at their backs, and Captain John loomed angrily in its frame. He had heard enough to know that Roderick was violating Godwin's wishes. Windmera was not to know. Not now, not yet! "Roderick . . . I think you have said enough!"

"No, Captain John, I have not. How faithful you are! Have you always been Godwin's dog?"

Captain John was across the room. Roderick was in his cups and easily handled. He shoved him roughly toward the door. "I have always been Godwin's friend . . . as he has been mine. You would be wise to be the same!"

Roderick stopped and shrugged off Captain John's hand. "May you rot! I am his friend . . . I would be . . . more."

Captain John watched Roderick's retreating form. So, it rankled still? There was poison festering in the lad, and when the carbuncle burst there was no telling what would occur. He turned to Windmera. She was staring but not seeing. Her mind was traveling in the past, searching for an answer.

"Best not pay any attention to the lad. He has been drinking deep," offered Captain John. She didn't reply, and he sighed. "I'll be locking your door, Mrs. Landon, and keeping the key . . . I think it'll serve."

"Yes, thank you," she agreed, but when she turned to the stillness of her dimly lit room there was a disquiet in her heart and there were questions plodding through her mind, and Windmera was such that she would not rest until she had the answers.

Twenty-four

Three days! Roderick had taken her away and they had been gone three days. The smooth lines of the *Apollo* sliced through the gray-blue waters of the St. Lawrence, its captain taut with purpose, his crew ready for the adventure. It had not been easy getting the *Apollo* from Perry. Friendship had not been enough. He and Jules had had to sign over the *Sea Hawk* along with several written notes, contributions if you will, to the war effort! And still, there had been a moment when Lance and Perry had faced each other stubbornly, each refusing to see the other's way of thinking.

"Perry . . . for God's sake . . . I need those papers!"

"I am sorry. Lance, don't you realize, at the very best they can only appear a pure forgery. How can we supply you with an English marque? You would be committing suicide going into an English port!" He shook his head. "You are a friend . . . Jules is a friend . . . do you think I will have a hand in this?"

Lance's face had gone white. If he had to ride overland to the *Sea Hawk*, precious time would be lost, time he could ill afford. He was furious that Perry should deny him in the name of friendship. Was he some child to be cautioned . . . controlled? He grabbed his commander-in-chief by his sturdy lapels and shook him. "You call yourself my friend? Perry! She is my wife! You have just the ship I need sitting in your harbor! You can't possibly have need of it."

Jules pulled at his son's hands, freeing Commander Perry. Gently he pushed at his son. "Perry . . . my son is distraught . . . you will of course understand. But he is right, you know. The *Apollo* is an English merchant . . . neat . . . sharp-lined . . . but scarcely armed. She has only recently been pulled into harbor and therefore will not be recognized widely as a captured vessel. Don't you see . . . it is perfect for our schemes."

"*You* approve of this?" asked Perry incredulously.

"We have no choice," returned Jules quietly. "Furthermore, I think if you go through the *Apollo*, you will find a ready English marque which we might be able to use to advantage?"

424

Perry paced. He was young for his commission, but highly capable. He was also something of a daredevil himself. He began to see possibilities.

"You know . . . the *Neuchatel* incident has you all fired up. Simply because one of our privateers has managed to capture an English merchant in the English Channel is no reason to suppose—"

"Stop it, Perry! More than one of our privateers has chased the English into their own waters with success! Besides . . . you are forgetting. My father's family is English quality. All I have to do is flash my name about . . . exhibit the family seals," argued Lance.

"And what of cargo? If you are posing as an English merchant vessel you will need cargo!"

"And I shall have cargo. A layer of Bajan sugar over several layers of straw. It will work, Perry . . . if only you will stop arguing and find me a capable crew!"

"I can't order the men to it . . . they will have to be volunteers," said Perry beneath a frown.

"Then let us get to it!" said Jules.

And they had. Eighteen men sailed beneath the captain's fine hand, and Ontario was securely at their backs. They passed through Kingston undetained, and the St. Lawrence was before them . . . as was the *Conrad*. Three days!

Oh, God, Windmera, my own Windmera. She pulled him onward, and not for a moment did he have a doubt that he would find her.

Ocean horses white and lovely formed for as far as the eye could see. Windmera huddled in her cloak and gazed into the sky. Clouds scudded in wild profusion, taking shapes to hide away the sun, whose mood was yet unknown. Lance. Lance. Lance. Her heart ached for him. Somehow she would escape Roderick. Somehow she would find her way back to her husband. Somehow . . . and then because she was alone and her path thorny and nearly too obscure to travel she gave over to emotion and began to sob. She bent onto her hands and leaned into the bulwarks, hiding her head from view, but her cries raked her body, and Captain John felt himself nearly beaten.

He told himself as he watched her distress that it was temporary, that she would come about, forget, settle down, and he knew he lied to himself. Godwin did to his daughter what Sara had done to him so long ago. Ironic and sad, but there it was. He had the power to turn the *Conrad* around . . . to take her back . . . but somehow he couldn't. It should be Godwin's decision. It must be Godwin's decision if ever this Hell was to end!

Roderick came up from his cabin. He'd been drinking heavily these days at sea. His cheeks and nose were red with the effects. His beard was dark and thick and his eyes glassy. He saw Windmera, and he heard her. She was bleeding. Good! Hadn't she made him bleed? She could have made him better. She could have healed his wound. She could have helped him forget Delia. But she would not! Why should he care what she suffered? Why? And yet he did. He moved toward her. He reached to touch, and then quickly withdrew his hand. "Windmera . . .?" he called.

She stiffened. "Go away, Roderick," she said, not looking at him.

"I can't. You can't. We will be forever bound to one another. Why can't you accept that?" He moved closer. "Once . . . once you wanted me, Windmera . . . once you needed me . . ."

"But I never loved you, and I don't now!" she breathed. "Do you think I could after what you have done?"

"What is so wrong with what I did? Didn't he do the same, this wonderful Lance Landon of yours? Didn't he abduct you from the *Southsea . . . from me?* What is so different in what I do?"

"Love! We love each other, Lance and I. That makes it different from what you do. You don't love me . . . you know you do not. You are doing something because of another's will, aren't you? Admit it! Roderick, I want the truth. Why did you come to Barbados? Why did you seek me out . . . ask me to be your wife? Why?"

He answered her quietly. What did it matter? "I tried to tell you the other night, but the good captain stopped me. Why do you think? Godwin of Ravensbury commanded a wedding. Godwin wished the marriage of Windmera de Brabant to Roderick of Ravensbury . . . and I was dispatched for that purpose. I am a pawn, as you are, my dear . . . but when I saw you I discovered that I wanted it too. I need to have you. I want you to have *my child . . .*"

She had her hand over her heart, as though to keep it from parting with her body. "But . . . why? Why would he want you to marry me? He doesn't know me."

Roderick glanced sideways at Captain John busy at the

wheel, and he sighed. "Windmera . . . your mother and Godwin . . . were lovers."

"How dare you!" she snapped, taking a menacing step toward him, raising her hand. He caught her wrist and held it firmly. "Hear me out. You wanted to know . . . so for once, listen! Yes, they were lovers, but Godwin had a wife . . . my mother. He wanted to divorce her and marry your mother, Heather. Mine had other notions, so she got rid of Heather . . . had her abducted, you see. Evidently your mother escaped and married Maurice de Brabant . . . but Windmera, she was already pregnant when she was taken out of Cornwall. She was carrying Godwin's child."

Windmera would have run had she been able. She was riveted to the deck beneath her feet. Her eyes stared long and hard at Roderick's face. It was the truth. She knew it. She was not Maurice's child. She knew this was so, but she wanted to rage against it . . . and then another thought dawned on her. "But . . . but what you are saying?" She could not form the words. They stuck in her heart never even making it to her throat. "Oh, my God . . ."

"Yes, you are Godwin's daughter. You are the flesh and blood he has pined for all these years. You are the daughter of a woman he adored more than life. You are a Ravensbury, and he would have you made one in name as well!" It was so bitterly said that Windmera had no doubts left as to its truth.

"Oh, my . . . oh . . . but then . . . how can he expect . . . why would he want his son to marry . . . he couldn't . . . we can't . . ."

He laughed without a trace of mirth, and it was a hard grating sound. "Ah, but we can. You see . . . I am no son of Godwin's!"

Windmera was in no condition for this shock. She felt her knees turn to sand beneath her. She felt herself sliding and could do nothing to stop the fall.

Roderick caught her. His hazel eyes were deep with intensity.

"It is a shock to discover oneself illegitimate. I found out about myself when I was scarcely ten years old . . . but one survives." He held her in his arms. "Windmera . . . you see . . . together we can make it all come out. Together we can set things right . . ."

She closed her eyes. "I . . . Roderick . . . how you must have been hurt. Oh, Roderick . . . I am sorry."

"Don't be. Now that you know . . . understand . . . you will help me, won't you Windmera?" He was pleading.

She opened her eyes and found his. Oh, how she pitied him. She had had a beautiful childhood. Maurice had been her father. This knowledge would never change that. She was content with the youth she had spent, it had made her whole enough to take this blow. Life had taught her enough to understand her mother. There were new questions now. There were the whys wandering about in her head, but they would be answered in time. Godwin . . . her natural parent . . . pining for her? How strange to think on it. Roderick . . . not Godwin's son and yet wanting to be . . . how pitiful. "Roderick . . . I would lie down for a time . . . please . . ."

"Of course," he said, helping her to the stairway, thinking that at last there was hope.

Captain Landon stood at the bridge, his hands clasped at his back, the wind in his face, the night lifting before his eyes. Had they outrun her? Had they succeeded in leaving the *Wasp* far enough behind? He and the crew had been awake throughout the night, this single purpose foremost in their minds, for it had been just as the sun set that the *Wasp* had been sighted.

Of all the ill luck! Captain Landon thought now, for of all the American sloops-of-war, this was the most renowned for its daring in English waters. He had met its captain, John Blakely, in Norfolk once, immediately after the *Wasp* had come from the English Channel. The Irish-born Blakely was fierce and quick-witted. He had attacked the English in their own den and had come off the victor. There was no doubt in Landon's mind that Blakely and his *Wasp* would pursue them into battle. Damn! For there was no gainsaying the fact that the *Apollo* was no match. The *Wasp* had over one hundred and seventy men to work its thirty-two-pound carronades and two long eighteens. If the *Wasp* drew up for a broadside the *Apollo* would have no choice but to surrender. Damnation, but that would mean explanations . . . and he could just see the look on Blakely's face!

The night mist was lifting, and Captain Landon went astern to put up his glass . . . and there in its circle was the *Wasp*. She had raised a white flag, and as she maneuvered he could just make out the words: "FREE TRADE AND SAILORS' RIGHTS!" As an English merchant ship he should have answered with: "GOD & COUNTRY: BRITISH SAILOR'S

BEST RIGHTS: TRAITORS OFFEND BOTH." But this was no time to prove himself a patriotic Englishman. He would have to tack and catch the wind if he was to get out of their sights.

The *Apollo* had the advantage of size, but the *Wasp's* captain was quick to realize this. With excitement working him up, Blakely whipped his crew into position and began tacking in order to catch their prey broadside. There was every good chance in Blakely's mind that they could get near enough to disable the smaller ship, but then Blakely did not realize he was playing with the captain of the *Sea Hawk*.

Landon noted Blakely's maneuver at once and countered it by calling out a sharp order to reach. In this way the *Apollo* caught the wind abeam. In this manner a sailing vessel can sail faster than in any other direction, but it was taking the *Apollo*, as Lance had feared, sharply off course. There was nothing for it, though, if they were to get away. He cursed softly to himself and thought that if Windmera did not hang in the balance he might even have enjoyed this. He studied the binnacle when he heard the watch call out that another ship was coming up fast. Up went the spyglass, and in its circle he found the British brig *Reindeer*. Low and long was his whistle. Sticky. The situation had become very sticky. He had just been contemplating staying on course and allowing the *Wasp* to board. A hasty explanation would be enough for Captain Blakely . . . after all, they were acquainted. It was a matter of deciding which course of action would cost him the least amount of time, but now with the British brig coming at him, there was no longer any decision to be made. It had been made irrevocably for him.

The crew of the *Apollo* was tense as they watched to see the outcome of this new addition to the scene. Every nerve in Lance's body itched to side with the Americans on the *Wasp*, but to do so would immediately label his ship a spy vessel, and there would be no safe entry for the *Apollo* in any English port. But . . . what was she doing? He watched in awed silence as he saw the big vessel wield its way and separate the *Wasp* from the *Apollo*. The *Reindeer* was drawing up to exchange broadsides with the *Wasp!*

This was ridiculous, thought Lance, feeling much like laughing and yet guilty over such a sensation. The British were drawing up to protect them!

The captain of the *Wasp* frowned. The *Reindeer* was inferior in firepower, but he had no wish to fight both a British brig and a British schooner without help. Perhaps it would be better to look for a single-ship engagement. To quick-clipped commands the steady crew of the *Wasp* began working the sails.

The captain of the *Reindeer* silently breathed a sigh of relief. It was his duty to protect what was obviously an English merchant schooner on its way to home port. However, the reputation of the *Wasp* was well known, and he had no wish to engage his one hundred and eighteen men against the reputed one hundred and seventy the *Wasp* maintained. And his weaponry was no match. His only hope was that the *Wasp* would not wish to find itself wedged between the *Reindeer* and the *Apollo* in English waters. Elsewhere, who knew, but certainly not even the *Wasp* would want such action here, so near the Channel. With much relief he put up his horn to advise the captain of the *Apollo* that they would be pleased to give them safe escort home.

Captain Lance Landon turned to his grinning crew. "What say you, lads? Shall we let them?"

Three cheers went up, and it is to be noted that all but the men of the *Wasp* were quite pleased with themselves.

Windmera sat on her bed contemplating her newfound knowledge. Godwin of Ravensbury . . . her father? Maurice de Brabant . . . her father? Who was she? Simply daughter of Heather? No! Godwin's blood ran in her veins, but it had been Maurice who had raised her, loved her. She was not a Ravensbury. In fact . . . she was no longer a de Brabant. She was a Landon! She was Lance Landon's wife. She would hold onto this thought, hold onto the dreams she had of the days that had passed with Lance. She would have them again. She must have them again.

Oh, Lance, I need you. In the quiet of her room she breathed his name, and his image floated before her eyes. The memory of his touch thrilled her, and she lay back wishing she were in his arms.

"Windmera . . . please . . . open the door!" It was Roderick, and his voice, laced as it was always these days with drink, sounded heavy and yet pitiful as well. He was begging her, and Windmera's heart went out to him.

She got to her feet, for she was no longer afraid of Roderick, and she opened her door. "Rod . . . what is it?"

"Windmera . . . please . . . let me in. Let me speak to you. Land's End is in sight. In a few hours we will be there

. . . docked and on our way to Ravensbury. Please, Windmera . . ."

Land's End? Within sight? Three weeks they had been at sea. Three weeks she had been apart from Lance, and Roderick was to blame. But no, not Roderick . . . Godwin . . her mother . . . no! She mustn't do this. Why must she find someone to blame? What good would it do? "Come in then, but keep the door open, Rod." Her voice was firm. She was in control, and he knew it.

He stepped into the room and ran his hand through his thick hair. He was not the same man she had fantasized about in Barbados. He was disheveled, and his self-assurance had gone astray. He was hurting inside, and there was more to it than the fact that she had rejected him. There was more to it . . . but what?

"Roderick . . . what is it? What is torturing you?" Her voice was gentle.

He stared at her a long moment and sucked in breath. Suddenly her attitude was clear. Too clear. "Damn you, Windmera . . . don't take that tone with me! You are not my sister . . . so don't take on the part!"

She drew back. Had she been doing that? Perhaps. "But Roderick . . . our situation is unique. We share a common bond."

"In what way? You little fool." He had her shoulders. "There is nothing now to bind us, but there can be. Windmera . . . don't make a failure out of me in *his* eyes . . . don't do that."

"Why should you care what he thinks? He hasn't cared for your good opinion. Roderick . . . this man you call my father has sent you out against your will to do his wishes not because it is best for you, not because it is best for me . . . but because he is obsessed with beating your mother at last!" She sighed. "Don't you understand that?"

"No! Godwin has been good to me all these years. Lord knows he had every reason to despise me . . . but he treated me like his own. The least I can do is make up to him for what my mother did. Windmera . . . she had yours sent away . . . she ruined Godwin's life . . . won't you help me in this?"

Compassion for him incited her next movement, for her hand went to his cheek. He clutched it there, and she allowed it. "Oh, Rod," she whispered, "I wish I could do what you want. Perhaps . . . if I had never known Lance . . . perhaps

I would have . . . but it would not have been right. We would not have been happy together, you and I. We were each meant for another."

He closed his eyes. Delia. He was meant for Delia, whose cornflower-blue eyes he could still see innocent in her love. Whose flaxen hair streamed in Bermuda's soft wind, whose heart had pounded against his own. He had given her up. How could he make Windmera see?

"Windmera . . . listen to me. I thought . . . I thought I loved a girl. Never mind who she is. I thought I would never get over her . . ." He hesitated. "But I know . . . if you helped me, I could. If I help you, you will forget Lance. Windmera . . . you wanted me once."

"You will never get over her if you really loved her, Rod . . . and I shall never get over Lance. History is repeating itself."

"What do you mean?" he asked, puzzled.

"Godwin has ironically managed to wield our futures so that they copy his own past."

"Then your answer . . . ?"

"Rod, how can I give you any answer but no? How can I?"

"He will force you to marry me."

"Let him try," she said, dismissing him from the cabin. He stopped a moment. He could force her into that bed. Captain John was busy on deck. He could force her . . . perhaps . . .

Windmera could read his mind. Quietly she picked up the butter knife she had been keeping near her pillow. "Don't even think it, Roderick."

He smiled wryly. "I see *you* have been . . . thinking of it."

She said nothing, and when he had at last left her to her peace she bolted the door and breathed with relief, wondering whether or not she would have been able to use the knife had he not decided to leave her.

Twenty-five

Satisfaction gleamed in Godwin of Ravensbury's dark eyes.
At last! Heather . . . Heather . . . our daughter is with us at
last. The words echoed joyfully in his mind. He stood upon
the very spot he had first taken Heather Martin in his arms
and made her his.

His home? It wore the mourning of the black wreath, for
Sara was dead. But Windmera was on her way to bring vivacity and life into his home. His daughter would walk
through his halls. He would hear her footsteps on the oaken
floors. See her skirts swish to music, watch her eyes. Oh, God
. . . could he bear the moment of meeting? His heart beat at
an unsteady pace, and his breath came in short spurts. His
own flesh and blood would soon be coming to him, for the
Conrad had docked and word had been sent that Roderick of
Ravensbury was bringing his bride!

Roderick's bride. That is what the town believed she was
. . . only Roderick's bride. Would they see Heather in her
face, as Captain John had done? What would they say? But
never mind, it didn't matter. She wouldn't know that she was
his daughter . . . though he longed to hold her, tell her. She
was his child. A woman grown . . . but his child. A sigh
coursed through his lungs. A sigh of satisfaction at last. His
daughter, child of Ravensbury, had come. The thought was
joy, the moment eagerly awaited.

What could she say to him? How could she meet his eye?
What would he look like, this Godwin of Ravensbury? He
had won her mother's heart. This is what her mother had
meant when she spoke of loving the man you marry. She was
moved by her own tragic love affair. What was this Godwin
that he would move Roderick so? Look at Roderick now,
across from her in the rumbling coach. There was sweat glistening on his creased brow, yet the coach was drafty and
cold. And there beside him, silent with his thoughts, sat Captain John. He was a good man, yet he had done this thing to
her. Out of loyalty to Godwin. All these people . . . dancing
to Godwin's tune? What sort of man was he . . . this man
who had given her life and would now control it?

The landscape. Rough. Cornwall was a rough and jutting land, strewn with mossy rocks and glistening cliffs. Beautiful and beckoning, but not her home. Her home was, could only be, in the arms of Lance Landon. And then Ravensbury loomed before her eyes.

Enormous! Gray and sharp in its lines. Frightening in its coldness, in its age. Bold. It was the word that came to mind as she stared at Ravensbury Castle, and then its lord blotted out all else, for he stood in the cobbled courtyard, waiting to greet the coach.

She stared hard, and was not displeased with what met her eyes. Godwin was certainly a man's man. Large, with faded red hair flying in the wind. Dark eyes that were bright with some emotion she could not name, and a smile upon his lips.

The coach had stopped, and a footman in blue livery opened the door for her. She could not move. Her limbs seemed frozen, her eyes could do naught but stare at Godwin, sho stood rigid, the smile dying on his lips as he saw his daughter's face. It was too much. He had been prepared to see a likeness to Heather, but this was too much . . . more than he could bear. This was Heather. Heather was coming to him. He reached out and gently, tenderly lifted her from the coach's opening, and holding her high in his arms he breathed Heather's name.

Windmera's heart rifted within her chest. How sad. How terribly sad, and all at once she understood everything and nearly forgave him for all he had wrought. "No, my lord . . . not Heather . . . but Windmera," she said softly, urging him to put her down, set her on her feet.

The voice. Heather's yet not Heather's. Of course. This was not Heather, but their daughter. Was he going mad? He put her down and blinked back a tear. He looked long into her eyes. Heather's violet eyes stared up at him . . . but somehow these eyes were different. Not in hue, not in shape, yet different. A fighting spirit lurked here, so unlike his Heather's tender soul. This one, their daughter, his and Heather's, would not be led. He saw something in Windmera's eyes, and it felt good, so good. "Of course, my dear. Windmera de Brabant," he said jovially, hugging her, reaching ·out for Roderick's hand with his other. Holding Roderick's hand, he gave it a mighty squeeze.

"Roderick . . . it is good . . . so good to see you!" He turned to his friend. "Captain John . . . you old goat, you are looking fit after your adventure. Come in . . . come in

434

. . ." But not even to greet either of these two men could he take his arm away from his daughter.

Windmera had wanted to correct him immediately. She had wanted to say, *"No!* Not de Brabant . . . but Landon . . . I am Mrs. Lance Landon!" However, an invisible force had managed to clamp her mouth. She could not form the words in her throat. She could not air the defiance she felt—not at that moment. Something in Godwin's eyes had stopped her. He was so genuinely happy. How could she spoil it for him? Roderick, too . . . he looked so apprehensive . . . how could she ruin the moment of his homecoming? She had the right. They had interfered with her life, her happiness, these people! Revenge? Justice? They were words, and these were flesh-and-blood lives she was dealing with. There would be time enough to explain all. Time enough to make Godwin of Ravensbury give it all up and see that she would never fall in with his plans.

Quietly she allowed him to lead her over the cobbled yard to the great front doors of the castle. A black wreath met her open gaze. Death? What did it mean? And then the doors, heavily studded and appearing impenetrable, clanged shut at her back. Oh, Lance . . . Lance, however will I find my way back to you?

The black wreath! Roderick had seen it at once. A strange sensation infiltrated his heart. What was it he felt? He knew what the wreath denoted. Sara was dead. His mother had died alone! Guilt skirted through his mind, etching pain in livid color. His face paled, and he moved quietly toward the brandy decanter while Godwin kept up a lively monologue at Windmera. Captain John said nothing, for he had seen both the wreath and Roderick's expression. It forboded ill.

"Godwin," said Captain John quietly, slowly, "Allow Windmera to be taken to her room. She is tired and would rest."

Godwin looked stricken. He didn't want her out of his sight. She was here, here . . . "But . . ."

"I am rather tired, my lord," put in Windmera quickly. Yes. Captain John should speak with him alone.

He patted Windmera's hand. "Very well, my dear." He went to a bellrope and presently a lackey appeared and was instructed to show Miss de Brabant to her rooms.

Again Windy wanted to correct him, and it was with supreme effort that she left the room without doing so. Leave it to Captain John to break the news to him. Allow Roderick to tell it in his own way . . . allow him to save face with his

435

. . . father . . . her father. How very disconcerting to think of the relationship that existed between the three of them! Oh, Lord, how she wished she could escape!

Roderick had downed a glass and was working on yet another. He had not been able to say more than a few words since the first meeting with Godwin. How determined he had been! This time, Godwin would not send him into submissive cowering! This time, he would speak his mind, do as he wished! And then, Godwin was there, and all resolves were shattered. And now, now how would he face himself? His mother had died, and he had not been here to ease her pain . . . to part in friendship. What was Captain John saying? He should listen, really. So he turned and raised his glass to the captain.

"Yes, speak up, man. Tell him that he has been using the wrong name. She is not a de Brabant . . . and oh, by the way . . . when did my mother pass on, as they say?" He was being flippant, because he was devastated, gripped by forces beyond his control.

Captain John scowled, but it was not surprising that Roderick should behave in this manner. "Godwin . . . when did Sara die?"

"Nearly five weeks ago," Godwin said quietly, turning to Roderick. "There was nothing you could do, Roderick . . . believe me."

"She died after I left Bermuda. I could have been here for her had I heeded Captain John. He told me she was ill . . . and I would not believe him." There was something in the recesses of his eyes. Roderick was breaking. His soul was coming apart. He attempted to control it. He shrugged his shoulders. "No matter. Death is death. She would have died anyway . . . is that not what you mean, sir?"

Godwin frowned. "Don't speak to me that way, lad. You are upset, it is understandable . . . but . . ."

"But rude, yes, I know. Now, on with the matter at hand. *Your daughter!*"

"Shut up, Roderick! Someone might hear!" snapped Godwin, taking a menacing step forward. Really, what was wrong with him? He had never been overly fond of Sara. He was behaving strangely.

Captain John came into it again. "Godwin. Before we go any further there is something you must be told."

Godwin gave him his full attention. "And that is?"

"Windmera has married the American who abducted her!" snapped Roderick before Captain John could speak.

Godwin spun around but could not speak. His daughter . . . married to some American? No . . . no . . . no! "You left him alive?" he hissed, his fury beyond belief.

"Godwin . . . she loves him . . ." said Captain John.

"Plague take him! The marriage will be erased! *I* will see to it," he said on a dangerous note, his voice low now, once again in control. "Before this week is out, Windmera will be wife to Roderick!"

Once again Roderick raised his glass, this time in mock salute to the man he had adored more than life itself. Inside of him there was a blasting of cannons. Flesh was being torn away as invaders slashed through to his heart. His mind dizzied with fragments of memories best forgotten, and somewhere far off he heard his mother cry. But there was Godwin before him, setting things to rights!

The crew of the *Reindeer* cheered and waved as they saw the *Apollo* sail into safe harbor. May was upon them, and more than one man on board wished he too were putting in for a night or two with a wench and some song. Their sighs hung in the dusk, for no such thing loomed ahead for them. They would continue to tour English waters and secure other British merchant vessels attempting to escape American savages.

Captain Landon could not help but smile to himself as he saw the large brig recede, and then he was staring up at Land's End. His first impression was of power. What majesty towered there! Awesome in its beauty, the meeting of crashing breakers and capacious rock. Somewhere behind that harsh wonder lay hidden his bride.

Tonight would find them docked. Tonight he would send McNabe, whose accent would allow him easy acceptance among the townspeople, to scout out the information he needed, and then, by damn, he would seek out Windmera, and God help any man who tried to get in his way!

A week had nearly passed at Ravensbury since Windmera had first stepped over the castle threshold. Godwin had been told, but not anything she had said had served to move him in his purpose. By what manner she knew not, he had declared her a free woman. Her marriage to the American was naught in English eyes. She was, he said, once again Wind-

437

mera de Brabant, and in the morning, she would be Windmera of Ravensbury! Yet she argued still.

"No! I won't do it. There is no minister alive that would marry an unwilling bride!"

"You are wrong, my child." He wanted to stroke the anger away from her face. Why must she be so obstinate? "I assure you I have much power in Cornwall. The man I have secured for the ceremony will not care a fig for anything you have to say. You needn't even be present if it does not suit you."

He was so calm. He was dealing away her dreams, and he was so calm. He didn't know yet. He hadn't been told that she was aware of her real parentage. She blasted him with it now. "How can you? You loved my mother . . . or at least I am told you did. She must have loved you . . . for I am living proof of that . . . so how can you put me through the same hell you have gone through yourself?"

He was stunned. He fell into the chair at his back and gazed up at her flashing violet eyes. It was so hard. Looking at her, he felt he was with Heather again. So many little things she did were in Heather's style, but there was much there all her own. She knew.

"Who told you?"

"Does it really matter? Godwin . . . how can you do this to me? I love my husband . . . he loves me . . . I am not in love with Roderick . . ."

"Enough! I won't hear it!"

"And will you tie me to Roderick's bed? Will you? Will you force me to take his seed and bear you grandchildren? Has it gone that far with you?"

"Stop! Don't you see? Your mother would have wanted this. She named you Windmera . . . knowing that one day I would find you . . . and understand that she loved me . . . still. You must . . . Windmera . . . you must see . . ."

"I see. You are crazed!" She ran from the room, but as she reached the great double doors, Roderick appeared and stood in her path.

"Go upstairs, Windmera. He won't like having to have you chased by servants . . . it won't do any of us good."

She thought quickly. If she ran out now, she could be easily caught. It might make them put a tighter rein on her in the future. She would have to seem submissive until she could get passage to France and from France to America. Oh, God . . . how could she ever? The answer came at once. You must! She turned quietly and put up her chin.

438

"As you wish, Roderick. Only tell him, will you . . . that he never was, never will be, father to me."

Roderick shook his head. "I would have given my eyes to hold the love he bears for you."

"Would you still, Roderick? Would you still?"

He frowned. The answer? He didn't know. He just didn't know any longer. He watched her take the stairs and was about to go out when Godwin's voice halted him.

"Roderick . . ." Godwin was slapping a letter into his open palm.

Roderick's brow went up. "Yes?"

"I was going through my mail . . . and remembered that this letter came for you while you were away. It is from Bermuda."

Roderick felt his entire body quiver. Bermuda. Delia. His Delia's hand? He came forward and reached out for it, blushing as he saw his hand tremble. Godwin noted this with surprise. "My dear boy, it is only a letter."

Roderick didn't answer. He took it quietly and slipped it into the inner pocket of his riding jacket. He then went outside and ordered his horse to be readied. He ached to open the envelope and devour whatever Delia had to say . . . but he mustn't . . . not here. He didn't trust his own reactions. He mustn't be seen reading this letter.

He rode away from the castle, and without realizing it made his tracks across Land's End. How often had he seen Godwin contemplating the Fates from just this spot? He stopped his horse on solid ground and slid easily off its back. Tethering the animal to a nearby bush, he took out the letter concealed in his riding jacket. For the first time he noted the scrawl was longer than Delia's hand. He still could see her handwriting as though it were yesterday when he had last received one of her quick little missives. He sighed and planted himself on the warm earth. May flowers gave off their scent all around. Oh, Delia . . . how I wish I were with you now, he thought as he slit the envelope and pulled out its contents.

Mr. Ravensbury:

I write this note not in my first moment of grief—but believe me, I am as bitter against you now, as I was on that terrible day.

I don't know if you have character enough left to you to read the following and be moved. Let us hope so. Let us hope that our Delia held enough power over you to draw now a twinge of guilt, of regret, for these feelings should be yours!

On the day you left her, Delia threw herself and the unborn child she carried into the sea! Neither survived.

                                                              Julia Hopkins

Roderick was stunned by the blow. Delia . . . dead? He saw the words float by. Neither survived. She had been with child . . . he would have had a child . . . Delia was dead . . . dead . . . Delia . . . ? Oh, God . . . I killed them! Such was the process of his thoughts, and then he stood up and raised his fist in anger, his voice in anguish. *"No! No! No! Not Delia . . . Please . . . No!"*

Roderick had been crumbling for weeks. His control over his emotions, a control he had begun forming at an early age, had held him together, but every man has his breaking point, and for Roderick it had come. His soul withered in his body, and his body was in Hell. He called for help, he called in terror, "Delia!"

Windmera paced in the quiet of her room. A small fire burned in the grate, giving off the only light in the darkened room. She had not gone down for dinner, and she had not eaten what had been sent up to her. She couldn't. Her stomach was churning, her head was reeling with rage. He said he loved her, this Godwin, this man who was her father, yet he would see her broken! But he would not succeed. Tonight she would escape. Beneath her robe she wore the gown Roderick had purchased for her when they had first landed in Cornwall. She couldn't bear to wear anything Godwin had purchased for her. Cash. She had very little, as all her needs had been supplied by the Ravensbury household. However, Godwin had been generous. He had given her a very fine set of diamonds, diamonds he told her were worthy of the occasion of her marriage. Well, she would take them along and use them for barter! But not the devil himself would deter her from her purpose.

Candlelight with its tallow aroma tinged the smoke-filled air. Revelry and music bounced off the weathered-gray plank walls in resonant trills. Jostling and bustling threatened to explode through the roof of the *Bull and Pen* as its amused patrons enjoyed themselves with wine, women and song.

McNabe was a small and wiry fellow. He mingled and wound his way through various sorts. In his sailor's dark woolens he blended in well with the crowd. From beneath his peaked wool cap he was able to spy out those he wanted without his own face leaving much of a mark. Thus far, all had gone well for the *Apollo*. Its captain had exhibited to the authorities his papers, and they had passed. Now all it needed was to find out what was happening up at Ravensbury Castle. But none of these coves would know. He needed a flash cove, and then in the corner of the large ale room he saw him. To be sure, Roderick's usually well-groomed auburn curls were in some disarray, as was his expertly cut clothing, but he had the look of nobleman about him, and McNabe was quick to see it. Quietly, easily, he tooled his steps to that corner table.

Roderick was in no mood to talk. After those first hours of wandering around the cliffs of Land's End he had made a determined path to this tavern. He needed drink and he needed to be away from Godwin . . . away from Ravensbury. He needed to forget that Delia was no more. He was attempting to do it in cheap wine. He looked up at McNabe. "You there! What the devil are you staring at?"

"Was I staring at ye, lad? Didn't mean no offense . . ." started McNabe, pulling up a chair.

Roderick frowned at him. He wanted no company. "Take yourself off, then, or I shall be offended."

"It could be I can help you . . ." said McNabe. This man would know about Ravensbury. He felt it in his bones. He was quality and was sure to know what was toward at the castle.

"Help me?" Roderick gave a mirthless laugh. "Yes, you can do that by loping off and leaving me . . . and don't call me lad! I am a man. In fact . . . I'll soon be a wedded man!"

"Getting married, are ye? Well, good luck to ye then," said McNabe, excited about this, but of course he was being ridiculous. Why should this man's getting married make him feel agitated in any way?

"Have you not heard? In the morning Roderick of Ravensbury takes to himself a bride!" said Roderick harshly.

"In the morning, ye say?" repeated McNabe, barely able to conceal his feelings. Why, this was Ravensbury himself . . . which would mean the captain's wife was up at the castle. He had to hurry back to the *Apollo*.

"Yes, a bride for Ravensbury . . ." It was a cold sound, and it sent a shiver through McNabe's body. "Get away from me now . . . dammit, get away!"

McNabe was only to pleased to comply. "Right, then, guv." And he was off. He had not far to go, but they would need horses, more than likely, and that would take a bit of time.

Roderick took another long gulp of wine. He needed the waters of Lethe's stream. He was in Hell . . . then why could he not find it? This hard displeasing wine was not nearly enough to pull him into forgetfulness. Would anything ever again be enough to enwrap him in oblivion?

Godwin brooded over Windmera in his library. Why was she being so stubborn? Roderick would make her an excellent husband. He had worried over the lad in those first days of his homecoming. Rod seemed to spend too much time in his cups, but then yesterday when he had been told of Windmera's annulment he had put the bottle away. He was being patient and good, and Windmera should appreciate that! Ah, Windmera. Nothing could reduce the joy he felt now. Nothing!

Love? Poor little girl. What did she know of love? At first she had thought she loved Roderick . . . hadn't she? She was willing enough to leave Barbados . . . come with Roderick and be his lady at Ravensbury. Why, if not because she loved him? What then was all this talk of loving the American barbarian? No, she was confused. The American had ravished her . . . and then for reasons he could only guess at the American had married her. She was a good faithful girl and imagined she owed him a loyalty. She was a sweet child . . . attempting to be true to her vows. She was Windmera . . . his daughter, her mother's image. But her will, well now, that matched his own, and this fact pleased him, very much! He sighed, full with his happimess, seeing nothing outside his own creation.

Captain Landon's jaw was set in a vicious line. McNabe had come with his news, and quickly they had set out to get horses from a nearby stable. They would have to work fast, but this left him unsure of himself. His intentions were to get Windmera and sail off without a hitch, without putting her in danger. This now would mean storming the castle, so to speak, and this could be difficult. If only he knew which room was Windmera's. Ravensbury was not expecting any trouble. It would be so easy. But the sorry fact was that he did not know her room. However, fate had lent a hand . . . and put Roderick out of the castle this night.

This would enable him to go right up to the front doors and request an interview with his lordship. He would say his name was Stanton. Yes, Stanton of Barbados, here with a shipment of rum and sugar. His mother had requested him to stop by and pay his respects to Miss de Brabant. They had not heard from her? Yes, this is the line he would take. It would have to do.

Windmera flung off her wrap and picked up her cloak. Godwin was in the library. She could easily sneak down the stairs and be out of the house in moments. There wasn't a horse in the stables she couldn't ride. Confidently she donned her cloak. The diamonds, all but the ring she wore on her finger, were sewn into the lining of her cloak. Softly she crept to her door and peeped out into the dark hall. Speedily she took its length and stopped at the landing. She would have to make sure Davies was nowhere about. And then she nearly jumped as the front door knockers sounded. Down she went into a crouched position.

She saw the butler open one of the doors, but could not make out the face of the distinguished gentleman that entered. There was something about his movement. Something to the set of his shoulders that caught her breath in her throat. Lance. She was seeing Lance everywhere. Was she going mad?

Lance stepped forward, allowing McNabe to follow. The butler politely if coldly put in at once, "May I help you?"

"Indeed," said Captain Landon, taking an imperious tone. "Tell his lordship that a Mr. Stanton of Barbados would like a few moments of his time."

Windmera's heart stopped beating. Stanton? This was Lance! The voice was Lance's voice. She peered through the wood balustrade and saw his profile. Lance! Lance! Oh, dear God, thank you! Lance! She could scarcely contain herself. She mustn't give him away. He was calling himself Stanton . . . of Barbados. What was his scheme? He must hurry before Roderick comes home. She would go down. She would manage somehow to identify her room. Lance . . . here? He had sailed right under the noses of the British! Was there ever such a man?

Davies stood at the library doors and announced Mr. Stanton to his lordship. Godwin was in no mood for visitors. He wanted to sit with his dreams, plan out the future of his children. But Godwin was ever a hospitable man.

Godwin frowned at his butler. "Stanton? What does he want?"

"Shall I inquire, my lord?"

"No. No. Send him in, then," said Godwin irritably.

A moment later he was going forward to meet the tall rugged young man who called himself Stanton. He scanned the handsome features and found that for no reason at all he rather liked him.

"How good of you to see me, my lord," said Lance easily. He was staring at the eyes. They were not Roderick's. Nor was the face. Perhaps then Roderick took after his mother.

"Yes, yes," said Godwin curtly, "But tell me, sir what brings you to Ravensbury?"

"Two things, sir. I am here with my vessel to dispose of a shipment of sugar and rum. It seems our agent was in error and our sale has gone awry. I was told in town that the house of Ravensbury might be able to take some if not all of it off my hands."

"Rum and sugar? I wonder who could have told you such an odd thing?" However, he quickly waved this aside. "No matter . . . I have friends who might be interested. But you said two things brought you here."

"Yes. The other is Windmera de Brabant," said Lance Landon quietly. Of course she would be known to someone from Barbados as de Brabant, not Landon.

Godwin's brow went up suspiciously. This was a very good-looking young man. Swarthy and bold. What had he to do with Windmera? "Explain yourself!" he said coldly.

Lance laughed lightly. "I see that I had better. I meant no offense, my lord. Miss de Brabant is a very close friend of my family in Barbados. We knew that she was engaged to marry your son and have been wondering why we had not heard the announcement of their marriage."

"I see. Well, they are to be married in the morning," said Godwin carefully. "Now, if there is nothing more, Mr. Stanton?"

"But I am afraid there is," said Lance blandly. "You see, my mother did ask me to look in on Miss de Brabant personally."

"I am afraid, Mr. Stanton . . ." started Godwin, only to be cut off by Windmera's voice. She had heard enough to pick up on.

444

"Mr. Stanton!" Windmera's angelic voice caused Lance Landon to spin around. He went hot and cold, and his knees turned to jelly. He did not know how he kept his hands off her. She did not know how she kept herself from running into his arms. She was coming forward, her hands were near his own, touching. Their eyes spoke poetry, but their lips told such lies! "Why, Mr. Stanton . . . how good it is to see you! Tell me how your trip went! Well, I hope?"

"Very well . . . and yours?" There was an underlining of meaning.

She sought to rest his mind. "My trip to Cornwall was uneventful. My captain kept me sheltered in my cabin for the most part." She turned and smiled at Godwin. "Captain John was very good to me, you know."

Godwin frowned. What was all this talk of trips? Testily he agreed, "Yes, yes. Captain John is an excellent fellow. However, it is late, and Windmera . . . you should be getting your rest. Your wedding is on the morrow."

"Oh . . . and I left a candle burning near my window drapes. I should go up at once." There, she had managed to give him the message. A candle would be burning in her window!

He understood at once. They thought alike, he and his bride. "Miss de Brabant . . ." he said, bowing over her hand. They turned, and there in the doorway stood Roderick of Ravensbury!

Twenty-six

The drink had clouded Roderick's mind. The ride home had helped to clear it, but he stood swaying a moment, attempting to ascertain whether or not what he was seeing before him was truth. Lance Landon standing and talking with Windmera . . . with Godwin . . . as though they were old friends? Absurd! What was this? What was it? And then slow dawning permeated his brain.

"Godwin! This man . . . this is Captain Landon! This is Windmera's American!" he shouted, but then he noticed a movement in the hall at his back. The small dark man who had moved out of his way when he had first entered. Damn! He dove into his Hessian and brought up his small pistol. He carried it always when he went out at night. It would stand him in good stead. "Don't move!" he ordered of McNabe. Then, quickly, as Davies came around to take hold of McNabe's shoulders, Roderick turned the gun on Landon and stepped slowly into the room.

They stood, each at bay. Davies was called in and instructed to tie McNabe to a chair. Windmera stood rigid. Godwin held her wrist, but she broke loose and moved near Roderick.

"Please, Rod . . . give it up . . . this is madness. I beg of you . . ."

"No! Give it up? Are you crazed? I will never give it up . . . *never!"* His voice was bitter in its depths. "Don't you see . . . her death . . . would have no meaning. It will all have been for nothing!"

Roderick's eyes found Landon again. How he hated him! If it hadn't been for Landon . . . Windmera would be his wife already. If it hadn't been for Landon . . . he would never have gone to Bermuda and destroyed Delia. The fault lay with Landon. He saw Landon's hand on the gun tucked in his waistband. "No . . . I think not, Landon . . . put it down . . . slowly."

"Not a chance," retorted Landon.

"Then you are a dead man, for mine is already drawn!"

What happened next took place in the splitting of a moment. Windmera screamed and lunged. Godwin saw what she was about. She could catch a bullet. His daughter would die, trying to save this American. He shouted her name and pushed her forward. The loud report of a gun echoed in the high ceiling of the room, and Godwin of Ravensbury was down.

In the shattering of a moment, the moment dies, taking with it at times more than life. Roderick dropped his weapon, and it smoldered at his feet. He ran forward and took up Godwin in his arms. Tears were already running down his cheek. He had mortally wounded the only father he had ever known. Could all this be happening? Perhaps he was caught in the web of a nightmare. Perhaps he would yet awake? He had not called Godwin father in eighteen years, but he did now.

"Father . . . please . . ."

Godwin's eyes were open. There was blood oozing from the corner of his mouth, but he was smiling. Pain. He felt a pain in his chest, but it was nothing to what he had suffered in the past. Soon it would all be over. "Never mind, Roderick . . you brought me my daughter. You completed the cycle. Never mind about the rest." He had taken pity on Roderick at last.

Windmera took up his hand and kissed it. She could say nothing. Words were inadequate. Suddenly he looked at her, and it was a long hard stare. She knew he was seeing some-one else.

"Oh, Heather . . ." he cried almost joyfully. "Heather . . . at last . . ." and Godwin of Ravensbury's life was at end.

Windmera released a choked sound and turned to dive into her husband's arms. He held her tightly, for her body was shaking beneath the weight of emotion.

Captain John walked in on this scene. He shook his head. So, at last, some peace had come to Godwin.

1815

Autumn in Mystic, Connecticut, had come. Gentle breezes carried leaves of russets and golds, spreading them over fading lawns. Mums bloomed in bright profusion in the Landon flower beds, for Windmera had taken an active hand in the gardening of her home. She stood now in the bright sun ap-

447

praising her handiwork with satisfaction, but it was not the flowers that held her eyes. It was her son!

He was just managing to walk toward his grandfather, who held out eager arms. "That's right . . . to me . . . to me, Shaun," cried Jules, thinking his year-old grandson an amazingly clever creation. Dear to his heart was this child of love. He sighed. It was too bad he didn't get to see Izzy's son, young Jim, as much as he'd like.

The fleet under Perry's command had embarked upon a successful campaign on Lake Ontario, but the British had retaliated by first attacking Sackets Harbor and then burning Buffalo to the ground. The town had literally been leveled, and Jim had felt he was needed there. So it was that Isabelle, Jim and young Jim Foster had remained to rebuild Buffalo, New York.

The war was over now. Trade once again flourished with the British. The industrial age was pushing forward. Waterloo had ended the reign of Napoleon, and the seas were open. So it was that Stacy Clayton made her decision. She had returned to find her estates in order and Monty Clayton on his deathbed. She left him there. She could have had her revenge, but it no longer seemed important. Her mind was consumed with the memory of Roderick, and with the passing of two years she discovered that time had not abated her feelings for him. Dreams of their days and nights together haunted her. She had to see him again. However, she would find in Cornwall a changed man, for Roderick of Ravensbury could never be the man he had been.

Captain John had taken a hand in Roderick's life. He talked, cajoled, reasoned, and these were balms, but the rough edges of pain were ever present, always ready to pinch and prick away at what was left of Roderick's soul, and he was a bitter man. There is no telling what Stacy could do with what was left of him.

Lance's deep-blue eyes devoured his wife. Forgotten were Roderick and Godwin of Ravensbury. She was the most lovely woman he had ever beheld. Her movements, her voice, her laugh teased him into sweet delight. Always he was drawn to her by a power he could not control. His hands found her trim waist and drew her against his broad chest. He bent his head and discovered the fresh delicacy of her neck. This was his woman, the mother of his child, his life.